HOME AGAIN

to

Texas Roots

A Contemporary Romance Novel

KAREN NEWCOMB
&
DAVID CARLTON, D.V.M.

PublishAmerica
Baltimore

First printing

At the specific preference of the author, PublishAmerica allowed this work to remain exactly as the author intended, verbatim, without editorial input.

ISBN: 1-4137-6311-1
PUBLISHED BY PUBLISHAMERICA, LLLP
www.publishamerica.com
Baltimore

Printed in the United States of America

HOME AGAIN

to

Texas Roots

A Contemporary Romance Novel

KAREN NEWCOMB

&

DAVID CARLTON, D.V.M.

CHAPTER ONE

Kristy Williams stood looking out her San Francisco office window where she said goodbye to the city she'd called home for the past seven years. Her gut was in her throat at the thought of being transferred to the Dallas office. Her reason for leaving Texas in the first place still lived there. Nick Chandler, the love of her life and father of her six year-old daughter, Nicole, was married and settled in Dallas. And to complicate things, her mother fractured her ankle, which meant Kristy had to spend time at the Chandler ranch to help the family during recuperation.

Kristy had been raised on the Chandler ranch, which was located in Texas near the Plains Caprock Escarpment that divides the High Plains on the west from the Lower Plains on the east. And where she'd learned the ranch ethic of hard work and perseverance. Her current company had given her time off to care for her mother and to get her affairs in order to move back.

"Miss Williams, am I interrupting?"

Kristy turned away from the window to smile at her secretary, Joshua. "Just recalling the first day I arrived in San Francisco."

"Pleasant memories I hope."

"Rather startling to be honest. Do you have my plane ticket?"

"Right here." He laid the ticket on the desk. "Is your dad meeting you in Lubbock?"

As a feeling of warmth swept over her, Kristy smiled. "He sure is. Joshua, thank you for being a great secretary. You've made my work so much easier."

He blushed behind his dark blond beard. "It's been a pleasure. I'm going to miss you."

Kristy hugged him and watched him leave her office. She gathered up the remnants of her belongings and quietly closed the office door behind her and to the last seven years of her life. She headed home to her two-bedroom apartment in the Marina district that she shared with her daughter.

When she opened the door Nicki was in her babysitter's arms crying. It broke Kristy's heart to see her daughter so upset about leaving the only friends and surrogate family she'd ever known.

"What about my horse, Mama, did she find a good home?" Large tears spilled down her cheeks.

"Nicki." Kristy pulled her tearful daughter onto her lap. "You met the new owners, didn't you think they were nice? I promise you'll have another horse. There are plenty of horses on the ranch and when we move to Dallas I'll see what I can find there."

Nicki's lower lip jutted out. "But, Mama, I don't want to leave Annie."

Kristy glanced up her friend and Nicki's babysitter. "You can talk to Annie on the phone every day, I promise."

"But who will take care of me when we live in Dallas?"

"We'll find someone you like. Until then you'll be at the ranch with Grandpa and Grandma."

Nicki's tears stopped. She looked up into her mother's eyes. "I know…but I'll miss everyone here."

As Kristy gazed into her daughter's pewter blue eyes Nick Chandler's face came into sharp focus. Her daughter looked so much like him it hurt to look at her sometimes. And Nick…didn't even know he had a daughter. "I know you'll miss everyone here but our family is in Texas."

Annie stroked Nicki's long blonde curls. "Honey, you know how much I love you and I'm going to miss you terribly, but your mother's right, your family is in Texas."

Nicki looked up at Kristy and wiped her eyes. "When do you have to leave, Mama? I'm all packed but I don't understand why I can't come with you."

Kristy hugged her. "Because, first I want to go to the ranch and make sure Grandma is okay. I'll get your room ready. On the weekends I have to drive to Dallas to look for an apartment for us. It'll only be for a few more days, then you fly out with Annie and Grandpa will pick you up."

"Will Annie stay with us?"

Annie smiled, "No darling, I'm just seeing you safely into your grandpa's arms. I have a new job I have to start soon."

Nicki's lip twitched. "I'm going to miss you, Mama." Her small arms laced around Kristy's neck.

"I'll miss you too baby. It's just a few more days."

That evening Kristy was alone in her apartment with the memories she and Nicki had created. The apartment was empty now, except for a sleeping bag and pillow her neighbor and friend Greg had loaned her. Greg had said his goodbyes earlier and was in such an emotional state he ran out of the apartment crying like a baby.

Kristy wasn't unhappy about leaving San Francisco because it had been a sanctuary for the past seven years. California had been a haven for her after she found out she was pregnant. The one man she'd loved her entire life had made love to her and married another. Yet Nick Chandler would be in her heart forever.

Once in the air Kristy felt her arms aching and her heart breaking. She'd never been without her daughter before and it was a strange and unsettling feeling. Her mind reeled as she looked out the window of the plane. Her heart raced and there was a knot in her stomach. She wouldn't stay at the ranch any longer than she had to. It was almost time for the spring round up and she didn't want to be anywhere near the place. In the past six years she only came home when she knew Nick wouldn't be there. Nick had married, and was now a prominent Dallas vet who only came to the ranch to help when he was needed a few times throughout the year. Kristy would always time her visits home in-between his, in no way did she want their paths to cross.

She'd been in love with Nick Chandler since she was just a little kid. She'd watched him grow into a man long before she'd grown into a woman. She was there as he mourned the death of his parents before going off to college and was there every time he returned from college to work the ranch. Nick was next in line to inherit the Chandler place. At the moment his uncle, Jack Chandler, ran it…almost into the ground, Kristy mused. Nick Chandler was twelve years older than her and probably thought she was just a snot nosed kid who tended to ask too many questions. A trait Nicki seemed to have inherited.

That never stopped Kristy from tagging along behind him when he came home from college during summer breaks. Her heart had always been with Nick even when he returned home one summer to let everyone know he was engaged to be married. A socialite, Kristy scowled, a real Dallas socialite. He was marrying a woman of money, education and a station in life that could equal his vet status. Kristy frowned and continued to look down at the passing earth. In Nick's eyes she was nothing but his ranch foreman's daughter he'd had in the hayloft and cast aside.

Her hand went to her throat where she clasped the heart shaped necklace she'd worn around her neck from the day Nicki was born. It held a picture of a perfect imaginary family, her, Nick and Nicole. Nicki was conceived from need and love on her part, but not so with Nick. He'd surprised her while she was cleaning the horse stalls one afternoon. He'd offered to help but one thing led to another and she found herself in the loft with him making love for the first time. Stunned, overwhelmed and so consumed with emotions, she gave up her virginity to the one man she would always be in love with. Even now, her body tingled at the thought of his calloused hard working hands stroking and exploring her body arousing her beyond what she thought capable.

Air turbulence over Las Vegas drew Kristy out of her reverie. She looked up as a stewardess asked if she wanted a drink. Kristy declined and stared out the window again. Her parents had only seen Nicki once, when she was about six months old. They'd met her in Lubbock and stayed over so they could get better acquainted with their new granddaughter. It was an unspoken rule that they were to remain quiet about Nicole. She'd sent her parents photos of Nicki on a regular basis, but now, to actually bring her to the ranch was something she wasn't sure about. After all, Nick's uncle did live there.

How, she wondered, would the ranch hands react when they met Nicole? Oh God, Nicki looked so much like Nick surely any one of them would suspect. She didn't want Nick to know. She never intended to tell him. He was married and probably had a very happy life with Mallory and their children. The Chandler legacy lived on in his children and the ranch that he cared so deeply about would have his children to keep it in the family. She would never do anything to disrupt that marriage no matter what she had to do to keep her secret.

When the fasten your seat belt went on and Kristy's heart began to race. She was returning home where she belonged, yet not for long, she had to move to Dallas and start the next phase of her life. For now, she'd be with her mom and dad and that made her feel very secure and happy. As the plane landed Kristy's heart lightened.

Joe Williams greeted Kristy with open arms that enveloped her lovingly. "We're glad you're home," he said.

"I'm glad to be home." Kristy laced her arm in her dad's. "Let's get my luggage and get out of here."

"How'd Nicki take to bein' left behind?" Joe asked.

"Not well. I'm anxious to find us an apartment in Dallas. In the meantime, how's Mom doing?"

"Not bad, she's hobblin' on crutches. Been practicin' so she wouldn't feel like a bother to you."

"A bother? Dad, I'm here to help out, give back to her for raising me. Lord, that couldn't have been easy living way out there in the middle of nowhere."

Joe chuckled and wrapped his arm around his girl's shoulder. It was good to have her home again...where she belonged. He could hardly wait for Nicki to come to the ranch because there were so many things he wanted to teach that child about her Texas roots. "Darlin', we need to pick up a few things in town before we head home. Your mom's got me playin' gopher these days."

Kristy laughed softly. "I can be the gopher now that I'm here. Does she need groceries?"

"Ah, daughter, you and your mother are always thinkin' of us cowpokes and our stomachs. She needs more flour and sugar. She plans on havin' you do the cookin' and can hardly wait to get you in the kitchen with her."

"Then let's do it."

Two hours later the older ranch battered pickup truck rolled across the cattle gate to the Bar C Ranch. The overhead sign was like a welcoming beacon to Kristy. She could hardly believe she was home again. She inhaled deeply of the fresh spring air and exhaled slowly. The floral scents and new grass filled her senses leaving her speechless. When the stone built house appeared in the distance she felt the sting of tears. She was now going to have to face her past one way or another.

Joe pulled the truck to a stop near the sweeping porch that skirted the front of the one hundred fifty year old house. "Well, we're here. I'll get the groceries, go in and greet your mother."

Kristy jammed her shoulder against the truck door to get it open and jumped out to run into the house. Her mother waited near the front door with open arms. "Oh, Mama, it's so good to be home."

Ellen Williams patted her daughter on the back. She knew how hard this was going to be for Kristy and had to admire her strength and determination. "Welcome home."

"Which room is Kristy's?" Joe asked Ellen.

"Her old bedroom…" she hesitated only briefly not wanting to mention it was next to Nick's bedroom. "It'll do."

Joe disappeared up the stairs with Kristy's suitcases. Ellen looked at Kristy and asked, "How was the flight?"

Kristy couldn't help but gaze around the familiar room at all the things she'd missed while living in San Francisco. "It was fine." She picked up a small bronze statue of a bucking horse about to throw its rider. A plaque at the bottom read *Nick Chandler, winner Amarillo invitational bronc riding 1984.* That's when he acquired that belt buckle he always wore. She slowly set the statue back on the table. It was just one more reminder of Nick.

"Do you want to go upstairs and unpack?" Ellen asked knowing full well everything in the house reminded her of Nick and all the Chandler's before him.

"Good idea. I'll be down in a few minutes."

The room was just as she remembered, only this time she'd share it with her daughter. She sat down on the edge of the double bed and folded her hands in her lap as her eyes scanned the walls. Seven years had passed, but her mother kept the room just as it was before she left.

A girl had left, a woman and mother returned. Her eyes wandered through the window toward the barn. What was it about Nick Chandler that made her love him so much? She'd never understood her attraction to him or why she'd never been able to love another man even when Hunter Taylor came into her life. She shook her head, now wasn't the time to analyze her emotions. She had to clear her head and emotions…she needed to ride.

"Mama, I'm taking Rascal out to the cemetery."

Before Ellen could stop her Kristy was out the door and headed toward the corral. She saddled Nick's horse and for the first time in days felt exhilarated as the rush of wind blew her long blonde hair across her back. Her heart raced and the sense of freedom overwhelmed her. She was home!

A short time later she knelt beside the graves of John and Mary Chandler, Nick's parents. With her hand she brushed away fallen debris and long dried flowers. She pulled what weeds grew there and walked just beyond the cemetery to a prairie of new growth wild flowers. She knew Mary would love the bluebonnets tucked in among the other colorful flowers. Without hesitation Kristy removed the necklace from around her neck put it to her lips before wrapping it around the stems of the flower bouquet.

"Mary, John, this holds a picture of your granddaughter, Nicole. I wish you were here to meet her. She's so much like Nick. I'm sorry he doesn't know about her." She carefully laid the flowers at the base of Mary's headstone. "I'm sure Nick brings his other children here to talk to you. He always said this was where his roots ran deep and that his children would always know where they came from. I'm sure you'd be very proud of him. Mama says he's a popular vet but that's about all she's told me. I love him so much…but it was never meant to be." Slowly, she stood placed her fingers to her lips then touched each headstone. She turned and mounted Rascal. There was one other place she had to visit.

As she stood on the ledge of the caprock overlooking the prairie she sucked in her breath and thought of her daughter. Nicki too had to know where she'd come from, where her roots had sprung. Yet, she couldn't take the risk of either Nicki or herself staying on at the ranch. She had to find an apartment as soon as possible and get them settled into a new routine…a new life.

The sun had dipped below the horizon when she returned to the house and unsaddled Rascal. Her emotions had lightened with the ride. She knew what she had to do and stopping at the ranch was just the beginning.

She helped her mother fix dinner that night but had Maria Lupe, the part-time housekeeper take it to the table. Kristy wasn't ready to face anyone that evening so she went upstairs, called Nicki and went to bed.

CHAPTER TWO

The next afternoon Kristy stood in a state of shock in the shadow of the barn as she watched small beads of sweat glisten off the steely naked back muscles of Nick 'Doc' Chandler. The sight of him left her stunned, gasping for air because she never expected to see Nick on her return home. Where had he come from? She'd only been away from the house a few hours when she returned home and walked into the barn. His taut washboard stomach strained and his forearms tensed with a thrusting grip. His heels dug firmly into the ground when he reached between the fleshy thighs of the horse and sliced two strokes against male organs before he released the ropes that bound the horse's legs. Kristy had seen the same scene before many times over in her twenty-seven years and while living on the Chandler's ranch. Watching Nick brought back some of those memories of him she'd hoped she'd forgotten.

She could tell he was angry by the way he walked away from the castrated colt. His spur rowels jingled as he angrily knocked the dust from his chaps with his silver-bellied Stetson.

"I'm out of here!" Nick yelled at his uncle, Jack Chandler. He pulled his shirt off the corral fence and slipped it on.

"But...but you can't just leave it's near dark," Jack protested.

Nick glared at his uncle. "Who gives a shit? Next time keep the damn corral closed and I won't have to fly all the way from Dallas to clean up your mistake."

When Nick looked up at the men sitting on the corral fence he shook his head. "What are you looking at?" He grumbled. "Maybe if y'all hog tied him once in a while the ranch might actually turn a buck or two."

"Ah, Doc," a tall stick thin redheaded cowboy said, "It ain't up to us to keep your uncle in tow. Shit, we all make mistakes."

"Yeah, but it doesn't cost you a cent. He let out fifty prized longhorns. Two of which died giving birth out in the bramble. Then he left the gate open to the mares and the colts went on a breeding frenzy. You've been around long enough to double check things." Nick pointed a finger at the man. "Next time, do it!" It wasn't a statement but an order.

He hadn't changed, Kristy mused. He was still giving orders and expecting them to be followed. Nick was right though, his uncle had cost the Chandler's plenty. She looked at the stone-faced cowboys sitting on the fence. They were the original breed of cowboys, hardworking, leather tanned faces, and as tough as nails when it came to working the ranch. But not one of them had ever learned to control Nick's uncle's stupidity when it came to using common sense.

Hat brims bobbed up and down. "Yes, sir," the men echoed one by one.

Nick mounted his horse and looked at the cowpokes again. The only difference around the cattle pens between today and 1894 was the models of pickup trucks parked along side the watering tank, and who now called the shots. These same men had taught him respect for animals, family and critters alike. They'd taught him how to ride, rope and shoot, how to take charge. He hated it when Uncle Jack screwed them over and he was left cleaning up the mess.

Kristy walked to the front of the barn and was about to go inside when Nick rode by. She quickly turned away so he wouldn't notice her and ducked inside the dimness. She'd been out on the range visiting her favorite places all afternoon and had no idea things could change so fast.

"Kristy?" Nick said and reined in his horse. He climbed out of the saddle and walked into the barn. "Kristy?" He said again and found himself staring at her back.

Kristy's heart raced so fast she wasn't sure she could even say hello to him. Steeling her emotions she slowly turned around and forced a smile. "Hello, Nick." She swallowed the lump that had formed in her throat. As she looked at him she couldn't recall a time when she wasn't in love with him. Beneath his hat she could see his hair as always needed a trim, but he never seemed to find the time to have it done. She longed to run her fingers through it.

"What the hell you doing here? I thought you lived somewhere out west."

She was totally knocked off guard by his presence. "I came back to help mom while her ankle mends. I got here yesterday."

He removed his hat and tossed it onto a barrel. "Yeah, I heard about her accident. I'm sorry. You look...beautiful." She'd changed in the seven years she'd been away. Now, she was what...twenty-seven? She was all grown up and more beautiful than ever. She no longer sported freckles on her sculptured cheekbones or on the slightly turned up nose instead, her skin was flawless. Her hair was no longer honey blonde but sun streaked and lighter in color. The blue-green color of her eyes stood out even more causing him to catch his breath.

"I heard you talking to the men. Is Jack the reason you're here from Dallas?" It was hard to look into those steely blue eyes of his and not think of Nicole.

"Then you heard. Christ, I don't think that man ever thinks anymore. He's running the ranch into the ground. I can't spend enough time here to change it." What he remembered most about her were her eyes that had torn into his soul so many years ago as they were doing now.

"I hear your vet practice in Dallas is a success. How's Mallory?" She regretted the words the minute they had come out of her mouth.

"Wanta take a ride with me? I need to get out of here."

"Sure. Let me saddle..."

He'd already thrown the saddle over the little mare. Together they rode out to what Kristy knew to be his favorite 'thinking spot' atop the Canyon. This time of year the mesquite trees had sprouted leafy green buds and the air smelled of new growth. It was an hour from sunset. Kristy knew this to be his favorite time of day. They dismounted and sat on the pasture grass. At thirty-nine, his six foot three muscular frame, and his tanned rugged good looks were certainly setting off her hormones, even if there were more lines in his face then she remembered. She longed to touch his thick trimmed moustache to see if she could remember the shape of his lips. She recalled only too well how they had felt against her mouth. There was a patience and a quietness about him that she had always been drawn to and never understood why.

"Coming home isn't something I do often enough." Nick said. "I try to get back here at least four times a year not only to work the ranch but to come out here to rekindle my spirit. God, it seems as if I need the renewal and don't know it until I'm here."

"I understand. I lived in San Francisco and I've missed this place so much over the years."

His head snapped up and he gazed at her from beneath the brim of his hat. "You're a big city gal now."

She smiled and shook her head. "No, no I'm not. I work for a big clothing company and I'm in marketing and advertising. But I'm all Texan at heart. My company is sending me to Dallas to work. I've come home a few times over the years and dreaded when I had to get on the plane to go back." She didn't tell him she'd always planned those visits when she knew he wouldn't be there.

He reached out and touched her waist length blonde hair. "It's really good to see you again." Kristy always had a calming effect on him and only now did he realize it. "Life in Dallas has been good to me financially, but physically hard at the same time. Today I started my day at a patch of dirt in Farmer's Branch, then onto a madhouse of citified poodles and a ferret, and ended up between the back legs of that horse cutting his balls off. I flew over two hundred miles to sonogram those dozen mares for pregnancy and castrated the three yearling colts Jack let loose. Man, Kristy, he hadn't realized he'd left the gate open to the mare pasture and the colts went on a breeding frenzy for weeks."

"I'm sorry," she whispered and gazed out at the flat prairie.

"My blood boils every time I think of Uncle Jack's carelessness. Those cows would have brought in tax money for next year. Now, it means I'll have to nearly double my work load in order to pay for my Dallas expenses and those of the family ranch."

She reached over to touch his hand recalling how gentle they were with the animals he doctored...and with her. "I remember a time

16

when you brought me out here and pointed out the area in front of us. I guess you must have been about twenty-four at the time and I was twelve? I had some kind of problem with Texas history and you thought this place would give me a sense of it. I remember you telling me Los Ciboleros once followed wild herds of buffalo and how ranches grew into empires. You pointed to the west where a lonesome town bordered the barbed wire fences of a three million acre Dos Amarillas ranch in the late 1800s. You also told me that until 1882 sixty thousand head of cattle grazed on the one million acres to the north and the El Guapo Ranch occupied 500,000 acres on the southern boundary in 1906."

He laughed at her memories. "Twelve huh?" He was sure he didn't have the same emotional reaction to her back then as he was having now.

"Don't laugh," she said, "there's more. You pointed to the east where jagged canyon floors stretched and you told me it was once home to Apache and Plains Indians alike. You said this place humbled you and the sight out there always took your breath away. As it does mine right now."

"There are times when I think I can see it all up here. The skies are as clear and vivid as anywhere on earth. I see the spectacularly colored panorama, the tumbleweeds that collect on the abandoned porches and the buildings in the square of Dickens. Here in the county seat, the population doesn't even support a school system, yet the limestone jailhouse, the one-room post office, the mud creek adobe houses are still there. The sandstone courthouse and that little café are still unchanged after decades. There is so much history all around us and we're part of it."

Just listening to his soft voice sent Kristy's heart pounding. "I also remember you telling me the plains are so flat they confuse the rainwater about which way to run. I always thought that best described this part of Texas. So why don't you come home to do what you've always wanted to do?"

How could he tell her why? She looked so beautiful sitting beside him staring off into the distance it almost took his breath away. "I had to rebuild my practice literally

from the ground up after my divorce. Mallory took it all. I had a choice to move back here and try to work a failing ranch or stick it out in Dallas and rebuild so I could save the ranch and be the best damn vet that I could be."

His news stunned her and she felt as if she'd been hit over the head with a bat. She turned to face him and tried to keep her voice calm when she said, "I didn't know you divorced Mallory. Mom didn't say a thing about it." She wanted to ask what happened but didn't think it was any of her business.

Nick broke off a blade of grass and rolled it between his fingers. "Mallory and I never should have gotten married in the first place. If I'd known her a little better...it doesn't matter now. We've been divorced for six years."

She inhaled sharply and looked away from him. Her daughter was six...his daughter was six. Why hadn't her mother told her he divorced? Did Mom think she'd rush home from San Francisco to let Nick know he'd fathered her baby? It was too late for that now...much too late.

"Do you and Mallory have children?" She found herself holding her breath waiting for his answer.

"No, thank God, she was too selfish for that. What about you, did you ever marry?"

She shook her head and pulled a few stray strands of flyaway hair from her face as the breeze moved about her. "No."

He couldn't believe that she sat there next to him. He wanted to reach over and touch her like he had that night in the hayloft of the barn where she gave up her virginity to him. Now, his heart raced as he looked into those blue-green eyes of hers. He could almost see her standing in the hayloft seven years ago ready to toss a bale of straw down to the stalls. He recalled how he couldn't resist climbing up there to be with her and the look of surprise on her face when he took her face in his hands and pressed his lips to hers. It was probably her first kiss. She had trembled as he unbuttoned her shirt and his hands sought her breasts. Had it only been lust on his part? Had he been so upset with the things going on in his life that he had to take it out on Kristy?

It might have started as lust, but when her arms went around his neck and her soft feminine body pressed against him his feelings changed. He wanted to make love to her, to feel her naked body next to his, to be the first man in her life. He recalled how frightened she was when he undid her jeans and tossed them aside. How she trembled as he took her hand to touch him for the first time and how her silky flesh felt beneath his calloused hands and how he ached when he slipped into her warm moist depths. He remembered how they moved slowly against each other until they were brought to peak of erotic heightened passion and back again. Yes, he remembered it all. He'd awakened a passion in her she probably didn't even know existed, until he showed her. He'd marveled at the sight of her trim shapely naked hips moving gently as he explored her body...her quivering flesh beneath his hands. And here she was, once again beside him. His heart felt like a jackhammer pounding against his chest. He felt his body harden. He was sorry that he would be flying back to Dallas in the morning.

Kristy felt herself flush and tremble as she gazed into his eyes. She wanted to tell him she'd loved him most of her life and that he had a daughter who looked so much like him and had his innate ability with animals. Instead, she forced herself to look away and say, "The sun's gone I think we should get back, don't you?"

When she started to rise he gently snagged her wrist and pulled her down on her knees beside him. "Wait." He rose to his knees and cupped her face in his hands. He had to know the taste of those lips again. His mouth slowly came down to cover hers.

As his warm lips touched hers something akin to an electric shock surged through Kristy to take her emotions by complete surprise. His kiss was warm and moist against her mouth and she savored the feel of it. When he gently coaxed her lips apart she allowed him to explore her mouth. Her arms went around his neck and she found herself being pressed tight against him. Every nerve ending in her body had come to life. When the kiss ended she found herself breathless and aching for something she hadn't had in a very long time.

"I'm glad you're back." He said, as breathless as Kristy. He ached to lay her down in the grass and take her but this wasn't the time, it was getting dark. "How long do you plan to stay?" He wasn't sure he'd be able to keep his hands to himself after that kiss.

Her eyes were still closed and she was trying to regain normal breathing. "Until mom's ankle mends." She was glad when he helped her onto the horse.

They rode back in dead silence with only the sounds of the wind, creaking leather and horses to interrupt their thoughts. Kristy wanted to know his touch again. Nick longed to make love to her. They rode back to the barn where Nick helped her off the horse. "I'll unsaddle them," he said.

She started to walk out of the barn but hesitated and turned back to look at him. "Thanks Nick, for everything." He had no idea what she was talking about and she wanted to keep it that way.

In the kitchen Kristy fixed a fresh pot of coffee and knocked on her parents bedroom door just off the kitchen, then opened it. "Mom, Dad, can I get you anything before I go to bed?"

Ellen said, "I saw you ride off with Doc. Do you think that was a wise thing to do?"

"We rode to the canyon and talked…nothing more." She wasn't going to explain her emotional reaction to Nick to her parents.

"He'll be flying back to Dallas in the morning. I think that's for the best."

"Mom, why didn't you warn me he'd be here?"

"Because we didn't know until he called and told your dad when he'd be landing. Did you tell him you're moving to Dallas?"

"I told him. I'm going to bed. There's a fresh pot of coffee brewing if you want any."

"Thanks, Kristy," Joe Williams said.

Kristy made her way upstairs to the bedroom she'd been given and opened the door to stand there a moment before going in and closing it behind her. She changed for bed and called San Francisco to talk with Nicki. After the half hour call she grabbed her robe and walked downstairs for coffee. She missed Nicki terribly and was always sad when she had to say goodnight to her beautiful little girl. She longed to hold her in her arms and kiss her goodnight.

Nick sat at the table, a mug sat in front of him. "Couldn't sleep?" He asked admiring long legs beneath a short robe. Though not particularly tall, maybe five foot five, her legs belied that fact.

She pulled a mug from the cupboard and filled it with coffee. She leaned against the counter and took a sip from the cup. "I haven't tried yet. I had some calls to make and just got through." She watched as his dark blue eyes pierced her gaze and it made her want to melt into the floor. God, how she longed to run her fingers through that thick mane of sandy sun bronzed hair, then along the cleft in his chin and over the dimple under one cheek. Just the thought of touching him made her weak in the knees. And until now she hadn't realized just how much his face was the mirror image of Nicki's. She had to get away from him and excused herself.

Once back in her bedroom she put the coffee on the bedside table and sat down on the edge of the bed. She had to stop her pounding heart. There was a soft rap on the door before it opened. She looked up to see Nick filling the doorframe. He came in and closed the door behind him. "You looked like you needed to talk."

Gathering her composure she smiled. "Thanks, but I don't think…"

He came to sit beside her on the bed. "It's been a long time."

His fingers brushed against her cheek ever so lightly causing a wave of yearning to sweep over her. She tried to back away. "It's late."

"I have to leave tomorrow at dawn. When are you moving to Dallas?"

She could hardly breathe. "I…as soon as Mom is up and around. I have to look for an apartment so I'll be driving there on weekends."

His fingers traced the outline of her jaw and neck. Her eyes closed. "Will you call me when you get there?" He wanted to lower his hands to her breasts and capture them but she looked upset and he didn't want to be rejected.

Kristy was glad when he removed his hands. "I'm not sure I'll have the time. And I know how busy you are."

"I'll make the time." He stood to leave. "Call me?"

To appease him she said, "Sure." She had no intention of calling him once she was in Dallas. It hurt emotionally when he left her room and closed the door behind him. She crawled into bed and turned out the light. How could she possibly love a man she hadn't seen in seven years?

Her thoughts went back to how Nick had always been there for her until she was "grown up" and then he seemed to shy away from her seeking comfort and support at college and later in Dallas with Mallory. It had broken her heart when he left the ranch. She always thought he belonged at the ranch and would always be there and that someday…someday, he would notice how grown up she'd become. It shouldn't have surprised her though that he never paid any attention to her back then, since she was just the ranch foreman's daughter.

Her heart ached at the memory of the last time she'd seen him just days before his wedding to the Dallas socialite. He'd come back to the ranch tense, drawn and not acting like the happy bridegroom she'd expected him to be. He seemed angry and upset and wouldn't talk to anyone on the ranch. Late one afternoon they accidentally met in the barn while she was mucking stalls. At first they talked about trivial events and things and she couldn't recall just how they ended up in the hayloft above. It wasn't planned but their lovemaking took her by complete surprise. It all seemed so natural and right as his skilled hands played over her virgin body to heighten and awaken every aching desire in her. She'd thrown caution out the barn door that day and never looked back. Neither had Nick. She never saw or heard from him again. A week later he was married. Her daughter Nicole was born nine months later in California.

Just like then, today wasn't planned. She never expected to see him here and it caught her emotions off guard. Something she didn't like. Since leaving the ranch she was always in control of her emotions. Or maybe, as she thought about it, she had simply buried them. Whichever, she found her body aroused and her emotions running the gamut from anger to desire. Thank God he'd be out of her life tomorrow. She didn't need this kind of emotional upheaval.

There was another rap on the door. Kristy turned on the bedside lamp. "Come in."

This time it was Ellen, her mother, hobbling on crutches. She came to stand by the bed. "Kristy, look at me, I know that look in your eyes."

Kristy sat up and plumped a pillow behind her back. "Mama, you promised me I would never have to be at the ranch at the same time as Nick. You promised!"

"Stop that nonsense girl. He's here because of Jack. He wasn't expected. I didn't lie to you."

"I know...but when I saw him...it caught me completely off guard."

"Look Kristy, I'm sorry. He only flew in this afternoon after Rex discovered the dead cows and the stallions in with the mares. Unfortunately, Rex thinks most of the activity happened within the past two weeks. You can imagine how angry Nick was to learn about it."

"He asked me to call him when I'm in Dallas."

Ellen frowned. "Do you think that's a wise thing to do?"

"Mom, I just don't know. I doubt I'll call him, there's no reason for me to. But I'll be living there with Nicki and he's bound to find out I have a daughter."

"What are you going to do?"

Kristy took a deep breath. "I can't hide Nicki forever, but I don't have to tell him either." She felt better now that she'd made a decision.

"I've asked Maria Lupe to come in and help out. Nick asked Joe if he thought you needed a ride to Dallas. You're damn dad said he thought you might. So...be ready early."

"Oh no, he didn't." Her gaze went up to the ceiling. "Should I rent a car to get back?"

"No, Doc said he'd fly you back. Kristy...be careful. I don't want to see you hurt again."

"Neither do I." She drew her knees up and rested her chin on them. "Neither do I."

Once her mother left, Kristy quickly packed what she would need in Dallas and went to bed. She didn't want to think about the consequences. She knew from before what could happen if she wasn't careful.

At four the next morning there was a soft tap on the door. Half asleep Kristy flew out of bed to answer it. Nick stood there dressed and ready to go. "Give me a second," she motioned for him to come into the room.

She grabbed her toothbrush and raced around the room gathering her jeans and a tee shirt. She hadn't closed the bathroom door as she peeled out of her night clothes and Nick stood in the shadows admiring the view of trim legs and white lace being slipped into jeans. He sucked in his breath when she pulled her nightshirt over her head and slipped into the tight fitting red tee shirt. His body reacted to what he saw and he swore beneath his breath.

Stepping back into the bedroom she said, "I'm ready." She smiled at him and threw the toothbrush into her purse then picked up her suitcase.

KAREN NEWCOMB & DAVID CARLTON, D.V.M.

Nick let out a sigh and under his breath said, "So am I." He pulled his jacket across the front of his jeans to hide how ready he really was.

Once they landed Nick taxied to where he kept the plane and helped Kristy out. "Do you have a place to stay?" he asked.

"I'll call a hotel, the company will pay for it."

They walked to his big red pickup with a metal vet pack filling the bed of the truck. "You can stay at my place I've got plenty of room."

She hesitated before getting into the truck. "I...I don't think that's such a good idea. I need to rent a car and check out apartments. I don't want to impose."

He started Big Red and pulled out. "I have a car you can use. It's no bother."

Again caught totally off guard and unprepared Kristy didn't know how to refuse him. "If you're sure."

He gave her a sidelong glance. "I'm sure." Then added, "We probably won't see each other anyway I'm usually too busy to do anything but catch a few hours of sleep at the house...if I'm lucky."

It was a quiet drive home with little conversation. Nick pulled into the driveway of his north Dallas ranch-style house and turned off the engine. He leaned back against the seat and rested an arm out the window. "We're here. I'm going to grab a cup of coffee and head for the clinic I have a busy day scheduled."

Once inside he led Kristy to a bedroom. "You can stay in here, make yourself to home."

She tossed her bag onto the double bed and followed him into the kitchen. "Here, let me do that." She took the coffee canister from his hands and asked where the pot was. He pointed to the corner of the counter. "Thank you for the offer of letting me stay here, I promise to stay out of your way." That was one promise she intended to keep.

He sat down at the table to admire the way she moved, almost like a dancer, he thought. He hoped she wouldn't stay out of his way too much of the time. He kind of liked having her there with him.

"Can I fix you some breakfast before you go?" she asked.

"Sure, I think there's food in the refrigerator."

She half-way laughed as she opened the refrigerator. There wasn't much in there but she knew he liked his bacon and eggs and just how he liked them. It wasn't long before he had a breakfast fit for a cowboy sitting before him. She poured him a second cup of coffee.

24

Satisfied with a full stomach, he pushed his plate back and finished the coffee. "Wish I had more time to talk but I have to get going. Thanks for the breakfast."

She smiled. "My pleasure." If there was one thing she knew how to do and do well it was cooking. Her passion since she was a little girl. She'd taken that passion one-step farther and even attended weekend classes at the finest cooking school in San Francisco and at some of the wineries.

After Nick left Kristy went into the bedroom to unpack. It was a comfortable room obliviously not decorated by Nick, but probably by Mallory. She showered, dressed and pulled out a Dallas phone book. First she would check into the office.

"Welcome to Dallas, Miss Williams," Tina, the petite brunette secretary said. "This is your office and I'll be your secretary. Is there anything I can get for you?"

Kristy looked out the glass windows at the Dallas skyline. It wasn't nearly as beautiful as San Francisco but it felt more like home. "Would you happen to know of any apartments for rent?"

"I'll make a list for you. You have a daughter don't you?"

"I do. Actually, even a small house might work."

"I'll see what I can do."

Kristy looked up to see a man in his late thirties standing in her office. "May I help you?"

"Hi, Kristy, I'm Matt Jordan, your boss."

Kristy smiled brightly and said, "I apologize for not recognizing you, but I do know the name. I'm very pleased to meet you."

Matt extended his hand to her and she took it. "I had no idea they'd be sending me the most beautiful woman in California...and with a hint of a Texas accent."

"Flattery will get you everywhere, Mr. Jordan."

"Call me Matt. Tina said you need a list of apartments and I'm having her working on that right now. I don't expect you to come in to work until your mother is back on her feet. How is she?"

"Actually, we have more help coming in so I can be to work as soon as I find a place to live and get my daughter out here."

"Then do you want me to send some of my files home with you so you can go over them?"

Kristy smiled. "I'd like that." Work would also take her mind off

Nick while she was staying with him.

"Could I interest you in some lunch?" Matt asked.

"I think I'd like that."

Over lunch Kristy learned Matt was a transplanted Californian himself, born and raised in Manhattan Beach, which would explain his stocky yet muscular blond surfer good looks. He graduated from Berkeley with a degree in business and marketing and went to work for the company straight out of college. He loved his job and missed California.

"I get back home as much as possible, which isn't often enough," he said.

"I imagine you feel landlocked here in Dallas."

He had a charming laugh and his blue eyes crinkled slightly at the corners. "Yeah, I do. Not a wave to be found. When will your daughter arrive?"

Kristy sipped her iced tea. "She'll be flying in today, mom and dad have offered to keep her there until I find us something here. I miss her so much." The thought of Nicki tugged at her heart.

Matt raised an arched eyebrow. "She's what six? I think I read that or was told that."

"She's six."

"You're a lucky woman to have a daughter. What about her father will he be moving here too?"

Kristy froze, she hoped he wouldn't judge her too harshly. "I'm single, Nicole doesn't know her father."

Matt leaned back in the chair and gave her his full attention. "Want to share the story?"

She shook her head. "It's best left the way it is."

"Then I won't pry."

"Thanks."

"How committed are you to company?" He watched the expression change on her face and knew she'd be the one he needed for the new endeavor he was about to undertake. With her blonde good looks and self-confident demeanor the clients would love her.

Matt's question caught her by surprise. "I've worked for them for seven years now, I guess you might call that committed."

"Are you open to other propositions if they come along?"

She shrugged, not understanding his meaning. "Of course, why?"

He winked and picked up the bill to sign. "I have something in mind that you would be perfect for but I don't want to get into it right at the moment."

Kristy couldn't imagine what he would have in mind for her.

CHAPTER THREE

Kristy spent the rest of the afternoon checking out two bedroom apartments. With Nicki in mind there was something wrong with every apartment she'd seen. She'd try again tomorrow. She returned to the office to gather up the files she needed to go over then headed for Nick's home.

Nick pulled into the driveway and noticed the car was still gone. Kristy hadn't returned yet. Looking up at the darkened house a pang of loneliness came over him. She'd only been there one day and already seemed a part of his life. He knew she had gotten under his skin seven years ago but hadn't realized she was still there until this morning. He slammed the palm of his hand against the steering wheel, turned the key over and burned rubber pulling out of the driveway. He needed to be with friends tonight.

"Well, howdy Doc!" Mavis Rhodes shouted from behind the bar of the Lone Star Saloon. "What'll y'all have?" She picked up a bar towel and wiped up spilled beer.

Nick leaned against the bar and thumbed his hat back slightly and said, "Beer. How are you, Mavis?"

"Ah, Doc, I can't complain. Arthritis acts up now and then but can't complain. Hear you've been busy at the ranch."

Word traveled fast. "Yeah, flew in flew out."

Mavis was the barkeep with a heart. A former model and singer she married the bar's owner some thirty years ago and had inherited it when the old drunk died. Mavis loved her job because she loved people. She knew everyone and everything that happened in this part of Dallas and some of what was going on in the other parts as well. She had a dry wit and keen eye and could spot a man with a problem the minute he walked into the room.

She sat the long neck in front of Nick wiped her hands across the clean half apron she wore and picked up the bar towel again. She leaned back against the liquor wall behind the bar and folded her arms across her chest. "Why are you so down, Doc?"

Nick took a long swig of beer and sat the bottle down heavily on the bar. "Don't rightly know."

A tight smile formed on Mavis' lips and spread across her face. "It's gotta be a woman. Nothing else could put that scowl on your face. And there's only one woman I know of that ever really got to you. I hear she's back."

Surprised, he glanced up at Mavis. "Shit if you ain't a crusty old gal. You seem to know everything about me before I do. She's back. In fact I have her staying at my place while she looks for an apartment."

"Doc…that's dangerous. You know that. Christ, that little Kristy has been in love with you since she was a mere kid. I hear she's not married." She could hardly wait to see the expression on his face.

Nick once again gave her a look of frustration. How the hell did she know so much? "Hell, she's no little kid anymore, she's all grown up in every way."

"So what are you gonna do about it?"

Nick's eyebrows drew together and a crease formed between them. "Mavis, have you always been this way?"

"What way?"

"You speak your mind even when it's not wanted."

Mavis gave him one of her smiles she was famous for. "Of course. How else could I survive in a business like this? You know she's got a kid don't you?" She waited.

The smile faded from his face. "No, I didn't know."

"Did you ever bother to ask if she'd been married or had children?"

Nick's heart was reeling. "I thought I would have known if she had." A kid? Kristy had a kid? How was he suppose to feel about that?

"She must have met someone in California."

Mavis gave him a sidelong glance and wondered how stupid one man could be. "Maybe. Why don't you ask her about her daughter when you see her again."

His head snapped up to see Mavis staring at him. "Daughter? Where the hell is the father?"

Mavis shrugged. "How would I know I'm just a barkeep." She walked away to greet another lonely looking customer.

Nick sat there dumbfounded. How could Mavis possibly know all this about Kristy when he didn't know? When Mavis made her way back down the bar she was polishing an imaginary stain with the bar towel.

"You know Mavis you're going to wear a hole in this damn bar one of these days."

"Going to the Cowboy Rodeo this year?"

"Probably, why?"

"Gonna ask Kristy?"

"I don't know, I hadn't thought that far ahead."

"What's she like? I haven't seen her in what…seven years now. I'll bet she's even more beautiful now than she was back then."

Nick picked up a pretzel and turned it over and over between his fingers. "She's a real beauty. She works for a clothing company and is moving here to Dallas to do something in publicity or advertising."

Mavis continued to question him. "How do you feel about that? I mean her moving here…with her daughter."

"I don't know. And why the hell are you so interested in her? Christ, I didn't even know she had a daughter until just now."

"I know love when I see it in a man's eyes. You can deny it all you want but I know the truth. Bring her in and let me see if it's still there in her eyes too."

The bar door flew opened and a loud feminine voice boomed, "Nick Chandler, where the hell have you been?"

Mavis frowned. "God, she's just what I don't need tonight. Jez Bevaca. The last time she came in she started the men a fightin' and they busted up half my place pretty good. Look, Doc, keep her in line or get her the hell out of here."

Nick grinned. "What's the matter, Mavis? See a little of yourself in Jez? You can't tell me men didn't do some fighting over you in the past."

Mavis slapped her shoulder with the towel. "You old charmer you. Go after Kristy. Keep Jez in line. Don't do anything you don't want to do. And one final bit of sage advice…follow your heart." She headed back down the bar.

Nick felt the sting of a heavy slap against his back, he knew who it was. "Evening Jez."

Her arms wrapped around his waist while her fingers dipped beneath the belt. "Nick, God it's good to see you…feel you."

"Cut it out, Jez. This is a public place."

Jez took her fingers out of his pants and sat down on the stool next to him. As usual, her long raven black hair lay heavy against her back and beneath the black hat with a large silver concho attached to the front. "So…where've you been?"

"No where but working. You been looking for me?"

"Yeah. I want you to take me to the Cowboy Rodeo in Guthrie. It'll be like old times. We'll make the black devil rock."

"You still got that old rolling black Ford brothel?"

"Hell it can't be considered a brothel if I'm the only one in there."

He didn't even want to think of the one and only time he and Jez were together. "I've got a date."

"No shit! You have not. You always take me." She leaned closer to him. "Then afterwards we can go dancin', we could go back to the truck afterwards and let me show you a good time." Her hand went to his back and her tongue went to his ear.

There had been a time when Jez did have an effect on him, but not tonight. In fact, he felt repulsed by her and gently unhanded her. "No, Jez. I'm not in the mood."

"Well get in the mood. It's been a month since I've had any lovin' and I'm ready."

"Always the bitch in heat. Go find someone else."

She pulled away. "You serious? Since when didn't you like to be man handled, shall we say?"

"I'm serious."

Jez really wasn't as crude as she pretended and Nick knew it. He's known her longer than he'd known Kristy. He and Jez had gone to high school together. Half Mexican, half Irish, Jez Bevaca was always fun to be with and passionate as all hell when she wanted to be. She hated her name, Jezebel, and the color red. She'd once said it had something to do with a Betty Davis movie her mother had seen when she was pregnant with Jez. In her teens she had been raped by a stepfather and from then on her whole personality changed. Nick liked Jez, not just for sex, but because he really liked her. They had been friends most of their lives. She was someone he could count on in the past and he was there for her more than once. Jez was also a hell of a horsewoman and even sang in bars when she got drunk enough to carry a tune.

Jez pretended to be wild because she liked getting men riled up enough to fight over her. She was known to make love with the hot-blooded passion of her Mexican half and at the same time use the wit and charm of the Irish half. She was flirtatious as all hell. She would tease her victims until they gave in to what ever she wanted and she wanted it all. Nick knew she'd been careful with the partners she'd chosen in the past but she was still a tease to almost everyone else and that's the reputation she had.

"Nick, what's wrong?" Jez asked.

Nick finished off the beer. "I flew in from the ranch this morning, put in a full day's work at the clinic and now I'm dead tired. So don't ask what's the matter."

"No, I've seen you after just such a day before, there's more."

Nick stood, slipped a twenty on the counter and started to leave. "I'm out of here."

"Hey Doc, you can't just walk out on me like that," Jez yelled over the already noisy room.

"The hell I can't." He headed for "Big Red" and home.

Kristy had come home to an empty house and was relieved. She'd stopped at the grocery store and picked up some steaks, potatoes and makings for a salad. She was so use to California cooking it was a way of life for her now. She fired up the backyard grill and put a dab of olive oil and garlic salt on the steak before she tossed it on the hot grate. She had no idea if or when Nick would be home but she made enough for two just in case he showed up. She'd also picked up a bottle of Texas grown Cabernet Sauvignon wine and opened it. She had just finished tossing the salad when the front door opened.

Kristy walked from the kitchen to see Nick toss his hat on a chair. "You look tired. Can I get you a beer? Or a glass of wine?"

She looked radiant standing there in form fitting jeans and tank top. How could someone so beautiful not be married? "Beer, thanks."

"I…took the liberty of buying steaks and I've got one on the grill, would you like me to fix you one?"

"Thanks."

She handed him a beer then took her wine and walked back outside. It was a beautiful warm evening. She could feel him watching her. When she turned around he was openly staring at her. Those pewter blue eyes bore into her and gave her a questioning look.

"Why didn't you tell me you have a daughter?" He asked in a tone that had a hint of hurt in it.

Stunned, she was afraid to answer him. Who told him? "I…I guess she's never come up in our conversations. How did you know about her?"

"Mavis."

She took the steaks from the grill and walked back inside to the kitchen. Nick followed her.

"Mavis, from the Lone Star?" Her stomach was in knots and her fingers shook. What was she suppose to tell him? Better yet, how was she suppose to tell him?

"How the hell did Mavis know when I didn't?"

They sat at the table. "My daughter isn't a secret. I suppose she could have learned about her from anyone that knew."

"And who the hell would that be? I didn't even know." He cut into the steak.

Kristy finished the wine and poured herself another glass. She needed all the courage she could muster. "I…ah…you haven't been in my life at all over the years, so I doubt anyone would have said anything to you."

He leaned back in the chair to watch her. "How old is she?"

She looked away from his gaze. "She's a little over six."

Nick didn't blink. "Six? Hell you must have found someone just after you left home."

Kristy didn't answer but stood and walked to the window to look out. "I can't say anything." Her stomach was churning.

"What's her name? Is she going to come live with you in Dallas?"

He needed some answers.

"She's already at the ranch, she flew into Lubbock this morning and dad picked her up from the airport. Yes, she'll be living with me here in Dallas."

"And her name?"

She turned to face Nick. "It's...Nicole, she prefers to be called Nicki."

Nick frowned. Who the hell? "Who's her father?"

Kristy's heart raced with anxiety. "That's not important. Nicki is the love of my life and together we've built a wonderful life for ourselves. She's bright and charming and has this unique love for animals. She was in tears when we had to sell her horse so we could move here. I promised I'd buy her another one. I'm sure dad already has her on one of the ranch horses." She was rambling on just to make conversation and to keep from facing any more of his questions.

Nick was stunned at her revelation. "And her father?"

"I told you it's not important. He has his life and we have ours." Oh, God, how was he going to react when he saw Nicki? Maybe he wouldn't recognize himself in her, but she was sure everyone else would.

"I told your dad I'd fly you back to the ranch this weekend. Suppose I'll get to meet her then?" Kristy was hiding something from him and he was going to get to the bottom of it. Even Mavis, of all people, knew her secret, so why wouldn't she tell him?

Kristy picked up the remnants of the meal and dealt with them before putting the dishes into the dishwasher. She made a pot of coffee.

"So did you go to your new office?" He asked.

"Yes, I met my boss. Matt Jordan is from California and we seem to have a lot in common. It'll be nice working with someone I like and can relate to."

"Did you look for an apartment?"

"Yes, but with Nicki there are some things I have to consider. I promise I'll be out of your hair soon. I can check into a hotel if you want me too."

He took the towel out of her hand and tossed it onto the sink counter. He tucked her hand in his and led her into the living room. "You don't have to move out. There's plenty of room here if you want to stay. You can bring your daughter back with you."

Kristy sucked in her breath. "I think mom and dad would like to keep her until I find a place for us."

They sat next to each other on the couch. His fingers played up and down her neck sending tiny shock waves surging through her. "Is she named after her father?"

Kristy looked away from him. Why was he questioning her? "Yes. But he doesn't know about her and if I have my way he never will."

"Why?"

"Because he's not the marrying kind. Nicki and I are doing just fine without a man in our lives."

Nick was about to ask her something when the phone rang. When he hung up he looked at Kristy. "Got a calf delivery at the Allen place. Wanta go with me? Wear something befitting a calf delivery."

They reached the Allen's ranch to find the cow standing knee deep in a muddy corral with a breach calf trapped in her uterus. Rain clouds billowed overhead. "Let's get her in the squeeze chute," Nick directed the farmer.

Large raindrops fell as Nick's hand scanned the contents of the cow's womb. Kristy cringed and walked toward the expectant mother's horns. Cecil Allen had secured the nose tongs to distract the Hereford from the pelvic exam yet she still bellowed with discomfort. Her uterine contractions pressured Nick's arm against her bony hip walls until his fingers went numb. "Hold her still," he yelled.

Kristy gently stroked the cow's head between her horns and spoke quietly to her. It seemed to work. "Just let Nick do his job and you'll have your baby in no time." She watched the cow's abdominal muscles strain with each contraction and she thought about her own delivery. If only she'd had him to comfort her back then instead of...She spoke again to the cow while she stroked her head. "It's going to be all right. Nick's here to help you." When the cow groaned Kristy grimaced knowing just how she felt. "It'll be over soon, I promise."

Sweat and rain poured down Nick's brow. "This sonofabitch is upside and backwards."

Kristy watched as both Nick's arms disappeared deep inside the cow and he pushed, tugged and winced with all his might. She started to croon softly to the cow singing a lullaby she'd sung to Nicki when she was a baby. Strangely enough the cow seem to react.

"I've got the front legs," Nick grunted, his nose pressed against the cow's tail bone. He reached in as far as he could.

Steam rose from the cow's back as the large drops of rain turned into sheets. Nick finally locked the tips of his fingers into the calf's nostrils and pulled the head and hooves into birthing position. "I've got it turned. Get the O.B. chains!"

Cecil Allen handed Nick the chains and he again dove deep into the cow's reproductive trace to retrieve the struggling newborn. The cow strained and bellowed loudly. Kristy crooned even louder and looked into the suffering brown eyes of the mother.

Nick followed his left arm with the chains looped around the fingers of his right hand. He grimaced and stretched. He twisted and grunted until taunt tails of the chains hooked into the O.B. handles. The double loops had been wrapped around the calf's forelegs. "I've got it. Cecil hand me the calf-jack."

Kristy was in as much agony as the cow. She found herself trying to coax the cow to breath slowly like she'd done with Lamaze. Hell, she had no idea what she was doing at this point she just wanted it to be over for her and the cow.

The farmer looked at Kristy and smiled. "Hey Doc, this one's not squeamish like the others. She have kids herself? The others say they never want kids after seein' something like this."

Nick was too busy to answer Cecil. He secured the butt-bar of the calf-jack into position. Nick grabbed the hand of the calf-jack and cranked with all his might. Afterbirth secretions splattered down the front of his coveralls when the newborn's head and forequarters came through the narrow pelvic outlet. Amnionic fluid odors filled the air but the rain quickly cleansed it away.

"Doc," Cecil calmly asked, "How does all that pass through sucha small hole?"

Kristy's face went pale. She didn't want to think about the same question she'd once asked when she saw her first calf born back on the ranch years ago. She had to admit though, it did help when it came time for her to give birth to Nicki. She'd been well prepared.

When Kristy watched and heard the sound of the calf slip from her mother the cow seemed to sigh with relief and Kristy fully understood that feeling also. The cow now had a bull calf to tend to.

Once again she stroked the new mother's head and thought she saw relief in those large brown eyes. The calf jumped to its feet. It was over. Now all they had to do was clean up and go back to the clinic.

"Thanks for your help back there. Old Cecil was amazed you didn't faint or something. I guess you've been at enough birthings to know what's expected."

She dried her hands and looked away from him. "Ranch life gave me a reality check on many things. Giving birth is just one of them."

He'd changed his clothes and was making notes in the file for his secretary. "Did you give birth alone?" He asked and went to check on an ailing dog in one of the kennels.

"I didn't have much of a choice. I did what I had to do."

"I take that to be a yes."

She hesitated, then said, "No, I had a friend with me."

"And where the hell was the man responsible for your condition in the first place? Shouldn't he have been there with you, taking care of you?"

Kristy petted the dog's head. "Nick, he was a married man."

His brows drew together with surprise. Nick finished his exam and put the dog back in the cage. "How'd that happen? That's not like you at all."

"It just happened."

"Where's the bastard now? Still married?"

She hoped he would drop the subject. "No, he's not."

"Then don't you think he should know where you are, shit, where his daughter is?"

"I told you he doesn't know about her. She doesn't know him."

He scowled. "And how the hell are you going to tell her when she does ask?"

"I'll have a story ready by then."

"A story? Is that what your daughter means to you? That you have to make up a story about her father?"

Kristy was getting angry. Why didn't he just drop the subject? Nicki was her responsibility, not his. "Nick, I don't want to talk about this. She's my daughter and I take full responsibility for her well being and happiness."

"And I'd like to kill the bastard who did this to you." Who was the man who took her after him? He wanted to kill the married bastard.

They walked out to Big Red and he gunned the engine heading home. Once there she quietly went to her room. She couldn't deal with his questions any longer.

CHAPTER FOUR

When the phone rang at six the next morning Nick rolled over in bed and picked it up. "Doctor Chandler," he said sleepily.

"Doc, it's Jack, we've got a little problem here at the ranch."

Nick groaned. "Oh shit, now what?"

"When can you get here?"

"Look, Uncle Jack, I've got a full week. My partner Brian and I will be there on Friday before we go to the Cowboy Rodeo. I'm dropping Kristy off." He couldn't imagine what kind of trouble his uncle could have created in such a short time. God, he was there only days ago. The phone fell silent. "Jack? You still there?"

"Eh…yeah."

"Well spit it out what's wrong?" Nick's arm went across his closed eyes as he waited to hear the latest crisis.

"Well, hell," Jack stammered. "It's just that when I got to my breakfast table this morning I was greeted by some small person who told me it wasn't polite to wear my spurs in the house. Or my hat! Can you believe it? I wear my spurs everywhere. And my hat!"

Nick was sure he was dreaming. Why would Jack call him about something like this? "What are you talking about? What small person?"

"Hell, I don't know who she is. Some kid about five or six was sitting at the table eating cereal when I got there. The house was all

39

dark and quiet…except for this little girl. The rudest damn kid I've ever seen, mind ya. She told me not to wear my spurs…that I'd scuff the floors up. Then she asked me if I had brushed my teeth. And why I smoked."

Nick chuckled silently. She must be Kristy's daughter. She must be something to upset his uncle so much. "Well what else did she say? Did she tell you her name?"

"That's why you need to come down. She won't tell me anything, just that I don't meet her standards as the man of the house."

"Good God, Jack, do you mean to tell me you woke me up at six to tell me some kid is making your morning miserable?"

"I wouldn't have called if I weren't upset. How dare they bring this young whippersnapper in here and let her talk to me this way. Although…you know, the kid seems familiar somehow. She said her name is Nicole but I was never to call her that."

"Then call her Nicki. She's Kristy's daughter, that's why she seems familiar."

"Oh Christ you mean to tell me Kristy has a daughter? Who's the daddy?"

"I don't know. You're on your own. Good-bye." Nick rolled over and put the phone down. Nicki must be some young lady to send Uncle Jack over the edge.

He didn't say…but did he take his spurs off? Shoot, Jack wore those damn spurs to bed. Mavis once told him Jack even made love with the damn things on. How did she know? The image caused chills to run up his spine. Not the spurs in bed, but Jack and Mavis making love. Well, now that he was awake he should start his day. Was that coffee he smelled?

Kristy heard the phone ring and automatically got up to make coffee. Yawning, she was about to go back into the bedroom to put her robe on over her night shorts and tank top when Nick walked into the room looking just as sleepy as she felt.

"Do I smell coffee?" he asked and stretched.

"It'll be a minute or two. Do you have to rush off to an emergency? I heard the phone ring."

Nick ran his fingers through his thick hair. "Oh hell that was Uncle Jack. Seems there's a young lady there that doesn't like the fact he's wearing spurs in the house or a hat at the table and let him know in no uncertain terms. She belong to you?"

Kristy hid her smile. "That's Nicki. Oh my God I hope she's not causing trouble."

"That crusty old fart could use a new viewpoint in his life. Your Nicki might just be the one to give it to him."

"Nicki's pretty opinionated for a six year old. She calls it like she sees it. She takes after her dad..." Her hands came up to cover her mouth, she'd said too much. She quickly turned to the cupboard to pull out a mug and filled for Nick.

When she handed him the mug his hands stayed on hers. "Who was the bastard that got you pregnant and left you all alone? How long after me did you wait?"

She sucked in her breath. "Seven years is a long time. I've made my share of mistakes. But Nicki isn't one of them. When I look at her I can see the man I love in her face and I will never regret her having been born."

"Do you still love him?" He dreaded the answer.

She looked away from his penetrating gaze. "Yes and I always will. Nicki is the bond we'll always have together."

He dropped his hand. He couldn't compete with someone that special to her. They'd had a child together. "Would you come to the Cowboy Rodeo with me and my partner Brian this weekend? We'll stop over at the ranch first. Maybe I can meet your Nicki. Hell, if she's got Jack this upset I think I like her already."

She started to walk out of the room back to the bedroom. She wanted to scream out at him that Nicki was his daughter and she looked so goddamn much like him it sometimes hurt to look at her own daughter. "I'll think about it. I'll need to see if mom can handle Nicki for a while longer."

Nick watched her long legs carry her back down the hall recalling how they fit wrapped around him when he made love to her. He needed a cold shower.

Nick arrived early at his Dallas, Twisted Trail Animal Clinic, yet the parking lot was full of old and new pickup trucks, a vintage Mercedes, a motorcycle and two bicycles. Coming through the back door he was greeted with the familiar sounds of cats meowing and dogs barking, not to mention the aroma of antiseptic. His technician, Joanie Sanders walked rapidly past him. "Morin' Doc." He removed his hat and hung it on the coat rack then slipped into his lab coat.

"Hey Doc, thought you weren't coming in until this afternoon," Joanie shouted over the animal noise. "Doc Walker will be glad you're back. He had an emergency run out to the Whiteley Stables. You could start with exam room one."

He watched Joanie open the refrigerator and take out a bottle of medicine before she walked to the work counter and started filling syringes.

"When is Brian coming back from the stables?" He walked to the door marked one and took the medical file out of the holder on the door.

"He's due back any time now."

Before going into the exam room Nick checked in at the receptionist counter to let his receptionist Cheryl know he was in. The reception room was full of waiting patients and their owners. A young boy stood up and walked slowly to the front of the counter. Nick glanced down at him and smiled.

"Mister..." the young boy said shyly.

"Howdy partner, what can I do for you?" Nick asked.

"It's something I found under some bushes and needs help?" The boy reached deep into his jacket pocket and pulled out a small helpless horny toad.

Nick asked, "Where did you get the toad?"

"I found it just layin' there."

Nick took the toad. "Well now this looks serious."

"Yeah," the youngster said, "That's why I brung him here." Tears streamed down his freckled face and he wiped them away with a slightly dirty hand.

Nick looked out into the crowded waiting room, then to Cheryl. She smiled and announced to the room, "We seem to have an emergency here, does anyone mind if this young man goes first?"

No one spoke out as Nick took the boy by his grimy little hand and lead him into the surgery room. The little boy's eyes grew large and round at the sight of the room.

"What's your name?" Nick asked.

"It's Joey Mitchell."

"Well, Joey, if you wait right here I have to get my nurse."

Joey's head bobbed up and down as his huge eyes roamed from equipment to equipment.

"Joanie, we have to save a horny toad that has a broken leg."

Joanie's gasped. "Where is it?"

"The patient's owner is waiting in surgery."

Joanie replaced the medicine in the refrigerator and followed Nick into surgery.

"Ah sir," Joey said, "are you gonna use all this stuff on the toad?"

"If I have to," Nick said.

"Well...ah...I ain't got much money," Joey said the words in a loud clear voice so there was no mistake.

Nick looked down at Joey. "I think we'll be able to work something out. But first I have to check his leg and see if it's broken." He gently examined the right rear leg of the toad while trying to hold the squirming toad down on the table. "How did you say he got hurt?"

"I don't know. Howie and me were riding our bikes when we saw it in the bushes."

Trying to distract Joey, Nick said, "Really?"

"Yeah, Howie's my bestus friend."

"Joey, why don't you go out in the waiting room with Howie while I take care of your pet."

Big tears started to slip down Joey's cheeks and his lower lip jutted out. "You ain't gonna put it to sleep are you mister?"

Nick picked Joey up in his arms and walked him over to the surgical table to where Joanie and the toad waited. "No, we're gonna take care of it. Tell you what, I'll let you see him once we fix him up."

"Thanks, mister." Joey jammed his hands into his pockets and followed Joanie back out to the waiting room.

After fixing the toad Nick returned to the waiting room to let Joey know about his toad. Joey reached in his pocket and pulled out four cents. Nick took one of the pennies. "One ought to do it. If you tell Joanie here your phone number she'll call you in two weeks to remind you to bring your toad back for me to look at."

Joey nodded and held his horny toad in his hands. "Gee Mister, you're cheaper than I thought." He turned and ran out into the waiting room to retrieve his sulking friend and show off the toad's splint.

43

Joanie shook her head and cleaned up the operating table. "Doc, you're such an old softie. You'd sure made a good dad. What about the toad's foot, will it mend?"

"If memory serves me that toad will sprout a new foot in a couple of weeks."

Later that day as he sat at his cluttered desk Joanie's words about him being a good dad hit home. He thought of Kristy. He wondered if she was at home yet. He dialed the number and she picked up.

"Hi, this is Nick."

Kristy blushed. "I wasn't sure if I should answer the phone or not but I called mom and she was suppose to call me back."

"Want to go to the Lone Star Saloon tonight?"

"Sure."

"Then I'll see you in about an hour."

"Would you rather I meet you there?"

"No, I'll be home shortly." When he hung up he found himself smiling. It was nice having her there. The house was no longer dark and empty when he came home and he liked that. She was a cook after his heart and remembered seeing her in the ranch kitchen growing up learning to cook at Ellen's knee. He hoped she wouldn't find an apartment any time soon he was just beginning to eat a well.

When he rolled Big Red to a stop and walked inside the place was as bright and as clean as a new penny. She'd even bought fresh flowers to sit on the table. "Kristy, I'm home," he said and strangely enough liked the way it sounded.

When she came out of the bedroom the sight of her took his breath away. Dressed in tight jeans and even tighter white tee shirt that accentuated her tan she looked every inch a Texan. She wore her white Stetson and cowgirl boots. Those trim legs and shapely hips sent chills up his spine.

"Ready for some two step?"

She laughed. "Oh I'm not sure I remember any of that but I could use a good night out. I've looked at so many apartments today my feet ache. I spent most of the rest of the day going over the files Matt sent home."

He put his arm around her waist. "Then let's head out."

Nick parked Big Red and escorted Kristy into the bar. Once inside there was total silence as the regular rowdy's looked at her. She made quite an impact.

"Mavis," Nick yelled, "mind if we take a table?"

Mavis' mouth dropped open when she saw the two of them together. My God, if he didn't get his hooks into her he was the biggest goddamn fool in the world. "Sure. Hi Kristy, good to see you again."

Kristy smiled and let Nick pull a chair out for her. When she heard chairs scrapping around the room she looked up to see at least six men heading in her direction. Five she recognized.

"Hi, Kristy," Dan Miller said. "Man, have you grown up. What the hell are you doing with Doc here?"

"Hi, Dan. Nice to see you again. How's your wife?"

"Gone."

"I'm sorry."

Dan raised an eyebrow and the corners of his mouth curved up into a smile. "I'm not. You remember these guys here?"

Kristy smiled. "I think so." She'd seen most of these guys at the ranch at one time or another.

When someone put money in the jukebox Dan held his hand out to Kristy. "May I Doc?"

Nick wasn't at all happy to see her look askance at him, but he agreed. He was even angrier when he saw Dan's long arms wrap tightly around her, drawing her hips to his and move about the room. She hadn't forgotten a thing about dancing and he could hardly wait his turn to hold her that close to him.

Mavis brought him a long neck and set it before him. "What do you think Kristy'll have?"

He couldn't take his eyes off Kristy. "I don't know she seems to like that red wine. Got any?"

"Yeah, but I think she's probably use to that California stuff. Why don't I fix her one of my margarita's, if I recall she use to like them."

"Sure, suit yourself."

"You're an ass, Doc, do you know that?"

He winced and looked up at Mavis. "Been called that plenty of times but not by you. What brought that on?"

"Can't you see how she feels about you? I could see it the minute you walked in here with her. She's crazy about you."

"She's in love with the father of her daughter, she told me that herself. I can't compete with that."

"Not only are you an ass but a blind one at that. Are you going to the ranch tomorrow?"

He frowned at Mavis. "How the hell do you know so much about my business? Yeah, Brian and I are going to drive there and go on to the rodeo. Why?"

"Kristy going?"

"To the ranch or to the rodeo?"

"Either."

"Yeah, to both I hope."

"Open your eyes when you get there. Now, why are you sitting here go and ask that filly to dance with you."

It wasn't easy pulling her away from Dan. But once he had his arms around her he didn't want to let go. She fit in them perfectly.

Kristy could hardly wait for him to ask her to dance because she wanted to remember how it felt to have his arms around her. He was good at slow dancing and held her tight against him. She inhaled his scent, laid her head against his chest and closed her eyes. She remembered every little detail about him. As they moved about the room she could feel his hardness press against his jeans and her stomach. She longed to free him and show him how much she wanted him.

"Nick," she whispered, "are you going to be able to walk back to the table?"

He grinned down at her. "Offering to be my shield?"

"It's a good thing it's dark in here."

Her perfume was driving him crazy as was the way she fit in his arms. No wonder he was reacting to her. When another slow song began he pulled her even closer to him and put his lips against her ear.

"Nick...I don't mean to make you uncomfortable."

"You aren't. This is my reaction to you. I haven't felt this good about anyone in years, I guess you bring back the memory of what we had."

She closed her eyes and savored the feel of his body next to hers. It might be a long time before she had the nerve to do anything to encourage him and right now, she loved being in his arms with his body wanting hers. When the song ended he walked behind her to the table.

Mavis brought Kristy a frosty margarita and set it before her. "It's so good to see you again, darlin', how ya doin'?" Her voice was soft and husky.

"I'm doing just fine. I'm moving to Dallas to work. Thanks for the margarita, you remembered."

"Darlin' there ain't nothin' I don't remember about you. I hear your darlin' little girl is at the ranch. Hear she's the spittin' image of her pa. How'd you manage to do that?" She watched Kristy's reaction.

Kristy looked down at the table and away from Nick. "Word gets around doesn't it? How'd you even know I had a daughter? As for who she looks like I've been told she's looks very much like her father."

Nick hated the thought of another man having made love to her. Why the hell was Mavis pushing it? What was in it for her?

"Hey Doc!"

Nick turned to see his partner Brian and his girlfriend Sarah saunter into the bar and up to their table.

"Sit down," Nick said and had Kristy move closer to him.

Brian held out his hand to Kristy. "Hi, I'm Brian, Nick's partner. This is Sarah, my beloved."

"Beloved hell, I'm his workhorse when there's no one else available. Like when you went with Doc to deliver that cow. Man, how'd you do it? I would have passed out and kept Brian away from me for months if I'd seen that."

"Ah, darlin' you know I love you," Brian said.

Sarah leaned over and kissed him. "I know you do. So, I hear you're from California, Kristy."

"No, she's from the ranch," Nick said. "She's only been in California seven years. She's back now."

Sarah raised an eyebrow. So this is the one that got away. Doc sure had good taste in women she'd give him credit for that. "Well, I'm glad you'll be living in Dallas. Does that mean we'll be seeing more of you?"

Kristy sipped the second margarita. "I'm not sure. I have a job starting in a couple of weeks. Nick's been kind enough to let me stay at his place while I look for an apartment."

"Oh, what do you do?" Sarah knew Doc well enough to bet Kristy wouldn't be sleeping alone for long.

"I'm in publicity and marketing for a large clothing company."

"Wow, I'm impressed," Sarah said.

Brian took a sip of beer. "Hey, my beloved, wanta dance?"

"Sure," Sarah said and soon moved effortlessly across the dance floor with Brian.

"Nice couple," Kristy said and finished the margarita.

"Yeah, Sarah's a bit high strung but nothing Brian can't handle."

"How long have you had a partner?"

Nick ordered another beer. "About five years. The practice has grown to the point we even need another vet but don't have the time to interview one."

"Well, if all the cases are like the cow I'm not surprised you need more than just Brian. Maybe one will show up."

He leaned closer to her and smiled. "Could you stand dancing with me again?"

She started to kiss his cheek but he turned his head and their lips met. It was like a shock wave being sent through them. Kristy was caught off guard by the warmth. Nick reached out and put his hand behind her neck pulling her mouth closer against his. He wanted her in the worse way. When the kiss ended all she could do was stare into those captivating blue eyes of his and force herself to breathe. He stood and took her hands in his before wrapping his arms around her and pulling her body close so they could move to the music.

Kristy glanced at Mavis and didn't understand the smile playing across her lips. Mavis had been a beautiful woman in her younger days and even now she was very striking. She was tall and slender and Kristy knew she had been a model at one time. Her blue eyes were lovely to look at. And surprisingly, Mavis seemed to know everything about everybody. Did she know about her and Nick too? And how did she know Nicki was at the ranch? Just how much did this woman know?

During one song Brian switched partners with Nick. Kristy found herself moving about the room with Brian. She liked Brian. He was shorter than Nick, about five foot ten, and about five years younger. His brown eyes crinkled at the corners when he smiled. "Are you going to the Cowboy Rodeo with us? Sarah will be there."

"It all depends on what I find at the ranch."

Brian laughed as he said, "I hear your little girl has Jack jumping through hoops at the ranch. That ought to be something to see."

She shook her head in disbelief at her child, so outgoing and opinionated. "I just hope she hasn't driven every one crazy by now. Nicki's pretty set in her ways. She's six going on forty, she seems to know what she wants and goes after it."

Brian looked into her beautiful blue-green eyes and said, "Does Doc know she's his?"

Kristy gasped and tried to pull away. "Don't say that…"

Brian held her close. "Once he sees her he'll know. Hell, Jack even figured it out. I know because he called the office and talked to me. Good thing Nick was out on call."

Her eyes closed and she said, "He was never suppose to know. I hadn't planned on coming back to Texas. I timed my visits to the ranch when I knew he wouldn't be there. Nothing's gone right since I've been here." She opened her eyes to see Brian staring intently at her.

"Kristy, your daughter has a right to know her father. Hell, he has a right to know her. I understand she's a pistol and a hand full. Serve him right you know." He chuckled at the thought of Nick actually fathering a daughter. Shit, it was going to blow his mind when he found out. Being so careless wasn't Nick's style. Therefore, Kristy must either be someone special or something happened that was so profound it wasn't planned.

"In my heart I know she needs to know him. But…for Nick, that's another matter. He doesn't have any kids and I'm not sure springing Nicki on him is such a good idea. It could backfire. He could turn away and we'll never see him again. It happened before."

"Shit, Kristy, he didn't turn away he was trying to make his marriage work. If he'd have known he wouldn't have married Mallory."

"He was already married to her when I found out. There was nothing I could do but take a job in California. I never knew they were divorced until he told me. I'm not sure what would have happened if he'd had known. I won't look back. I have his daughter and together we've managed to have a good life."

"There's not a ranch hand who will say anything to Doc. Neither will I, but you'd better be prepared to tell him the truth tomorrow when we get there. From what I hear there's a lot of Nick in her, enough for him to recognize his own kin."

"We'll have to wait and see won't we. If he doesn't recognize himself in her then I'm not going to say a thing."

Brian danced her back to Nick and he took Sarah in his arms. At the same time both pagers went off and each man looked down. "Ah, shit," Nick said, "same as mine, Brian?"

"Banyon place?"

Brian nodded. "Must be horse trouble. Let's roll."

Nick looked at Sarah and asked, "Will you take her home?"

"Sure."

Brian kissed Sarah on the cheek and headed out the door to Big Red.

"Let's finish our drinks, Kristy. This is what it's like being involved with a vet. Everyone in the area depends on them."

"I know. Nick's always been one to jump in and do what needed to be done. I grew up watching him work on the ranch long before he went off to college to become a vet. After he left for school I hardly saw him, except on his vacations and then he worked even harder on the ranch."

"Both men amaze me with their work ethics. Rain, shine, snow, sleet, just like the post office these vets are out there saving animal's lives." Sarah raised her beer and clinked it against Kristy's margarita glass. "Here's to the men we love."

Kristy tried to protest, but failed. Later around midnight Sarah dropped her off at Nick's house and she promptly fell into bed. She was exhausted.

CHAPTER FIVE

Nick started to knock on Kristy's open door early the next morning. But before he did he watched her lying there asleep. Her long blonde hair lay spilled out in every direction and she snuggled with her pillow. One long leg had been thrown over the covers and lay there bare and beautiful. He longed to stroke her flesh. He rapped softly and watched as she opened one eye.

"What time is it?"

"Four. We need to get started if we're going to make it to the ranch and get some chores done."

She stretched and as she did Nick felt his body respond to her. Would it ever end for him? How could he stand being so close to her yet so far away? She climbed out of bed and brushed past him as she headed for the kitchen. He was so amazed by her graceful demeanor that he followed her into the kitchen. It was like she was on automatic. She brewed a pot of coffee.

She rubbed her forehead. "I think I need an Excedrine, I seem to have a bit of a hangover."

He smiled and went to stand before her pulling her into his arms and allowing her sleepy head to rest on his shoulder. "I'm sorry we had to bail last night." He loved the way she fit in his arms. He was surprised by the overwhelming emotions that swept over him as he held her.

"How's the horse?"

"Fine. Did you stay out late?"

"No, Sarah brought me home around midnight. I like Sarah and Brian. Think they'll get married?"

"I'm sure they will in time."

She started to pull away but he didn't want to let her go. "Thanks for being here," he whispered against her ear.

She looked up at him. "What?"

"You've made this house pleasant to come home to. Before you came it was just a dark place to spend the night. But now…you've filled it with life. And you can cook too. Why don't you move in? There's no need to find an apartment. There's plenty of room here. Nicki can have a horse out back if she wants one."

"But…that's too much of an imposition on our part. I don't think you need a six year old under foot." She had to convince him she couldn't possibly move in with him.

"Just think about it."

"Thank you for the offer…but you'd better wait until you meet my daughter before you offer to let us live here. She can be a handful."

"Then go get ready. Brian and Sarah will be at waiting for us."

Kristy took a quick shower and had just stepped out to dry herself off when Nick walked into the room. He stopped short and she heard him gasp for air. "I'm sorry, I thought…" Oh hell, what he was looking at took his breath away. Naked and still glistening from the shower he wanted to volunteer to dry her off himself.

Kristy pulled the towel around her. "I should have closed the door. I'm sorry, I'm just so use to living alone I forgot you were here."

"Don't be sorry. I like what I see." He turned on his boot heels and left the room.

Kristy quickly donned a pair of jeans and tee shirt and pulled her hair into a pony tail. When she walked into the kitchen Nick was sitting at the table sipping coffee.

"I'm ready," she said.

God, so was he. Had he been a fool to offer to let her stay with him? He couldn't take having her walk around naked without hauling her off to his bedroom. Better yet, move her into his bedroom.

Kristy's heart pounded as they drove into the ranch. She could hardly wait to see Nicki and hold her in her arms but at the same time she dreaded what Nick might think.

The minute he stopped the truck and got out Nick headed directly to the corral to saddle Rascal. He wanted to ride to the family cemetery to pay his respects to his parents, which was his custom upon returning to the ranch. Kristy was glad to see him ride out. She'd remembered the locket she'd laid at the base of his mother's headstone. She doubted Nick would even notice so she relaxed and looked around for her daughter.

"Mama! Mama!" Nicki screamed from the front porch and ran into Kristy's arms.

Kristy picked her jean clad daughter up in her arms and hugged her so tight she never wanted to let her go again. She saw her father and mother standing there waiting. Brian and Sarah drove their truck up next to Big Red and walked to where Kristy stood with Nicki in her arms. Both were smiling.

"Nicki, this is Brian and Sarah, what do you say to them?"

Nicki stuck her small hand out and smiled, "It's nice to meet you." She looked at her mother and asked, "Who was that man that rode off?"

"His name is Nick, he'll be back, you can meet him later."

Nicki squirmed and Kristy put her down. "I want to go play, Mama."

Brian was grinning from ear to ear as he said, "Ain't no way Nick won't know who her daddy is."

Kristy just shrugged and said, "Nick's as blind as they come sometimes, we'll see."

Kristy, Sarah and Brian followed Nicki to the barn where she showed off three new retriever puppies before leading them to a new foal. When she walked into the stall as if she owned it Kristy held her breath.

"Oh it's all right, Mama, his mama doesn't mind me being in here." She took her small hand, stood on her tiptoes and reached up to run it along the mare's neck.

Nick hunkered down before his parent's side-by-side graves and said a few words. When he stood he noticed a dried bunch of wilted wildflowers with something shiny tangled among the dead stems at the base of his mother's headstone. He picked it up to see a heart attached to the chain. When he opened it he was rather surprised to see a picture of himself and Kristy on one side, and on the facing side, a picture of a beautiful little blonde girl. The necklace must belong to Kristy, he thought, and that must be her daughter. She sure was a beautiful little thing, just like her mother. He was about to snap it shut when he took a second look at the little girl. A sudden image of his first grade photo flashed through his memory and he felt his heart stop before it pounded furiously in his chest. It couldn't be. He snapped the locket shut and shoved it in his jeans pocket. Kristy had some explaining to do.

As he rode up to the corral he noticed Kristy, Brian and Sarah in the barn. He dismounted and walked to where they were making over the new foal. What he didn't expect to see was the cutest little blonde cowgirl dressed in blue jeans and pink tee shirt. Her long hair was pulled away from her face and held in place at the back of her head with a pink bow. She was in the stall with her hands all over the new foal. He watched her carefully. She had gentle hands. He could tell by the way she ran them over the foal. As he watched she almost took his breath away. It was like watching himself in a time warp. How the hell?

He must have made a noise because without prompting Nicki looked up, then walked out of the stall and over to Nick where she held her hand out to him. "Hello, my name is Nicole, only you can call me Nicki. Mama says your name is Nick."

Nick held his breath. He took one look at the little girl presenting her hand to him and in an instant knew he was looking into the face of his own daughter. My God, how could Kristy have kept this from him? She had to have been pregnant when she left for California…when he married Mallory. He took Nicki's hand in his and shook it. "Yes, that's right, my name is Nick. How old are you Nicki?"

Nicki put her hand in her hip pocket and the other to her chin. Nick almost sucked in his breath as he watched her because she had his mannerisms too. "I'm six years and a few months old. I'm in first grade. Mama says we're moving to Dallas so I'll have to go to a new school, of course, I won't mind because Mama says I can have another horse here." Nicki continued to babble but Nick didn't really hear her, it was like he was looking into a mirror of himself at that age.

"And what do you do?"

It was only when he realized she'd stopped talking that he answered her. "I'm a vet. Do you know what that is?" He couldn't take his eyes off her beautiful little face and those dimples that formed when she talked. His dimples. She was going to be a real heart breaker when she grew up.

Nicki's long blonde curls bounced as she nodded. "Oh yes, I know. My mama told me all about being a vet. She told me my daddy is a vet."

Shocked by the news, he asked. "Oh, and what else did she say about your daddy?"

Nicki looked up at the man standing there giving her his attention and said, "That he's a very special man but he couldn't be my daddy. I don't know what she meant by that but as long as he's special to her, then he's special to me too. My mommy loves him you know."

"She does? Did she tell you that?" Nick looked beyond Nicki to where Kristy stood. Why did she have such a shocked expression on her face?

Nicki continued to ramble on. "Yes. Every night when she tucks me into bed and reads to me she says my daddy loves me because she loves him. Do you think that's true? If I've never met my daddy then how can he love me?"

Nick picked her up in his arms. "Oh your daddy will love you even if he's never met you."

Nicki pointed to Kristy, who was standing there stunned at the sight. "Mama called last night and said she was going to cook for all of us tonight. Do you know my mama can cook real good? She's been teaching me too."

"Yes, I know. Your mama is something very special." He walked to where everyone stood and set Nicki down. He looked deep into Kristy's eyes. "Why didn't you tell me?"

Ellen and Joe had come into the barn and Ellen spoke up. "There's time for such things later. Right now, my daughter has promised to take over the kitchen tonight. Thank God, Maria Lupe is good, but not as good as my daughter."

Joe put his arm around Kristy and the other one around Nicki and walked them toward the house.

Nick stood beside Brian watching their retreating backs. "Why the hell didn't she tell me?"

Brian looked at him and answered, "Because you married Mallory. What else could she have done? No one told her when you divorced the woman. She thought all these years you were still married. She would only come home when she knew you wouldn't be here."

Nick scowled at Brian. "How the hell do you know all this?"

Brian just grinned. "Mavis, of course." He lied.

Nick shook his head. "How the hell does she find all this stuff out? Now I know why she said some of those things to me. She even knew about Nicki, didn't she?"

"Oh yes, she knew. What are you going to do now, Doc?"

Nick's hands slipped into his hip pockets. "Hell if I know. I have a six-year-old daughter I have to get to know. I asked Kristy this morning to stay at the house and not to find an apartment. I like coming home to find her there. I never dreamed her daughter was also mine."

"Give it time, Nick, she's worth it or haven't you figured that one out yet?"

Nick and Brian walked toward the ranch house.

Nicki headed toward Rowdy sitting on the porch rail. Scamp, Cotton and Tex were seated on the steps. "Well, young lady," Tex said, "have you met everyone?"

"Oh yes, I have, thank you. Can I get you boys something to drink?"

"Well, little miss," Scamp said, "You have any ice tea?"

Her hand went to her hip pocket and the other to her chin. "I believe Grandma made some this morning, I'll see what I can do." She skipped into the house with her long blonde curls bouncing against the middle of her back.

Nick stood at the bottom of the steps and looked at the grinning cowboys. "What are ya'll looking at?" he growled. "Chores done for the day?"

"Take a look at yourself. Your goddamn hand is stuck in your jeans pocket and I expect the other one to go to your chin if you actually have some thinkin' to do. Like you she makes statements rather than ask unnecessary questions." Scamp laughed a heavy deep-throated laugh. "She sure pulled one over on you. That little girl is like a breath of fresh air around here. And chores are done."

"Crap," Tex added, "she's got us removing our goddamn spurs before she'll let us in the dining room. No more chawin' tobacco either. She says it makes our teeth yucky and we smell bad. We're only allowed to chaw when we're in the bunkhouse or on the range. She's got Jack takin' his hat off before she serves his dinner. I think the old boy likes the kid now that he knows she's yours."

Kristy slipped past Nick and into the house. Ellen followed her into the kitchen. Nick followed.

"Would you excuse us, Ellen, I need to talk to Kristy in the other room." He took hold of her arm and pulled her into the den, which Jack used as his office.

She stood quietly with her hands at her sides. "I'm sorry," she said. "I never meant for you to find out about her."

"How could you not tell me? How could you let me go on running the bastard down that got you pregnant and deserted you? Because that bastard is me. You knew before you left the ranch. Did anyone else know?"

She shook her head. "No one knew, not even my parents. I only told them after she was born."

"How could you go it alone?"

Tears filled her eyes and threatened to fall. "Because I didn't have you. Mallory did. I didn't know you were divorced until you told me. I probably would have told you if I had known...but I didn't. My baby and I did just fine. She's my world."

He just shook his head in disbelief. "She's something. I can see why you didn't want me to meet her."

"That wasn't it...I was afraid you wouldn't like her, that you might think I got pregnant on purpose and so many other things I didn't want to face."

His hands cupped her face. "You told me you loved her father, that every time you looked at her you saw him. I'm her father. Are you telling me you love me?"

She swallowed hard. "I've always loved you, that never changed. And when Nicki came along it made me love you all the more. I won't ever act on these feelings though, it's not right for me to think I could."

He couldn't believe she actually loved him. Why the hell didn't he sense it? Slowly, his head lowered and pressed his lips to hers. "I asked you to move in with me. Will you do it now?"

"Nicki doesn't know you're her father. I don't know…"

"She'll have to hear about me sometime. She tells me her father loves her because you love her father. Is that true?"

She looked away. "I wanted her to feel she was loved by both parents. Even if her father wasn't around, I wanted her to feel his love through me."

"I've got a lot to let soak in. Man, this news has me reeling. I never thought for one minute I got you pregnant."

Ellen knocked at the door. "Kristy, *your* daughter is out here giving us orders again, do you want to handle it?"

Kristy smiled and sighed. "She's the most determined little girl I've ever met, so much like her…father."

She walked into the kitchen to find Nicki ordering her grandfather to pull the sugar off the pantry shelf. "Grandpa, the other shelf. The boys want sugar with their tea."

"The boys?" Nick whispered as he stood behind Kristy.

"She has her ways."

"Grandma, would you mind handing me those glasses next to you." One by one she counted the glasses and put them on the tray. She tried to pick up the big pitcher of ice tea but wasn't strong enough. "Mama, would you help me?"

"Sure, honey. I'll carry the tray for you. Is there anything you've forgotten?"

Nicki looked at the tray. "No, I don't think so. I'll stay outside and play for a while. May I go look at the horses in the barn?"

"Only if Grandpa goes with you. You remember how to…"

"Oh Mama, I know all about horses. Grandpa will take good care of me."

Kristy carried the tray out to the front porch and set it down on the rattan table there. "Help yourself…boys," she teased.

Tex said, "Hey, say it with feeling like little Nicki does."

Rex took a glass and smiled. "Don't forget to take those spurs off before you go inside."

Kristy had no idea Nicki would take over so fast. She made a mental note to tone her daughter's habits down to a dull roar before she alienated everyone on the ranch.

Kristy walked back into the kitchen where her mother waited, Nick and her dad were gone. "So, what do you have planned for me to cook?" she asked.

Ellen smiled, "Fried chicken, mashed potatoes, milk gravy, snap beans, your biscuits and I had Maria Lupe bake six apple pies."

Kristy pulled on an apron and started prepping. "I've always loved this kitchen, Mom. It was the one place I found total contentment and security when I was little. I always felt safe here." She handed her mother a huge basket of green beans to snap.

"Yep, you were always underfoot here. You use to hide over there in the pantry when you got scared during our spring thunderstorms."

Kristy found the three heavy cast iron skillets she'd use for her fried chicken and put them on the stove. She cleaned, floured and seasoned the vast amounts of chicken they would need and sat them aside while the oil heated in the skillets. Her mother had already peeled the ton or so of potatoes and had them diced and in a large pan of boiling water. Kristy then measured the ingredients into the huge bread bowl for her biscuits.

"I'm glad you're here, Kristy. We've missed you. I know all this hasn't turned out the way you wanted, but it's over now. What do you think will happen?"

Kristy took the pliable biscuit dough and rolled it out on the large wooden board that normally rested against a cupboard in the pantry. "Nick knows…what else can I say? He asked us to move into his home with him. Of course that was before he met Nicki." She gently kneaded the dough a few times before rolling it out to the proper thickness.

"And?"

"It's a lot to think about." With a round biscuit cutter she pressed firmly down into the dough.

"What's to think about? You'll be a family."

Putting the biscuits onto baking sheets she set them aside. "No, Mom, we won't be a family. This has been a shock for Nick. I think he has to take some time to let all this sink in, he has to get to know Nicki. You already know she's a handful. I think it would be for the best if I take one of those apartments I looked at. I don't have a car and it would be closer to work."

"Oh pooh, what's a car got to do with it? You can go out today and buy one. As for being closer to work, why would you want to be? I know you well enough to know you bring enough work home to keep you from thinking about the things that really matter."

Kristy put the chicken pieces one by one into the hot oil. "Mom, work and Nicki are all I've known for years."

Ellen put the beans in a large pot of boiling water and hobbled back to the table where she put a lettuce and tomato salad together. "Nonsense, things have changed. You're going to have to tell Nicki about Nick, so why not do it while you're living in his house?" She reached for the store bought tomatoes and began slicing.

How could she get her mother to understand that she didn't feel at ease forcing themselves on Nick. "Mom, I have to do things that are comfortable for me."

"Do you want us to keep Nicki so you can go to Guthrie with Doc and Brian?"

"Would you mind? It would give us a chance to maybe talk some." She knew she would have to explain everything to him. It wasn't going to be easy.

"He's been alone a long time you know. He's been waiting for someone but he just didn't know it. You're the someone and I don't think you know it."

Turning the chicken she glared at her mother. "Mom, I'm not ready for any kind of long term commitment just yet. So drop the subject."

"Can I do anything?" Sarah came into the room.

"Sure," Kristy said, "set the table and…Oh hell, you know what to do."

Sarah smiled and winked. "Yeah, I know what to do."

Joe came into the kitchen scowling. "That granddaughter of mine is so danged strong willed I want to throttle her."

Kristy sighed and removed the chicken onto wire racks to drain. "Now what has she done?"

"She wants to buy Doc's horse that's about to foal in the barn. Says she can treat it better then any of us on the ranch. Where does she get her attitude from?"

Nick walked in at that point. "Obviously from me. So what does she want to pay for it?"

"Oh who the hell knows, Nicki can talk anyone into anything so be careful."

"Can I take anything to the table?" Nick asked.

Kristy pointed to the food waiting on the counter. When she removed the biscuits her dad grabbed one. "Couldn't wait?" she asked.

Joe said, "I'd better get out there, *your* daughter has the *boys* lined up for 'clean hand' inspection as she calls it. And...they're removing their goddamn spurs just as she ordered. Jack's even doin' it."

Kristy looked at Nick. She couldn't hide her smile. "Thanks, Dad." Ellen hobbled out of the room.

Nick came to stand behind Kristy and put his arms around her waist. "Thank you."

Kristy was trying to open a quart jar of Ellen's homemade strawberry jam. Nick put his hands on hers and loosened the lid. "Thanks for what?"

"For my daughter."

Kristy froze at his words, they sounded so strange coming from his mouth. Words she never expected to hear from him. She hesitated then said, "I think you should get to know her before you thank me."

He turned her around and gazed down into her eyes. "Will you give me that chance? I mean to get to know her?"

"She doesn't know you're her father yet."

"All the more I should get to know her and she should get to know me. Bring her home with us."

"Nick...I'm thinking of taking an apartment...you have no idea what you'd be getting into."

"No, no apartment, not now. I don't care what I'm getting into, I have to get to know her and I can't do it if she's living in some high rise. She needs space."

"Here, take this jam and put it on the table everyone's waiting."

"Not until you tell me you'll bring her home with us."

"I'll think about it."

He grabbed her arm. "No, you're coming back home with me."

She jerked her arm away. "And I wonder where Nicki gets her strong willed attitude. I still have a life to live. I'll think about it."

His hands went up in surrender. He also smiled. "You'll be coming home with me."

Kristy closed her eyes and wished she had a smart comeback for him. Instead she grabbed the biscuits and walked into the Chandler dining room where every ranch hand, her parents, Nicki, Jack, Brian and Sarah waited for the two of them. Nick held the chair for her and he sat at the head of the table next to her.

After Jack gave grace, Nicki said, "So let's eat!"

The table came alive with familiar voices all talking at the same time. To Kristy this was heaven. This, sitting around the dinner table with family and friends was what she missed so very much in California. She didn't miss the dust, the heat, or the barbed wire fences. And she didn't miss the scent of cow manure, which Jack called 'money on the hoof'. She had missed the sound of everyone talking at once, telling what they'd done that day or planning ahead for tomorrow. This was the time of day when problems were solved and the future planned. She took a moment just to sit back in her chair, take in the scenario and savor it in her mind. Her daughter deserved this…to know where her parents came from and how they became who they were. She deserved family.

"So, Nicki," Nick said as he scooped mashed potatoes and gravy onto his plate. "What do you do for fun in California?"

Nicki seemed to ponder the question. "I win blue ribbons."

Nick stopped in mid bite. "Blue ribbons?"

"Yes, didn't Mama tell anyone? I win blue ribbons at the horse shows." She sat up straighter in the chair filled with phone books.

Nick's mouth dropped open. "Really? How many do you have?"

Kristy was busy passing bowls around the table and noticed Brian staring at her. She looked away.

Nicki put her hand to her chin as if she were thinking. "I think we put fifty in a box."

Nick's fork hit the plate. He glanced at Kristy. She said, "Nicki's been on a horse with me since she was a year old. She's been showing since she was four…and winning."

"Mama, without my palomino will I still win?"

Kristy took a deep breath and explained, "As you grow older it won't matter what color your horse is. I'm sure we'll find a beautiful horse for you to work with."

Ellen excused herself and left the room, but came back shortly with a framed picture in her hand. She handed it to Nick. It was a picture of Nicki on her Palomino, dressed in silver and white western attire. Her blonde hair beneath a white hat set off the distinct coloring that blended with the color of the horse. She held a blue ribbon against the horse's neck.

"You're a real pretty little girl, Nicki." He couldn't get over her. His heart swelled with an unaccustomed sense of pride.

Nicki sat up proudly. "Thank you, Nick, do you think my daddy would be proud of me?"

Kristy closed her eyes and leaned back in the chair. Nicki had an insatiable need to know about her father but until now she couldn't satisfy that need. "Nicki," she said, "of course your father would be proud of you. I've always told you that."

Nicki looked at her hands in her lap, then up again. "I know, Mama." She looked up and across the table at Nick to stare at him for a moment before she said, "That man there…Nick…he's my daddy isn't he?" She pointed at Nick.

Kristy gasped so hard she found herself holding her breath. "Nicki!" She looked at the others around the table and thought she saw smirks. "Why would you say that?"

Nicki leaned forward and looked directly at Nick. "Because I look like him. You always kept his picture next to your bed."

Kristy felt lightheaded and at a lost for words.

Nick asked, "Nicki, would you like for me to be your daddy?"

Her hand went to her chin. "I have to know you first. I need a special daddy."

Kristy rose and took her plate in her hands. "Enough, Nicki. We'll talk about this later." She left for the kitchen. She could hear Nicki's remark as she left the room and it tugged heavily at her heart.

"But, Mama, he is my daddy."

Kristy all but threw the plate into the sink. Her entire life was being turned upside down and it was tearing her gut apart. Ellen came to stand behind her. "March yourself back in there and tell her the truth, if you don't I will."

Walking back into the dining room Kristy looked at her daughter. Straight-armed she leaned heavily against the back of one of the chairs. "Yes, Nicki, Nick is your daddy. But he doesn't know you yet…"

"When will he get to know me?" Nicki asked with confidence.

"Nicki…it takes time."

"When we take you back to my house with us," Nick said, his tone gentle but firm.

Kristy didn't like him making decisions for her but when she looked at her daughter's face she knew she had to go along with it…for now.

"Mama, will we be living with Nick?"

"For now."

"Will I have a horse?"

"Sure," Nick said.

"We'll see, Nicki," Kristy reminded her.

"When will we go home?"

Nick said, "When your mother and I get back from the Cowboy Rodeo in two days. We'll come back here to pick you up. Can you be ready to move by then?"

The hands went to the chin. "I think I can. May I give you a hug?"

Nick moved his chair out as Nicki climbed off the phone books and made her way around the table to hug him. Kristy watched Nick's eyes close as he responded to Nicki's hug. She had to leave the room. Joe followed.

It was a warm evening when she stepped outside. She inhaled deeply and closed her eyes. Joe put his arm around her shoulder. She said, "There's nothing quite like an evening in Texas on the ranch."

"Nothing," he said. "Unless it's seeing my granddaughter hug her father for the first time."

She rested her head against his strong muscular shoulder just as she'd done so many times growing up. Her dad always made her feel safe and secure. "What now, Dad? I can't let her think we're going to be a family."

"Why not?" Joe hugged his daughter. It was good to have her home again.

"Because I don't know if it's what either Nick or I want."

He removed his arm and turned to face her. "What are you talking about? It's what you've always dreamed of."

"No, Dad, not this way. I wanted to be romanced and won before I got married. I want to be loved and wanted. I don't want to go into any kind of relationship because I have to for the sake of my daughter. Couples today don't have to marry just because they should."

He sounded outraged as he bellowed, "They do in this part of Texas!"

"Dad, I don't live in this part of Texas," she reminded him and walked away.

CHAPTER SIX

Early the next morning Nick, Kristy, Brian, Sarah, Joe and every ranch hand on the Bar C headed for the Cowboy Rodeo with loaded horse trailers in tow. Nicki and Ellen stood on the porch to wave goodbye. Maria Lupe arrived just as they were leaving.

Nick turned over Big Red's diesel engine and looked over at Kristy. "So when were you going to tell me about Nicki?"

She put on her sunglasses and looked away from him. "When hell froze over."

"That soon?" He poked a finger at the brim of his hat.

She didn't look at him. "God, Nick, life is so complicated."

"It doesn't have to be."

"What the hell are you talking about?" She asked angrily.

"Yeah, you're right," Nick mumbled, "I swore I would never get married again, not after the Mallory disaster.

"Who said anything about marriage?"

Was he being rejected automatically? "Why not?"

"Because we don't know each other any more. I...I can't explain." She grew quiet. "Marriage is never the answer." She loved him beyond words but would never force him into anything.

After a long silence between them Nick asked, "What's she like?"

Kristy couldn't look at him but continued to stare out the window at passing scenery. "Oh Nick, she's so precious. She's smart, outgoing, determined, and compassionate. She loves animals, especially horses. There's a gentleness about her when she's with an animal…very much like you."

Nick glanced over at her briefly. "She has your coloring, except for the blue eyes."

Kristy smiled. "And everything else about her is you."

He just shook his head. He couldn't believe he'd fathered such a beautiful little girl. "I could have helped out financially, why didn't you let me know?"

She looked off into the distance. "Nick…I wasn't about to upset your marriage in any way. I honestly didn't know you weren't married anymore. Nicki has been my reason to work hard, to better ourselves, so I could give her everything she needs."

"That can change now."

"You're not obliged to help out, I make a good living for us."

Nick scowled. "I know I'm not obliged. Hell, she's my daughter. I want to get to know her as my daughter." He also wanted to get reacquainted with Kristy. A warm rush of emotion swept over him as he glanced at her. He realized that, even though she'd been out of his life for seven years, she had always been with him.

An hour later Nick looked in his rear view mirror and expected to see one of the ranch trucks behind him, instead he spotted a ravine black truck and matching horse trailer with a sleeper cabin soaring toward Big Red. Dark tinted glass shielded the driver's identity but Nick knew who it was and cringed. Jez Bevaca was the last thing the Cowboy Rodeo needed. Christ! And with Kristy sitting beside him he knew there was going to be trouble.

Once they reached Guthrie, rigs were parked side by side as Jez pulled hers close to Big Red. She stepped from her rig dressed in skintight jeans and even tighter black tee shirt. "Howdy boys!" In a matter of minutes every unattached cowboy flocked to her door. "Yeah, yeah, but y'all are too late. I've done got my pistols loaded and my sights set. Where's my man?" She headed for Big Red.

Nick saw Jez heading his way and quickly grabbed Kristy's arm and headed her for the safety of Brian and Sarah.

Kristy couldn't have missed Jez Bevaca if she wanted to. Jez hadn't changed a bit the past seven years. Loud and boisterous were the only words she could think of to describe the woman. She used her sexuality to attract men. Her goal was always to get Nick notched on her rig. She was sure Jez had one notch at least and probably trying for more than one.

Jez spotted Kristy and pointed her boots in that direction. "Well look what came all the way in from California boys! If it isn't Kristy Williams herself."

"Hello, Jez," Kristy said, arching a brow.

Jez looked Kristy up and down. "So who'd you come with, Joe?"

"More like the entire Bar C ranch. You here alone?"

Jez's hands moved up and down her thighs. "Not for long." She turned and walked away.

Kristy knew it was going to be a different kind of event with Jez there. Maybe she could pick up some pointers.

Sarah came to stand next to Kristy. Her hands rested on her hips. "I've only been dating Brian for two years and I've had to fight that woman off him more than once."

"Jez isn't really anyone's competition, Sarah. That is if the men aren't drunk. She's not the type they'd take home for keeps."

Sarah laughed and said, "Well, that's one way of putting it. Who the hell can compete with that body of hers? They may not marry her but she can sure give them what they want in bed."

"Sarah, I strongly suspect you're all Brian needs in his bed, so don't look for trouble. Jez has her aim set for Nick this time. It's up to him to take it or leave it."

"And how do you feel about that?"

"I won't know until I see them together. I have no ties on Nick."

"The hell you don't. You have his daughter."

"Sarah, I have never used my daughter as leverage and I don't intend to do it now that he knows. He's free to do what he wants and he knows it."

"And what about you? Are you just as free?"

"You bet I am."

Sarah gave Kristy a high five. "Good for you!"

Fetch and brand and bronc breaking were on the schedule for the day. There were no stopwatches for the teams of cowboys who had to rope, tie and brand as many cows as possible by the end of the day.

Fifty-mesquite wise pasture bred wild Watusi cattle, each weighing five hundred pounds had been turned loose from stock trailers on a thousand acres.

Kristy and Sarah watched as the Bar C wranglers snubbed their hats, spurred their horses and charged to rope and brand their first steer. Nick and Brian were partners, but Brian was tending to Billy Joe's gelding. While Nick waited he watched the cowboys and steers scatter among the gopher holes, and rattlesnake infested canyon terrain. Once he saw Jez heading his way Nick spurred Rascal and headed out. When Brian saw him leaving he yelled, "Wait for me!" and nudged his own horse after Nick.

Jez stood with her hands resting on her hips. "You'll be back, Doc!"

A cowhand said, "He's gotta be plum blinder than a polecat in a snowstorm not to notice you, darlin'" His eyes skimmed over Jez's skintight jeans that left nothing to the imagination.

When Brian took one look at Jez his lariat sailed over a fence post instead of the steer. Nick yelled at him, "Hell, son, keep your eyes on the cattle. Put your mind on the grass not on her ass."

Laughing, Kristy and Sarah walked to the chuck wagons where cooks were preparing a feast of skillet browned cornbread and red bean chili for the night's festivities. Sarah took two cups of coffee and handed one to Kristy.

"We might as well wait it out at the truck. Want to play some cards or something?"

"Sure." Kristy watched as Jez headed for her trailer with some young horny cowboy in tow. "Sarah, there's victim number one for the morning."

"Hope she doesn't ride him too hard he's bullridin' in the morning."

"He'll have all night to recover. She'll have number two in there in the next thirty minutes."

"Oh hell, Kristy, what do men see in her? My God look at you. You're better lookin' with a better figure."

Kristy gave Sarah a sidelong glance. "You don't see any of them lining up to be with me, do you?"

"Don't think they don't want to, I saw the looks in their eyes when you stepped out of Big Red. If it's action you're lookin' for this is the place to find it. I think what's keepin' them away is they think you're with Doc. Are you?"

"I came with Nick. As for my sexuality…I'm more than comfortable with it."

"You would be you're gorgeous! I have to work at what I've got."

Kristy thought Sarah was extremely attractive and Brian was lucky to have her. She was petite, had soft brown eyes, long straight brown hair and an outgoing personality that fit to Brian's more introverted way of looking at life. "Work or not, you have it all going for you and Brian knows it."

"Yeah," Sarah grinned at Kristy's take on things, "he does, doesn't he."

That night the men were exhausted after their long hard day in the saddle. But there's nothing like whiskey tainted coffee to perk a tired cowboy up. That, along with campfires, harmonicas, guitars and a few fiddles thrown in really brought them to life. Kristy was amazed at the number of single cowgirls that had made the long trek from all over north Texas just to have their pick of the litter. It seemed to her that this was a mating rodeo. Billy Joe's sister made an overt move on Brian once she'd had six beers and it set Sarah into a defending rage. For the rest of the evening Sarah's arm was laced with Brian's. Sarah was defending her territory. It made Kristy smile to see Sarah's determination to keep her man for herself. Sarah was lucky to have such a man in her life.

Jez emerged from the shadows like she was queen of the damn arena. Jez wore the tightest black leather pants Kristy had ever seen. They looked like polished skin stretched tight over her body and tucked into her concho fringed knee-high moccasins. Her thin silk black blouse was tied just below her breasts and it wasn't hard to see erect nipples aimed at the slightly tipsy cowboys. What she didn't like seeing was the way Jez made her way to Nick and pressed those same braless breasts against his back.

"Kristy?"

She turned to see a young cowboy she'd known most of her life. Jett Rydell was only a few years older. He held out his hand to her. "Hi, Jett."

"Can't waste the music."

His arms went around her and they danced to about the only slow tune played all night. He smelled a bit of whiskey and tobacco and his hands roamed up and down her back.

She tried to make conversation with him but all he seemed to want to do was feel her up. She didn't like that one bit. "Jett. If you want to dance with me, then dance. Leave the rest of my body alone."

"Sorry, Kristy. You just look to good not to touch. You here with Doc?"

"Why do you ask?"

"Cause, look at him and Jez. She'll peel those pants off for him in a minute if he asks."

Her heart was breaking. Jett was very observant. "My dad's here or haven't you noticed. Why would you think I'm here with Nick?"

His thin shoulders drew up then down and he pulled her tighter against him. "I don't know just a hunch I guess." She felt his hardness press against her and she didn't like feeling uncomfortable. Jett was not her type.

When the music stopped she said, "Thanks for the dance, Jett. Have a good evening." She turned and walked away thinking maybe she shouldn't have come after all. She headed back to where Big Red was parked.

"Better watch Jett," Nick said, "he's always had a crush on you." He handed her a cup of coffee.

Kristy was surprised to see Nick standing there without Jez. She took the coffee and sipped. She almost choked on the whiskey taste, but it warmed her belly nicely. "He told me Jez would peel those pants off in a minute if you wanted her to."

"Oh hell, she can peel whatever she likes, Jez isn't the one I want."

It was late and only the older cowboys who'd been there and done that, had settled into their sleeping bags for the night. The younger ones wooed and teased what was offered to them. Kristy noticed Jez make her way back to her black beauty with Rowdy from the Bar C ranch clinched in her grasp.

Kristy swallowed hard. Nick's hands were on her arms moving up and down torching every nerve ending in her body. He led her beside Big Red where he'd laid out his sleeping bag. "And what did you do with my bag?" she asked.

He'd had just enough drink to make him feel bold. "I want you with me tonight." He had zipped the two bags together to make one.

"Why?"

"Why not?" Nick unzipped the bags and took them apart. "There…satisfied?"

"No."

"Hell, I never know what you want," Nick grumbled. Women! He'd never understand any of them.

"Kristy!" Jett yelled from two trucks down, "Wanta come over here?" He was now as drunk as a skunk.

Kristy laughed. "He never could hold his liquor."

"He wants you as much as I do. As any man here does."

Surprised by his remark, she asked, "What are you talking about?"

"Jez may flaunt it, but you're what every cowpoke here wants in his sleepin' bag tonight." His hands reached out to her.

"Is that's why you want me? I'm just another piece of ass to you?"

He stood back. "California's turned you into someone I don't really know anymore."

"That's my point exactly, Nick. We don't know each other. I don't think we ever did. I'm so drawn to you sexually and emotionally there was a time I would have done anything for you."

He was stunned by her confession. "And now?"

She looked away from him. "It hasn't changed. But you need to know who I've become. Yes, I had your daughter, but I've also grown emotionally. You don't have a clue as to who I am."

His hands clasped hers and he pulled her down on the ground to the sleeping bag. "Let me get to know you." His hands ran slowly up and down her thighs.

She smiled. "Then you better find a place that's a little more private. I can hear dad snoring less then five feet away."

Laughing he picked up the two sleeping bags, grabbed her hand and headed off into the distance where he was sure no one else slept.

Nick could hardly believe he had Kristy all to himself. He doubled the bags, yanked off his boots and tossed his hat onto a low limb.

Kristy took her time. She touched his shirt, unsnapping one snap at a time. When her hands traveled up his stomach and across his chest she heard him suck in air. She could feel his heart beating and was sure hers was beating just as hard and fast. A hand drifted down to his jeans and fought with the huge belt buckle in the way. Once it was out of the way she flicked his jeans to lay them open. She felt his hands moving up her back to her head where he pushed the hair from her face. "Oh God," he moaned and pressed his mouth to hers as they slowly sank down onto their knees. He cupped her face in his hands. "Kristy, let me love you."

She took his hardness and stroked with a firm grip, allowing her thumbs to massage the underside of the tendon like sheath until she could see his eyes glaze over and his breathing become shallow. It wasn't long before she found her clothes peeled away and his hands moving with deliberate slowness over her body. His mouth played along her neck and shoulders while his hands made their way lower across her taut stomach downward. His fingers teased her until she was wet and ready. Still on their knees she guided him to where she wanted him and felt as if her world was spinning out of control as her hips moved against his. His arms wrapped tight around her back and hips to pull her closer as he moved back and forth until he couldn't stand it any longer and lay her gently onto her back. He dove deeper into her warm moist depths until he couldn't hold back. Unleashed and uncensored, Kristy joined him on the journey to paradise and back.

"My God!" He gasped raised his head to look down into moonlit eyes. "You're just as I remember. Only now you know what it's all about." His next thought was how the hell did she know? His hand took her breast, which had matured since he'd known them and he loved the feel of her silken flesh. He'd never be able to get enough of her. He liked the way she'd held him and took him, giving in to what he wanted.

A flush of excitement swept over her as his hand slowly caressed her breast, his thumb brushing against the nipple. She couldn't believe after all these years he was here with her, in her arms making love with her, giving himself to her. She closed her eyes and savored the way his hardness created the exotic state of arousal that took her breath away and unleashed her inhibitions. She needed him to make love to her. She needed to feel connected to him. To her surprise she felt his body react and that was all it took for her to wrap her long legs around him and encourage him to once again seek what they both wanted. When he couldn't go on any longer he held her in his arms not wanting to lose the connection he felt with her.

Totally satisfied and relaxed she snuggled against him. "You're like a stranger to me," she said in a voice filled with spent passion.

He kissed the top of her head that nestled against his chest. "You just showed me how much you love me. I certainly hope you don't do that for strangers."

She tipped her face to look at him. "Are you sure it isn't that I needed to be made love to?"

"Kristy, I know the difference. You made love to me."

"Then you know more than I do."

"What are you saying…you don't love me?" He felt hurt.

"No. I'm just asking how you can tell the difference."

"Oh Jesus, woman you're as exasperating as our daughter." He wrapped both arms around her and hugged her tight.

"And you're such a cowboy."

"Oh God, I hope so." He moved against her knowing she was embedded deep inside his heart and soul and he never wanted to lose her again. He also knew no woman had ever satisfied him like she did and now he knew why.

When dawn came they could hear the camp stirring somewhere in the near distance. Kristy woke to find Nick staring at her. "Thank you for last night," she said.

"My pleasure for sure. How do you feel this morning?"

"Like my body was floating on a cloud all night."

He was feeling pretty satisfied himself this morning. "Do you think it could get any better than last night?"

She laughed and tried to roll away to get up but he wouldn't release her. "It might if I didn't have rocks beneath my butt."

"I don't want to let you go. I love this feeling of you in my arms." He was also as hard as a rock again.

She moved slowly against his hardened passion and it wasn't long before they were once again dancing to a sultry rhythm that suited them. They each gave and took from the other while exploring each others bodies. When Kristy arched upward she felt as if she were riding on the crest of a California wave and she didn't want the heightened state of nirvana to end. When the excitement ebbed Nick brushed damp strands of hair away from her face.

In a husky breathless voice, he said, "You're mine, you know that don't you?"

Just as breathless, she whispered, "What you don't know is that I've always been yours, right from the start."

"Guess we'd better get up before they come looking for us."

"How would you explain us?"

He grinned. "That I've just discovered something I lost and I was getting to know her."

She rolled over and pulled on her jeans before pulling on the tee shirt. She ran fingers through her thick mane of hair and knew she must look a mess. She watched as he slowly rose and pulled on his jeans. Would this be the one and only time for them? Oh God, she hoped not, she needed to feel his body embedded with hers.

"Oh Christ!" He doubled over. "I'm not ridin' bulls today."

Playing innocent she said, "Why not?"

He shot her a warning glance. "Mind if we leave early?"

She smiled. "Not if..." She looked up to see Brian and Sarah standing there grinning. She felt herself blush red. How much had they seen...or heard?

"Problem partner?" Brian said and put his arm around Sarah.

"Not really," Nick groaned.

"Do you know what your problem is partner? You don't get it enough."

Sarah gave Kristy a thumbs up. "Good goin', girl." The couple turned and walked away.

Nick rolled up the sleeping bags, pulled his hat from the limb and headed back to Big Red. He looked at Kristy. "You do know that by now the entire camp knows what happen between us last night."

"Do you care?"

He grinned. "Not at all." They headed back to the truck to stow their gear.

He hadn't taken two steps from Big Red when he heard, "Doc...Doc!" Billy Wayne shouted.

"What is it?"

"It's Bobby Jo's mare, Side Wynder. She's choked. Ya gotta come quick, Doc."

Nick grabbed his medical bag from Big Red and followed Billy to the corral. Brian grabbed a gallon of mineral oil, a bucket of water and an assortment of various sized naso-gastric stomach tubes.

Nick and Brian approached the mare with caution. Side Wynder's neck stretched to the ground and she coughed violently trying to dislodge the foreign objects stuck in her throat. Without warning the sorrel mare panicked, gasped for air, choked and crashed to the ground. The earth shook. Her hooves cut a violent path through the air. She tried to stand again as sweat and sand rolled off her body.

"Doc, be careful!" Sarah yelled.

Kristy noticed Jez emerge from the black devil wearing nothing but baggy sweatpants and a tee shirt that read Property of Psychotic State University, NO BITING. Rowdy followed close behind zipping his jeans and pulling on his boots. She would bet her bottom dollar Jez didn't have as good as time as she'd had last night.

Nick grabbed the mare's halter and tried to help her to her feet, but failed. Brian was able to tap her jugular vein with an eighteen-gauge needle to administer a stabilizing does of tranquilizer and muscle relaxants. Nick stroked the mare's neck to steady her and could feel several large boluses wedged in her esophagus.

"What the hell did she eat?" He asked.

Billy Wayne said, "Some old cattle alfalfa cubes. I saw 'em on the ground when I tied her up but I thought they was rocks. I didn't think she'd…"

"Doc," Brian said, "here's your stomach tube."

Nick took the rubber tubing and passed the hose through her left nostril and down the esophagus to the first hard dry alfalfa bolus. Brian held the mare's halter. The tube stopped, stuck. Nick couldn't budge the blockage. "Give me some water." Nick flushed a combination of dissolving solution and water into the swallowing canal. Side Wynder panicked. Her eyes dilated with horror.

"Look out!" Brian yelled as the helpless animal gagged, coughed and frantically went berserk.

The horse reared and backed into the fence pawing at the air, the knee sent Nick flying. Kristy screamed and ran into the corral where she helped Brian with Side Wynder's lead rope.

Nick dusted off his sleeves and repeated the process avoiding the horse's panic stricken attacks. Nothing worked. The dried alfalfa cubes were like five petrified rocks. Nick looked at Billy. "Shit! This isn't working I'm going to have to cut them out."

Billy grimaced, but Bobby Jo, said, "Do whatcha gotta do, Doc."

Billy held the lead rope while Kristy stood next to him. Nick injected a local anesthetic and sliced a deep incision. Brian assisted as they pulled each of the obstructions out one by one. Brian blotted the wound and handed Nick suture material.

Kristy smiled with pride. Sarah ran up and hugged Nick and Brian both when they were finished.

"She'll be fine, just keep an eye on her," Nick said to Bobby and Billy.

"Thanks, Doc."

"I'm out of here," he said to Brian and pulled Kristy by the hand toward Big Red.

"Oh hell so are we," Brian grabbed Sarah and followed.

"See you back at the ranch?"

Brian nodded. "Yeah, I don't want to miss any fireworks."

After loading Rascal, Big Red headed back to the ranch. Brian and Sarah followed. Kristy thought she recognized her dad's pickup somewhere down the road. She was sure Rowdy would show up sooner or later after Jez had finished with him.

Nick was silent as they drove. Suddenly, he said, "We'll spend another couple of days at the ranch. We need to get the roundup done."

Kristy knew it mean branding, vaccinating, dehorning, worming and culling the herd. "Who's back at the clinic?"

"Brian and I hired a third vet. We'll see how he works out while we're at the ranch. If we like him we'll keep him."

It was late afternoon when they arrived back at the ranch. Nicki ran out and threw her arms around Kristy. "Mama, I'm glad you're home."

"Oh me too, baby." She hugged Nicki as tight as she could.

Nicki looked at Nick. "Well?" Her hands went to her tiny hips and into her back pockets.

"Well what?" Nick asked and his hands went in his back pockets.

"Aren't you going to hug me?"

Nick smiled and opened his arms taking Nicki into them. "There, that tight enough?"

Nicki smiled and Nick was amazed that it was his smile he was looking at, right down to the small cleft in her chin and a dimple beneath her cheekbones. Her eyes were as pewter blue in color as his.

"Mama," Nicki said. "Do I have to keep calling him Nick?"

Kristy frowned. "What do you want to call him?"

Nicki looked at Nick. "Daddy."

Kristy glanced at Nick. "I...I don't..."

"I'd like that," Nick beamed with pride. "Yeah, I'd like that." He grabbed Nicki's little hand in his and said, "Let's go take a look at the mare."

As they headed for the barn Nicki looked up at him and said, "If you're my daddy, then does that mean I still have to buy the foal from you?"

Kristy was near tears as she watched the two of them walk to the barn. From the back they not only looked alike but walked alike. Oh God, it was going to be something to watch Nicki grow into the woman she was meant to be. She just hoped Nick would be in her life.

Ellen came out onto the porch. "How come you came back early? Where's Joe?"

"He's coming behind us. Nick wanted to leave early. Nicki has him in the barn bartering for the foal."

"I had Maria Lupe get your rooms ready. You might want to help me with dinner."

"Sure, Mom. What do you have planned tonight?"

"With half the ranch gone I hadn't planned on much. How about ranch burgers."

"Sure." She couldn't keep her eyes from the barn. She hoped Nicki wasn't giving Nick a bad time. She loved them both so much it almost hurt. But she needed more from Nick then just mind blowing sex. How could she possibly convey that to him?

CHAPTER SEVEN

Most of the cowhands showed up later...about suppertime. Kristy hadn't expected them, but there was always more than enough food to be had and no one went away hungry. Once she'd finished the dishes and put on a fresh pot of coffee it was time for Nicki to be tucked into bed.

"Okay, Nicki say good night to everyone."

Nicki who had been sitting on the floor playing a game by herself said, "Mama...I don't want to go to bed."

Kristy frowned. "Well, I'm sorry but it's that time of night and you need to be in bed."

Nicki stood and looked around the room until her eyes settled on Jack. "Then I want Uncle Jack to tuck me in tonight."

Jack who had been half asleep with a full mug of coffee in his hands almost fell out of the chair he was in when Nicki made the announcement. Kristy thought she saw Nick gasp for air at the request.

"I ain't tucked no one in before," he said, sounding mighty grumpy.

"Oh it's not hard, Uncle Jack." Nicki walked over, took the mug of coffee out of his hand and set it on the table before she took his hand in hers. "You sit on my bed while I go into the bathroom and put my jammies on, then you pull the covers up around my neck and kiss me goodnight."

Kristy watched as they walked hand in hand up stairs together.

"Is that all there is to it?" Jack asked.

"Pretty much." She turned around and waved to everyone in the room. "I love you."

Ellen shook her head. "That child is unbelievable. She's even got that old crusty grump eating out of the palm of her hands. Doc you're going to have to keep an eye on that girl when she grows up. Oh God! I don't even want to think that far ahead. Come on Joe let's go to bed."

Kristy walked into the kitchen, poured coffee into two mugs and brought them back into the living room where she handed one of them to Nick.

Nick leaned back in the chair and propped his boots up on the footstool. "How'd you do that?" He took the mug from Kristy.

Kristy looked perplexed. "Do what?" She sat in the chair Jack vacated across from Nick.

"Produce me?"

She'd always wondered that herself. "You put her in me, what she is is a direct result of you. I guess you produced yourself. She's always amazed me by the things she's done and that outgoing personality of hers had everyone loving her in San Francisco."

Brian and Sarah came into the room. "It's beautiful outside tonight, you two should go for a walk. The stars are so bright," Sarah lamented.

Nick said to Brian. "Everything's ready for tomorrow, why don't you two turn in early?"

Brian grinned and ran his hands over Sarah's butt. "I could use a good...night's rest."

Jack came back downstairs and stood on the bottom step. "What am I going to do when you take her away?" He turned and walked back upstairs to his bedroom.

When the phone rang Kristy answered it. "Hi Kristy, this is Matt. I've got a proposition for you. I'm going to start my own agency, want to join me?"

"You've got to be kidding? Why would you want me?"

"I know your work. I know you could work at home for a while until I get an office set up. I've got so many clients I can't handle them all. You're good at PR, I've got several clients who want that service too. What about it? I'll give you a raise right now."

Kristy stood there with her mouth open. "I'll do it. I don't have to think twice if I can work from home for a while. Nicki and I are still getting acclimated to Texas. Thanks for thinking of me."

"We'll have to meet next week. Thursday good for you? I'll be looking at office space all next week."

"Just call and let me know when and where, I'll be there."

"I'll let you chose your own secretary."

Smiling, Kristy put the phone down. She turned to Nick. "I've just been offered a better position and more money."

"Oh yeah?"

"Matt's starting his own agency. I can work at home until we find an office."

"Then you'll be coming home with me?" he asked, grinning.

"If you don't mind…at least for a while."

He took her by the hand. "We'll turn your bedroom into an office."

"Then where will I sleep?"

He grinned. "Beneath me."

"Oh no…" she whispered as they walked outside to enjoy the stars.

Stepping off the porch Nick tightened his hand around hers. "How does it feel to be home again?"

Kristy inhaled the fresh night air. She could smell the distinctive aroma coming from the barn and heard rhythmic boot heels marching along the wood plank porch leading to the bunkhouse door. "Strange, after all these years. Especially being here at the same time as you."

As they walked slowly past the corral a horse snorted. Somewhere in the distance a lonely coyote howled for her pup. In a tree a nighthawk screeched. Kristy hadn't felt this happy in years. She'd made love with Nick last night and tonight they were enjoying the silent beauty of the ranch together.

"It was bound to happen someday. Aren't you going to miss San Francisco?" he asked and put his arm around her shoulder.

"What I miss is a Texas night like this. There are no cars honking angrily at other cars. No gunshots or sirens. No bright lights or crowds. Just pure natural sounds in the evening quiet." She leaned her head against his shoulder. "I can't remember…is Dallas full of noise?"

"Not where I live."

They walked past the open barn door and hesitated. Both had a flash from the past. Nick hugged her. "That's where it all started, in there."

Kristy lowered her head. "Something so innocent…and beautiful….changed my life forever."

They walked past the barn toward Ellen's vegetable garden where planted seeds were sprouting tiny buds. Ellen insisted on long rows of leafy vegetables, tall blocks of corn and tomatoes, lots of tomatoes, unlike the cardboard tasting tomatoes from the grocery store.

Nick felt her chuckle. "What are you remembering?" he asked.

She looked up at him. "Old Jake. He always said a cowpoke lived on steak and beans, not domestic weeds."

Nick recalled that conversation from when he'd come home from school one summer. "Seems to me Ellen's reply was 'What do you think beans are, Jake'. He claimed he never met a cow he didn't like or a bean he couldn't handle. But he also picks his teeth with barbed wire and uses rattlesnake milk to cut the metal taste from the tin cup he carries in his saddlebag."

Kristy laughed. "I remember as a child I thought Jake had actually built the old ranch house. That shock of white hair and leather-like skin gives him his aged appearance. He just makes the ranch life seem fuller with his cowboy knowledge and wisdom. I've noticed Nicki asking him questions. Probably the same questions I asked him at that age."

"I once heard you ask him why he had white hair. I don't remember his answer."

She shook her head. "Neither do I. I can't believe how I've missed the feeling of open spaces and starlit skies at night."

"Don't get to use to it, you'll be in Dallas in a couple of days and back to work."

They turned around and headed back toward the house. Kristy had no idea if, or where, this relationship would go, but tonight she was very content.

The sun hadn't yet peeked over the horizon as Nick stepped onto the front porch. He hadn't felt this good in years. It promised to be a very busy day.

"Mornin', Doc," Old Jake said then spit tobacco juice on the ground. "All of 'em are ready to go."

"Horses or men?"

"Ah shoot, Doc, you always was a mornin' person. Both, men and horses. They know you want a dollar's worth of work every day even when they only have two cents worth to give."

"How late did the others get in?"

"Most came early…only Rowdy came back late. Said something about Jez. I hope to hell he didn't get her hooks in 'em."

"Me too," Nick said. "Where's my uncle?" He dreaded the answer.

"He's already in the pickup. Hell, I heard those spurs a jinglin' around three this mornin', and I've done closed two gates behind 'em."

Nick hurled the last of his coffee onto the ground and set the cup on the porch rail. Thank God Kristy had fixed the coffee this morning he was almost too exhausted to get out of bed. He could hardly wait to get her and Nicki home to Dallas and settled in.

"Hey, Doc!" Rowdy yelled, "Someone takin' the copter out to round 'em up?"

"Yeah, Joe is. I hear most of the herd's in the canyon. I've got forty men ready to handle them once they're out in the open."

"Hey Doc," Rowdy yelled again, "have fun at the rodeo?"

"Did you?"

"Times a wastin'," Old Jake yelled and headed for the saddled horses.

Nick looked at the Bar C hands standing among the neighboring ranch hands. Their gear was worn by years of use and they rode horses that were as seasoned from years of roundups. Each horse stood saddled and tied to the fence. Like their owners their range-weathered skin was thicker than the mesquite briars in the pastures. Nick was at ease among these men and he knew he could depend on any one of them. He wished to hell he could stay on at the ranch now that he knew he had a family in the making. Nicki needed to know she had roots.

In the next few hours Nick slipped into his Doc persona as he heard the sound of rumbling hooves echoing through the canyon. He waited at the pens for the cows. The State veterinarian drove up to the pens and stepped out of the truck. He had come to help with the testing for any disease.

"Mornin', Doc, how's it goin'?"

"Howdy Frank, so far so good."

The first two hundred cows emerged from behind the canyon wall just as the chuck wagon cook slapped breakfast onto metal plates and took the boiling coffee from the open fire.

"Ah shit!" Manuel spat. "Ain't nothin' worse than raw bacon and burnt coffee."

Cowboys rode out of camp in different directions leaving dust clouds hanging heavy over the corrals.

"Start runnin' them through the chutes," Jack Chandler yelled with authority.

Nick, Frank and Brian took their places at the chutes. Nick and Brian took blood samples from the ventral tail vein of each cow as Frank logged the identifying information. Heifers and steers were wormed and calves dehorned, branded, and vaccinated. Gates slammed open, then slammed closed. Boots in cow dung was the order of the day. Lariat loops sailed, ropes pulled taunt and scents of branded hide rode the winds. By noon they knew they only had two more batches to work. It was hot dirty work. Eight hundred cows and calves had been ear-tagged, tattooed and tested.

They stopped just long enough to each fix a plate of beans and corn bread washing it down with the strongest coffee on the Texas plains. Then it was back to work. By the end of the day the only thing Nick wanted to do was go back to the house and fall into bed. Every muscle ached. But it was a good, honest kind of ache. Until he thought of Kristy and suddenly going home had a new meaning.

Kristy and Ellen knew the men would be exhausted at the end of the day when they returned from the lower pens and they were ready for them. One by one the men straggled dead tired and with muscles aching into the kitchen for a quick sandwich and coffee before dragging themselves off to the bunkhouse.

Nicki stood next to her mother to hand "the boys" a beer if they wanted one and coffee and cookies if they didn't.

Before Nick went into the house he stood just outside in the darkness to watch his little bit of a daughter actually giving the dead tired cowpokes sympathy and cookies. Man, she was going to be something when she grew up. Just like her mother. And what the hell was he going to do then? How was he going to protect his daughter from men like him? Hell, how was he going to protect her mother from men like him? His future stood in that kitchen but if Mavis spoke the truth, he'd have to win Kristy even though he knew he had her heart. But how? Hell he was too busy to go courting like a normal man. Having her living with him would make it easier even though there was danger in those arrangements. Was she the marrying kind? Hell, was he the marrying kind? Did he ever want to marry again? It looked to him like she'd done just fine without the benefit of a ring and piece of paper. Nicki was more than normal for a child without a father. He could thank Kristy for that. Watching Kristy took his breath away. She was not only beautiful, but elegant.

"Good night, boys," Nicki said as the cowboys left.

Ellen chuckled. Kristy just shook her head.

When Joe came in Ellen not only grabbed a sandwich for him but immediately took him off to bed where Kristy knew her mom would have to force him to eat then remove his boots and thick socks. She'd seen him drag home time and time again only to be so tired he'd fall across the bed in a dead sleep. Ranch work was hard. Even though the ranch work ethic had been instilled in her she was glad to be in advertising now so she could support herself and her daughter in a comfortable manner.

"Anything left for a tired hungry vet?" Nick asked.

"Well," Nicki said, "what would you like? We have ham sandwiches and coffee."

"That sounds mighty good."

Nicki handed him a sandwich. "Mama said I have to go to bed now. I'll tuck myself in tonight. I love you." She reached out and hugged a weary Nick then Kristy.

"Thanks, baby," Kristy said.

Nick took the sandwich to the table and sat down. He was exhausted and it showed in every dusty line etched on his thirty-nine year old face. He tried to eat but couldn't.

Kristy gently took his face in her hands and kissed him. "You need a bath. You smell like cows."

"You offering to give me one?"

She laced her arm in his and led the way upstairs to his bedroom. A few minutes later Nick slipped into the hot steaming water and let out a heavy sigh as he rested his head against the back of the old fashioned cast iron tub. He looked at Kristy. "What'd you put in the water it feels kind of tingly."

"Something to relax the muscles. I picked up a few secrets living in northern California near all those wonderful spas."

"Feels great."

Kristy was sure it did. She stood to leave but he snagged her hand. With closed eyes he said, "Don't go."

"I was going to turn your bed down so I could give you a back rub."

He opened one eye and asked, "Something you learned at those spas?"

She smiled. "You know it. I couldn't work all week in San Francisco then play cowgirl on the coast on weekends without the very skilled hands of…" She thought of Greg, her very gay and very dear friend and masseuse who lived in the same building as she and Nicki.

Nick's eyes flew open. "Of who?"

"Never mind. I learned well, you'll see."

Thirty minutes later he toweled off and walked into a candle lit bedroom that smelled strangely of some type of flower. He liked the smell. Kristy wore a short robe that barely covered anything and clung to her naked body like a silken glove.

"You're not leaving tonight, are you?" he asked. She'd slept in Nicki's room last night and he regretted it.

She motioned for him to lie on his stomach and when he did she stripped the towel from him. "It all depends. Do you want me to stay?" She straddled his back, warmed the lotion in her hands and rubbed it on his skin. As she gently kneaded out the knots in his pressure points he moaned like a new born calf. He had so many knots she wasn't sure one session would be enough.

"I want you to stay," he groaned as he began to relax beneath her skilled hands.

Her hands and fingers worked their magic from his shoulders to his lower back until she could feel him relax. When she went for the glutes he flipped over.

"You let someone massage that part of your body? Who was it?"

She smiled and teased, "Butts get saddle weary don't they?" It wasn't his rear she was now focusing on. She watched the change in his expression as she ran her thumbs along the underside of his hardness and followed by some tender loving, and very skilled, hand care.

"Yeah but I…" Her hands were doing some intriguing things to him and he couldn't help but respond. "Hell, surely this ain't part of a massage?"

Grinning, she said, "Only in most men's dreams." What he didn't know was what she was doing to him she'd only done to one other man and was curious as to what his reaction would be. She soon found out as he rolled her onto her back and slipped inside to be taken to the one place they shared together. Something she hadn't done with the other man.

When he raised his head to gaze into her eyes he said, "I don't ever want any other man doing this to you." He took the plunge and showed her how much he needed her.

Nick woke the next morning and realized he hadn't slept like that in years. When he turned expecting to find Kristy, she was gone. He wasn't disappointed for long. She came walking into the room carrying a steaming mug of hot coffee.

"Good morning," she said. "You slept like a log last night, how do you feel this morning?" She sat down on the bed beside him.

His hands crept up her bare thigh to her hips. "Like I'm gonna need a lot of those California massages."

She grinned and teased, "Oh that was just one kind of massage…there are more, some I think you'll like even better."

He took a sip of the hot brew. "It couldn't get any better."

"Sure it can, you just don't know it."

He raised an eyebrow. "How would you know?" And who the hell taught her all those things?

She stood and shrugged the silken robe to let it fall to the floor. "Trust me." She climbed back into bed and took him in her hands to watch his eyes glaze over before he turned to her to pull her hips against his. She longed to tell him he was the only man she'd ever known. That she'd loved him so much she'd never been able to let another man enter his playground.

An hour or so later she asked, "When do we leave for Dallas?"

He sighed. "When ever we want. Should be soon though, Brian and I need to get back to the clinic."

She looked deep in those blue eyes. "I'm going to miss the ranch. But to tell you the truth I've grown accustomed to city life and I kind of miss it. Maybe when I'm old and ready to settle down I'll come back here to be with mom and dad. Right now Nicki and I need to visit malls, eat in restaurants and see a movie now and then."

"Is Nicki coming with us?"

"No."

"Why not? Christ, we have a daughter to think of."

"You're not ready for fatherhood that's why. Our daughter is just fine."

"But I don't want to lose you."

"You won't."

"Think about it."

"That's all I've ever thought of for seven years. I wondered what kind of life you and Mallory had together. I wondered if you'd given her children and if you were happy. I thought she had every thing I ever wanted. After I had Nicki I realized my life hadn't ended as I thought it would. I knew I was strong enough and had been given the moral foundation needed to raise my daughter alone. I dreamed about being in your arms at night until it almost tore me up inside. Then one day I woke up and said no more. You belonged to Mallory. I envisioned you were making love to her at night, not to me."

"If only I'd known," he whispered.

"It wouldn't have made a difference. You had your vet practice to keep you busy I doubt you had time to think much. That's why Sarah and Brian aren't married yet he's too busy. He's lucky to have found someone as understanding as Sarah."

"Yeah, he is."

She ran a finger down his chest. "Maybe someday you'll be just as lucky. But remember my life doesn't revolve around you at this stage of our relationship. It revolves around my daughter and her needs. I need to start a home for her and get her in school again. Then I need to find someone to watch her after school when I'm at work. The only difference this time is we'll be living with her father for now."

"And forever if I have my way."

"I won't make any promises. And neither should you. I don't want Nicki to be disappointed. She's my first priority."

"I think we should hit the road before everyone on the ranch is banging on my bedroom door."

She kissed him before she pulled on her robe and went to get dressed. She hesitated and turned back to him. "I suppose Nicki could come with us."

Nick shouted, "Yeehaa…that's great."

"We'll see." She wasn't at all sure she had made the right decision, but dreaded being away from Nicki even more.

Leaving the ranch was harder on "the boys" and Jack than anyone else. Old Jake actually had tears in his eyes when Nicki put her little arms around his neck and kissed his weathered old cheek.

"Now, Jake," she said, "you will take care of the mare and call us when she's about to foal won't you?"

"Sure, little miss," he said.

Kristy had to literally pry Nicki out of Jack's arms to strap her into Big Red. "We'll call you when we get to Dallas," she reminded her parents.

With Brian and Sarah following, they hit the road for Dallas.

CHAPTER EIGHT

"Which room is mine, Mama?"

Kristy looked to Nick for help.

"How about this one here? I think we'll turn that one into an office so your mother can work at home for a while."

Nicki looked up at Nick. "Is that one your room?" She pointed to the master bedroom.

"Sure is."

"Then Mama should sleep in there too. Your bed big enough?"

"Nicki!"

Nick nodded. "I think the bed's big enough. Do you want bunk beds in your room?"

Nicki's hand went to her hip pockets. Nick's went into his hip pockets. "No," she said, "I'm a girl I want twin beds so in case I make friends I can have sleepovers."

"Oh God," Nick groaned, "sleepovers?"

Kristy ran her hand up his arm. "Don't fret it. You always have the clinic to hide at. Besides, this arrangement might not be permanent remember?"

"Don't say that. I'll adjust."

"You shouldn't have to."

Nicki tugged at Kristy's shirttail. "Mama, will we find someone to stay with me after school like with Annie?"

Kristy picked up Nicki's suitcase. "Yes, I promise, she'll be just as nice as Annie." She put the suitcase on the Nicki's twin bed and opened it. "I'll let you unpack...unless you want some help?"

"No, Mama, I'm a big girl now I can handle it."

Nick sat on the edge of the bed. "Are you too big to give your daddy a hug?"

Nicki stood before Nick. "No, Daddy, I'm not." She wrapped her arms around his neck and hugged with all her might before kissing his cheek. "Are you going to marry Mama?"

Horrified, Kristy yelled, "Nicki!"

"We'll see."

Nicki returned to her unpacking. "That's good. Someday I want a brother to play with. Mama said that I couldn't have a brother until she got married."

Nick's eyes shot up to Kristy. "You said that?"

"Never mind. I think I'll make coffee."

Nick followed her into the kitchen. "You want more children?"

"She asked me that a couple of years ago, it was the story I told her."

"There's some truth to it isn't there?"

"Not really. I think Nicki is enough if I don't have any more children. I can't imagine having more than one like her. I'd be scattered in so many directions I'm not sure I could handle it."

When the phone rang it was the clinic and Nick was out the door in a flash. Kristy had some decisions to make. The first thing she did was to call Matt and asked him if he knew of anyone who looked after children.

"You know, I do. My sister Gracie just flew in from California to spend the rest of the year here to get her life together. She might be interested. Why don't you bring Nicki to our meeting Thursday and I'll bring Gracie."

"How's the office hunting going?"

"I think I've found one but I want you to see it first."

"Where do you want to meet Thursday and what time?"

"Meet me at Cuba Libre downtown and make it about eleven.

The next thing Kristy had to do was find the school to get Nicki into. By the end of the day things were coming together. Nicki was out back checking out the empty corral after declaring she needed a horse at Nick's as well as at the ranch. When she came back inside she had a baby chicken in her tiny hands.

"Look, Mama." She held the fuzzy yellow bird up to her face.

"Where'd you get that?"

"In the corral. I didn't see a mother. What should I do with it?"

Kristy wasn't sure what to tell her. "For now let's put it in that basket over there. I'm sure Nick will have some kind of chick start if he has chickens. Let's go back out there and see if we can find the hen."

They couldn't find the mother bird so Kristy thought it best to keep the chick in the kitchen until Nick got home.

Nick found himself anxious to leave the clinic that night and didn't realize it until he pulled Big Red into the driveway and saw his house lit up. He sat there a moment just to savor what he was about to walk into. She'd have supper started, he could tell her about his day and she could tell him about hers. Maybe he could spend some time with Nicki before they put her to bed. It was the thought that came next that caused his body to react.

When he opened the kitchen door he could smell supper. Nicki was on her hands and knees looking under anything that wasn't nailed down and Kristy too was on all fours in the living room.

"What the hell?" he said. "You gals lose something?"

Nicki got to her feet while Kristy sat on the floor looking exasperated. "I can't find the chick," Nicki said. "It was in that basket by the stove and it got out."

"What chick? I don't have any chickens."

Kristy looked at him. "You do now…only we can't find it."

"I found it in the corral," Nicki said and got back down on her hands and knees.

Nick stuck his hands in his back pockets and enjoyed the view as he watched Kristy's jean clad butt stuck up in the air while she ran a hand under the couch. "If you'll sit and listen for a few minutes you might hear it peeping."

"We tried that," Kristy said. "I give up. Nicki go wash up for dinner, if it decides to show itself I'll call you."

Nick watched Kristy wash her hands and go to the stove and take out a batch of biscuits to go with the chicken fried steak, mashed potatoes and gravy. "Don't move," he said quietly and watched her freeze with a hot pan of biscuits in her hand. He leaned down and with a flashlight looked in the crevice between the range and the cupboard. "There it is warming its little fuzzy body next to the stove." He scooped it out.

"Fine, you deal with it. Your daughter's had me on the floor most of the afternoon looking for the blasted thing. Have any chick start?"

"Where'd this thing come from anyway? Yeah, I have some in the barn."

"I don't know but if she's anything like you this house will be turned into a vet clinic in no time. I swear to God my apartment in San Francisco had every stray dog and cat in the city for a while. My vet bill alone looked like the national debt. I'll try to keep it to a dull roar while we're here. At least I won't have to deal with sea birds and sea mammals living in Dallas."

"Think she's going to be a vet?"

"You tell me, weren't you just like that at her age? They have a marine mammal rescue volunteer group we were involved with. We also belonged to the sea bird rescue association. You should see her clean oiled sea birds. Or rounding up orphaned seal pups."

"Nicki," he yelled, "I found it."

She came running down the hall to look into his hands. "Mama said it needs to be warm since we can't find the hen. What do you think?"

"Come with me. While your mama's putting supper on the table we'll go out into the barn and look around again."

When the two returned they didn't have the chick with them. "I take it you found the hen?"

Nicki's eyes lit up. "A whole bunch of them. We put it back. The mama was there. Daddy says we now have a flock of chickens and I can take care of them. He'll buy some food for them tomorrow. Mama can I collect the eggs when they grow up?"

Kristy smiled. "Of course. And do you know what that means?"

Nicki let out a whoop. "Angel food cake!"

Nick washed up and sent Nicki back into her bathroom to do the same. "I'll have a vet that can cook on my hands. I can hardly wait."

After supper Kristy cleared the table and put the dishes in the dishwasher. "Come on, Nicki, you can take your bath and watch television for a while if you want. We have a busy day tomorrow."

Nicki cocked her head and looked up at her mother. "If you start the tub and put the bubbles in I can turn it off myself."

"Well...are you sure?"

Nicki nodded. "I'm trusting you," Kristy reminded her.

"I know, Mama." She skipped off down the hall into her bedroom.

"Doesn't she ever walk?" Nick asked.

"Not if she can run, skip or hop. There's a fresh pot of coffee, I'll be out in a moment."

Kristy returned to find Nick in his office going over paperwork. "Come in," he said.

"I won't bother you if you're busy."

He pushed his chair away from the desk and motioned for her to sit on his lap. She had the urge to laugh. "I'm not sure this is a good idea." She wiggled herself comfortable and knew she was right. "I think I've found someone to watch Nicki after school. Matt's sister is living in Dallas for a year and she's looking for work. Nicki and I are meeting with them tomorrow. I've also enrolled her in school."

He kissed her neck and ear. "You've had a busy day."

Her arms went around his neck. "And no doubt you have too. How's Brian? I talked with Sarah today and she's exhausted after our trip."

"Aren't we all?"

"I've been meaning to ask you, do you know of a good storage place in Dallas?"

His brows drew together. "Why?"

"Our things from California are being shipped next week. I thought at first I'd have them sent to the ranch but if Nicki and I find an apartment I'd rather have our things here where we can get to them."

His muscles tensed. "I don't want you moving to an apartment. Hell, I want the two of you here. We can store things in the barn if we have to."

Kristy put her head on his shoulder. "Nick, we have to be sensible about these arrangements. We can't go on playing house forever."

"Why not?"

"I have some unpacking to do." She stood to leave but he grabbed her hand. "I'm tired Nick, after I put Nicki down I'm going to soak in the tub before going to bed."

"I'll put her to bed."

"Are you sure? She'll talk your ear off if you let her. You have to be firm with her…"

"I'm sure I can handle one little six year old."

An hour later, Kristy had just slipped into the tub of scented bubbles when Nick came into the bathroom looking exhausted. She smiled up at him. "Told you so."

He shucked his jeans and the rest of his clothes and slid into the tub facing her. She locked her legs around him. "She asked me which came first the chicken or the egg."

Kristy chuckled. "I hope you didn't tell her about the rooster part."

Nick's eyebrow rose. "How'd you know?"

"You've got a lot to learn."

"You should have warned me." His hands moved up and down her bubble slippery thighs.

"I tried. What else did she ask?" His hands were driving her crazy.

"If it took a rooster to make a baby chicken when was she going to get her brother." He pulled her closer to him.

"She's a broken record. I've tried to tell her…" He slipped into his favorite area taking her breath away. "That I'm…not…going to…" His lips came down on hers as water splashed onto the floor and nothing else mattered.

Kristy and Nicki met with Matt and Gracie over lunch at Cuba Libre.

Gracie was as beautiful as Matt was handsome with a southern California tan and long sun streaked blonde hair. "Why did you come to Dallas?" Kristy asked.

"I turned twenty and realized if I stayed I had to go into my father's insurance business. I didn't want that. Big brother here offered to help me out. I'm not sure what my calling is yet so I've given myself a year to find out."

"Gracie," Nicki said, "I like that name. Even with my front teeth out I can still say it. Do you like kids?"

Kristy just looked at her daughter who had taken charge of the interview.

"I do, especially six year olds with missing front teeth. What do you like to do after school?"

"Well…first I have to do my homework if I have any. Then Annie and I would go to the marina or the wharf…except we don't have a wharf here. I don't know…maybe I have to find new things to do after school."

"You like water then?"

Nicki quickly bobbed her head up and down.

"Matt has a swimming pool at his house. If it would be all right with your mother I could pick you up after school and make sure you do your homework, then we could go swimming. Can you swim?"

"Oh yes. Mama and I lived on a sailboat for a little while so I had to take swimming lessons and wear my life vest when we were on the boat."

Gracie took Nicki's hand. "I'll bet we could order some dessert so why don't we go find out what they have. What do you like?"

"Ice cream."

"Oh me too. With chocolate and whipped cream?"

Nicki laughed, "And a cherry on top."

Matt looked at Kristy. "That's some daughter you have. Can you tell how much Gracie likes her?"

"I think Nicki feels the same way. What's Gracie's story?"

Matt sighed, leaned back in his chair and plucked at the napkin on his plate. "Her boyfriend is the story. She got pregnant and he dumped her. She had an abortion and needed to start over. Now you can see why she and Nicki hit it off. Gracie's going to make a great mom one of these days, but she needs more experience first."

"She'll get it with Nicki. She asked Nick which came first the chicken or the egg and he made the mistake of telling her about the rooster. Nicki has an obsession about wanting brothers and sisters. I think Gracie is just what she needs."

"And?"

"And what?"

"Are you going to give her brothers and sisters?"

Kristy toyed with the straw in her ice tea. "I'm not sure. I have a new life to start here in Dallas."

"You're living with her father, what does he say?"

"It's not up to Nick at this point. I have to get to know him all over again and I don't want to rush into anything."

"I can certainly understand that. Then I can expect to get one hundred percent from you?"

She scowled. "Of course you can. Don't ever doubt that for one minute. I'm use to being independent and I want to be able to keep working regardless of what my personal plans are."

Matt added, "Sometime soon I'm adding a Los Angeles office. You have no idea how many Nashville stars are asking for my help. Hell, I'm not even sure how they heard about me, but they have and I have to move on it fast. How would you feel about traveling back and forth dealing with clients?"

She smiled. "I think I would enjoy the change of scenery between the two states. As long as I know Nicki is okay I don't mind traveling."

"Good. I knew you'd be worth the price I'm offering. As soon as the gals get back let's take a trip to the new office I rented. I think you're going to like it. You can start interviewing secretary's if you want."

"Did I ever say thank you for the offer?"

"You did. You'd better give Nick head's up about the California office and the type of people you'll be dealing with. If he's as macho as the rest of the men in this state he's not going to be too happy having you deal with big public figures."

"I...never thought of that. He'll just have to understand that I have a career as well as a daughter to raise. I'll feel him out though because I don't want to go into any kind of relationship if there are restrictions."

"Good."

After lunch Matt, Kristy, Nicki and Gracie visited the new offices.

"I must say the view from here is spectacular," Kristy said looking out the all glass office.

"Thought you'd like it. I'm only taking three offices. We can expand later if we want to. I have one other talent coming on, Hunter Taylor." He watched her expression change and he knew what he'd heard had been right.

Kristy held her breath when she heard a name from her past. "Wow, how'd you get him?"

"So you know him?"

Kristy nodded. "I worked with him in San Francisco for a while. I thought he moved to Orange County."

"He did that's how I got him. He needed a breather, so I made him an offer he couldn't refuse."

"I think you're making a habit of gathering all of us misfits and using us to your advantage. Good business sense. Is Hunter in town now?"

"Yeah, he is."

Kristy wasn't sure what to tell Matt about Hunter except she dated him for a while when she first moved to San Francisco. She remembered Hunter very well and would always be grateful to him for befriending her when she had no one else.

"Matt...about Hunter."

He smiled at her. "I already know the story. How do you feel about seeing him again?"

"In truth...I don't know. It's been a long time since we lived together."

"Nick know?"

"No, and I don't see any reason to tell him unless...I guess I should tell him. I have no intention of ever lying to Nick."

"I can hardly wait to meet this vet of yours. I hear he's really something, his reputation is this town is outstanding."

"You can look at Nicki and tell that much, she's so much like him."

Matt touched her shoulder. "I think you should take him out and get him drunk before you tell him everything. He might be more understanding."

Oh God how she dreaded this evening.

She inhaled as she looked at the Dallas skyline. "I'd better collect my daughter and head home. Thank you for recommending Gracie, I'm sure she'll work out just fine."

"Yeah, me too. Good luck."

Kristy looked back over her shoulder and said, "I hope I don't need it."

Gracie brought Nicki into the office after exploring the other two. "Do you think it would be all right if Nicki spent the night with us? What do you think Matt?"

He shrugged, "It's fine with me. I have a date for the evening and she's certainly more than welcome."

"Please, Mama."

"Tell you what, Gracie can come back to the house with us and you can pack an overnight bag."

Nicki jumped up and down with joy.

CHAPTER NINE

Nick called and left a message on the machine saying he would be working late at the clinic. Once Nicki and Gracie left, Kristy decided she'd surprise him at the clinic. She was totally surprised to see the jet-black pickup of Jez Bevaca parked in the lot just outside the back door. Did she even want to go inside? After sitting there for at least ten minutes she couldn't bring herself to go inside for fear of what she might run into. She turned the car on and headed for the Lone Star Saloon.

"Hi, Mavis," Kristy said, "I guess it'll be a beer tonight."

"Sure, honey. Where's Doc?" She could tell by the look on Kristy's face something was wrong.

"At work."

Mavis flipped off the cap and set the long neck on the bar. "Wanta talk about it?"

Kristy took a sip of the beer. "I don't think so."

"Hey, honey, if you can't tell old Mavis your troubles who can you tell?"

Kristy smiled at the woman she'd always liked. "Mavis, I have a feeling that's why this place is the popular watering hole you've made it to be. What do you know about Jez and Nick?"

Mavis slapped the bar towel hard across the wood. "That woman ain't nothin' but trouble with a capital T. He ain't at the clinic with her

100

is he?"

"Why do you ask?"

"Honey, she ain't what he wants or needs. Say, how's that precious little girl of yours? Have a picture I could see?"

Kristy knew Mavis was trying to change the subject. She reached into her purse and pulled out her wallet to lay it open to Nicki's picture.

Mavis sucked in her breath. "My God she's the spittin' image of Doc. How'd he take the news?"

Kristy looked hard at the woman. "You should know, you know everything else." Then she said, "Look, I'm sorry. I wasn't being unkind. But you seem to know more then anyone else in this town and you're usually right on the money." She didn't understand the softened expression that crossed Mavis' face as she looked at Nicki's picture.

"Ain't no use runnin' a bar if you can't get into everyone's business, now is there?"

"Kristy!"

She turned to see Jett weaving his way toward her. "Mavis, I don't want any trouble with him."

"Then how about that tall handsome gent staring at you in the corner over there?"

Kristy's gaze followed Mavis' direction and she sucked in her breath. Hunter?

"Kristy!" Jett yelled, "Let me twirl you around the floor!"

"Jett leave her alone," Mavis yelled back at him.

Hunter was five years older then Kristy. He was six foot four, muscular, dark-haired and had the sexiest greenest eyes and longest lashes she'd ever seen in a man. The first time she saw him was shortly after moving to California when she was as lonely as she could be. He was like a breath of fresh air and it wasn't long before he was taking her to dinner on a regular basis. When he tried to make love to her she had put a stop to it. She'd felt guilty knowing she was pregnant with Nick's child and she wasn't going to lie about it. Hunter seemed to understand but that didn't keep him from trying over and over again. Hunter had taught her a lot about sexuality, hers and his, but she had never actually done the deed, even though they had lived together for ten months.

"Hi, Kristy," he said smiling warmly at her. "Matt said you were in town." He reached out and touched her cheek before pulling her into an embrace. "Dance with me?"

She didn't try to pull away from him especially when Jett reached for her. "Sorry, Jett. Hunter's an old friend of mine from California."

Jett weaved, his head bobbed back and forth. "Doc know bout this?"

Hunter danced her to the opposite side of the bar. "God, it's good to hold you in my arms again. You look beautiful."

She smiled up at him. "And you look just the way I remember."

His laugh was infectious. "How old is Nicole now?"

"Six." She gazed up at him. "Matt surprised me when he told me you were coming to join us."

"Yeah, I know, it took me by surprise to know we'd be working together again. I somehow get the impression...well, let's just say...never mind."

"Kristy!" Another gent yelled from across the bar.

"Oh hell, leave her alone, Dan!" Mavis yelled.

Hunter laughed and kissed her ear. "It seems you're a wanted woman in this place, want to go somewhere else?"

"They're just old friends I've known most my life. Does it make you uncomfortable?"

"Not as long as you're in my arms."

"Have you seen our offices?"

He gazed down into those beautiful blue-green eyes of hers that had always tugged at his heart. "Yeah, mine's next to yours. I think Matt planned it that way. He said you've agreed to trip out to California when the other branch is open. True?"

"True. Why?"

"You can stay at my place when you get there. I promise I won't be there at the same time if you're uncomfortable being around me."

She looked up at him. "It's been years since we lived together. I'm not uncomfortable with you." She wasn't sure that was at all true. She could feel her heart step up a beat or two as he held her tight against him. She didn't have the same reaction to him as she did with Nick, but it was true then, as it was now, she was physically attracted to him and recalled the feel of his very skilled hands and mouth as they played her body.

102

"Matt says you're living with Nick. True?"

"For now. He found out about Nicki and thought this might be the answer so he could get to know her."

"Are you going to marry him?"

"I don't have any plans for marriage. Why do you care?"

Hunter stopped and looked down into her eyes. "You know damn well why I care."

"Kristy!"

She looked over Hunter's shoulder to see Brian and Sarah walking toward her.

"Hunter, this is Brian and Sarah. Brian is Nick's partner at the clinic, Sarah is his girlfriend. Brian, Sarah this is Hunter Taylor."

"Join us?" Brian asked.

Hunter gazed at Kristy and lifted an eyebrow in a way she so well remembered. "Sure," she said.

"So," Sarah started off, "where's Doc?"

Mavis came to take their order and brought Kristy another bottle of beer.

"He's at the clinic. Jez's truck was in the parking lot so I came here. I ran into Hunter and just about every one else I know in Dallas."

"Hunter," Brian said, "how do you know Kristy?"

Hunter took Kristy's beer in his large hand wrapped his long lean tanned fingers around the bottle and took a sip. "We use to date." He knew that would stir up a hornet's nest and he didn't give a damn. At least he hadn't said they'd lived together. He was more than interested in her and always had been. The timing hadn't been right before but it damn well might be now.

"Date?" Sarah's eyes grew large with attention and she leaned against the table resting her chin on her hand. She wanted to hear more. She was also looking at the most gorgeous man she'd ever met. He had the long and square face that was straight out of the movies or a magazine ad. He had the most sensuous mouth she'd ever laid eyes on, and God, those green eyes were framed by the longest lashes she'd ever seen. What she wouldn't give to know the feel of those large hands and long fingers on her body. Sarah found her heart racing.

"Yeah. When Kristy first moved to San Francisco seven years ago. We're working together again here in Dallas." His arm went around the back of her chair and when she didn't move away from his touch he let his fingers linger against her shoulders.

Brian leaned back in the chair and gave her a suspicious glare. "Kristy?"

"Oh Brian don't look so bothered about it. Hunter and I are working for Matt. Matt's sister Gracie is going to take care of Nicki while I work. It's like one big happy family."

"Yeah, I'll just bet."

"Brian!" Sarah poked his stomach. "She's single."

"Well she shouldn't be."

Now it was Kristy that took offense. "I don't need your help. I've done just fine without it."

"Ah, Kristy, you know what I mean."

"Yeah, Brian, I do. Look, what ever happens, happens. I just don't know what I want at the moment. I do know I have no intention of jumping into something that might not last. I hardly know Nick anymore."

Brian's eyes roamed lazily over her body making her blush. Sarah poked him in the stomach again. "Leave it be, Brian," she ordered. "We came here for some fun now let's have it. Dance with me." She pulled him out of his chair and onto the dance floor.

Hunter leaned forward and ran a finger down Kristy's arm. "What your friend Brian was telling me was that you and Nick are screwing the hell out of each other and you're off limits to me."

She smiled. "That's one way of putting it. I'd forgotten how possessive the men in Texas are. I think I've been in California too long."

He leaned back in the chair and took her hand in his. "Oh hell, I was one of the straightest guys you knew in San Francisco no wonder you were attracted to me."

"And if I hadn't of been pregnant and you married…who knows where it could have led to. But, it didn't happen and here we are now in Dallas debating what to do with each other."

He winked. "I don't have to debate, you know what I'd like to do with you."

The image of his mouth against her breast made her nipples become erect. She took a deep breath and sighed. "I can't. Not while I'm involved with Nick."

"I understand. I'll keep my hands to myself. But you know how I feel about you."

"Yes, I know."

Sarah came back to the table. "Wouldn't you know it, one night alone with him and he's paged. That damn clinic!"

Kristy reached out and patted Sarah's hand. "Don't fight it. Brian loves you and you know it. He and Nick are the best vets in town that's why people call them. Stay here with us and get to know Hunter. Mavis! Another round."

"So, Sarah," Hunter said, "how long you been dating Brian?"

"Too long I think. For about two years now. He keeps saying we'll get married but I think he and Doc are married to their clinic." She took a long swig of beer. "How about you Hunter? Are you married? Married to your work? Any kids?"

Kristy smiled at Sarah, she could see how hurt she was.

Hunter grinned at Kristy before looking Sarah straight in the eyes. "I was married. I'm not married now. I'm not married to my work. I don't have any kids. Anything else you'd like to know about me?"

Sarah sat back in her chair and gave him a good long sober look. "How long you been in love with Kristy?"

Kristy gasped, she didn't want to get into hers or Hunter's background together.

"Seven years. Anything else?"

Sarah leaned forward against the table and rested her chin on her hands. "That's a long time to be in love with someone you don't see."

Hunter looked over at Kristy and took her hand in his. "I had memories to live on. Don't you think she's worth the wait?"

Kristy wanted to disappear.

"That's how long Doc's cared about her. Only he was as blind as a bat when it came to seeing it. He and Brian are just alike. They don't know what they have until they lose it. Too fuckin' bad."

Hunter's eyebrow rose. "I'm not going to put the moves on Kristy if that's what you're thinking. I respect her too much for that. But Nick will have to know we're working together and we did date once upon a time."

Sarah looked at Kristy then to Hunter and thought they were beautiful looking together. He was dark and handsome, she blonde and gorgeous. "I take it you didn't know she was pregnant at the time?"

"Kristy was honest with me. I wasn't as honest with her. I was married back then. What you may want to know is that I was with her when Nicole was born. She needed someone and I was there for her. I took her to the hospital and I stayed with her during the delivery. I brought her and Nicole home from the hospital. Kristy and I broke up and I haven't seen her since."

"Wow, that's really something. That you would do that for her when you weren't even the father."

"It didn't matter to me. She was alone in a very crowded and somewhat unfriendly city at the time. She was scared to death and I didn't want her feeling like she didn't have a friend in the world. It was no big deal. I'd do it all over again if I had to."

Sarah finished her beer and ordered another. "Nick, the ass, should have been with her instead of with that gold diggin' socialite he married. She wasn't good for him but he couldn't see it at the time. She took him to the cleaners and got everything he had to give and then some." She frowned, "Wow, I have trouble watching a cow being born I can't image watching a human coming into the world."

Hunter took Kristy's hand just as he did that night and placed it to his lips. "It's a beautiful thing. It's not like I was at the business end of things, I was there holding her hand coaching her to breathe and giving her the encouragement to go on when she didn't think she could. There was nothing sordid or unnatural about it. I was lucky to see Nicki the minute she was born. I even got to hold her for a few minutes."

"Wow," Sarah said again. "Wanta hold my hand if I ever give birth?"

Kristy laughed. "Sarah, I think I'll be driving you home tonight so if you want another beer go for it. I know how upset you are with Brian. You have to understand, Hunter was a married man at the time, but he was also there for me when I had no one else." She looked at Hunter and smiled. "There was Greg...but he would have passed out at the thought of giving birth. Although he was there helping us after we came home."

Hunter laughed and said to Sarah, "Greg was Kristy's gay friend who loved her but had such feminine traits he would panic at the sight of a spider."

"I think I'll keep all this to myself. Brian and Doc would never understand what he did for you. Hell, Doc would be so pissed."

Mavis brought another round of beer. Hunter said, "Put it on my tab." Mavis gave him one of her famous smiles. Kristy knew he'd been accepted.

Sarah brushed a falling strand of brown hair from her face. "Why do you suppose Jez is at the clinic tonight? Shit, you know she's got the hots for Doc."

"Yes, I know, Jez always has. But does Nick feel the same about her?"

This wasn't the first time she'd wondered about Nick's feeling for Jez. Was she stepping in where she didn't belong?

"Brian once told me Nick...I'm sorry. I think I've had too much beer."

"Don't be sorry Sarah, Nick is a big boy he can screw who ever the hell he

wants."

"No he can't. You're back in his life. He wouldn't do anything to mess that up."

"We'll see won't we? Hunter did you say you had an apartment in town or staying with Matt?"

"I have a penthouse apartment." He gave Kristy a look that seemed more like an invitation that she understood all too well.

Sarah, in her own messed up way, said, "Think I'll ever get to see it?"

"Sarah!" Kristy said.

Hunter laughed that infectious laugh of his. "Tell you what, when we have an open house at the office you'll be invited to my place. Bring Brian."

"Oh pooh on Brian. I'm drunk. Kristy wanta drive me home now?"

"Sure. Hunter, thanks for this evening. I'm glad we'll be working together."

Hunter walked them to Kristy's car and opened the door for Sarah. He pulled Kristy into an embrace and kissed her long, hard and passionately. One hand went around her waist while the other held the nape of her neck. He plundered her mouth and her soul. He didn't want her to forget a thing about him or what they had once shared.

She came up breathless and quickly got into the car. "Good night," she said to him.

Once she pulled into Brian's driveway she had to all but carry Sarah from the car. Brian wasn't home so Kristy assumed Nick wouldn't be home either. She helped Sarah into the house.

"Can I make you some coffee?"

"No, Kristy, I think I'll go straight to bed. Thanks for this evening and…Hunter. God how I like saying his name…Hunter! He's like one of those beautiful Norman's in ancient history. Hunter," she slurred his name. "I watched him kiss you…Texas men don't know how to kiss like that. Wow, I could feel it all the way to the toes of my boots."

Kristy laughed. "Frankly I've always wondered who would name their kid Hunter. But it fits him."

"He's gorgeous, Kristy. Those green eyes! Don't tell Brian I said that."

Brian opened the front door and walked in and when he took one look at Sarah asked, "How much did she have to drink anyway?" He took Sarah's arm.

"Obviously too much. Take her to bed Brian, love her and don't ever let her go."

He smiled his understanding. "Thanks. If you're wondering about Jez…don't, he doesn't want her you know that."

Kristy turned to leave. "Tell Sarah how much you love her." She left and went home.

Nick still wasn't home but Kristy was too tired to think about it. She showered and climbed into bed where she fell asleep almost instantly.

When she felt Nick's arms go around her naked body and press boldly against her she woke up enough to turn toward him and wrap her arms around his neck.

"Where's Nicki?" he asked and kissed her neck.

"With Gracie…" She inhaled what certainly didn't smell like Nick's scent. Her eyes flew open just as his hand went inside her thigh. She jerked away from him reached over and turned on the lamp. "Maybe you should have showered before you left the clinic. I know Jez's perfume when you reek of it." She jumped out of bed grabbed a robe and walked out of the room.

"Oh Christ! It's not what you think." Naked, he followed her.

She spun around to face him and he almost fell into her. "I have a nose, I can smell Jez all over you."

"Nothing happen."

"If you mean you didn't have sex with her…that's your choice, but you still smell like her."

"You know how she is, she was all over me I kept pushing her away."

Kristy looked at the clock. "It's two in the morning, and you're just now unwrapping her from around your neck? God, how stupid do you think I am?"

"I'm not use to having to explain myself."

"I know you're not. That's why I think it's best if I move out. You shouldn't have to explain your actions to anyone."

"No, don't do it. I need you here."

She shook her head. "I'm sorry, Nick, I have to move out. I can't get caught up in my emotions like this. We can still see each other, it's not like I'm leaving…" What was she saying? Of course she'd be leaving but not permanently.

His head snapped up. "What were you going to say?"

"I stopped by the clinic earlier to tell you I'm going to be doing some traveling to southern California to meet with clients. It wouldn't be more than a day or two at a time. I'll be staying at…a friend's place while I'm there. And just so you know, I'm going to be working with a gentleman I dated while I was in California. He's now here in Dallas. When I saw Jez's rig in the parking lot I waited for a while then went to the Lone Star. Hunter was there. So was Brian and Sarah."

Nick felt as if he'd been shot through the heart. "We can't be over, we never got started. Who the hell is Hunter?"   "Nick, we're not over, we can still see each other."

"Hell I want more then that and you know it."

"Then you'll have to court me just like you would anyone else you're interested in. I want you more then you'll ever understand but I also have a life to live. For your information Hunter was in the delivery room when your daughter was born. He helped me when I needed you the most. He was married at the time and there was no real involvement with him, but he was and still is a very dear friend to me. Sarah fell head over heels over him last night so you'd better warn Brian to treat her better or he'll lose her."

"Have I lost you?"

"No you haven't. If you'll shower Jez off your hide I'll show you how much I need you."

"What else do I need to know about this Hunter person?"

"That he's in love with me."

"Oh my God." He couldn't hit the shower fast enough. With his schedule how the hell was he going to win her back?

"But, Mama, I thought we were going to live at Nick's?"

"You'll see Nick as much as ever I would imagine, but because I'm not married

to him I think we should live alone. I've found a nice apartment for us and it's closer to Gracie and Matt. You'll still be going to the same school and Gracie will be picking you up every afternoon."

Nicki's hands went to her hips. "I was afraid this would happen. Nick should marry you so we could stay with him."

"I don't want him like that, Nicki. He's not an animal you can trap." Nicki ran into her room and slammed the door shut.

Kristy's heart was breaking for her daughter. She never should have moved in with Nick in the first place.

Nick didn't come home that night or the next. He said he had one colic surgery after another that kept him at the clinic. Kristy could only assume he was giving her space so she could pack her things and get out of his house. She asked Matt if he would loan her his car so she could move what she and Nicki had. She wanted to make the move while Nicki was in school.

When the doorbell rang she thought it was Matt and opened the door.

"Hunter!"

"Matt said you needed help moving into your new place. He asked me to do it. What can I do to help?"

Kristy pointed at the few suitcases sitting at the door. "That's all we have here. I have a truckload waiting at the apartment. I guess I'm going to have to buy a car this week."

"I have a couple of them so use which ever one you want."

It hurt Kristy to take one final look around Nick's house and slowly close the door behind her. But before she left she wrote her new address and phone number on a tablet and left it near Nick's phone where he was sure to see it.

Her new apartment was comfortable but it wouldn't be a lifetime thing. Just until she could figure what she wanted to do with her life.

"Where do you want these?" Hunter asked holding four suitcases.

"Put them anywhere, I'll deal with them later." She went to a large window to look out at the city. "New home, new city. I'm wondering if I'll ever find what I'm looking for."

He came to stand behind her and put his hands on her shoulders. "You will. It'll be interesting to see how he tries to win you."

"Who, Nick? He may not even try. I wouldn't blame him if he didn't. I told him about you, that you were there when Nicole was born, that I had dated you for a while. I didn't tell him we'd lived together."

"What'd he say?"

"Not one damn word."

"He had a lot to take in. It might be different once we meet."

She smiled as an idea popped into her head and she turned to him. "How would you like to meet one Jez Bevaca?"

"I can tell she's not worth meeting, not compared to you. Hell, why not? If I'm going to try to win you I might as well throw everything we have into the mix and see how it turns out."

"Let's go to the Lone Star Saloon I need some fun tonight." She was going to set some ground rules!

CHAPTER TEN

When they walked into the Lone Star Saloon and their eyes adjusted to the smoky dimness Kristy looked around the room.

"Hunter! Kristy!" Sarah yelled, and waved at them from across the bar as they walked in. "Over here!"

"Hang on to your hat, Hunter, Sarah's alone and gunning for bear."

"Where's Brian?" Kristy asked as they stood next to the table.

"Who the hell knows? He and Doc probably took off to some pasture south of Dallas. I'm glad you're here." She motioned for Hunter to sit next to her. She looked at Kristy. "I heard you moved out of Doc's house. He's devastated ya know."

"Then he shouldn't have come home at two in the morning smelling like Jez Bevaca."

"No kidding! You don't think he actually...ya know."

Kristy shrugged. "I wouldn't know."

"You mean you couldn't tell?"

This wasn't something she wanted to get into with Sarah. "I'll be right back, I want to say hi to Mavis. Beer, Hunter?"

"Sure. Tell me Sarah, you come here much?" Hunter was giving her his undivided attention and Sarah seemed to thrive on it.

Kristy walked to the bar and sat down. "Hi, Mavis. What's the latest gossip?"

Mavis opened a couple of beers and set them before Kristy. "That

Doc's miserable."

"Good."

"I see that tall drink of water is with ya. I hear you dated him. Want to know more?"

Kristy leaned forward and pulled Mavis close to her. She kissed her on the cheek. "Mavis I love Nick, but I know he's too old to retrain to suit me. If I have to let go then I will. As for Hunter, right now he's just a friend. But guess what? I'm going to introduce him to Jez so point that woman's boots in our direction if she comes in."

Mavis let out one long belly laugh. "Doc'll never know what hit 'em. Are you sure Hunter knows what he's in for with Jez?"

Kristy nodded and smiled. "He's more than capable of giving Jez what she wants."

Mavis raised an eyebrow. "And how would you know?"

"Call it intuition and leave it at that."

"Kristy!" Jett yelled. "God, girl, I can never get enough lookin' at you."

"Leave her alone!" Mavis shouted.

Kristy grabbed the two bottles of beer and walked back to the table where Sarah and Hunter waited. Along the way more than one man she knew reached out to put his hand on her butt where she sidestepped most of their attentions.

Sarah grinned and said, "I wish they'd do that to me when I walk by. How's it feel to know they want you?"

Kristy laughed and looked at Hunter. "I don't want them touching me. I haven't encouraged them either."

Hunter said in a low husky voice, "It's a slow one, want to dance?" He held his hand out to Sarah and watched Kristy look amused and grateful.

Sarah flushed and looked at Kristy. "I...can I?"

Kristy shrugged and nodded. "He's a free man go for it." She watched as Sarah's face lit up being held so close to a man most women could only dream about.

When she heard loud commotion coming from the front of the bar she knew, Jez must be there. She sat patiently waiting. It wasn't long before tight pants, long legs and the scent of perfumed horse stood beside her table.

"Hear you wanted me to meet someone? Where the hell is Doc? I don't suppose he told you I was with him the other night..."

"Have a beer on me, Jez. Nick's not my business anymore."

Jez slid her butt across a chair and grabbed a beer. She gave Kristy a long hard stare. "That true? Doc's not with you anymore? What happen?"

Kristy looked at Jez. She was one hard looking horse woman. "You should know, he came home smelling just like you. My heart's not up for breaking anymore. I've moved on."

"Hey, Love," Hunter said and pushed his chair as close to Kristy as possible. Sarah took the other one, she was dying to see what was going to happen next.

"Jez Bevaca I'd like you to meet Hunter Taylor. Friend of mine," Kristy said with a smile and watched the thunderstruck expression on Jez's face.

"Nice to meet you, lovely lady," Hunter said and took Jez's fingers and put them to his lips. He was doing this for Kristy, he told himself. The woman before him wasn't the least bit attractive to him.

"Yeah...yeah...Hunter is it?" Jez stammered and blushed. "Where's Kristy been hidin' you?" She was now giving Hunter her full and undivided attention.

"I haven't been in Dallas all that long. Kristy and I go way back...to California."

Jez's eyes widened and a smile played across her brightly painted red lips. "Way back huh? You follow her here to Dallas?"

Hunter let her fingers slip back to her lap and wasn't sorry. The woman looked as hard as nails and as easy to lay as anyone he'd ever met. She wasn't soft and as untouched as Kristy. "No. But we are going to be working together again."

Jez pursed her lips. "Oh? Wanna dance?"

Hunter let his fingers graze lightly over Kristy's shoulder pushing the hair away from her face. He longed to reach over kiss her and plunder that mouth that gave him so much pleasure in their past. "Sure."

Sarah looked at Kristy once Hunter had Jez encapsulated securely in his arms. "My God could she get any closer to him and not be part of him?" She sighed heavily, "Oh what I wouldn't give to see what's under those jeans."

"Sarah! Think of Brian."

Sarah grinned impishly, her soft brown eyes crinkling at the corners. "Oh I know what's in his jeans and I don't think it would measure up to Hunter. What's he like…you know."

Kristy paled. "I know what's there but I can't really say…we never had that kind of relationship. Silly I know, but it's true. I was in love with a married man, dating a married man. Do you think there's a pattern going on there?"

"Oh hell you're all single now. What if he wants to?"

Kristy leaned forward toward Sarah. "Then I'll let you know how it measures up!"

"Kristy, can I have this dance?" Nick said and held out his hand.

Surprised to see him and Brian standing there her eyes slowly climbed to his gaze. She could hardly breathe once she was in his arms. She closed her eyes and laid her head against his chest. "Did you get my new address and phone number?" she asked. "I'd like to give you a key too."

He didn't want to do anything but hold her in his arms and never let her go. "I did. I don't want to go home anymore. It's just a dark place to sleep again. How's Nicki? Why didn't you take the car? You'll be needing one."

"Just hold me tight, Nick."

His lips pressed against her cheek and his hand moved up and down her back holding her tight against him. Their legs entwined as they slow danced around the room. She could feel his hardness straining for release and pressing against her and she wanted him in the worse way.

"Who's that with Jez?" he asked glancing in Jez's direction.

"Jealous?"

"Hell no. Who is he?"

"Hunter Taylor." She felt Nick's grip tighten around her as if he was suddenly claiming her as his own.

"So that's the one."

She looked up at him. "The one that what?"

"That was there for you when I should have been."

"Nick, don't have any regrets. You loved Mallory and you married her before I knew I was carrying Nicole. I was so miserable in San Francisco once I got there. Hunter was…a friend."

"The hell he was. I must have seemed like some old red neck country clod compared to him. I can't blame you for wanting him."

"I didn't want him, I wanted you and I couldn't have you. I couldn't have Hunter either, he was married too."

"That didn't stop him did it?"

"From being my friend and helping me when I had Nicole? No, it didn't."

"And how about now?"

Her gaze went to his. "I'm offering you a key to my apartment and my bedroom if you want it. If you don't, just say so and I'll move on with Hunter."

"God, woman you're infuriating! No wonder Nicki is so stubborn. I'll take that key because I don't want anyone else in your bed including that stud muffin from California."

"Jez made it clear to me she was at the clinic with you the other night. She hasn't changed in all the years I've known her. She wants you and a ring on her finger. What do you think she'd do if you actually did propose?"

"It ain't going to happen."

"I was just asking."

"Well, don't."

"A marriage of convenience isn't what anyone wants or needs."

"You're gonna make me do it all aren't you? Don't you think I'm too old to start from scratch?"

She placed her lips against his and put her arms around his neck. She molded her body to his. "Men are never too old to start from scratch. Haven't you ever wanted something bad enough to make an extra effort to get it?"

"Maybe I'm insecure when it comes to women."

"Women? You must have said the right words to Mallory."

"And look where it got me?"

"Not all women are like that. Some of us actually love you." Again she pressed her lips to his and savored the warmth of them. When the music stopped they went back to the table.

Jez still clung to Hunter. Kristy thought she saw Jez's hand trying to slip into his back pocket. "Hey Doc," Jez said, "you met Hunter here?" Without letting go of him she pushed him down onto a chair and promptly sat on his lap. Her arms remained looped around his neck.

Kristy smiled at Hunter, who gave her a look of being

uncomfortable.

"Nice to meet you, Nick," Hunter said and extended his hand.

Nick took it and said, "Likewise." He looked at Jez. "Why don't you pull up that extra chair and give him some breathin' room?"

"Ah sugar…that wouldn't be any fun." She did it though, but quickly slipped her arm around Hunter.

"So did you meet Hunter, Doc?" Sarah beamed as she sat down next to him.

"What'd you do with Brian?"

"He went to order another round of beer."

Kristy looked at Nick. "How's the new vet working out?"
"Pretty good. Thought I'd take next weekend off and fly to the ranch. Think Nicki would like to go with me? I need to check on the mare."

Kristy felt a sense of disappointment that he hadn't asked her to go. "I think she'd love it. Jack calls her every night asking when she's coming back for a visit." Kristy looked at her watch. "I think I'd better call it a night. Nicole is staying with Gracie again tonight but I need to start unpacking. Thanks for the evening."

Nick stood. "I'll see you home." He made it a statement.

There was no way Jez was going to let Hunter leave and Kristy felt sorry for him. "I'll talk with you tomorrow," she said to him.

"Let me know which car you want to use I'll have it delivered to you."

Kristy winked at him and smiled. "I will. Thanks again."

In the parking lot Nick looked at her and said, "Did you do that to him on purpose?"

"Do what?"

"Jez."

"I think he could do worse."

"What you mean is he's running interference for you."

"Look, you don't have to take me home if you don't want to. Hunter can do it."

Nick took hold of her arm. "I'm sure he can. Get your butt in Big Red, we're going home."

Nick drove them to her new apartment.

"Well, how do you like it?" she asked as she walked from room to room in the apartment turning on the lights.

Nick walked behind her turning them off. "It's okay for now. Would you stop for a second and look at me?"

Kristy stopped and turned toward him. "What do you want me to do?"

He took her face in his hands. "Love me."

"Nick, I do."

"Then show me."

She took him by the hand and led him into her new bedroom. The only thing she'd done to the room was plug in the bedside lamp. She turned it on. "I'll have to find some bedding."

He sat down on the edge of the bare mattress and removed his boots then hurled them across the room. He watched as she opened box after box until she found what she was looking for and he helped her make the bed.

"Tried your tub yet?" he asked with a smile.

She grinned and walked into the large bathroom that had a window looking out over Dallas. She found some scented candles and lit them, then filled the tub and put scented bath salts into the water. She turned around to see Nick peeling out of his clothes. It wasn't long before he had her out of her clothes and they were melting in the warm relaxing water.

She wrapped her legs around him. "Why didn't you ask me to fly to the ranch with you?"

His brows drew together. "What? I did ask."

She shook her head. "No, you asked if Nicki would like to go with you."

"I thought you'd come along too."

She leaned toward him and ran a sea sponge across his lightly furred chest. "Your problem is that you take me for granted. Don't. We're not some old married couple who assumes one will do what the other wants. It doesn't work that way when you're twenty-seven. I want to be asked. I want to be needed. Frankly, I feel like the proverbial saying why buy the cow when you're getting the milk for free. I'll take whatever you'll willing to give to me...for now...but."

Her scent sent his head reeling. Was he really so set in his ways that he couldn't see what she needed? He drew her legs tighter around him and ran his hand over her stomach and inner thigh. "I want you now, tomorrow, for a lifetime."

118

Nick spent the night loving her over and over again. He hated it when dawn came and he had to leave her. He looked at Kristy now sound asleep and brushed a strand of still moist hair away from her beautiful face. "I love you," he whispered, "I've loved you since the first time I held you in my arms. You and Nicki have become my reason to plan a future. I want to give Nicki that brother she desperately seems to need. God, Kristy, I love you." He placed his lips against her forehead. He knew she heard nothing; he wished he could make those same declarations to her when she was awake. But for now he was afraid of getting hurt again.

When Kristy woke Nick was gone and she felt as if part of her body was missing. She called Gracie, then showered, dressed and went to the office.

There was a soft rap on her office door and when Kristy looked up from her computer Hunter stood there looking worse for the wear. She grinned. "Well?"

"You owe me big time for last night."

"Why? Was it that bad?"

"Let's just say if I hadn't of been around you all evening nothing would have risen to meet the occasion."

Kristy laughed and leaned back in the chair. "Don't tell Sarah she'll be jealous."

Hunter rubbed his temples and lowered himself onto the couch stretching those long legs out before him. "Why would she be jealous?"

"She asked me what you had in those jeans of yours because she found you to be very desirable."

His gaze shot up to hers. "And…what'd you tell her?"

Her lips spread into a smile. "That I knew but wasn't telling."

"You still owe me for last night. I don't ever…and I repeat this…don't ever want anything to do with that woman again. Let Nick have her. Although I can't imagine why he'd want her."

She pretended sympathy. "Too much woman for you? They say bull riders can stay on all night."

"Too well used. She expected far more than I wanted to give her. Man…I don't see what those cowboys see in her. Besides, I'm no bull rider. I ride the waves! She wanted to get it up and get it on." He paused and seemed to think for a moment. "That might have been a good thing you know. Slow and go with her would have turned me off. I can say one thing about you gals that ride horses you've got thighs strong enough to crack walnuts."

She chuckled at the thought. "Frankly, I never did understand their interest either. But, I'll bet she can buck." Kristy laughed out loud. "Look, I'm sorry I didn't expect it to go that far. You could have said no."

"I needed release, it's been a while. You're not available...yet."

Kristy leaned over the desk toward him. "Show me your tongue, Hunter," she said.

He gave her a hint of a smile and raised an eyebrow. "Want me on my knees?" he teased, recalling some very pleasant memories in and out of the shower.

A vision flashed to mind that caused her to blush all over. "No, just show it to me." She grinned as he stuck his tongue out. "Maybe if the stud was still there you could have shown her how she could double her pleasure, shown her what...If the tongue stud is gone then I'm assuming the other one is gone?" Her gaze went to his jeans.

"Ah shit, I'm glad I wasn't wearing that thing last night, took it off years ago. Show me yours."

Kristy stuck her tongue out. "It's gone. These people who ride for a living only know one way, fast and furious. They live hard and love hard. Shoot, I can't imagine Jez knowing much about a good time other than what you said, get it up and get it on. They couldn't even begin to understand what slow erotic hands can do or..." she smiled at him and blushed.

He rose from the couch and pulled her up from the chair where he clasped her hands in his. "You've given me more pleasure with that beautiful mouth of yours, these eight fingers and oh God, these two thumbs then any other woman I've ever had." When his mouth covered her thumbs, he sucked and drew off slowly, he could hear her gasp. He could tell, she remembered.

"Don't, Hunter..." A shock wave jolted through her body and she was taken back to another time.

"Has Nick found out what pleasure these create?" Her thumbs went back into his mouth to slowly draw them out and return them back to his mouth.

"Don't...I..." She found it hard to breathe.

Matt opened the door and walked in. "Good, I'm glad you're both here. I want the two of you to fly out to LA. I've found an office but I want the two of you to look at it first and get back to me." He took one look at Kristy's thumbs in Hunter's mouth and the expression on her face and laughed. He leaned back against the doorframe and folded his arms across his chest. "Ah shit, I certainly know where this could lead, save it for California."

Kristy's mouth dropped open and she yanked her hands away from Hunter as if she'd been burned. "But why both of us?"

"Because I have two potential clients meeting you there. One, a beautiful up and coming star for Hunter, and the other is an older sports team owner for you Kristy. Charm them, wine and dine them. Win them over and if we get their business it'll pay for six months rent out there. I've already booked your flight. If you want I can book hotel rooms but since you have a place out there Hunter I was wondering if you might want to use it."

Hunter looked up at Matt. "You'll have to change the flight to John Wayne Airport since I have a house in Newport Beach. Kristy can stay with me."

"But…"

"No buts, it's a done deal." Matt stated. "Gracie's already prepared Nicki and she's agreed to stay at the apartment with her. Go home and pack, I'll call and let you know when you have to be at the airport. I'm counting on the two of you to win those clients over. Hell, we could all be very rich by this time next year."

"I'd better call Nick, he wanted to take Nicki to the ranch with him this weekend."

Hunter looked at her. "Then let him. We'll be back by Monday or Tuesday at the latest. I'll pick you up later."

After Matt and Hunter left she called the clinic but Nick was out. She left a message with his service then went home to pack. She tried his home number but again there was no answer.

CHAPTER ELEVEN

Kristy arrived home to find Nick waiting for her. "I tried to reach you at the clinic," she said.

"Yeah, I got the page. Thought there might be something wrong with Nicki."

"No, she's fine, Gracie will bring her home tonight and stay with her until I get back from Los Angeles."

He scowled. "Los Angeles? What the hell you going to do out there?"

"Wine and dine some potential clients and hope they like me. Matt says this trip will set us up for the rest of the year. And...that means I can stay in Dallas with only an occasional trip to California."

"Does this mean Nicki can't fly to the ranch with me?"

"She can go with you. Your daughter loves you very much if you haven't already noticed. While you're there why don't you get her to show you how she wins blue ribbons. I don't want her to get too rusty if she's determined to show again. Keep your eyes open for a good cutting horse too."

"Why?"

"That's my passion. My blue ribbons are packed with Nicki's."

Nick was amazed at her. "When do you leave?"

"As soon as Matt calls. Hunter..." She turned around to face him. "Look, I'm sorry but he is part of the team. He's wooing an up and coming starlet and I've been given an over the hill sports team owner."

"Where will you be staying?"

"Do you trust me?"

"You're not tied down."

"No, but my heart is, it's tied to you and our daughter. I'm staying at Hunter's house in Newport Beach. I'll have my own bedroom."

"Door have a lock?"

She shrugged her indifference. "I don't know I've never been there."

He went to the refrigerator and pulled out a beer. "I can't tell you what to do. I'll try not to think about the two of you sleeping in the same…house."

She wrapped her arms around his neck. "I've waited a long time to share a bed with you and you alone." She moved away from him and picked up the mail to thumb through it. "Did I tell you Hunter made it with Jez last night?" She pretended she was reading an envelope.

Nick had just taken a long pull of beer and at hearing the news spewed it clear across the room. Kristy tried to hide her smile. "Is the man crazy? He didn't."

"He said I owed him big time and that he never wanted anything to do with her again. Seems she made demands for something he wasn't willing to give. Although I think he appreciated her get it up and get it on style. He said he didn't want to spend any more time with her than was necessary."

Nick shook his head and wiped the beer off his shirt and chin. "Didn't you warn him about her?"

"He said it had been a long time and needed…"

Nick sat down on the couch. "I guess he made her night."

"He made something."

Nick looked up at her. "You think it's funny don't you?"

"Not really. I never asked him to do it. I told him Sarah was more than interested in him but knew he wouldn't act on it. Besides, if Brian doesn't do something he will lose Sarah, she's tired of waiting. She even asked Hunter to be in the delivery room if the time ever came. Of course she was teasing but deep down I wonder if she knows Brian will be too busy."

"Sarah knows what she's getting into."

"Yeah, she does. I have to pack. I hope I can find my California clothes…and shoes. Although, southern California is so much more informal than San Francisco, I'll just have to make do with what I have. I wonder if I should pack my bikini?"

Nick followed her into the bedroom and watched as she pulled a suitcase from the closet and opened it. "No bikini," he ordered. "Hunter doesn't need any encouragement."

"You're right, we won't be there long enough to get a tan." She quickly moved her hand across the hanging clothes, and mumbling to herself she said, "I'll need…at least one, no two cocktail dresses." She pulled a shimmering white mid thigh dress from the closet and laid it across the bed. She chose a black mid thigh dress and tossed it onto the white one. She chose two pairs of heels and one sensible pair. "It's probably in the seventies so I'll take a sweater, two pairs of slacks and…" She turned around to see Nick holding the white dress up to look at it. "What are you doing?"

"Would you put this on for me so I can see how it looks. I'd like to have the memory so I can think of you while you're gone."

She smiled and pulled the tee shirt over her head and let the slacks drop. She stepped into the shimmering gown and zipped it up. "Of course I'll have nylons and with heels and makeup I'll look different." She drew her hair up and held it.

Nick stood back and admired what he saw. She was the most beautiful woman he'd ever seen. He didn't want to think of her on Hunter's arm in that gown. The dress accentuated every detail of her body and he felt his body reacting.

She dropped her arms and her hair fell back down her back. She slowly unzipped the dress and stepped out of it to lay it back across the bed. She reached for a robe but Nick stopped her.

"Don't," he said. "I want to love you before you go."

Her arms went around his neck. "I've had more loving since I've come home than any time in my life. You were worth waiting for." Her lips pressed against his and she felt his hands unhooking her bra. He drew her down onto the carpeted floor and passion took over.

By the time Matt called she was packed and the bags waited at the door. She didn't have to leave until early the next morning. She hated having to say goodbye to Nick but he got an emergency call from his service and Big Red went flying down the road.

*   *   *

Gracie brought Nicki back to the apartment that evening.

"Mama," Nicki said, "am I going to fly to the ranch with daddy?"

"Yes baby, you are and I want you to be a good girl. Help grandma too."

"Oh, I will, Mama. I love daddy and miss living with him. Will we ever live with him again?"

Kristy hugged her questioning daughter. "Maybe someday we can live together. I'm going to call you at the ranch every night. I should be home Monday or Tuesday. "

"Okay, Mama. I love you." She hugged Kristy before going off to bed.

Kristy offered Gracie a cup of coffee.

"I don't know about you but I think I'd rather have tea tonight," Gracie said.

"I guess we're just too Californian aren't we. I keep a stash of tea bags on that second shelf there. Help yourself to anything in there."

"I love that daughter of yours, she's such a kick to be around. She makes me forget my problems. Do you think she misses San Francisco and her friends? She really hasn't said much about it."

Kristy sat down in a comfortable chair. "I think Nicki is one of those people who can fit in anywhere. I know she must miss Annie but she hasn't said much to me either."

"Who's Greg? She mentions him sometimes."

Kristy laughed as Greg's face came to mind. "He was our very, very gay masseuse friend who lived next door to us. He was more feminine than I am. He taught Nicki how to brew and pour a proper cup of tea. You see he was also very British. So, if you ever want a proper high tea ask Nicki. Although I wouldn't know where to get double clotted cream in Dallas. She even has a beautiful little tea set he gave her. Then her other friend Mikiko gave her a Japanese tea set and she can also show you the involved ritual to their tea ceremony. San Francisco really was a diverse playground for that little girl. She's been exposed to culture that no native Texan could understand. She adapts so well though."

"Believe me I know that. I was having all kinds of trouble just understanding these people but Nicki always asks them very politely to say it again or slow down when they speak. She has the patience of a Saint. She soaks up culture like a human sponge. She even asked me to take her to a museum the other day."

"That was one of our favorite things to do on weekends. That is when we weren't in Marin County riding our horses along the beaches and trails or cleaning sea birds. Have her tell you about the baby seals she helped to round up. She loves animals and doesn't seem to have a fear around them. I took her to UC Davis when they had their annual picnic and we visited the vet school. She was fascinated by the whole department. I can see Nick in her over and over again."

"And what about you? What do you like to do?"

"I loved showing my cutting horse. I loved the art galleries. The wharf and that wonderful sour dough bread we would buy to go with our crab meals. I've met some very nice people who were far from straight but once you got to know them their talents were so diverse and amazing. I have to admit I'm not sorry to be away from there, but I do miss the friends we made along the way."

"You're not thinking of inviting them to visit are you?"

"I don't think they'd be as understanding out here. No, maybe someday we'll go back so we can visit. Nicki does get nice cards and notes from Greg, who encourages her to remember to raise the little pinky when she's drinking tea. And…to always be a lady. Did you ever notice how gay men look so much better in makeup than we gals? I learned a lot of tips from them. Greg's life partner is a female impersonator."

"I know San Francisco is a far cry from Manhattan Beach. The beach is where they hide their sexuality behind rich posh doors. The straights that go behind those doors pretend not to notice. My own dad would have a fit if he thought I knew any gays."

"Nicki knows only that there are some men who are better at being women and they've showed her the manners of the upper crust so to speak. Nicki will do well in any situation."

"You bet she will. She's looking forward to going to the ranch with Nick. She chatters on and on about her daddy. It's like she's trying to make it all right. I sometimes think she's trying too hard. From what I've seen of Nick he's in no hurry to settle down and raise a family."

Kristy smiled. "I think you've hit the nail on the head. He has only himself to answer to and that's the way it's always been. He's expected to provide for the ranch anyway he can. I wonder if he'd even make a good husband at this stage of his life."

"And? If he doesn't want to settle down, what then?"

Kristy inhaled and sipped her tea. "I don't know. I've loved him for so long that he's the only man I've ever wanted. And to be truthful...I've never been asked by anyone else to marry them."

"I've seen the way Hunter looks at you. Matt told me he was in love with you. Would you ever consider settling down with him?"

"I would have to be in love with him. I don't know if I could do that. I admit I'm physically attracted to him and I always was. I also knew he was safe because he was married."

"But, he's no longer married."

"I know. I'll just have to see how it goes with Nick. I do know one thing, I can't and won't wait forever. I want more children. I don't know if Nick does. I know Hunter said he wanted them."

"You've got a few years to worry over that problem."

Kristy smiled. "I do, don't I. Why don't we turn in? Hunter should be here around six. I've made up the guest room for you. And thank you Gracie for taking care of my little girl."

Gracie hugged Kristy and disappeared into the guest room. Kristy climbed into her lonely bed to think about the things she and Gracie had talked about. She realized that she missed talking about personal things with Greg. It was nice to have a man around to talk to and not have to worry about him wanting her. She kind of missed that. She made a mental note to call him when she got the chance.

The next morning Kristy woke Gracie to let her know she was leaving and went in to kiss Nicki.

"Oh you're awake," Kristy said. "I'm leaving now." She hugged Nicki tight.

"Good bye, Mama, I'm going to miss you."

"I know, baby, I'll call you tonight when you get home from school. Gracie's awake. I love you." She kissed Nicki and walked out the front door.

Nicki picked up a picture book and opened it to read.

"Good morning bright eyes," Nick said when he arrived and

peeked into Nicki's room to find her sitting on the bed.

"Morning, Daddy. Mama's gone."

He went to sit beside Nicki. He put his arms around her and hugged her. It was nice to have a daughter to hug. He missed having her living with him and he missed her mother.

Hunter opened the door to his beach house and promptly opened every sliding door and window in the place to let in the warm sea breeze. Kristy stood in the middle of the room enjoying the ocean view.

"Well?" he said, "what do you think?"

"I'm impressed."

"It's the only thing my ex-wife didn't take from me. Make yourself to home." He picked up her bag and headed down the hall to a bedroom. "You can stay in here."

"Isn't this your room?"

"I'll take the guest room. You deserve the best I've got."

"That's not necessary."

He took her hand. "Of course it is. This is almost like old times. Hey, want to take a walk on the beach?"

She kicked her shoes off and they were out the door.

That evening they dined at the local seafood restaurant highly known for their famous dishes. Kristy was in heaven eating a crab dish. By the time they'd had dessert and coffee they were exhausted and went home.

Pouring over their dossiers on the perspective clients Kristy found herself yawning.

"Did you call Nicole?" Hunter asked.

"I did. She's excited about flying to the ranch. Nick's a pilot. I don't think I've ever had her in a small plane before so I hope she takes to it."

He ignored Nick's name being mentioned. She was here with him and if he had his way he'd make the best of it. "She will. You look tired."

"I am. I'm kind of nervous about the meeting tomorrow. It seems the only thing this guy wants is some advice on licensing a few things. Shouldn't he see a lawyer for that?"

"I am a lawyer."

Kristy's mouth dropped open. "I didn't know that."

"Happened after us. I prefer the marketing, PR aspect of things, but Matt thought he could use a legal eagle in the firm. Your job tomorrow is just to win him over to our firm."

"Well, you've got more confidence in me than I seem to have in myself."

"You'll do just fine. Why don't you turn in?"

"I think I will, good night."

By the time she and Hunter found the restaurant Zucca on Figueroa Street in Los Angeles she was a nervous wreck. What she wasn't expecting was the man representing the elder team owner. Ricardo Ventana almost took her breath away. Young, Latino and very well spoken he treated her with a great deal of respect. When she presented the agency's proposal he asked all the right questions and she was able to answer them. After a two-hour lunch he reached over and took her hand in his.

"Thank you, Miss Williams, for the lunch and the conversation. I'm sure Arthur will agree to go with your agency. Should we be calling here or the Dallas office?" He pressed a kiss to her fingers before putting her hand back on the table.

His dark eyes held her mesmerized. "Dallas...for now. We're still setting up the California office."

"Will you be heading up the California office?"

"No...I don't think so."

"Too bad. I would like to see you again."

Now Kristy was beginning to feel a bit uncomfortable and wondered how Hunter was making out. "Maybe you'll come to Dallas. We'll do lunch."

"I would like that," he said.

Ricardo escorted Kristy to where Hunter and his client waited. They all walked into the bar to celebrate the signing of their first clients. The local noon news was just coming on and the lead story was tornados hit the panhandle of Texas. Kristy let out a gasp and grabbed Hunter's arm.

"Go call!" he ordered.

Kristy's feet couldn't get to the nearest phone fast enough. Gracie answered the apartment phone. "This is Kristy, have Nick and Nicki left yet?"

"No..." Gracie seemed to hesitate. "Kristy, you've got to get to the ranch. I've got Nicki. Nick, Brian, Joanie and Sarah took out of here like bats out of hell. It seems the ranch was hit."

"Oh my God! Keep a close eye on Nicki. If you hear from Nick tell him I'm on my way. I'll call the ranch."

"Don't try. Nick had to use a short wave to get through. I hear it's bad, Kristy. Hurry."

When Kristy returned Hunter could see her distress. "How bad is it?"

She swallowed hard. "I don't know. Gracie said she has Nicki but Nick and Brian had to get to the ranch it was hit by a tornado and it was bad. I have to get there! Nick's going to need help...my parents are there."

Ricardo took her arm. "Then you can use my plane. I'll call the airport and have the pilot get it ready."

Her mouth dropped opened. "It's just a small runway...oh thank you!"

They excused themselves from the starlet and headed to the Burbank airport.

Ricardo asked, "What do you think you will need? I have a medical doctor who could go with you."

Kristy was on the verge of tears. "I'm not sure what they'll need. Nick is a vet and so is Brian, they're on their way now. The nearest doctor is miles away and will probably be swamped with patients. Are you sure your doctor won't mind?"

Ricardo smiled, "No, I won't. My grandfather owns the team, I'm his team doctor. We must go now." He made the call to the airport from his cell phone.

Hunter grabbed Kristy's arm and pushed her into a seat on the Lear jet. Tears streamed down her cheeks before she could stop them. Hunter held her hand.

She looked at Ricardo. "I'm not sure you can land a jet at the ranch the runway is probably mud by now."

"Then we'll head for the largest airport and order a helicopter. If you will excuse me I have some phone calls to make and some supplies to order. Don't worry."

Kristy looked into Hunter's green eyes and found some comfort in

them. "If anything happens to any of them…"
"We'll get there as fast as we can."

CHAPTER TWELVE

When the call came in from Old Jake at the ranch Nick was getting Nicki ready to go. He told her what had happened and that it was important that he go to the ranch without her. Nicki had put her arms around his neck and kissed him on the cheek. 'Go Daddy, take care grandma, grandpa and the boys,' she'd said. His heart had melted as he recalled the locket he kept in his jeans. He raced off to the clinic.

Brian and Joanie had the necessary supplies ready to go by the time Big Red pulled into the parking lot. Henry the new vet would stay and tend to the patients. Joanie would go with him while Sarah rode with Brian. Brian had seen his hometown turned into a pile of rubble when he was a child and knew that tornados in Texas were as common as hurricanes in Florida, only much more unpredictable. Nick's own mother died in just such a storm when her car had been thrown from the highway near Lubbock.

Big Red resembled a missile on the road. Nick mashed the accelerator to the floorboard. He had no idea how bad the funnel cloud had damaged the roots of his and Nicki's heritage. He had Joanie keep trying to get through on the mobile, but there was no response. They drove by one disaster sight after another until Big Red rumbled across the cattle guard leading into the seventy thousand acre ranch.

"Look out!" Joanie yelled. "The road's washed out!"

"Hold on!" Nick shifted into 4-wheel drive and gunned the engine to rush headlong into the waves of water. Muddy rain refuge and debris crashed against the hood and onto the windshield. The wipers left mud streaks.

Joanie pointed out the window. "What's that?"

Nick slammed on the brakes and veered to a stop. "Shit." To their left laid three torturously mangled dead Longhorn cows. Mesquite trees were shattered into toothpicks and they could see where the twister touched down. From atop the caprock he and Joanie could see more of Mother Nature's fury. Adjacent to the obliterated roadway was the contorted steel of the windmill from the west pasture. Yanked from concrete anchors Nick knew the six-inch, hundred-foot girders had been swept several miles. Huge wood splinters perforated the large metal windmill blades.

"Look," Joanie pointed, "there's a fawn nestled in that clump of wildflowers. I wonder what happen to the mother?"

They stopped the truck and got out. Brian pulled up beside them.

Sarah screamed and they turned to see what was wrong. "There...ther..." she pointed to two dead rattlesnakes hanging from the broken branches of a lone still standing oak tree.

Uncle Jack's pickup truck lay crumpled at the base of the cliff. Fenders of a John Deere tractor were wrapped around an uprooted fence post. Sprigs of barbed wire had snapped and were embedded in flat rock boulders pushed to the lip of the gorge.

"Jesus!" Brian said, "The wind must have been something to do all this."

A 40,000 pound cotton picker machine lay broken and Nick knew the gin where the combine had been parked was sixteen miles away.

"Anyone tried to get in touch with Kristy?" Sarah said.

Nick picked up the fawn and put it on the front seat of Big Red. "Ain't had time," Nick replied. "She can't be more than three days old," he said of the fawn.

In the far distance Nick could see the old white frame church, only the steeple and cross now stood. The cowboy's bunkhouse was leveled with only a few chimney bricks standing. He let out a sigh when he saw the rock ranch house still standing. The main barn looked salvageable from where he stood. But farm equipment and livestock were scattered everywhere.

Mud spun beneath Big Red's tires as they made their way slipping and sliding to the house. It was near dusk and the fawn squirmed in the seat. Joanie stroked it's head and said, "Whoa, you're gonna be all right."

They drove past Jack's smashed truck. Images of his mother's car flashed through Nick's mind. "Boy, I hope he wasn't in that thing."

When they pulled up to the house and walked in Ellen had candles burning. Rex said he'd disconnected the gas butane tanks and electricity to the house and barns.

"They air lifted Jack by helicopter to the hospital in Lubbock. Doc, I'm so glad you're here." Ellen was in a state of semi shock.

Nick laid the fawn he'd carried in on the floor and glanced around the room. "Get her some colostrum from the freezer," Nick ordered.

He looked around the place to see cabinet doors torn from hinges and two giant wood ceiling beams collapsed.

"Doc, we ain't got no birthin' milk. Hell, we ain't got no freezer," Roper said.

Ellen retrieved a pitcher of goat's milk from the kitchen. "I was going to pour Jack a glass before..." she choked on the words.

"Joanie, use the milk for the fawn. Is there anything left? Plywood, horse trailers, anything?" Nick asked.

Rowdy said, "Storm got it all, Doc."

"Where's Joe, Rex, Cotton, Roper, Old Jake, Scamp?"

Cotton walked into the room. "There's a helicopter landin' out there. Doc, Jack got busted up real good. He's at the hospital in Lubbock. Want us to..."

Brian looked out the door to see Kristy running as fast as she could toward the house. "My God it's Kristy...and Hunter...and some others."

Nick raced out the door and pulled her into his arms. "Your mom is fine. I don't know about Joe yet."

She clung to his neck letting tears fall down her cheeks. "I...we heard."

Inside the house she hugged her mother. "Where's dad?"

Ellen gave her a stoic looked. "He and Jack are both at the hospital in Lubbock."

Nick asked, "Boys, where's the pregnant mare?" He could see hay bales scattered about the pasture.

Roper yelled, "We turned her loose, Doc."

Nick stopped dead in his tracks. That was Nicki's horse. The hay loft door swung open and fell to the ground. "Hell, we got a ranch to run. Call the hospital."

"We ain't got no phone, Doc."

"Use the mobile in the truck."

Ricardo and Hunter raced up to the front porch. "Nick," Kristy said, "Ricardo is a doctor. He had his jet fly us to Lubbock. I knew we couldn't get the Lear in here so he hired a helicopter from there. Do any of the men need attention? Or have they all been taken to Lubbock?"

Nick held out his hand to Ricardo. "Thanks for your help. I think everyone's fine here but you might want to take Kristy and Ellen to the hospital." He turned around and looked at Roper, "Find what horses you can and find that mare." He reached out to Kristy and put his arms around her. "Go to Lubbock. We've got to put this place back together so we've got a home to come back to."

She gasped as she looked around the broken interior of the house. "Oh Nick!"

Ricardo and Hunter escorted Kristy and Ellen back into the helicopter and took off. Nick watched them leave. The rain started again as the men mounted to ride out. It came down in torrents making it hard to see anything in front of them but time and time again they saw the evidence of Mother Nature's reckoning.

"Hey, Doc...look at this," Cotton said. A dead calf with a neighbor's brand was discovered by lantern light.

Another yelled, "Damn!" Rowdy had found a toppled oil derrick spewing "black gold" high in the air. Nick yelled for him to shut down the pump.

"Let's call it a night, we've done what we can." Nick's rain slicker was soaked with oil and rain. His face, along with the other cowboys was smudged with mud and his arms splattered with blood. Briars had cut through his boots and his feet were wet to the bone. He pulled the brim of his hat forward. When they spotted a small herd of cattle he said, "Let's move them out!"

Old Jake had built campfires so they would have some guidance to come back to. When the cattle were put into the only corral left standing Nick and the rest went inside to stand by the hearth and dry out.

"Hear from Lubbock yet?" Nick asked.

Old Jake seemed to stutter. "The doc's say...they say Jack'll be crippled."

"What the hell happen?" Nick yelled.

"Both of his legs was busted." Cotton said. "His spine was broke in his lower back. He was trying to save the mare when the twister hit. We didn't have no warning. The funnel dropped from the clouds like a whip and caught him in the barn. Hell the force of the winds musta blown him hard against the stall planks. He didn't want anything to happen to Nicki's horse. We found him buried under some boards from the hay loft. He never had feelings in his legs. The doc in Lubbock said his back was broke before them big old beams fell on his legs." Cotton took a deep breath. "Doc, Jack's spine was dislocated nearly three inches...the doc said. He never felt nothin'"

Nick looked at Old Jake's pale face. "What is it? Did you get ahold of Kristy and Ellen?"

"Yeah. They've also discovered Jack has a brain annerism."

"A what?" Nick asked. "You mean a brain aneurysm?"

Old Jake nodded. "Ellen said the doc's said the bubble could have been there for years."

"That would explain why he was so forgetful." Nick shook his head. His whole world was torn upside down.

"Jack's only got a fifty fifty chance, Doc. Ellen said he was still in surgery."

The room grew quiet. Nick looked at Brian, Sarah and Joanie. "The boys can take care of what needs to be done here. I have to get to the hospital, do you want to come along? I think Kristy's going to need us."

"We'll come," Sarah automatically said.

"We'll finish up here." Old Jake said, "When we do we'll come to the hospital. Give Kristy our love. Does Nicki know about any of this?"

Nick shook his head. "No, I'll let Kristy tell her when we know more. Who the hell was that doctor with her?"

Heads shook, no one knew. Rowdy said, "Who was the other tall dark haired man with his arms around her?"

Sarah spoke up, "Hunter is her old bo and he'd do anything for her. She's lucky they were together when she heard the news." She laced her arm with Brian's. "Let's get goin', Kristy's gonna need us."

Old Jake remarked, "I'm givin' Mavis a call she'll want to know."

Nick turned and threw a scowl at him. Why would Mavis want to know? Was Old Jake the one feeding her information all these years or was there more to it?

It was close to dawn before they reached the hospital and walked inside to find Ellen and Kristy sitting quietly at Joe's bedside.

Nick touched Ellen's shoulder and she jumped with a start. "How is he?" Nick asked.

"He got hit in the head by a barn timber while trying to rescue Jack. Doctor's say his skull is broke. They won't know about his condition for a few more days. Doc, get Kristy outta here. Her friends tried to take her back to the hotel but she wouldn't budge. You make her go, we can't have her getting' sick over this. Nicki needs her."

"Are you all right, Ellen? Is there something I can do for you?"

Ellen shook her head. "No. Just take care of Kristy."

Before he woke Kristy he wanted Ellen to know, "Old Jake was calling Mavis when I left, what's that all about?"

Ellen stood to pace about the room and pulled Nick out into the hall. "Oh God help us. I think you should know something Doc, in case Joe doesn't make it. I...don't know how to..."

Nick led her to a small waiting room and offered to get her some coffee. "No," she said. "I have to tell you. Joe and Mavis...have a daughter. It happened, I was told, at the cowboy rodeo so many years ago."

His knees almost buckled and he sat down beside Ellen. "Are you telling me Kristy is..."

Ellen nodded. "Yes. You can see the resemblance if you look hard enough. God, Doc, if I could have given Joe a daughter I would have, but I couldn't. When Mavis found out she carried Joe's baby she came to me and asked me what I wanted her to do. I told her to give the baby to me, Joe and I would raise it together. And that's what we've done. We did what we thought best. Kristy's had a good life. We intended to tell her all along but kept our mouths shut too many years and it became impossible to tell her."

"How could you have done such a thing to her?"

"Mavis knew she and Horace couldn't have raised her. You know how Horace drank. Mavis always had a thing for Joe and followed him to the Cowboy Rodeo. She and Joe…well you know how things can get out of hand at that thing. Joe couldn't do right by Mavis because we were married and so was she. She asked us to take Kristy and raise her and that's just what we did."

"Mama! What didn't you tell me?" Kristy stood there glaring at Ellen and Nick.

"Kristy…I…" Ellen got up and walked back into Joe's room.

Kristy was numb. She was angry. She was hurt. "I don't even know who I am anymore." She turned and walked as fast as she could down the hall and into the elevator. Nick tried to follow. By the time the elevator opened she was gone.

"Let her go, Doc," Ellen said. "She's got to let it soak in."

"She shouldn't be alone at a time like this."

"I don't think she will be. That friend of hers, Hunter, gave her a key to his room."

"Which hotel?"

Kristy couldn't get out of the hospital fast enough. She grabbed a cab and headed for the hotel where Hunter was staying. Nothing made any sense. It was like she'd just lost her identity and now she didn't know who the hell she was. No wonder Mavis knew everything about her. No wonder she wanted to see the picture of Nicki. Oh Christ! Nicki was her granddaughter. Mavis and dad? She shut her eyes tight and tried to think of this year's cowboy rodeo. If she hadn't been there for Nick he and Jez might have created a new life, something she was sure Jez would have done to keep Nick with her. She knocked on Hunter's door and when it opened he spread his arms and she ran into them.

"How's he doing?" Hunter asked.

"They don't know anything yet. Hunter…I found out…Oh God! That Joe is my dad but Mavis is my mother."

Hunter dropped his arms to his side and stood back. "You've got to be kidding? Mavis from the bar?"

Kristy paced around the room. She nodded.

Hunter sat down on the couch to think about it. He looked up at her. "I think I can see the resemblance. Mavis is tall and was very beautiful. You can see it in her face. She's no trashy barkeep, just a nosey one and now you know why. Does Nick know?"

Again she nodded. "I overheard mom…telling him. She's afraid dad won't make it and wanted Nick to know."

"Joe's going to make it you know that. Ricardo checked with the doctors and they told him the same thing. Jack is another matter though."

Her hands went to hide her face. "What's Nick going to do without his Uncle? And, oh no…Nicki loves him so much." She sat down on the couch. "This has been one hell of a day. How can I ever thank Ricardo for his help? Did you call Matt? Did you get the starlet to sign with us? Oh hell, I don't know what I'm going on about…I…I'm numb."

Hunter hunkered down and put her feet on the couch removing her shoes. "Why don't you try to get some sleep? You'll need a clear head in the morning. Yes, the starlet signed on the dotted line before all hell broke loose, Ricardo said he was going with us. Matt's ecstatic and sends his regrets and sympathy to you. He's also given us the time we need to get over this. I'm flying out tomorrow with Ricardo and back to the beach house. I'll gather your things and bring them back to Dallas. Are you going to be all right?"

"I don't know anything anymore."

He picked up a light throw from the bed and covered her with it. He sat in the chair beside the couch until she fell asleep.

Nick sat beside his uncle's bedside. Jack Chandler was in grave condition. Tubes of every sort monitored his critical condition and dripped life support medications as he lay there. He was glad Kristy was gone he didn't want her to see Jack under these conditions.

He reached into his jeans pocket and pulled out the locket he kept with him at all times now that he knew the truth. He opened it to see his beautiful little girl's face looking at him. God, he'd grown to love her. It hadn't taken Jack that long to fall in love with her either. He opened his uncle's hand and put the locket in it before curling his fingers over it. "Nicki's with you Uncle Jack. Hell, pull through for her."

Nick dosed off only to be awakened by the neurologist. "I'm sorry Doc, but I don't think your uncle will ever go home."

Nick frowned. "Was he busted up that bad?"

"No, they fixed his bones, but the aneurysm isn't operable. It could rupture at any time."

"Then can he die in his own bed on the ranch?"

"In a few more days. Nick, I'm sorry. But there's nothing else we can do."

"I understand. Thanks."

Ellen came into the room. "I never thought I'd see Jack like this."

"Me, either."

Ellen said, "I called the hotel to see if Kristy was there. Hunter said she slept for a few hours then up and left. He doesn't know where she went. He and that doctor, Ricardo, are flying back to Los Angeles this morning. He'll bring Kristy's things back to Dallas with him."

"He cares about her, you know that don't you?"

Ellen nodded. "I could tell. What's their story? She's never told me a thing about her life in San Francisco."

Nick took the locket from Jack's hand and opened it. "I didn't know she was pregnant when she left us. She met Hunter and he was there for her when Nicki was born. Hell, he fell in love with her even though he was a married man."

"So were you, Doc."

"I know."

"Kristy's never had any regrets about Nicki. When she called to tell us she'd had a baby girl it took us by surprise until her dad figured out it had to belong to someone on the ranch. That's when we knew, she'd only loved one man on the place and had since she was a little girl. It made no difference to her that you were so much older. No, not to Kristy. Hell, if we could have told you we would have. We did call you but Mallory always intercepted our calls. So…you never knew."

His guts felt as if they were being torn inside out. "I never should have married that woman. Kristy and I were only together that one time when I came home shortly before I married Mallory. It wasn't suppose to happen but it did and that gal's became embedded inside my heart and soul and she's been trapped there all these years. When I stepped into the barn that day and looked into the eyes of that little girl, I knew she was mine." He looked into Ellen's deep brown eyes. "I have to get to know Kristy all over again, and Nicki. Maybe…then we could marry."

"That's what Kristy has always wanted. She told Joe she wouldn't marry you because she wanted to be asked, to know that she was wanted for herself and not because of Nicki. She's never loved anyone but you Doc. In some ways she's a lot like Mavis. Mavis was a beautiful woman when she and Joe dated in high school. Then I came along and tore them apart. Mavis went to New York and became a model. She came back one spring and ended up at that damn rodeo lovin' Joe. Joe and I'd had a fight, that's why I didn't go." She looked up at Nick. "How do you feel about Jez?"

"Jez?"

"Yes, Jez. She thinks you're in love with her. She'd do anything to get her hooks in you."

He thought about it for a moment, then said, "I love Kristy."

"Then you should tell Kristy you love her. She told me just recently that you've never said the words to her. I can't imagine her not saying them to you."

"I never expected to see her again. I certainly never thought she had given me a daughter. It's taken some time to soak in."

"Kristy will be more confused than ever now that she knows the truth. She's had a lot to deal with these past seven years, and now to find out she's not mine…" Ellen shook her head. "I hope we don't lose her. I couldn't bear having her move back to California with our Nicki. I love them so much. But I also know a woman can stand just so much without breaking."

Nick stood. "Will you be all right here? I'm going to find Kristy." She nodded. "We'll be fine."

CHAPTER THIRTEEN

Nick never looked back. There was nothing more he could do at the hospital. He rumbled Big Red across the cattle guard and parked in front of the house. Several neighboring ranches had sent help and cowboys were milling around waiting for orders.

"Scamp, take Milley's boys and start building a new bunkhouse," Nick directed.

The cowpokes from the Double Barrel spread unloaded rolls of barbed wire fence. "What do you want us to do, Doc?"

"Rex, you and Cotton help Billy Wayne's crew repair the barn and corral. I'll check on the mare as soon as I find Kristy. Where's Rascal? Where's my saddle? Oh hell, I'll take the jeep."

Scamp said, "Doc, we ain't got no jeep no more."

Nick dropped Big Red into 4-wheel drive. He had a mission and he was sure he knew where Kristy had gone. She was hurt, alone and upset. She no doubt felt confused and isolated. He knew those feelings all too well and he was damn well going to be there to console her. Big Red came to a stop at the family cemetery. He stopped long enough to say something to his parents buried there. "She's up there, Mom, Dad, I can feel it. I wish you were here to see your granddaughter. She's something to behold."

He noticed horse prints. Kristy had Rascal. He climbed up the trail where rocks crumbled beneath his feet. When he got to the top he spotted her sitting near the ledge. She always gravitated to his secret spot and now he realized why. Because it was his place and she wanted to be close to him. He could see she'd been crying. Her long hair floated on the breeze around her shoulders. She was the most beautiful thing he'd ever laid eyes one and she was all his...if he wanted her, and he did.

Kristy heard footsteps and turned to see Nick climbing down to the ledge. "How'd you know where I was?" She wiped her cheeks free of tears.

He sat down behind her and pulled her back against him. He pulled her hair free of her neck and kissed it. "Did you think I wouldn't know where you'd be? This is the one place...Are you all right?"

She shook her head and continued to look out over the Texas plains. "I don't know anymore. It was stupid of me to run away. Nick, what do you want with me? What do you want me to do? I can't go on the way we are. I'm not cut out to live this way."

"Nicki and I want..."

"Doc!" Rowdy's voice drifted upward from the bottom of the ravine. "Doc! Doc! You up there!"

"What the hell do you want, Rowdy?" Nick's voice echoed off the canyon wall.

"It's the mare, Doc! We found her and she's tryin' to foal! She's got problems!"

"Oh Christ! What else could go wrong? I'm comin', Rowdy. Kristy, my truck is at the cemetery. Meet us back at the barn." He mounted Rascal and gigged him.

She watched as Nick rode away with the setting sun at his back. She made her way back to the cemetery and stopped at Mary and John Chandler's side-by-side graves. "Your son deserves better than me. But Nicki and I love him so much."

Nick found Crystal Slipper pacing in her stall. He stood and watched what she might do. "How long she been this way?" He asked Rex.

"Ever since we found her."

Nick looked at the clock on the tack room wall. He watched

Crystal's flanks strain with labor contractions and figured it would be another hour. "Has she been down?"

Cotton answered, "Off and on, Doc."

Nick entered the stall. "Whoa, girl, whoa," he crooned to the anxious mare. His hand reached out to stroke her sweat stained jowl. "Cotton, fetch me a halter. Whoa, girl, whoa."

Crystal pawed the ground and seemed to be trying to avoid the pain of uterine contractions. She suddenly dropped to the ground onto her side and strained. Her hindquarters flexed and stretched. She strained.

"Cotton, fetch me some soap and water," Nick said.

The mare rolled onto her back and her hooves pawed at the air. She suddenly rose and shook the dust from her withers before straining again. Nick heard the rumble of Big Red's diesel and he knew not only would Kristy be with him but he'd have his medications if they were needed.

Kristy raced into the barn to see Cotton set a bucket of water in the aisle. She grabbed the halter from Cotton and went to Crystal stroking her nose and saying soothing words to the horse. She watched Nick raise Crystal's tail then wrapped it in a plastic sleeve. He scrubbed his arms with the soap and water and slid his hand into the horse. Kristy cringed. Even if it was a horse, that had to hurt.

"Where the hell is that right leg?" Nick mumbled and continued to identify what was inside. "Damn, I'd rather have it comin' backasswards."

Cotton looked at Kristy and said, "What do ya feel, Doc?"

He glanced to Kristy. "The left forequarters are jammed in the pelvic inlet. I feel the head, neck and one foreleg. The right one's nowhere to be found. It's probably pushed down and back. I just can't quite reach it. Every time I get close she contracts and smashes my arm."

Kristy continued to stand at Crystal's head and stroked her neck. She would forever recall her own labor every time she saw an animal contracting. Her thoughts went to Hunter. How he'd held her hand against his cheek and spoke softly to her encouraging her not to bear down but to relax. How he massaged her stomach and back until it was time to deliver and then was even more the tower of strength to her.

Nick groaned and grunted as he stretched with all his might. "Without that hoof it'll never come out."

"Oh baby, relax let Nick do his job."

Nick's fingers were numb. He worked blindly. With his left hand on the foal's skull he tried to push the baby back into the uterus. Crystal strained and tried to pace. Kristy held her tight and kept her in a standing position.

"Look out!" Kristy yelled as Crystal staggered and started to fall. "Nick, get out of her!"

"I almost had it," he said. Nick peeled off his shirt. "Damn, I've got to get that foal."

Crystal laid flat on the ground where her pulse and breathing increased dramatically. Kristy knew what this foal meant to the ranch income. She also knew Nicki had laid claim to it. Without a quick delivery and a healthy baby Nick would think the ranch was doomed. What could she do to help? Her mind raced frantically. She placed her hand along the side of the horse's belly and stroked.

Nick spread his shirt beneath Crystal's tail to lie down. "She'll probably stand and kick my head in but I've got to try one more time." He locked the soles of his boots against the stall wall for added leverage then he reached as far as he could into Crystal's uterus. He grunted and twisted and grabbed for all he was worth. "How the hell," he grumbled, "can something so small cause so much trouble." He finally identified the front knee joint and guided the foreleg to its proper birthing position.

Kristy could tell Nick had turned things around. She could feel the horse strain one more time before she stood up with the baby half way out. Kristy whispered, "You can do it."

Nick grabbed the foal's front legs with a forceful tug. "Here she comes!" he yelled.

Kristy smiled and hugged the horse. "You have a little girl, my beauty."

"Yeah," Nick said "and she's marked just like Crystal."

Crystal Slipper turned to inspect her newborn and whinnied. Kristy had tears in her eyes. "It's a little girl." Those were the same words Hunter had whispered to her as Nicole was laid on her stomach. He'd said 'she's a beautiful little girl'. If only Nick had been there to see his daughter come into the world.

Cotton grinned. "She is the spittin' image of Crystal, Doc, four white socks and a perfect star, stripe and snip."

Wiping his hands clean, Nick said, "I think we'll call her Crystal Locket." He reached into his jeans pocket and pulled out the locket.

"Where'd you get that?" Kristy asked. "I left that at your mother's...."

"I know." He handed the locket to Kristy while he washed up and dried off his arms.

"I wore that all the time I was in California. The only difference is Nicki's picture. I replaced her baby picture."

Cotton looked at Kristy. "You have that much trouble birthin' that daughter of yours?"

Kristy smiled with memories. "No one was jamming their fool arms in me if that's what you're asking. No, my labor wasn't that long or that bad. Well, that's the way I remember it six years later. I'm sure I didn't feel that way at the time."

Nick came to her and put his arms around her. "How big was she when she was born?"

"Seven pounds six ounces. She was one week early and was twenty inches long."

"And Hunter? What was he like?"

"A rock. His wife would have had a fit if she'd known he was showing me that kind of kindness. But without him I don't think I could have brought Nicki into this world alone. I only wish you could have been there."

"With the next one, I promise."

Her mouth dropped open. "I doubt I'll have a next one."

Cotton let out a belly laugh and headed out the barn door. "Oh hell the loft's still in tact, go make another one. This ranch is gonna need a lot of new Chandler's just to keep it in the family."

"We will rebuild this ranch you know," he said. "Even if it means I have to work harder than ever in Dallas, we will rebuild."

Kristy put her arms around him. "I know you will. Rowdy's cranked up the generator so we have refrigeration again. I stopped at the store on my way home and bought some food. I'll make you a sandwich and coffee. No doubt you'll be out here most of the night."

He walked into the tack room and found a shirt he'd left there. "You know the ranch life well. Kristy, are you okay? About Joe and

Mavis I mean."

She gazed at him with tears welling. "I always felt close to Mavis and I didn't know why. Now I do. Mom told me Mavis and dad dated in high school and had been sweethearts. That when she saw him the first time she knew she had to have him. I think back to the last rodeo when I gave myself to you so completely. Of course I already have your daughter, and she will always know who her parents are. I also think of you and Jez and what might have happened in the past."

"Jez and I don't have that kind of past."

"I'll have to take your word for it."

"Kristy." He took her by the arm. "Cotton's right you know, the loft is still there we could make our second one only this time I'd know it."

She shook her head. "Maybe someday I'll consider it. I want to make sure you'll be around when the time is right."

"And when the hell do you think the time'll be right."

She smiled a knowing kind of smile. "Oh we'll know." She placed her lips on his and held him tight. "I'll get you something to eat."

The woman was frustrating the hell out of him. What did she want from him?

Kristy made her way into the kitchen. If Nick only knew that she was now making enough money to help out so he wouldn't have to work so hard...would he accept her help? If she presented the fact that Nicki was biologically a Chandler and would someday probably inherit part of the ranch, would he accept her help? Probably not. Nicki didn't have the Chandler name and may never have it. She'd wait to offer her help, she needed to feel him out first. Her body ached at the thought of making another baby in the hay loft. She shook her head, hay loft or not, she would give him another baby someday...if he really wanted one. For now, what he wanted was something to eat.

Kristy spent the night in Nick's arms in the stall next to the new mother and baby. When she woke the next morning, black rain blew at dawn. She went into the house and started breakfast. The kitchen was still in tact but they'd brought out the propane camp stoves since the electricity was still off as was the gas to the house. She knew the cowhands would want their biscuits to go with their country gravy and brought out the Dutch ovens and put them in the hearth embers.

Nick headed for the smell of food and strong coffee and found

Kristy removing the Dutch ovens from the hearth. He took both of the heavy cast iron pans and walked into the dining room.

"Is the baby okay?" Cotton asked and piled sausage, bacon and ham onto his plate.

"Purdier than a speckled pup," Nick replied as he scooped scrambled eggs and bacon onto his plate.

Ellen walked into the house with Mavis. Chairs scraped against the hardwood floor as the cowboys stood.

"How's Joe?" Rowdy asked.

"He's awake and up to go good. Told me to get back to my chores here at the ranch," Ellen replied. She tossed her water soaked jacket onto a chair and took Mavis' jacket from her.

Kristy stood rooted, she didn't know what she should do.

"Sit down," Ellen said, "finish your meal, there's work to be done out there."

"Mama...can I get you a plate? Mavis?"

Both women shook their heads. "No," Ellen said, "we ate earlier."

Kristy left the room and went upstairs to the bedroom. She felt awkward now that she knew the truth. She looked up and watched Mavis come in.

"It ain't gonna change you know that," Mavis said. She found a chair to sit in.

Kristy folded her hands in her lap. "I've lived twenty-seven years believing I was me...now I don't know whether I'm me or someone else."

"Darlin', Joe's still your pa, it's just you have two mothers now."

"Great, how do I explain this situation to my daughter who is too young to be so confused about who to call grandma?"

"I hear that Nicki of yours is capable of understandin' just about anything thrown at her."

"Nicki's young. I'm just plain confused."

Mavis patted Kristy's hand and left the room to give her time alone.

Kristy had no feelings left in her to give to anyone. Since she'd come back to Texas her whole life had been turned upside down. She wasn't suppose to run into Nick, she wasn't suppose to let him know about Nicole, she wasn't suppose to give herself so blatantly to him, she wasn't suppose to love him with all her heart...but she had. It wasn't working out and she had some serious decisions to make once she got back to Dallas.

Nick's uncle Jack died in his sleep with his boots on shortly after returning to the ranch. Only ranch hands and the immediate family were present. He was a simple man with simple needs. The ceremony was held at the Chandler cemetery and few words were spoken. From cemetery hill there was a symbolic view of the wide-open spaces. Jack's hand carved red cedar coffin was fancier then he would have wanted. It had the ranch brand burned into the lid signifying a cowboy always rides for the brand, even in death. The coffin set atop bales of hay overlooking the wide-open spaces and endless blue skies of Texas. It had been lined with Navajo Indian blankets and the handles were fashioned from stirrups. It was draped in the Texas flag.

They watched as Jack's horse, Coyote, was slowly led up to cemetery hill with the boots turned backwards in the stirrups. As was the custom, they slowly unsaddled the horse and turned him loose to roam the prairies, which meant the freedom of the cowboy spirit.

Even though Jack's death was not unexpected, Nick, Kristy thought, took it the hardest. To see him with tears in his eyes was a humbling site. Weren't they all now thinking about their own mortality? She also knew this was the end of an era, and now the fate of the Chandler ranch rested firmly on Nick's shoulders. He was the last living male Chandler.

Nick and Rex used their lariat ropes to lower the casket into the grave. Nothing else was said as each person there dropped a handful of dust into the grave. A simple wooden cross was erected to reflect the modest heart of a good man.

"Hell," Old Jake muttered, "now he's leavin' the gates in heaven open."

Kristy didn't even return to the house after the funeral. She jumped in her rental car and sped off to Dallas. She had to get away. Too much had happened. She no longer knew where she fit in.

"Are you sure this is what you want to do?" Hunter asked Kristy.

"Yes. Nicki's out of school next week and I need to get away.

Matt's already agreed to let me spend the summer in California. I'll be willing to rent your house from you."

"It's yours, no charge. You're running away."

"I don't care anymore."

"Who's going to watch Nicki while you're working?"

"Gracie's going home with me."

"Then you've got your summer all planned out."

"Hunter…I have no plans. I'm on automatic."

"What about Nick?"

"To hell with Nick. To hell with them all."

CHAPTER FOURTEEN

Kristy and Nicki left without so much as a word to anyone in the family. She was running and she knew it. She had to let the family get on with their lives. She'd disrupted an entire family by returning home. She was confused, hurt and upset over something she had no control over. Running seemed to be the easiest way out.

As the plane descended into the John Wayne Airport Nicki argued, "Why couldn't I say goodbye to daddy? Or grandma?"

"Nicki, I told you…"

Nicki pouted. "No you didn't tell me anything except we were spending the summer at Hunter's house. It's not fair. I wanted to spend more time with daddy. And why isn't Gracie here with us?"

"We'll make arrangements for you to fly back when your daddy can clear his schedule. You know he's a busy man. Gracie will be here tonight. Come on, Matt has a limo waiting for us."

"What's a limo?" Nicki asked and grabbed her backpack.

Kristy pointed out the window of the airport. "You see that big car out there?"

"Yeah."

"That's a limo. And the driver is holding up a sign with our name on it."

Fifteen minutes later they were thanking the driver, Ron, and tipping him after he carried their bags into the house.

Nicki's eyes were large as she looked around the house. "We have the ocean to look at. I think I'm going to like it here. Do you think they have a marine mammal rescue here?"

"Oh no, Nicki, don't get started on that again."

"Then how about horses?"

"Hunter gave me the name of a stable somewhere around here we'll check it out. He said there are plenty of horseshows too."

Nicki pouted. "It's not Texas."

Kristy was getting irritated with Nicki. "You were born in California."

"Yeah but you and daddy are Texan. Grandpa and grandma live in Texas. I want to go home."

Trying to find some patience with her upset child, Kristy said, "Go find a bedroom you like. I'll let you call your dad and grandma tonight."

"The big bedroom is yours." Nicki made it a statement. "That one will be for Gracie and I'll take this one. Where will Hunter sleep if he comes out?"

"Hunter is letting us use his house for the summer. I doubt he'll be coming out here."

"Mama…"

"Yes, Nicole, what is it now?"

"Why did we leave Dallas?"

Exhausted, frustrated and confused, Kristy said, "The weather! Now leave it at that."

Nicki frowned and headed for her chosen bedroom. She didn't slam the door, but she made it known by her actions she was one unhappy little girl.

When the phone rang Kristy answered it. It was Hunter.

"He's on the rampage," Hunter said.

"Who, Nick?"

"Yeah. I didn't know what to tell him when he stopped by the office."

"What did you say?"

"I told him you'd gone to California for the summer. He turned on those boot heels of his and headed out the door."

"I'll let Nicki call him tonight."

"Are you all right?"

"No, but I'm a survivor."

"Hey, put on that white bikini of yours and go lay on the sand, it'll renew your spirits."

Kristy looked out the window at the crowded beach. "I think I'll skip the bikini...if you could see the hard bodies out this window you'd be here in a moment's notice."

"Well, at least work on a tan over the summer. I'll be flying out there in a week or two. But...I'll stay at my sister's."

"You're making me feel bad."

"Don't. My sister only lives a few yards away from you. Turn to your left and look out the kitchen window."

Kristy did as he said. "Yes?"

"See the blue house with white trim?"

"Yes."

"Go over there and introduce yourself to Linda, my sister and her husband Mel."

"You've got to be kidding! Why didn't you tell me you had family here? I've been feeling guilty for taking your house out from under you." She heard his charming laugh as she hung up.

Later that night Gracie appeared with suitcases in hand and Nicki showed her the bedroom. Then Nicki was allowed to call Nick.

"There's no answer at daddy's." Nicki sounded disappointed.

Kristy dialed the Chandler ranch and when Ellen answered Nicki became animated and made herself comfortable in the middle of the floor where she talked and talked. It was dusk and the sunset was spectacular.

"Gracie, I'm going for a walk on the beach to enjoy the sunset."

"You think it's safe?"

"I can always scream."

Kristy grabbed a lightweight sweater and tied it around her neck. With the sun going down it was still warm but there was a nip in the air. She walked up the beach until she came to the Newport Beach pier and wandered out onto it. After that she checked out the local businesses that flourished along the highway. She found a seafood restaurant she was sure she, Nicki and Gracie would want to try out soon. Then she turned and walked back down the beach. When she passed the blue house she saw a couple sitting on the deck and walked up to them.

"You must be Linda and Mel. I'm Kristy Williams, I'm staying at Hunter's house for the summer."

"Oh my gosh," Linda said. "You're just as beautiful as Hunter said you were. Come on in."

Mel asked, "Can I get you a drink?"

Kristy shook her head. "No, I went for a walk up the beach and I have to get back. But thank you."

Linda said, "Why don't we plan dinner later in the week. I understand your daughter and nanny are with you."

Kristy nodded. "Yes, they are. I should get back. It was real nice to meet you. Thanks for the dinner invitation."

When she walked into the house Nicki was in tears and Gracie was trying to console her. "What happened?" Kristy asked and rushed to Nicki's side to put her arms around her to comfort her.

"Ellen upset her. She told her Nick couldn't call because he didn't have the phone number."

Kristy pulled Nicki into her arms. "That's why you're going to call him and give it to him. I don't see a problem here."

"He's not answering his phone," Gracie said.

"Let's call his service they'll give him the number."

Once they called Nick's service and left their new phone number Nicki settled down and finally went to bed without much of a fuss.

Kristy opened a bottle of wine poured a glass, handed one to Gracie and flopped down onto the sofa. "I don't think I'm cut out to be a mother," Kristy said. "Hell, I can't deal with these upheavals anymore."

Gracie laughed. "And to think you're just getting started. What happens when she becomes a teenager?"

"Oh my God I don't know and I don't want to think that far ahead. I'm just sorry I had to take her away from Nick, but it's for the best right now." She changed the subject. "I met Hunter's sister and brother-in-law tonight."

Gracie gave her a funny look. "Where'd you meet them?"

Kristy pointed toward the kitchen window. "They live in that blue house. I was talking to him on the phone and that's when he told me."

Laughing at the thought Gracie said, "He's a devil in disguise. God, he's the best looking man I've seen in years. He seems so crazy about you and Nicki."

Kristy gave Gracie a hard glare. Did Gracie have a thing for Hunter like Sarah did? "Gracie, Hunter has been my friend and confidant for a while now, and I adore him, but I'm in love with Nick and he knows it. I don't know where, or even if, this crazy relationship with Nick is going to go anywhere, but I intend to ride it out no matter what."

"I admire your tenacity, Kristy. I can't imagine what it feels like to fall in love with someone and have those feelings become a part of your life."

Kristy finished her wine. "I can't help my feelings for Nick. I love him. I've always loved him and will always love him."

A week later Nick hit the Lone Star Saloon like a train roaring through. He glared at Mavis. "To hell with her!" he all but yelled. "I'm not chasing any woman that doesn't know where her roots are planted."

"Whoa!" Mavis frowned and handed him a beer. "Hell, she's had 'em uprooted and doesn't know where she belongs anymore."

"Then she can stay the hell in California. I'm movin' on with my life."

Mavis slapped the towel hard against the bar as she looked toward the front door. "Then I suppose you'll be movin' on with Jez, cause she's got that look in her eye and you in her sights."

"Oh shit." Before he could move Jez was all over him.

"Hey, I hear your girlfriend went back to California with her kid."

Mavis gave Jez a look that could kill. "Leave 'em alone, Jez."

"Hell no, I ain't gonna do that, can't you see he needs some companionship."

"Not the kind you have to offer him, Jez," Mavis added.

"Why'd Kristy leave? You too much man for her? Maybe she left for Hunter."

"Leave it be, Jez," Nick growled in no uncertain terms. "Where is she, Mavis?"

Jez slapped him on the back. "Ah hell, you don't even know where she's at?"

Mavis started to come out from behind the bar but when Jez saw the look in her eyes she took off to where other men waited for her.

"Damn bitch," Mavis mumbled. "No upbringin' worth a damn."

Nick sat back and looked at her. "I can see the mother hen coming out in you. Your chick's flown the coop." He suddenly thought of Nicki and the baby chick. His heart was breaking.

"Ah hell she'll be back. Kristy knows where she belongs and why."

Nick scowled. "And she took my daughter with her. I'll never forgive her for that."

"What was she suppose to do go without her? No, she'd never leave that precious child behind."

"She could have left her with me. I could take care of her."

"Oh like hell you would. You don't have time to do anything but chase after yourself and your patients. No, she's better off with Kristy. Kristy won't keep her from ya, you know that."

"I don't know a goddamn thing anymore." He drained the bottle and slammed it down onto the bar. "Give me another."

Mavis pulled the cap and set another in front of him. "You can't just sit here and drink night after night."

"Why the hell not? There's nothing to go home to. I won't be going back to the ranch until the fall and I have a broken heart."

Mavis rolled back on her heels and leaned against the liquor wall. "So you admit it. Your heart's broken. Well, well, that's a starting point wouldn't you say?"

"I don't know how to handle a broken heart. It hurts like hell."

The expression on Mavis' face softened. "We've all been there, Doc. What'd you do last time it got broken?"

"Married Mallory." He tossed a twenty on the bar and left.

Kristy answered the phone long after everyone else was asleep. "Hello," she said in a quiet tone.

"Why'd you do it?" Nick yelled.

"Why not do it? There's nothing left for me in Texas."

"Nicki's a Chandler, she needs to be here to get to know me and her family."

"Nick," she said in a soft, calm voice, "Nicki's last name is Williams." She hung up.

Williams? He scowled. Oh holy hell, Nicki didn't even have his last name! He dialed Kristy's number again. When she answered he

156

said in his own way, "Why the hell doesn't she have my last name?"

"You figure that one out for yourself, Nick. Good night." She hung up again.

Nick looked at the phone in his hand. The woman was driving him crazy. How could he love someone so much and be so angry with her at the same time? Nothing made any sense. Somehow he had to get through to her. Nicki needed to have the Chandler name to protect her heritage.

Until he could figure out what he was going to do Nick threw himself into his work. Cheryl, his receptionist hadn't been with him more than six months and until now he wasn't sure what to do. His receptionist had no concept of time, mileage or money management. His gasoline bills had doubled some weeks, tripled other weeks. Since she'd been there his days seemed to go on forever as he traveled from one barn call to another like a rat in a maze. Brian was having the same problem. Just to tell her the problem wouldn't solve it he realized. No, he had to find another way. Hell, there were times he found himself ricocheting and crisscrossing four counties exhausting what daylight was left. He and Brian often passed each other on the road.

On the wall behind the reception counter he put a huge map of the Dallas area. He'd remembered this idea from the summer he worked on the King Ranch in South Texas. Windmills were numbered according to the wilderness sections of land; thumb tacks would mark barns along the outskirts of the city roads. With the same idea in mind the Dallas map would show Cheryl what part of the countryside he or Brian was working.

Nick opened a box of red thumb tacks and placed one tack at the location of each prominent barn. A total of forty-two. It was a start. Today...she would soon learn she'd be riding in Big Red with him. He went into the office to start some paperwork until she arrived.

He picked up his pen and started to write on a chart when he noticed Nicki's picture on his desk. He automatically picked it up. She was such a beautiful little girl. He wondered what she would be doing today? Did she miss him as much as he missed her? He put the picture in his vest pocket. She would be near him that way.

When Cheryl came in Nick heard her groan, "Who put that thing on the wall?"

Nick walked into the reception room. "I've got Sarah covering for you today, you're going to be riding Big Red. Go get a pair of overalls and put them on."

Cheryl craned her neck at him. "Me?"

Nick thought if they started at the most aristocratic barn she might remember the large animal clients and would recognize the importance for more efficient scheduling. Colonial Bend Stables, in Los Rios, on the west side of Dallas County was their first stop. "Sneaky Gobblin has to be tube wormed," Nick said and wished it were Kristy helping him out.

Cheryl's eyes grew large as she looked at the beautiful Austin stone barn, which housed the horses of the rich and famous. "Boy," Cheryl said, "this place is nicer than my home."

Each stall was freshly bedded with deep pine shavings and scents of high quality alfalfa hay circulated beneath ceiling fans. Automatic watering systems bubbled clear spring water for the horses to drink. Every horse stood perfectly groomed. Sneaky Gobblin was seventeen-hands tall, a massive hunter-jumper full of pent up energy. The horse had been 'tubed' many times before and normally he didn't object. But today he seemed to sense Cheryl's lack of horse experience. Or maybe it was her big Texas puffed hair, Nick couldn't be sure, but when Cheryl's reflection caught the eye of the horse in the pooling water bucket the horse's ears perked. Nick took note and was shocked when Gobblin grabbed a lip full of her hair sprayed monstrosity.

Cheryl screamed and the horse jumped. "Why that no good sonofabitch," she yelled as she fell into the shavings. "He did that on purpose!"

Nick tried to keep a straight face but couldn't. He helped her to her feet and hustled her out of the barn.

Next on Cheryl's schedule for the day was T.J. Storms' hovel over thirty miles to the east side of Collin County. When they stepped from Big Red Cheryl gasped at the foul odor and the sight of the staggering rent-line stable owner weaving his way to them. Baby piglets, fighting cocks, and diarrhea afflicted dairy calves roamed loose within the dilapidated fences and crumbling leanto of a barn.

"T.J.," Nick said, "this is Cheryl. She answers the phone at the clinic."

Slurring T.J. said, "Oh, I know you. Howdy, Missy." He wiped calf scours from his hand and extended his shaky grip to her.

Cheryl took one whiff of whiskey fumes and nearly fainted.

"What's the problem, T.J.," Nick asked.

T.J. weaved and pointed to the calves. "Them calves got the squirts, Doc."

Nick looked at Cheryl. "They've got Coccidiosis, each one has to be orally drenched with medicine."

Cheryl looked dumbfounded. "Huh?"

T.J. said, "Gal, you gotta catch 'em by their head and tail. Hold 'em for Doc."

Cheryl gingerly touched a calf's rump and it promptly kicked her in the shin while showering her coveralls with yellow watery diarrhea. "Oh yuck!" she yelled but continued to hold onto the calf.

Nick looked at her knowing she was getting a valuable lesson. "Welcome to veterinary medicine."

After being knocked down more than once Cheryl was finally getting the hang of holding on. "I like answering phones better."

After T.J.'s they drove north, then south, then back across Denton County. Back and forth, back and forth. By now even Cheryl was getting dizzy. Nick waved at Brian as his truck headed in the opposite direction. "Wasn't that Doc Walker?" she asked and looked at what had been a perfectly manicured set of nails.

"Yep."

Once they returned from the rounds to the clinic small animal patients waited them. "I get your point!" Cheryl said and headed for the shower.

Nick and Brian saw nineteen more clinical cases and helped eleven Golden Retriever puppies come into the world by caesarian section before their day ended.

"Where's Sarah?" Nick asked Brian.

Brian grinned. "Sent her home. I've had a hard day and need some tender lovin' care when I get there. She'll make things all better."

Nick envied Brian tonight. He too needed some tender loving care that only Kristy could give him. He thought back to the 'California' massage she'd given him at the ranch and felt his body harden. He dreaded going home to the hollow sound of an empty house again. How much longer could their stubbornness go on?

When the phone rang at midnight his head hit the headboard with a thud. He picked up the phone and rubbed his head at the same time. "Doctor Chandler."

There was silence, then Kristy said in a soft voice, "I'm sorry to be calling so late."

He turned on the bedside lamp. "Kristy? What's wrong? Is it Nicki?"

"There's nothing wrong...I just wanted to hear your voice."

"It's good to hear yours too. How are you? How's Nicki?"

Again silence. "She misses the hell out of you and when she can't reach you I find her in tears sitting on her bed. What are we going to do, Nick?"

His heart felt like there was a wrench around it, tightening. His arm went across his brow. "What do you think we should do?"

"Hunter's flying out here tomorrow and back to Dallas in a couple of days. He could bring Nicki home with him, Gracie would come along and they could stay at the apartment."

Hunter! The man was beginning to get on his nerves. "Then why not just send Gracie and Nicki home alone?"

"Because..."

He shut his eyes tight. He knew...it would mean Hunter would then stay behind and she was vulnerable. "It's a decision only you can make." He quietly hung up.

CHAPTER FIFTEEN

Early one warm afternoon Hunter answered the door of his beach house to find Sarah standing there. "My goodness," he said, "what brings you way out here? Don't just stand there, come on in."

Sarah brushed past him and set her suitcase down in the middle of the room. Her eyes grew large as she scanned the room and gazed at the stunning furnishings, the art work on the walls and the very expensive statues sitting about. "Wow, this is some place you've got here. Where's Kristy?"

"She hasn't come home from work yet. Can I get you some ice tea?" She sure was pushy for a Texas gal, he thought. Had Nick sent her out here to check up on them now that Nicki and Gracie had returned to Dallas?

Sarah walked around the room admiring the art work and bronze statues. "Sure, thanks."

He thought he might as well put her mind at ease. "In case your wondering, we aren't living together."

Sarah knew that was probably true. "She sent Nicole and Gracie home to the apartment. I've never seen Doc look happier then when Nicki ran into his arms. It's a shame."

Hunter handed her the tea. "You're as transparent as they come, Sarah. Did Nick send you out here to keep an eye on us?"

Sarah gave him a big innocent smile. "No. I thought Kristy might be lonely so I came to see what California livin' was all about. I don't think Nick even knows I've flown out here. He probably wouldn't care anyway."

Hunter laughed and that captivating smile of his caught Sarah completely off guard. He was the most handsome man she'd ever laid eyes on and wished she could win him for herself. She loved Brian, but Brian was committed to his vet practice, not to her. She didn't want to end up like Kristy…wanting someone so bad that she had to wait to get him. No, that wasn't her style. She wanted things when she wanted them, and sitting around waiting for Brian to make up his mind drove her crazy.

Hunter said, "Hell, I'm staying next door at my sister's house. About the only thing Kristy and I are doing together is have dinner…which by the way, you're invited to tonight."

Sarah sipped her tea and pointed a finger at him. "But you'd like to do more than that wouldn't you?"

Hunter raised an eyebrow. "I've made no secret of how I feel about her. Until she gets over that lame brained cowboy no man will ever have his way with her."

Now it was Sarah's turn to laugh. "That lame brained cowboy is a broken man and just too damn stubborn to admit it. I swear when they get to be his age they get plain stupid."

Hunter picked up her suitcases and took her hand to lead her to Nicki's bedroom. "Got a pair of shorts in there?"

"Yeah, why?"

"Put them on, I'm going to take you for a walk."

"Ooh," she smiled and closed the door so she could change.

The next time she saw Hunter he too had on shorts and his very masculine legs were as tanned as any she'd seen, so were his arms and face. The tan made his green eyes stand out even more. His dark hair had reddish bronze streaks highlighting it. He spent a lot of time in the sun she assumed. She could hardly keep from staring at him. God, if Nick could see them now. He hadn't sent her to be with Kristy but knew he'd be forever grateful to her for taking the trip when he couldn't. Maybe he'd even give Brian some time off so they could get married and have a short honeymoon. Yeah, right, it was just a fantasy in her mind and she knew it.

They walked down the beach weaving in and out of sunbathers

and children making sand castles. "Wow, this place is something. I've never seen the Pacific Ocean before and so close to your house."

Hunter took her small hand in his. Give her his best charm, he thought, treat her as Brian never would...or could. Sarah and Kristy deserved some male attention paid to them. "Yes, that's the Pacific Ocean all right. We'll walk across the street to Balboa Bay after we walk along here for a while. So, you've never been to California before?"

She shook her head. "Never been out of Texas before."

"What's your first impression?"

She looked around her. "That everyone's so tan and beautiful. Pull the jeans off a Texan and you get fish belly white legs...like mine."

He laughed out loud. "White maybe, but you have beautiful legs. How long do you think you'll stay?"

She looked up at him. "Maybe until I get a tan?" She loved how her small hand fit into his large one. She wondered what it would be like to have a roll in the sand with him while she was visiting? How could Kristy stand to be so near such a hunk of man and not want to be touched by him? Was she crazy?

They crossed a busy two-lane road and walked to the bay side where a ferry crossed back and forth. He pointed across the water. "That's Balboa Island. Shit, most of the tourist don't even realize you can drive there. I guess they like the romance of the ferry."

"It's so beautiful. The water, the sky...the people."

"I'll take you and Kristy out on the boat. Show you where John Wayne and his family use to live. A lot of the dead stars had homes down here at one time or another. It's a great place to get away to. Today's celebrities like the gated communities we have around here, but I find this old established area fits my personality better."

"I'll bet it does. You have a boat too?" Her mouth dropped open, he was just full of surprises.

He grinned down at her and touched the tip of her turned up nose with his finger. "Yeah, I have a boat too. Tell you what, why don't we stop at the grocery store and stock up for a dinner cruise. Kristy will like that."

"Oh my God, I've died and gone to Valhalla!" And she was going there with Hunter, her version of the God of Love!

When Kristy opened the front door and saw Sarah sitting on the couch next to Hunter sipping white wine she couldn't believe her eyes. "Hi!" She grinned and tossed the briefcase onto the table next to the door. "It's so good to see you. Why didn't you let us know you were coming out?"

Sarah was close to feeling as if she were in a state of perpetual happiness. "I wanted to surprise you. Instead, Hunter surprised me. He said we could go on a dinner cruise. Wow, what a tan you have!"

Kristy laughed softly. "Dinner cruise? Then let me go change. Did you go to the store?"

Hunter nodded and winked at her. "Got everything we'll need. Even stopped at your favorite bakery and let Sarah pick out dessert."

Sarah sat there grinning from ear to ear. "Y'all know…I may never go back to Dallas with this kind of treatment."

"I'll be right out." Kristy was exhausted, but never too tired to go out on Hunter's fifty-foot yacht for dinner. She knew Sarah was being treated royally and she would forever be grateful to Hunter for it. She wondered how Nick was and did he know Sarah had come to visit? She pulled on a pair of white cotton slacks, striped red tee shirt and tied on her white deck shoes. She walked back into the living room to see Sarah mooning over Hunter. She couldn't help but wonder how Brian might feel about that? "I'm ready. Where's the food?"

Hunter pointed to the kitchen. "We're ready." He picked up the sacks of groceries in one hand and took Sarah by the other hand and led her into the garage.

Sarah's mouth dropped open again.

Hunter pointed to the sleek silver convertible sports car and opened the door letting Kristy get into the back and putting Sarah in the front seat. He put the groceries in the back seat with Kristy.

"Do we have far to go?" Sarah asked. Her face lit up like a Christmas tree.

"Nope." Hunter smiled and looked in the rear view mirror at Kristy who looked dead tired. He wanted to make that tiredness go away and he knew he could given the chance. He wanted to massage her back to relax her then run his hands over her entire body until she was writhing beneath him for release.

A few minutes later he pulled into the yacht basin and parked.

"We could have walked over here," Sarah said sounding disappointed.

Kristy laughed. "And carry all these groceries? I don't think so. Come on, let's get on board and let Hunter wine and dine us while he plays captain of his ship."

Hunter fired up the heavy motor of the boat threw it in reverse and backed out of the boat slip. Once outside the breakers he slowed the boat down to a crawl. "You don't get seasick do you, Sarah?"

Kristy grabbed a seasick patch and quickly slapped it behind Sarah's ear. "This will help. I don't want your first boating experience to be a bad one."

Sarah sat on deck relaxing and sipping white wine. Kristy went below to fix a delicious crab salad for them and brought it back up on deck. Hunter dropped the anchor through dinner and they watched as the sun set on the horizon.

After a dessert of cheesecake and coffee Hunter said, "Want to try your hand at steering the boat, Sarah?"

They weighed anchor and Sarah sat in the captain's chair and steered the boat. Kristy had never seen such a big smile in all her life. Sarah was enjoying the experience, especially when Hunter kept his hands on hers. "It's not much different from a car," he said, "except we have props and you aim into the wave."

Sarah laughed. "I can't believe I'm doing this!"

Kristy enjoyed watching Sarah experience something so foreign and new to her. She hoped she would stay with her awhile, she missed Nicki terribly and Sarah would help take her mind off her daughter. The last time Hunter had them on the yacht it was Nicki he let steer the boat. Kristy could still hear her daughter's laughter as Hunter held Nicki on his lap and put her small hands on the wheel.

"Maybe we can go to Catalina this weekend," Hunter said.

Sarah broke out in song, "Twenty six miles across the sea…"

"See, you're Californian at heart and just don't know it," Hunter mused.

"Well I could certainly get use to this lifestyle…that's for sure."

Hunter looked back at Kristy who sat on a chaise lounge looking more beautiful than ever with her long hair flying on the sea breeze. She looked so forlorn and lost. He knew how much she missed Nicki, shit so did he.

When the stars came out, Hunter turned on the running lights and they headed back to the docks but not before they wandered around the bay for an hour to let Sarah enjoy the lights reflecting off the water. He was sure Sarah was having an adventure of a lifetime.

"Oh how I hate to see this day end," Sarah complained.

"We'll have to do it again," Hunter reminded her and helped her onto the dock.

Two couples passed them as they walked to their own boats. They nodded at Hunter and the women before slowly walking away.

He laced each woman's arm in his. "You know, I consider myself the luckiest guy in the world tonight, with two beautiful women on my arm."

Back at the beach house Kristy poured Hunter a brandy and asked Sarah, "Would you like a brandy or coffee or something else?"

Perking up and much too excited to even think about sleeping Sarah said, "I think I'll try a brandy."

"Good," Hunter said and led her out onto the deck on the ocean side and where the patio furniture had nautical theme upholstery.

"Kristy, I don't want to go home."

"Then stay awhile. Actually, I'll only be here until Nicki's school starts. I'm going to miss this place. I've grown to love it too."

"How about you, Hunter, you going back to Dallas too?" Sarah was feeling the warmth of the brandy and loved the bold uninhibited way it made her feel.

"Sure. I have a job there. I'll always have this place to come home to when ever the mood strikes."

Sarah leaned close to him. "What mood?"

Hunter leaned close to her. "Any mood." He brought his mouth to hers and gave her a kiss he was sure she wouldn't soon forget.

Sarah came up gasping for air and quickly took another large sip of brandy. Brian never kissed her like that!

Kristy knew Hunter was teasing Sarah, but also knew Sarah could be led down the wrong path if she wanted to go that direction. Hunter looked up at Kristy and winked.

"So, did you have a good time tonight, Sarah?" he asked.

Sarah's eyes were closed and she was still savoring the kiss of a lifetime. "Oh my yes."

Kristy shook her head warning Hunter to be careful. He understood, but he wanted Kristy so bad he hurt. He stood and took Sarah by the hand. Kristy let out a gasp. Sarah was pleasantly numb and allowed herself to be led into the house and down the hall to a bedroom. Hunter discreetly closed the door shutting Kristy out. Kristy felt just awful for what she knew was the wrong reason on Hunter's part. She tried to reason with reason. Sarah was single with no real promise of marriage from Brian. Didn't Sarah deserve at least one good time…She finished off the glass of brandy and walked out onto the beach, it was none of her damn business.

An hour later Hunter came to sit down behind her and put a leg on either side of her. "She's asleep."

"Why'd you do that?"

"Because I can't have you."

She leaned back against his chest and rested her head while looking out at the dark ocean where the frothy white caps of the incoming waves glowed iridescent. "Hunter, if I could love you I would. My heart belongs to Nick."

His arms folded around her and his chin rested on the top of her head. "And so does your body. He doesn't have a clue as to how lucky he is. He's blowing it. If only, are the two words we keep saying to each other. I've loved you for years and I'm trying to find the same thing you seem to have with Nick. Whatever the hell that is. If I have to bed other women after being around you then that's what I'll have to do." He placed a kiss on the top of her head and hugged her tighter against him. Her perfume filled his senses and if he could he would throw her back onto the sand right then and there to make love to her. He knew she'd never allow that.

"But Sarah? You knew she had a crush on you in Dallas. My God, now she knows what it feels like to make love with you. How's she going to recover when she goes back to Brian?"

"That's not my problem."

"Have you made love to Gracie yet?"

He pressed his mouth to her ear. "No."

"It's probably just a matter of time."

"And you know how to stop me…at any time."

Kristy halfway turned to look at him. "If only…"

He pulled her to her feet and they walked back into the house. He kissed the top of her head and held her tight against him. "I'll see you in the morning." Then left and walked next door.

Kristy picked up the phone and dialed Nick's number. "Doctor

Chandler."

"Hi."

"Hi yourself. I heard Sarah flew out there today."

"Yeah, she's had quite a day. I'm sure she's going to be as red as a lobster by the time she leaves here. And how long do you think she'll be here?"

"Hey, I didn't send her out there."

"Too bad, it would have told me a lot about you."

"We're not going to fight over the phone are we?"

"No," she whispered and longed to be held in his arms. "How's Nicki? Did they have a good flight?"

"She's everything I could ever ask for and more. I tucked her in at the apartment and waited until she went to sleep before I came home. What did you and Sarah do today?" He wanted to keep her on the line as long as possible. He needed to be connected to her any way he could.

She ached to be in his arms. "Actually, she's been with Hunter all day. I was at the office. We took her out on the boat for a dinner cruise. Hunter let her steer it and she was having a ball."

"Boat too?"

"Yes. We might go to Catalina this weekend."

"Catalina huh?"

"Yes."

"You can sleep on this boat?" He asked trying to keep his voice calm.

"Well, yes, it's a fifty footer with sleeping cabins and stateroom."

"Must be romantic to sleep on the water with the motion of the ocean stirring you."

"Why don't you fly out and join us?" she asked.

"I have to work."

"I figured that's what you'd say."

"It was good talking to you. You want me to tell Nicki anything?"

"Only that I love her."

With a rage of pent up emotion he wondered, did she still love him too?

She hung up and went to bed, but she didn't sleep. All she thought about was Nick making love to her.

The next morning Sarah wandered out of the bedroom and into

the living room where Kristy sat sipping coffee. It was Saturday and she was watching the early morning joggers along the beach.

"Good morning, Sarah, sleep well?"

Sarah blushed. "Why'd I do that?"

Kristy walked into the kitchen and brought Sarah a cup of coffee. "Probably because you needed to."

Sarah smiled. "Oh God, did I ever need that. He was...the best...I've..." She put the cup to her lips. Kristy got the picture.

"I talked to Nick last night and asked him to come out so we could go to Catalina together."

"Yeah, and what'd he say?"

"He was working."

"Of course! Those two men..." Sarah finished the coffee and went for a refill.

Kristy stood looking out the sliding glass door. "They've hired a third vet, you'd think they could take some time off. Even a weekend."

"Kristy, what are you thinking about me now?"

Kristy turned to look at Sarah then walked over and hugged her. "Sarah, obviously you needed Hunter. I'm not going to say anything else. How are you going to feel when you go back home?"

"You mean to Brian?"

Kristy forced a smile. "You said you wanted to know what Hunter was like, and now you know. Of course Jez knows too."

"Oh man, do I ever. How can you pass that up? Doc's no saint, you know he has his share of women, not just Jez. And what do you have to compare to if you only have Doc? What do you mean Jez knows too?"

Kristy let her gaze go to the window to watch the sun glistening off the water. "Nick is the reason I can pass it up. And yeah, Jez knows."

"Surely you've done it with Hunter? At least once?"

Kristy definitely wasn't going to say a thing. "I think I'll walk to the grocery store this morning, you want to go along?"

"Okay, okay, I won't ask again. God, what am I going to do if I see him again?"

"Oh you'll see him again, he's on the deck now." Kristy thought Sarah turned two shades of red.

Hunter walked in and kissed both women on their cheeks. "Got any coffee?"

Kristy motioned toward the kitchen. "I'm going to the store you want anything special?"

"Nope," he said and smiled at her.

Sarah quickly dressed and went to the store with Kristy. What had she expected from Hunter when she saw him again? All she'd gotten was a kiss on the cheek and a hello. She felt cheap for one thing. And he barely acknowledged her because he went straight for Kristy. Shit, he was notching his belt with everyone she knew…except Kristy.

Later that afternoon during a quiet time Kristy sat on the couch thinking about Hunter and Sarah. Sarah had been brave enough to go after what she'd wanted…so why couldn't she do the same thing. If Nick wouldn't come to her she would go to him.

Kristy packed an overnight bag and headed for the airport.

CHAPTER SIXTEEN

Nick entered his office with Nicki and pulled up a chair. He needed to go over a few files.

"I like your office, Daddy. Did you kill the deer and put its skull on the wall?"

"No, I found it. Makes a pretty good hat rack don't you think?"

"Yeah." She ran her hand over the shiny spittoon and made a face. "Why does that clock run backwards?" She pointed to the wall.

"It's a Texas Aggie clock, where I went to school."

"I'm going to UC Davis. They're called aggies too. I hope their clock doesn't run backwards cause I have trouble telling time when it goes the other way. I met the nice man from the veterinary department and he told me I needed real good grades to come to his school. I liked his school, it was close to home and had wide open spaces around it." She paused, put her hand to her chin, cocked her head, then said, "But I don't live in California anymore, does that mean I have to go to a Texas school?"

Nick leaned forward against his dark heavy desk, given to him by Uncle Jack when he left his law practice behind, and rested his chin on his hand. "No, you can go to any school you want to. How come you were at Davis?"

"Mama took me to their picnic, she was thinking of going there. They have an animal rescue center and we wanted to find out more about it." She looked around his desk. "Daddy, you need a picture of me and mama on your desk." She made a comment about his photos on the walls and thought there should be more horse pictures. "Will you show me your animals?"

"Okay, let's go to the kennel. I have to check on a dog." He took her by the hand and led the way. Putting the dog on the exam table he couldn't help but notice how reserved Nicki seemed. "Is there something bothering you, Nicki?"

"No. I miss mama, that's all."

"Did your mama say when you'd be moving back to the apartment?"

"Yes. At the end of August. She said I needed to get ready to go back to school then."

"How do you feel about moving home?"

Nicki sat down in a chair and rested her head against the wall. "Okay. Only I don't know where home is anymore. I don't like that."

"Would you like to come back and live in my house again?"

Nicki's eyes lit up. "Oh yes. But mama won't do it."

"Maybe we can convince your mama that's where she should be."

Nick put the dog back in the cage and washed his hands. Nicki didn't look like she felt too good. He put the back of his hand against her forehead and it was burning up.

"Are you sick?"

She nodded. "I didn't feel good when we flew here. I feel kind of sick to my stomach."

Nick dropped everything and rushed Nicki back to his house where he put her to bed. He called Joanie and asked her what to do for a fever and upset stomach. "Hell, Doc, I don't have any kids, how would I know?"

"You're no help!" He called the apartment and no one answered. Where the hell was Gracie? He put some ice cubes in a plastic bag, wrapped a kitchen towel around it and handed it to Nicki. "Here put this on your forehead."

"Daddy, mama usually puts a thermopeter in my mouth."

"Thermometer," he corrected and realized with her front teeth not yet grown in the word was hard for her to say. What the hell was he suppose to do now? If she were an animal he'd know exactly what to do, but she was a human child.

"Anyone home?" Kristy yelled as she opened the door.

"Mama, Mama!"

Kristy knew the sound of distress and ran into Nicki's bedroom to find her in bed. "What's wrong?"

"I wish the hell I knew. She said she has a fever and upset stomach. I...don't know what to do."

Kristy looked up at him. "Well do you have a thermometer that doesn't go up the
backside of an animal?"

"No, but I can run out and get one."

"Then do it."

Nick was out the door in a flash. Kristy looked at Nicki. "When did you start to feel sick?"

"When we got off the plane."

"That was five days ago and you're just now letting Nick know you're sick?"

"I didn't want to worry him. I have a sore throat too."

"I think you might have caught a bug. Do you want to sleep?"

"Yes, Mama I think I do. When I wake up can I have some ice cream?"

"Maybe after you eat some chicken noodle soup."

"Will you make it?"

She pulled the sheet up around Nicki's neck and pressed her hand against her forehead again. She'd wait until Nick returned before she made any kind of medical decision. Nick returned with a medical doctor who prescribed an antibiotic and told them to keep her in bed for a couple of days.

Later that night Nick had an emergency and Kristy sat curled up on the living room couch and sipped hot cocoa with big fat marshmallows in the cup.

She dialed the apartment and Gracie answered the phone. "Hi, this is Kristy. Take a couple of days off, I'm at Nick's and Nicki's sick. How do you feel?"

Gracie groaned, "Probably as sick as Nicki. Whatever it is we picked it up on the plane. I'll be fine, you take good care of our girl."

"And you take care of yourself. I'll be over tomorrow to see what you need."

Nick returned home around midnight. "You still up?" he asked.

"How's Nicki?"

"Sleeping like a log. Gracie has the same symptoms and suspects they picked the bug up on the flight back here."

"She scared the hell out of me. I don't know how to take care of sick kids."

"So where'd you find the doctor?"

"I treated his horse. We traded services tonight."

"Can I get you anything to eat or drink?"

"No." He put his arms around her and pulled her close. "I thought you were boating to Catalina today?"

"Nick, we have to talk."

"All right, let's go into the bedroom."

"No, let's talk out here," she said and curled up on the couch again.

"Don't look at me like that," he said, "I feel guilty enough having her sick."

"It's not your fault. It's a normal part of being a kid. She gets sick once in a while."

He hunkered down before her and took her hands in his. "Yeah, but not on my watch."

"Look, I flew home to apologize to you for running away like I did. I was confused and upset. I needed space away from the family. I..."

He moved to the couch beside her. "You had a shock. Mavis said your roots had been pulled up and you didn't know where you belonged anymore. Has that changed?"

She sank back into the couch cushions and thought for a moment. "Mavis. I can't get over the fact she's my biological mother. It took me a while to understand that I am who I am because of my upbringing. Just as Nicole is who she is because of what I've given to her." She gazed into those blue eyes of his and lost herself in them. "I guess having a biological parent only means they gave you life, what you make of it is far more important."

"You're not talking about yourself anymore are you?"

She shook her head. "No, I'm talking about Nicole."

"What about her?"

"I can't keep moving her from state to state, from ranch to apartment. I need to find a permanent home for her and myself. I'm thinking of buying a house."

He stood up and frowned down on her. "Here or California?"

"I can't keep her from you, it wouldn't be fair. She and I both love California but she needs to be here so you can watch her grow into what she'll become."

"Then move in here with me," his words were almost a plea.

She shook her head. "No. This was Mallory's house that you bought for her. I want my own."

"I can understand that. I can sell the place and we'll look somewhere else. I want my daughter living with me."

"And what about me?"

"Man, that goes without saying."

She looked beyond him and thought back to California. "I've learned something about myself over these past few days that bothered me."

He sat back down beside her. "What's that?"

"That I couldn't allow myself to be with any other man...no matter how much I wanted or needed to be with him, I couldn't do it. You're always with me and have been since the first time in the hayloft. I hate myself for the way I feel. I've robbed myself of any chance to know if I can find happiness with Hunter. Hunter is a man who loves me unconditionally, but he's also a man that needs to have a woman when he needs her. So far I've managed to pawn him off on Jez and..."

"And who?"

"That's not important..."

"Good God it was Sarah! Holy hell, Brian can never know that she...made it with Hunter. It would kill him."

"I warned you and I warned Brian but neither of you would listen. Look, I know
there have been other women in your life other than Jez, and I'm sure Brian's had his share too. Hunter gave her what she needed. Unfortunately it was because he couldn't have me. Now, Sarah is riddled with guilt and shame. She knows that she was a stand in because I wouldn't let Hunter bed me, and I think she's kind of afraid to come home. She feels that somehow Brian will know what she's done...and probably still doing. I was there, Nick, she needed to be with Hunter for all the right reasons, but for him it was all the wrong reasons. What I'm saying is I can't go on having an affair with you with nothing to look forward to in the end. Nicki needs to know her

father."

Nick's grin spread into a smile.

Kristy was almost in tears. She would have to settle...for Nicki's sake. "We'll move back in here with you temporarily. I fully intend to buy myself and Nicki a house."

"When?"

She leaned back into the couch and thought for a moment. "I can't come home until I finish with my clients which should be at the end of summer. That's only a few weeks away."

He took her hands in his. "How do you feel about what Sarah's done?"

"I don't feel anything. At first I felt responsible but I couldn't have stopped either one of them unless I'd given my permission for Hunter to take me into the bedroom...and I couldn't do that. Sarah told me that I would never have anything to compare to if I didn't change my feelings."

"And what'd you tell her?"

"That I didn't want to make comparisons I knew what I wanted. If I'd wanted

Hunter I would have done it seven years ago when he came into my life. I will tell you this one thing about Hunter and myself, he showed me, no...taught me, what a man wants and how to go about giving a man what he needs. He taught me about myself. There's something else...Hunter and I lived together for a while."

Nick was numb. He looked at the grandfather clock. "It's late we should turn in. I'll check on Nicki. You go to bed."

"Nick."

He turned to look at her. "What?"

"I left Sarah with Hunter and I feel as guilty as hell."

"Don't. Brian will never hear it from us."

"Thank you." She walked into his bedroom and threw open her suitcase. She hated living out of the thing, and most everything was in California, some still at the apartment. Oh hell, she swore silently and tossed the suitcase on the floor. She stripped out of her clothes and climbed into bed naked. If she had to get up to check on Nicki she'd borrow Nick's shirt.

When Nick climbed into bed beside her he took her in his arms and held her. He knew she was too upset to push for more and he didn't mind just holding her. She was coming back and she'd agreed to move back in with him. What more could he want? How was he going to feel when she found a house?

Late Sunday afternoon Kristy took Nicki back to the apartment and tucked her into her bed. Gracie too was on the mend.

"I brought some of my chicken soup for the two of you to finish off. I'm sorry I have to get back to California but I have to meet with a client tomorrow afternoon."

Gracie tried to smile. "Don't worry about us, we'll be okay. Nick's been great with her."

"Sit down, Gracie I want to ask you something."

"What is it?"

"How do you feel about Hunter?" She wanted to see Gracie's reaction to her question and wasn't disappointed.

Gracie tugged at her lower lip. "Why do you ask?"

"You're in love with him aren't you?"

She nodded. "He doesn't know."

"Gracie, you sometimes have to go after what you want. I flew home to let Nick know we'll be moving back here. I want to buy a house so Nicki can put down roots. Nick asked me to move back in with him until I find a house and I said yes."

Gracie's mouth dropped open. "But...why?"

"Because of Nicki. I love Nick and I always have, I want to make a life with the two of them."

"But Hunter..."

"Gracie, Hunter and I are not meant to be and he knows it. I'm spinning my gears moving back and forth between states and it's not good for my daughter."

"Would you continue to work?"

"Of course and I'll still need you with us. Hunter will be coming home next week."

Gracie blushed. "I..."

Kristy smiled. "Leave it to me. I'll put a burr under his saddle and point him in your direction. You're just too darn shy for your own good, but I can understand why."

"I think dating scares me a little."

"Hunter will make it easier for you. Once I'm out of the picture he'll be looking elsewhere, I guarantee it."

Gracie gave her a long hard stare. "You care about him don't you?"

"I care. He and I will always remain friends, but my heart is with Nick. I'm going to check on Nicki before I go. Take care and I'll fly home next weekend."

"Kristy…thank you for caring."

Kristy smiled. She was going to enjoy watching Gracie come out of her shell.

Hunter and Sarah met Kristy at the John Wayne Airport.

"How's Nicki?" Hunter asked as he kissed her cheek.

"She and Gracie are getting better. They're looking forward to us flying home in a couple of weeks."

"I miss that kid," he mused.

"Did the two of you go to Catalina?"

Sarah beamed. "Yes, we did, it was beautiful over there. I had no idea it was cow country. Did you see Brian when you were home?"

"No, only Nick. I stayed with him and Nicki."

Hunter opened the door and took her suitcase into the bedroom for her. When he came back into the living room he folded his arms across his chest and stared at her.

"What have you done, Kristy?"

"Anyone want a glass of wine?"

"I'll get it," Sarah said and left the room.

"I've agreed to move back in with Nick. I want to buy a house so Nicki can settle down and not be uprooted so much of the time. We can live with Nick while I look for a place."

Hunter nodded. "That's understandable. Did he say he loved you?"

"No."

He shrugged. "Then you must know what you're getting into. I won't stand in the way. You going to keep working?"

Sarah came in and handed them each a glass of Merlot. Kristy said, "Yes. Why?"

"With me?"

"Yes."

He grinned. "Good." She was going to need him to lean on.

"To our last few weeks in Newport," Hunter said and raised his glass.

Kristy and Sarah raised theirs. Kristy reminded him, "We'll be back."

"We'll see. Think Nick will let you come back?"

Kristy hadn't thought that far ahead. What was she giving up for her daughter? "I…hope so. I'll still have to deal with some clients out here. I still have my own life to live, I'll just be living it at Nick's for now." She hadn't realized how she actually felt until she'd said the words and she'd noticed a hint of resentment there.

Hunter took a sip of wine. "How about you Sarah, you going to end up married living on a ranch somewhere pregnant and isolated?"

Sarah looked thunderstruck and paled. She collapsed into the closest chair. "My God, I never thought of that either. Nursing sick kids and animals…Oh Kristy…just when I thought I knew what I wanted."

"Yeah…me too." Kristy walked to the kitchen and grabbed the near full bottle of wine and poured herself and Sarah another glass. Without Nick's love what was she letting herself in for? Her knees felt weak and she found herself on the couch. "Hunter just painted a picture of…what?"

Hunter smiled. He'd given both of them something to think about. Hell, Kristy may have grown up on a ranch, but she didn't belong there anymore, except for an occasional visit now and then. Sure, she'd probably be fool enough to have a couple more kids only because the cowboy wanted his name to go on forever. He'd watched her bloom and grow over the past seven years. When she walked back into his life in Dallas he could see what she'd become. She was no longer some ranch foreman's daughter and she knew it. She loved city life where she could come alive after a hard day at work. She was highly respected among their clients and because of her gorgeous looks and outgoing attitude she brought in more clients than anyone else in the firm. Word of mouth did wonders in this business and she lived up to everything anyone said about her. Their male clients wanted her seen on their arms, just like he showed off the female clients. Matt knew what he was doing when he hired both of them. He wondered if Kristy even knew? And what would Nick be offering her? Had he even bothered to tell her he actually loved her? No, the man was a blind jerk. He wanted his daughter and that was probably all, if her mother came with the package even better. He'd never offer marriage, and it was time Kristy faced that fact. He liked the fact she'd be living in her own house, it would mean he could visit.

"We have a couple of weeks left." Hunter casually mentioned and watched the expression on their faces darkened. He raised the wine glass to his lips and sipped the fruity brew. Yes, he'd given her something to think about all right...to his advantage.

Kristy could hardly breathe. "I..." She looked at Sarah who seemed to be stressing too.

Tears welled in Sarah's eyes. "Kristy...have we made our beds and now have to lie in them? Oh God, I don't think I ever want to see the inside of a veterinary clinic again. The smell alone is enough to make me want to run in another direction."

"Then look for another job. I could use a new secretary in Dallas." She suddenly perked up. "That's it Sarah, come be my secretary."

"You're kidding."

"No, I'm not, ask Hunter."

Hunter grinned and raised an eyebrow. "She does need a new one, the last one is getting married."

"Oh great," Sarah moaned, "everyone but me has someone."

Kristy looked at Sarah and said, "You have Brian. I...don't have anyone."

Hunter finished his wine. "That's good because we have more clients than we know what to do with in Dallas, you're not going to have any time off for months to come." He could see Kristy's shoulders relax with the news. "Those Nashville types heard you're in Dallas and are bombarding Matt to let them at you. That means you'll have to be their escort and show them a good time in Dallas. You can't let Matt and the agency down."

Kristy looked up at Hunter. She almost felt grateful to him. "Hunter...take us out to dinner and make us feel better."

"A woman after my own heart. Get your things and let's go."

Dinner was more somber than it should have been and by the time they returned home both women were miserable. Hunter said his good night and left them. Sometime after one Kristy still couldn't sleep and walked into the living room to find Sarah sitting there.

"Couldn't sleep either?" Sarah asked. "Kristy, what the hell are we going to do?" "Oh hell I don't know. I've made my commitment to living with Nick and I suppose I have to honor it for Nicki's sake. He makes me so mad."

"Who Nick? Or Hunter?"

"Nick. He seems so...how do I put it?"

"Like he's stuck in the mud?" Sarah added. "Like his life is on automatic and nothing seems to matter except what he wants?"

"Sort of. He's reached every goal he ever set for himself...except to make the ranch self-supporting. He doesn't know that I've earned enough money just these past few months to more than cover his expenses out there. He'd never consider taking money from me to help out. No...he's such a damn bullheaded cowboy. It would mean he wouldn't have to work so hard and could devout more time to the ranch."

"What's with their egos? Brian's is just as bad. If he's not fixing up some downtrodden beast he's flirting with the cowgirls."

"He and Nick have probably screwed every good-looking cowgirl in Dallas and the surrounding counties. They'll be running on empty before we get them. Then I look at Hunter and he has it all going for him. He too has reached all his goals, except for me. He has money and power and prestige, yet he's willing to settle down and offer me a life I can only dream about. He's loved Nicki since the day she was born. He's been a stand in dad that Nicki has come to love and knows she can count on. Am I crazy for loving Nick?"

"Honey, our hearts lead our heads sometimes and I for one can't explain it."

Kristy paced about the room. "I'm having so many doubts about myself right now. I know I'm doing all this to give Nicki a real family life. That's important...don't you think?"

Sarah sat there looking blank. "I suppose. Let me ask you this one thing, when you were out here...before going back to the ranch and running into Nick, were you really happy? Were you this confused and miserable?"

Kristy had to think about that question hard and long. "I was happy. But no, no I wasn't confused, because I felt safe with my secret. I didn't have to please anyone but my daughter and myself. I didn't have to answer to Nick or my parents. I knew I loved Nick, but…that's just it, things have changed and I'm not sure I've handled them the best way I could have."

"What do you think will happen with Nick? What are your dreams?"

Kristy tried to laugh but couldn't. "I suppose we'll move into a new house and I'll…"

"Yeah, I know," Sarah interrupted, "come home after a day of working, cook dinner and say goodbye to Nick as he rushes out the door to some emergency. You'll bring work home then go to bed and try to wait up for him but you'll fall asleep. It'll all start over again the next morning until you're ready to scream."

"My, you paint a pretty ugly picture. Is that what it's like being with Brian? I'm not giving up my job so I'll at least have my own life."

Sarah nodded. "Yeah. Maybe if you start showin' horses again at least you'll have something to look forward to on weekends…when you're not back to muckin' stalls and tending horses. Then you'll smell like a stable when you go back to your clients on Mondays."

"I'm not sure I want to do that either. Those rich bitches back home are truly worse than the ones out here. I don't think I ever made one friend at those blasted shows either here or Dallas. I did win blue ribbons though, so that put them in their places."

"Oh hell, Kristy, it was your looks that turned them off. I know the types, see 'em all the time. Real snobs and for no good reason except their husbands give them everything they want because they have a mistress on the side. Not only do the men have their mistresses but the women have their…toy boys, whatever they call them in Dallas these days."

"What's our alternative?" Kristy asked. "We stay the merry single broads until we're old and gray and no one will want us…or we just try to have a happy family life. I do love Nick with all my heart."

Sarah nodded her understanding. "Yeah, but has he ever sent you flowers? Or asked you to have a nice dinner with him? Has he ever taken you to a movie where you could hold hands? No, and neither has Brian. They take us for granted. Shit, we're lucky to get a night out at the Lone Star and then we have to put up with those goddamn beepers on their belts." She grinned. "At least Brian's vibrates."

"To Nick and Brian those things are a waste of time. That just shows you they don't know a damn thing about women."

"So what do you think we should do?" Sarah now sat upright and ready to hear some good news for a change.

"Go back to Dallas and make the best of it, I guess. Sarah, I'm going to try to get some sleep. I have two clients to meet with tomorrow."

"Good night." It wasn't what Sarah wanted to hear. What were they going to do?

CHAPTER SEVENTEEN

Hunter knocked on Kristy's bedroom door at six the next morning. She rolled over and opened one eye. "What are you doing here?"

He stretched out on top of the covers and rested his head against his hand. "I wanted to know how you were this morning."

Her eyes focused on the bedside clock. "At six in the morning? Hunter, you're a crazy person."

"Yeah, but you love me for it."

"I love Nick."

"And where is Nick?"

"Hunter, I don't want to get into this so early. I have a one o'clock client. I set it up that way so I could sleep in, now what do you want?"

"You."

"Hunter, go away."

"If that's the way you want it." He rolled off the bed.

"No! Wait," she said, she wanted to talk to him about Gracie.

He jumped back into position and leaned over her grinning from ear to ear. "You're finally agreeing?" he teased and put his hand under the sheet.

She turned over to face him. "No, I'm not. I want to ask you how you feel about Gracie." She watched his face soften at her name.

"Why do you ask?"

She scooted to a sitting position and plumped a pillow behind her back. Hunter reached over and cupped a breast. "Stop it, Hunter." She moved his hand away.

"So why do you want to know how I feel about Gracie? You said yourself it was just a matter of time before I took her to bed."

"I think she actually cares about you. She thinks you're a tease and called you a devil in disguise. I think that pretty well sums it up."

His long finger made a path up her arm to her chin. "You know, it's strange, but I've looked at Gracie in a different light from the others. She's kind of fragile."

"Do you think you could ever care for someone that fragile?"

"I don't know. I guess I could find out."

"Hunter, don't just go after her for all the wrong reasons. You and I will always be close. Nicki loves you, I love you in my own way, but what you need is someone who loves you as unconditionally as you love me. I think Gracie can give you that if you'll give her a chance."

He gazed into those blue-green eyes of hers and found he was losing his heart to her all over again. "What is it about that cowboy that makes you love him so much?"

Kristy leaned her head against the headboard and looked up at the ceiling. "I remember the first time he got inside my heart. He was shoeing a horse and I was about nine." She laughed and allowed Hunter to rest his head against her shoulder. "All I could see was his tight rear sticking up and those muscles rippling on his bare shoulders."

"At nine?"

"Well, there was nothing sexual about it at that age. But I thought he was the best looking man I'd ever seen. I think he was twenty-one at the time. Just back from his second or third year of college. He'd changed so much since leaving the ranch."

"And then what?"

Kristy took a deep breath and sighed. Did she even want to think back to that time of her life? "He kept leaving the ranch and coming back to work it during summers. And every time he came back as I grew up I would hide in the hayloft of the barn where I could lay on my stomach and watch him work the animals in the corrals. He got older and so did I. I knew…my heart was with that man from day one."

"Tell me about the first time."

"No, Hunter."

He reached up and brushed the strands of hair from her neck. "Yes, Kristy."

"I look back and realize how hard ranch work is and I wonder why I had the guts to ever leave. It meant my parents had to work harder after I left.

"Go back, Kristy, and tell me about the first time."

She closed her eyes and relived it over in her mind. "I'd been cleaning the stalls. I must have smelled like horse manure and fresh straw…all I know now is that I didn't smell the way I do today."

Hunter inhaled her scent and had to agree with her version. He loved her wearing the perfume he'd introduced her to. "Go on."

"Nick was getting married the next week. But for some reason he showed up at the ranch. He looked mad and miserable and I couldn't figure out why. He wouldn't talk to anyone at the dinner table and would ride off alone to be by himself. I rarely saw him. That's why I was so surprised when he showed up in the barn that day. He started to help me clean the stalls. He'd taken his shirt off so he wouldn't get it dirty I suppose. When I went up into the loft to throw more straw bales down I turned around and there he stood. I…" It hurt to think back.

"Go on."

"Hunter, I can't."

"Sure you can."

"Why are you doing this to me?"

Hunter grinned and kissed her bare arm. "So I'll understand. I know what we had, but I need to know what stopped you from fully giving yourself to me. All those times we came so close to it, but you always pulled back. I want to know what kind of love for one person does that."

"When I turned around he stood there ready to take the bale from me. Somehow our eyes locked and the next thing I remember is lying in a pile of straw. I was almost twenty and I don't think I'd even been kissed yet." She turned to Hunter. "That's what it's like growing up in isolation. Twenty and never been kissed."

He chuckled. "Boy, did he see you coming."

"I don't think so. When his lips pressed against mine I was so scared and so happy at the same time. I had this cowboy in my arms that I'd loved for so many years. Yet at the same time I knew he was marrying Mallory the next week. I suppose in the back of my mind I knew it was a one shot deal...so to speak. I wanted to know him, his body, his lips, his hands. I was taken completely by surprise when we made love. It was the most incredible thing I'd ever experienced. I had no idea what a man felt like. When flesh met flesh...it was beyond belief. I think we stayed up there most of the afternoon and late evening. He made love to me over and over and I couldn't believe it. I wanted to...learn it all. I didn't even help mama with dinner that night. I didn't want to let him out of my arms because I knew when I did he'd be gone forever and back into Mallory's arms."

Hunter's arm lay across her stomach. "And?"

"And I was right. The next morning he was gone, I was deflowered as they say, and I went on with my life. I never saw him again after that."

"But surely..."

"No. When I suspected I was pregnant I didn't tell anyone. I answered an ad in a Dallas paper that led to a job in California. By the time I packed my bags I was nearly three months along. Once I got to San Francisco and found that tiny apartment that took most of my pay check, a man named Hunter had befriended me."

Hunter put his arms around her and hugged her as she snuggled against him. "You were so refreshing to see and talk too. I thought an angel had walked into my life...and she had this very soft southern accent."

"The first time you touched me my hormones were raging. When your hands and mouth did all those wonderful things to me I wanted to get Nick out of my system but something held me back. I wanted to love you Hunter, I really did."

"I remember. That's when you told me you were pregnant."

"And you didn't tell me you were married."

"I couldn't. You would have walked out of my life for good and I didn't want that."

"Is there something wrong with me?" Kristy asked with sincerity. "Why do I love that man so much it hurts?"

"If you hadn't had Nicole do you think you'd still feel the same way about Nick?"

"I can't even answer that question. I do have Nicki."

"I remember the time when she first started kicking. You'd say she seemed as stubborn as a mule by not letting you sleep at night. I remember staying up rubbing that extended belly of yours to quiet her down. I recall Greg and Jed coming over with their stretch mark lotion and insisting they take care of you. Two effeminate males going through your pregnancy with you. You were loved by a lot of us, you know that don't you?"

She smiled at the memories he described. "I do and I think that's what made my life bearable back then. I didn't have any family and all of you became my extended family and support system. Even after I found out you were married. You were all so different from anyone I'd ever met on the ranch. You scared me but fascinated me at the same time. It was like I'd stepped into a different world, one that I never knew existed."

"You had stepped into a different world. When Laura found out about you she hit the roof. She accused me of all sorts of things. Our marriage had been long over by that time and it was just a matter of monetary settlement. I was rich and she wanted it all."

Kristy looked up into Hunter's eyes. "When did she find out about me?"

"When I went into the delivery room with you. Her father was a doctor and one of the doctor's on staff called him. They thought you were having my baby. I never told them any different even after Nicole was born."

Kristy's mouth dropped open in surprise. "But why?"

"Because I cared about you and didn't about them. They still don't know."

"Oh my God."

"It didn't make any sense to deny it. You and I separated ten months later and I never saw you again until Matt brought us back together. I can't tell you how many times I thought about you and Nicole. I missed the two of you so much when we split. There was a hole in my heart and in my life."

"Our lives have certainly taken some strange turns haven't they?"

He kissed her bare arm. "Yes. Am I going to be invited to the new house?" He felt her stiffen.

She inhaled sharply. "I think it's time to get up."

He held her arm. "You didn't answer me."

"If there is a new house…you'll be invited."

He released her arm. That was all he wanted to hear. "What if I ask you to marry me?"

She stood beside the bed and looked down at him. "Why would you do that when you know my heart is with Nick?"

"Because I'm the one who loves you. We could give Nicki a stable family life. Hell, she'd be a Taylor with all the benefits I have to offer."

"Hunter, I can't."

"Then what's Gracie like?"

"Why don't you find out on your own?"

He grinned and lifted that eyebrow of his. "Okay, I will. There's something I should warn you about back in Dallas."

Kristy frowned hoping it wasn't bad news. "What's that?"

"Those Brit rockers living in Nashville have a thing for southern women with soft accents and long legs. Why the hell do you think they're asking Matt for you?"

She frowned. "What are you talking about?"

"You know the guy I'm talking about. Claims he wants to be country. Christ! The man has a cockney accent, how the hell does he expect to become country overnight. He told Matt he would only sign with the agency if you were his rep. I'm telling you this to warn you about him. He's got this reputation for getting what he wants and I think he's set his sights on you."

"Then I'd better get ready to fend them off." She recalled Robert's hands all over her trying to undo her blouse, her slacks and how Hunter always jumped in to save her. Oh God, why did she have to keep fending them off? All she wanted was Nick and she couldn't even get his damn attention.

"You'll get a wedding ring on that finger if you'll let me put it on you. Otherwise be prepared to fight the Brit off you." Hunter laughed and climbed under the covers inhaling the perfumed scent she'd left behind. "Mind if I catch some shut eye? Got up too early this morning."

Kristy picked up a small cushion from the chair and tossed it at him before she hit the shower. When she came out Hunter was fast asleep.

By the time Hunter woke up it was after one o'clock. He stretched and pulled Kristy's pillow closer to his nose where he inhaled her scent. God, he wanted her and he was as hard as a rock.

"Kristy, are you still asleep?" Sarah opened the door and gasped. "Hunter!"

He smiled, spread his arms and pushed the covers aside. "She's gone. Come here."

Sarah was stunned, shocked and yet she staggered into Kristy's bed and allowed Hunter to make love to her once again.

It rained in Dallas. No it poured. Nick was impatient as hell that morning and didn't know why. Was it because he knew Kristy, Sarah and that goddamn Hunter would all be flying home later today? Nicki had chattered her way through breakfast about the house he was considering buying and she sounded so much like him he had to tune her out. Something he didn't like doing. Even Gracie, who was normally the rock Nicki clung too, was nervous and edgy. Could it have something to do with the weather? He wondered.

He walked through the back door of his clinic where Joanie handed him a strong cup of coffee. Cheryl put two charts in his hand. "Mrs. Quinn's in number one," Cheryl said.

Joanie said, "She's got two cats."

While sipping the coffee Nick heard, "Terry leave Alex alone. He'll get down by himself."

Assuming Terry and Alex were cats he finished off the coffee and handed the cup back to Joanie. Then, without looking at the charts assumed Terry was the male cat and Alex was the female cat. He was dead wrong. When he opened the door he noticed two cats restrained in pet carriers. Alex and Terry ran loose. Oh shit, he thought, more kids, that's all he needed to start his day.

Terry was about six-years old and the cutest little girl he'd seen outside of Nicki of course. But she was a talker. "I'm gonna be a nurse!" was the first thing she said as she tugged on his white lab coat.

"You are?" Nick said and lifted a three-year old Alex off the exam table.

"Yeah," she tugged again, "I'm gonna be an animal nurse." The pitch of her voice almost shattered the glass medicine bottles displayed on the shelves.

Nick's head was beginning to throb. He wiped the cookie crumbs away from the examination table. "What's wrong with your cats?" he asked Mrs. Quinn.

"Boris," she said as she grabbed Alex by the arm, "is the yellow cat and has been spitting up hairballs for the past few days. Missy, the gray cat, needs her annual shots."

"Yeah," Terry screeched, "Boris barfs a lot. Don't he, Alex?"

Alex was missing. Nick noticed Alex playing 52-card pickup with the Feline Leukemia brochures on the floor and didn't know whether to treat the cats or tranquilize the kids. How did mothers do it?

"Are you a real doctor?" Terry asked. "Do you have any Cokes? Can I listen to my heart? What's that thing?"

Nick retrieved his stethoscope and wrapped it around his neck. "I'm an animal doctor," he said patiently.

Alex jumped from the floor onto the exam room chair then off again as if he was superman. "Look at me..." he yelled and went flying through the air. Right before he crashed. Mrs. Quinn scooped him up off the floor unharmed only to let him bang on the animal crate claiming he was now a drummer.

Nick took a deep breath and walked to where he kept the vaccines. He had no idea Terry had followed him until she opened her mouth and the questions seemed endless. By now his own daughter seemed a saint in his eyes. Nicki was not only polite and well mannered, but only asked questions when she didn't understand something. Terry didn't shut up until she saw Nick pick up a needle. He grinned and she winced.

Nick pulled Missy out of the cat carrier and gave her the shot but when he went to put her back into the case he had to pull Alex out. Missy hissed, Terry clung to his lab coat and he was trying to pull Alex out of the box. Once he got Alex under control he slipped the cat back into her cage. By now Alex was poking his fingers through Boris' crate and shaking it.

"Kitty, kitty," Alex yelled.

Poor Boris was trying to become invisible at the back of the crate. When Mrs. Quinn yelled at Alex to keep his hands off the crate her voice set off the dogs in the kennel, and in turn, scared the hell out of Boris, the cat.

When Boris hissed at Nick who was trying to coax him out of the cage Mrs. Quinn said, "Boris has always had an attitude problem.

Boris, I'll whip your butt if you hiss like that again."

Nick was convinced Mrs. Quinn was more embarrassed by her cat than the antics of her unruly kids. About that time Alex decided to play Superman again and the repeated crash of metal exam chair against concrete floor unnerved both Nick and Boris.

"I thought I told you to sit still!" Mrs. Quinn yelled. "And pick that sticky sucker up off the floor. Terry was doing her damnest to get Nick's and her mother's attention and started yelling.

Nick tried to dump Boris out of the crate about the same time Alex wrapped his sticky sucker holding hand around Nick's shin. Boris refused to slide out of the crate. Nick could certainly understand why. When he looked inside the fiberglass carrier all he could see was Boris clinging with suction cup paws to the roof of the thing. Nick shook the box, then shook it again. Nothing happened except Alex then grabbed Nick's other leg and almost knocked him off his feet. Nick was getting more and more frustrated. Finally Boris lost his battle with retreat and hold and fell out of the crate onto the exam table feet down. Nick quickly covered the cat with a towel. Alex started to wail. Terry started to cry.

When Nick felt Alex let go of his leg he saw him disappearing out the door with about forty of the Feline Leukemia brochures crammed in his back pockets and barking like a dog. Nick quickly took Boris' vitals and gave Mrs. Quinn some hairball medicine. Nick walked Mrs. Quinn, her cats, and Terry out into the reception room to turn them over to Cheryl. That's when he noticed Alex had climbed up on the pet food display and had another lollipop in his mouth. He could hardly wait until he saw their tail lights leave the parking lot.

"Need more coffee, Doc?" Cheryl smiled and handed him a mug.

Nick slid his hand into his pocket only to discover a well-licked lollipop had stuck to his palm. God help him, he thought, why would anyone want kids! Then he thought of Nicki and smiled. That's why, because they would be his. His mood lifted. On to door number two.

Joanie smiled and said, "It's Ms. Hamilton." There was a hint of devil in that smile Nick thought.

"Is she here to show off her latest tattoo or her latest animal?"

"Well, you're close. She seems to have acquired an over weight guinea pig she calls Shelly."

Nick knew that he was in for in more surprises than one. Jessica

Hamilton was an attractive, well-endowed, young woman who worked at the local bar and kept her horse at a stable near the clinic. She also sported tattoos is some very strategic places on her body and always offered to show him her latest. He'd treated her horse and her various other animals at different times so he thought he knew what to expect. Joanie had already gone into the exam room while Nick stood just outside the door looking at Shelly's chart.

"Doc's gonna flip when he looks at my latest tattoo," Jessica said.

"Oh I'll just bet he will," Joanie replied.

Jessica asked, "Can I put Shelly down?"

"Sure," Joanie said.

Nick could imagine Jessica showing her latest tattoo to Joanie. He waited to hear Joanie's response. He didn't hear a peep. He opened the door and walked inside. Thinking the guinea pig was still in the pillowcase he untied the knot, which would have freed the thing. Instead, nothing emerged. The pillowcase was perfectly still, yet it bulged so he knew the guinea pig had to be in it. He opened the case thinking Shelly was at the bottom but what he saw, and retrieved, was Jessica's lacy underwear. Nick retrieved each neatly folded bra and underpants one at a time. Joanie stood there laughing.

Nick looked at the women. "Where's the guinea pig?"

Joanie shrugged. Nick tossed a pair of red silk panties at her. "Here," he teased, "you might need these someday." Joanie headed out the door laughing herself silly.

By now the exam table looked like some goddamn display case of a lingerie shop. He looked at Jessica. "Oh my God!" she screamed and ran out of the room.

Nick picked up a hot pink bikini thong and wondered why anyone would want to wear that? Wearing nothing wouldn't be as uncomfortable. He started cramming the items back into the pillowcase.

Jessica was beet red by the time she came back into the room with an identical pillowcase, only this one moved.

As Nick untied the knot he teased, "I hope there's a creature in here, there's just not enough of this silk material here to save."

While Nick checked Shelly out he could hear Cheryl, who had joined them, Joanie and Jessica discussing her tattoos. "Hell, Doc's seen everything else I own."

Nick looked up to see Jessica pull the waist band of her shorts down to her bikini line. "What do ya think of this, Doc?"

Cheryl's eyes were glued to the tattoo of a Texas flag that had Don't Mess With Texas stenciled across it. Joanie just shook her head as she watched Nick's eyes. He tried to move his gaze from Jessica's taut stomach back to the guinea pig.

Nick said, to Shelly, "Kinda makes you want to get down on your knees and salute the flag."

Cheryl gasped. Jessica smiled as her eyes met Nick's and pulled the shorts back up.

Joanie grabbed the chart and headed out the door. "Maybe Kristy ought to paint a surfer named Hunter on her breasts and make 'em dance across the waves."

That remark certainly took the fun out of Nick's day. Jessica watched Nick put Shelly back into the pillowcase. He was glad a simple case of ear mites was in exam room three.

But before Jessica left the room she said, "I'm always ready for you, Nick."

Nick could hear Joanie's reaction to that remark and he just smiled at Jessica.

CHAPTER EIGHTEEN

Nick held Nicki's hand as they waited for Kristy to get off the plane. What he didn't like seeing was the way Hunter held her arm as they moved along the concourse.

"Mama!" Nicki yelled.

Kristy opened her arms and Nicki went flying into them. "Oh baby, I've missed you!"

"Me too, Mama. Hug daddy too?"

Kristy smiled broadly and rushed into Nick's arms. "I've missed you," she whispered in his ear.

Nick's eyes closed as he held her tight and kissed her with the passion of a long starved man. "I'm glad you're back," he said.

Disappointed, Kristy expected him to say as much. "I'm glad to be back too."

Sarah patted Nick on the back. "What'd you do with Brian?" She almost dreaded the answer.

"Sarah!" Brian was making his way to her with a huge bouquet of yellow roses in his hand.

Sarah's eyes grew large with surprise and she gave Kristy a quick glance. What had Kristy said...or done the last time she'd been home. This wasn't like Brian at all. She was near tears when Brian opened his arms and she ran into them.

"Oh God, how I've missed you!" Brian said and all but swept

Sarah off her feet.

Hunter put his hand in the middle of Kristy's back to get her attention and said, "I'll catch you at the office. Have a good day."

"Hunter!" Nicki yelled.

Hunter turned around to see Nicki fly into his arms and hug him before he put her back down. "Where's Gracie?" Hunter asked.

"Oh she's home waiting for us. Hunter. I miss you."

Hunter ran his hand over the top of her blonde head. "I miss you too. Hey, do you think I could take Gracie out to dinner sometime?"

Nicki's hand went to her hip and the other to her chin. "I think Gracie would like that. Give her a call."

"Thanks, Nicki,, I think I'll do just that." He gave a wave and was off.

Nick couldn't let go of Kristy. He never wanted to let go of her again. With his arm still wrapped around her waist he said, "Nicki and I have a surprise for you."

Kristy smiled and put her lips to his cheek. "And what would that be?"

"Want to tell her, Nicki?"

Nicki was beaming from ear to ear. "We found a house, Mama. But daddy said we can't buy it until you see it too. Mama, I like the house. Gracie likes the house too and she can have a little house all to herself."

Kristy looked at Nick, confused. "A little house?"

"What she's trying to say is that it has a guest house that would be ideal for Gracie."

"Well, when can we see it?"

"How about now? Let's get your luggage."

The small ranch wasn't far from Dallas and Nicki loved showing Kristy around the place. The house was more than Kristy could have hoped for and there would be plenty of room to entertain her clients. She wondered how she was going to tell Nick about that? How would Nick feel about overly obsessed rock stars, country western singers, actors, product people and sports stars showing up at the place expecting to be royally entertained by Matt, Hunter and herself? She really had to think about this one. She made a mental note to call Matt when they got home, they would have to entertain elsewhere, but where?

"Well, Mama? Do you like it?"

Kristy smiled at her charming daughter. "I love it. I'm not sure I can afford to pay this much money for a place."

Nick gave her a funny glance. "Why would you pay for it?"

"Because it was my idea. You don't need to spend your money on us...you've got the ranch to think of."

Nick jammed his hands in his rear pockets. He turned and walked outside.

Kristy followed. "I wasn't trying to insult you Nick. I also wasn't trying to get you to buy us a house. I just don't want to live in Mallory's house."

He stood looking out over pastureland and envisioning a few head of horses out there. "Where would you get this kind of money?" he asked.

Kristy swallowed hard and went to stand before him. "I don't think I ever wanted you to know this, but I've made more money this year because of the client's I've brought in than I need. I've made so much Nicki's college fund is full for the first time since she's been born. Matt's agency has taken off and it's mostly because of my clients. They seem to like me and tell others that become clients."

"Are you sure it's not Hunter funding things?"

Kristy's mouth dropped open in surprise. "Why would you even think such a thing? Hunter's rich on his own, but I can tell you he doesn't make as much money as I do with the agency. His client's are all beautiful young up and coming females. While mine are established...people."

"People? Like that doctor you flew to the ranch?"

"You mean Ricardo Ventana?"

"Yeah, him."

"Nick...Ricardo's grandfather owns that ball team, Ricardo is the team physician. I do have a few younger clients, but mostly not." She certainly wasn't going to tell him about the horny out of control musicians she handled.

Nick shook his head. "No, you're not paying for this place, I'm going to do it. I'll stay at my old house."

"All right. I'm not going to argue with you, we have a daughter that needs a place like this to settle down on. If money is a touchy subject with you so be it, I won't mention it again. Just remember...what's mine is yours, including Nicki." She turned and walked toward the barn where Nicki was playing.

He wanted to kick himself in the ass for being such a male chauvinist. But hell, that was the way he'd been brought up. He intended to be the provider, not Kristy. He could fully understand how she'd always provided for herself and Nicki, but she didn't have to do that now, they were his responsibility.

Kristy walked inside the barn with Nicki. "Wow, this is pretty nice, don't you think?"

"Yes, Mama, I do. Are you and daddy fighting again?"

"No. We're having a difference of opinion."

"Oh okay."

Kristy looked up at the small empty hayloft above. A smile crossed her face.

"What are you smiling at?" Nick came to stand behind her, then followed her gaze upward. "I see," he grinned.

Nicki raced back outside to check out the small pond when a duck drifted across it.

"Nick...we can't always make love in a hayloft," she teased.

"Why not?" His arms went around her waist to pull her back against him.

"Well...I was hoping someday..."

"Could put a bed up there."

She turned around and laced her arms around his neck. "I don't think so."

He pulled the hair away from her neck and placed warm butterfly kisses along the nape. "When do you want to move in?" He thought he felt her tense.

"Whenever my schedule is cleared enough. I may have to wait just a little while longer."

"Guess we've waited this long a while longer won't matter."

Kristy put her lips to his. Then said, "I have no doubt we'll figure this out. That precious little girl out there wants us to be a family and she wants...a horse."

"I thought she wanted a brother?"

"It's easier to give her a horse."

He gave her that knowing kind of grin. "Oh I don't know about that, seems we did it right the last time around."

Kristy walked away from him, but said, "Sheer luck!" as she looked back over her shoulder.

"I'll give the realtor a call, tell them you're taking the place. Right now I need to get back to the clinic. I'll drive you gals home...first. Where's home, my house or your apartment?"

"Where do you think?"

He winked, "My place."

"No, it's still the apartment." She had a lot of thinking to do.

Gracie came to stay with Nicki while Kristy went to the office.

"Matt," she said, "Nick is buying a small ranch just outside Dallas and I'm guessing that's going to be my permanent home. He'll keep his own house."

"I'm glad your back and planning on putting down roots. So what's the problem?"

"I thought about entertaining the clients out there but knowing my clients I think it's best if I entertain somewhere else. I have an idea but I want to talk to Mavis about it first."

Matt's eyebrow rose. "Oh?"

"I think it should be on neutral ground, don't you?"

Matt laughed that charming laugh of his. "Meaning the good vet wouldn't understand a Brit or anyone of those musical types trying to get you out of your clothes."

"Neutral ground. I had Hunter fending them off in California, but here in Dallas..."

He nodded his understanding. "And Mavis just might want to give some of the new talent a try to get them started?"

"If we remodel the club. What do you think?"

"You're a genius. How much more country western could you get than the Lone Star Saloon?"

"Would you be interested in investing in some of the remodel? I'm going to offer to do some of it myself. After all she is my biological mother and I feel I owe her something. This idea could bring in a lot of money for her...and us."

"Sure I would. I wonder if Hunter will go along with it too."

Kristy closed her eyes dreading his answer. "Do you want me to ask him or will you?"

"Oh hell, you do it. I'm off to Rome tonight. Would you believe we've picked up six Italian companies who find Dallas irresistible. Japan's coming on strong too. Send them cowboy hats to make it official and they sign on the dotted line. God, I love this city!"

"Matt, to change the subject...how would you feel about Hunter and Gracie getting together?"

Matt's smile faded. "You tell me how'd I feel."

"Happy?"

"Not if he's aching for you and screwing everyone else. Shit, he had your fingers in his goddamn mouth as if he was remembering."

"I admit Hunter has been a playboy in the past, but I think he's willing to settle down when he meets the right woman. As for me...I'll still be seeing Nick."

Matt stood and looked out the window. "Seeing Nick? Although I have to wonder..."

"Wonder what?"

"How the clients will react when they find out you're still single."

"They all know I'm not available to them. I've made that very clear."

He nodded. "Yes, of course, you're right."

Kristy stood to leave. "Have a good trip to Rome. By the way...are any of those Italian men going to be my clients?"

Matt grinned. "What do you think?"

"Oh God! Nick won't like it when the Italian invasion gets here."

"Then get married or get pregnant, do one or the other."

"Thanks Matt...you've been so much help," she was kidding. "I'll talk to Mavis and get her feel on things and I'll see you when you get back." She started to walk out of his office but hesitated. "Matt, you're going to hear about this from Hunter so I might as well tell you myself. He's asked me to marry him."

"And you expect my sister to make him happy? That man has to work you out of his system before he'll accept any other woman."

Kristy walked into her office and sat down at her desk.

"You busy?"

She looked up to see Hunter standing there. "I thought you went home."

"And I thought you went home," he responded.

"Good God, just look at us, we're workaholic's just like we were San Francisco."

"I understand you went to look at a ranch with Nick and Nicki."

"Yeah, I did. When I offered to buy it Nick jumped down my throat."

"And?"

"I told him to buy it. I can't win with him. I don't think he understands I've been taking care of Nicki and myself for seven years now and I feel guilty letting anyone take care of us."

"Don't feel guilty, it's his choice. I assume he'll be moving in?"

"Sit down, I want to talk to you about something I just spoke to Matt about."

Hunter pulled a chair closer to her desk.

She toyed with a pen on her desk. "I wouldn't feel comfortable entertaining at home. How would you like to invest in expanding and updating the Lone Star Saloon?"

His eyebrows came together. "Mavis owns the place doesn't she?"

Kristy nodded. "Look at all that talent we're being bombarded with, most of them don't have that hit record yet, but want the exposure we can give them. What better way than to set them up performing in a well-known improved place to show. their talent. Matt's willing to invest, so am I."

Hunter started to laugh and leaned forward toward Kristy. "It's the Japanese isn't it? Matt told you about them coming here."

"Not really. But yes, they will want to be entertained. I'm more worried about the Italian's."

Surprised at the news, Hunter now leaned back in the chair. "What Italian's?"

"Matt's flying to Rome tonight, he says he's got six companies signing up with us."

"Oh good Lord no wonder you need a place to take them."

"Not me...us. I have no intention of doing this alone and you know it. Maybe the Italian's will be beautiful women instead of men."

Hunter smiled and lifted an eyebrow. "That would be nice."

She tossed a paperclip at him. "I can't believe how big this agency has gotten this past year. I've never seen anything like it. Do you think Matt will hire more of us misfits? I think we're going to need help."

Hunter gave her a long hard stare. "We could start our own agency with you at the helm."

Kristy's mouth dropped open. "Why are you bringing that up?"

"It would give you some breathing space."

"No...not right now, we owe Matt."

"Okay, but in a few years we'll do it." Hunter looked at the clock on the wall. "Shouldn't you be getting home it's almost six o'clock."

"Oh crap! I'm going to have to watch this type of work habit." She shut down the computer.

"Gracie watching Nicki?"

"Yes. And why don't you call her tomorrow and ask her out to dinner. Or do you want me to invite you to dinner?"

"I think I'll call."

"Good idea. Good night."

Kristy was out the door and headed home but stopped at the Lone Star on the way. Nick's truck was parked there. So was Jez's.

Kristy walked up to the bar and sat down. She didn't see Nick or Jez.

"Hi baby, what can I get you?" Mavis asked.

"I want to talk about a business proposition with you."

"Business?"

Kristy closed her eyes and leaned forward putting her face in her hands. "Where are they, Mavis?"

"Honey, let's go to my office and talk some."

Kristy followed Mavis into a small office and sat down.

"So what do you want to talk about?" Mavis asked even though she knew she'd have to explain later.

Kristy took a deep breath. "I...I guess there's no way to say this except to say it. Matt, Hunter and I want to invest in you and this place. We want to remodel and add to it. We want to expand the office and hire a staff of people for you to run the place."

Mavis threw the bar towel on the desk and leaned back in her rickety old chair. "Why?"

"To tell you the truth it's because I'm being selfish. I have a lot of well known and up and coming clients in the music business. We want a place here in Dallas where we can showcase them. We now have clients coming in from all over the world that need to be entertained while they're in town, so we thought if we combined the two…we'd all get rich and you'd be doing me a huge, huge favor."

Mavis lost the ability to talk.

Kristy quickly added, "You'd still be running the show, it's your place."

"Could we upgrade to a kitchen and restaurant as well as a bar and dancing?"

Kristy smiled broadly. "Yes, anything you want. You mean…you're agreeing?"

Mavis leaned over and took Kristy's hands in hers. "You're my daughter and I would do anything for you. But…I don't want to lose my current customers, they kind of depend on me ya know."

"Maybe we should build a new club and restaurant next door and keep this one as it is. It's dark and private and…"

"They're in the other room drinkin'."

"Thanks, Mavis. I'll contact an architect and a designer and let you talk to them. Frankly, I don't care what it costs I'm going to be one of the major investors. You plan it the way you want."

Mavis stood up and came around the desk to pull Kristy into her arms where she hugged her tight against her. "You're the most beautiful thing I've ever created. Thank you for believing in me."

Kristy hugged her back. "You're my mother. Nicki's grandmother."

"Now go out there and get your man."

Kristy walked into the dim area of the bar and sat down where she knew she wouldn't be seen by either Nick or Jez. She'd already made up her mind…no matter what she witnessed she wouldn't allow herself to get upset. But, she told herself she had to see what Nick was like on his own when she wasn't around. She had no claim on him now, or ever.

Nick was sipping beer. Jez had her arm around his neck with her hand running up and down his thigh. Even in the dark she knew what Jez's hand was doing under the table. When a second cowgirl sat down next to Nick the only thing Kristy could do was smile. They knew a good thing when they had it, she mused. But it was Nick's reaction that took her by surprise. He kissed one, then the other and leaned back in the booth.

"Don't just sit there, dance with me."

Startled, Kristy looked up to see Hunter holding his hand out to her. "How long have you been standing there?"

"Long enough to know what kind of treatment he's getting under there."

She smiled. "Well, let's go out there and give them all a shock."

Hunter held her so close in his arms that they almost became one as he slowly, deliberately moved her around the dance floor. There was no way Nick and his ladies could miss them. Hunter's hands were resting possessively on the cheeks of her butt without so much as a breath of air between their bodies, deeply embedded in her hip jeans pockets. His mouth brushed up and down her neck and her arms were around his neck.

"I just talked to Mavis," he said. "I hear she's going along with us."

Kristy smiled. "She's doing it for me. We've got our work cut out for us."

"You should see what they're doing in that booth now."

"I don't want to see. When this song ends get me the hell out of here."

"I don't think so. Jez has seen us. What's going to happen with Nick now?"

"Nothing. I'll…"

"Mind if I cut in?" Nick growled. "You might want to get your hands out of Kristy's jeans."

"Nick! Stop it," Kristy said.

Hunter gave Kristy a slight bow and walked back to talk to Mavis.

Nick pulled her into his arms. "How long you been here?" He didn't sound too happy to see her.

Kristy forced a smile. "Long enough to know that bulge in your jeans isn't from me."

"You weren't home."

"So? Does that mean you have to come running down here for some attention to detail?"

"Why are you here? Shouldn't you be home fixing Nicki's dinner?"

"I was on my way home. I had a business deal to talk over with Mavis. I was going to tell you about it tonight, but I think now is as good a time as any."

He scowled and tipped the hat back on his head. "What business?"

"I tried to tell you earlier I've become a fairly wealthy woman. You wouldn't agree to let me help buy the house so I'm...we're, Matt, Hunter and I, are going to invest in this club. I have clients I can't possibly bring home to entertain and clients who need their talents showcased. This will solve our problems. We'll become even wealthier."

Nick stopped and stood there staring at her. "Are you telling me you don't need me?"

"No, Nick I'm not telling you that at all. You have a choice. I don't. I can't keep fending off British musicians going after me. You're married to the clinic. So I have to settle on living alone with Nicki in the new house. I sat here watching you with Jez and the other one tonight thinking to myself that I should turn and run as far from you as I could. To just leave you to hell alone, I have no hold over you. But, I did that once and you were still here in my heart. I can run for the rest of my life but you'll still be with me. Nicki needs both of us. "

"Let's get the hell out of here, I've got some explaining to do."

CHAPTER NINETEEN

The move to the new ranch wasn't all that complicated. Nicki loved the ranch and Gracie was more than happy to have her own place out back where she could entertain when the mood hit her, which wasn't very often, but she did like the privacy the small house afforded her.

The club renovations became a giant headache but went on, as did the new club being built next to the Lone Star. Nick was more confused than ever about his relationship with Kristy yet marveled at everything she'd accomplished over the years they'd been separated. What he didn't like was her involvement with the California stud muffin, but he wasn't going to fight it either. He knew he had her love. At least that's what he was thinking. The one thing that he hated was having her live by herself. He missed Kristy's presence in his house and he missed Nicki. What he missed most was the home cooking and honest loving.

At the clinic one afternoon he received an emergency call from Nicki's teacher who asked if he could possibly stop by their classroom after school, that Nicki would be there waiting for him.

Nick wondered if he should call Kristy? No, he decided they'd called him and it was up to him to see what the problem was.

"Afternoon, Mrs. Lukens," Nick said in his best professional manner and noticed Nicki with her head stuck close to a goldfish bowl.

"Thanks for coming, Doctor Chandler." She pointed toward Nicki. "Your daughter recommended your services as a vet. I'll let Nicki explain to you."

"Hi, Daddy. The bird is losing its feathers and our goldfish is sad."

Nick took one look at the not so healthy animals and said, "I think it might be cheaper to just replace these animals with healthy ones rather than pay for medicines."

"No, Daddy…we kids want these animals."

"All right, Nicki, I'll see what I can do." He examined the bird first. After determining it had mites he dusted the bird's feathers.

"What about the goldfish, Daddy?"

Nick was perplexed at that question.

"His name is Nemo, Daddy."

Nick picked up the fish bowl and held it up against a light. "Nemo's swallowed something."

"What?" Mrs. Lukens gasped.

"Yeah, look there's something red in him."

"What is it and can you get it out?" She asked.

Nick tried not to laugh. "Look, with all due respect, the only fish I've ever operated on…ended up in a frying pan."

"Daddy!"

"All right, I'll try something." But what? Nemo wasn't two inches long and a half inch wide. He picked Nemo up by his tail and tried to shake the red thing loose. Nothing happened. He tried to flush the object out but that didn't work either. Then he wondered if it was possible to actually drown a goldfish, so he stopped.

He glanced to Nicki who was watching him intently. In desperation he squeezed Nemo's mid section until his eyes bulged. When Nemo puckered he inserted a forcep down his open throat and grabbed hold of the tiny red object. "There, I got it out." He put Nemo back into the bowl. "He'll be as good as new. Seems someone decided put a piece of crayon in the bowl and Nemo ate it."

Nicki ran up and threw her arms around his neck. "Thank you, Daddy."

Nick picked her up in his arms and looked at the teacher. "You need to change the bird's diet for vitamin deficiencies and put it under a red lamp to prevent him from plucking his feathers around the irritated areas on the skin."

"How much do we owe you?" Mrs. Lukens asked.

Nick looked into his daughter's eyes. "Nothing. I'll call it a donation to modern science. I think I'll take my daughter home now."

"Thanks again. We'll see you in the morning, Nicole."

"Good bye, Mrs. Lukens," Nicki said.

Hugging Nick's neck Nicki pressed a kiss against his cheek. "Thank you for saving Nemo, Daddy."

"You like animals don't you?"

Nicki nodded as Big Red pulled out of the school parking lot.

"Do you know what time your mama's going to be home?" he asked.

Nicki grinned revealing her dimples. "Yeah, she's home right now."

"Then let's head in that direction."

"You mean you don't have to go back to the clinic? You can come home with me?"

Nick suddenly realized he was missing out by not spending more time at Kristy's. Nicki now had her horse in the corral and working with a trainer every day. He hadn't seen her on it once. He missed the hell out of not having Nicki living with him.

"Yeah, I'm coming home for the rest of the day. Let me give Brian a call."

Kristy was baking chocolate chip cookies with big chunks of extra chocolate added when she felt arms go around her waist from behind. "What are you doing here this time of day?" she asked.

Nick grabbed one of the warm cookies. "I performed a crayonectomy on a goldfish in Nicki's classroom." The cookie went into his mouth and he savored it.

Kristy smiled, turned around and put her arms around his neck. "I see. Now your daughter is recommending your services?"

He removed his hat and sent it sailing onto the kitchen table. "What are you doing home? Boy that sounds good…home."

"I'm usually here when Nicki comes home. After I know she's settled in with Gracie I sometimes go back to the office until I have to be home again to fix dinner."

"I didn't know that you would be here, I just assumed you were at work all day."

"I put in my ten hours and then some. I'm trying to give Nicki more of my time. Of course if our paths crossed more often you'd know these things. Are you leaving again? Or would you like a cup of coffee to go with those cookies?"

"I promised Nicki I'd watch her with her filly. Brian's covering. I'll take that coffee...and some more cookies."

Kristy laced her arms around his neck. "She'll like having you watch. She misses you."

"How about you?"

"I miss you. I think we're both to blame for that." She pressed her lips against his. "Think we could find some time for each other after Nicki goes to bed?"

He brushed kisses along her neck. "Do we have to wait that long?"

"Mama!" Nicki came running into the kitchen. "Come look at Gracie."

Kristy grabbed Nicki's arm, "What's wrong with Gracie?"

"Nothing. I put her on Crystal Locket. Come look."

"You left Gracie sitting on your horse?"

"Yes, Mama."

Kristy grabbed Nicki by the hand and raced out to the corral.

"Krrrrrriiiis...what do I do now?" Gracie groaned, holding her breath.

"Oh hell," Nick smirked, "that horse can tell you're scared of it by your butt movements. Relax."

"Whaaaat are you talking about?"

Kristy started to laugh. "Nicki get in there and get her off." She climbed onto the corral fence to watch.

"Ah Gracie, let me walk you around," Nicki urged and took the reins to walk the horse. The two-year old filly had been in training for months. She was still hot blooded, but gentle and broke.

Kristy quickly said, "Think of a surfboard, Gracie, you're sitting astride the board in the water with Hunter behind you, waiting for that next wave to come in. You're not nervous he's behind you just like Nicki's in there for you. Relax in the saddle."

Nick watched Gracie's whole body start to relax. What the hell did Hunter have over these women? He'd certainly seen the difference in

Sarah since she'd been with him. Actually, now that he thought about it, Sarah seemed more understanding of Brian than she had before. Maybe it was guilt? Brian didn't seem to mind.

"Good," Kristy encouraged. "See, it's just like riding the waves."

Gracie was grinning from ear to ear now. "You're right it's not much different than when Hunter had us on the boards."

Nick glared at Kristy. "You surf too?"

"We all surf, Daddy."

Nick put his hand on Kristy's butt and rubbed it. "No wonder you had that bikini line that's disappeared." He didn't like envisioning Hunter lying on a surfboard behind her with her bikini clad butt stuck up in his face.

Nicki held the horse while Gracie all but fell off. She walked to the fence to stare up at her parents. "When will I be getting a baby brother?"

Kristy looked at her beautiful little girl. "I don't think that's going to happen, Nicki."

Nicki jutted her lower lip out. "But,Mama, we have a house now, I should have a baby brother."

Nick threw his hands up in the air and headed for the barn to feed the other horses. Kristy followed. "What's the matter, Nick? Too much too soon? Nicki too out spoken for you? She speaks her mind when she wants something."

"Don't you think you should think about it before jumping into having another baby?"

What a pigheaded old fool. She turned and started to walk away. "Yes, I think I should do just that." She headed out of the barn then hesitated and turned around to look at Nick. "Want to move in with us?"

Kristy wasn't even aware of the bucket of oats slamming to the floor or his movements toward her until she felt his arms go around her and his lips on hers.

"About damn time you asked," he growled and kissed her again.

Several weeks later in Kristy's office she stood there staring at Hunter. She was just now breaking the news that she was once again living with Nick.

"You've done what!" Hunter yelled at Kristy.

Sarah, who was now Kristy's secretary, sat on the couch watching total devastation cross Hunter's face.

"You knew I'd eventually move in with the man. I love him."

"I know, but Gracie says you're thinking of giving Nicki that baby brother. You can't do that!"

"Hunter, I don't understand your reaction to my news?"

Hunter paced around the office with anger written all over his face. "Of course you understand it. What now? You can't just go off and have another baby, we need you here and you know it."

Kristy took a step toward him. "Hunter, I have no intention of quitting work. I may change my mind about having a baby, my feelings are so up in the air at this time of my life. With the club ready I'm going to be busier than ever." She went to stand before Hunter and took his hands in hers. "Nothing's changed between us."

"Everything's changed between us." His piercing gaze bore right through her. "I was all you needed in the past. I was your rock. I was there for you when you needed someone. I'm walking you through that damn cowboy's courting, if you can call it that, and now I feel as if I'm losing you. You can't give him another child."

Sarah was stunned and amazed at Hunter's confession. She knew he'd always had a thing for Kristy but Hunter actually needed to be needed by her. He truly was in love with her.

"I said I was considering it. I would never let Matt or the agency down, you know that. I still need you in my life, that hasn't changed. We have history together."

Hunter took her face in his hands and kissed her with the passion of a jealous lover, his tongue plundering what used to be his. "There, just remember what we had." He stalked angrily out of the office.

Kristy leaned against her desk and looked at Sarah. "We've got to find him a woman."

"Why? He's a great toy boy for me."

"Because he needs one in the first place, and in the second, he'll try to destroy my relationship with Nick. I've waited all my life for Nick and no one...no one is going to come between us."

Sarah picked up a folder and headed into the waiting room and to her desk. She tossed the folder onto her desk and spun around to look at Kristy. "You're breaking a lot of hearts, Kristy. That J. C. Norton that you've booked into the club is a prime example. Good God, I swear there's drool coming out of his mouth instead of pretty music when he's around you."

"Sarah, J.C. is younger than I am, I'm giving him the break he needs. He's grateful, that's all."

"Yeah, and I'm blind too."

"Did you get ahold of that record producer in LA?"

"Yeah, I did and yes, he'll be here."

"Good. Were you able to reach Drummond and check on his flight?"

"Yes, I did that too. I ordered a limo to pick him up and get him to the hotel. Matt said someone would pick him up and deliver him to the club's opening tomorrow night. Oh yes, Matt also told me to let you know that Italian...Guido Piazza would be at the club too."

"And you, and Brian?"

"I wouldn't miss it," Sarah grinned. "Sure do like working for someone that can get me free entry to some good country western music. I hope Brian can make it...but you know how that goes."

"You're just as much a part of this team now as the rest of us. In fact, you're my right hand at this point. I hope Nick and Brian will want to join us, if not...I'm not going to stew over it."

"Thanks, Kristy, that makes me feel good about myself." Sarah poured a cup of coffee and walked back into Kristy's office. "What do your parents think of you and Nick living together?"

"I'm not sure they were very thrilled to hear the news but dad said, bet Nicki's happy...I believe were the words he used."

"I talked to Nicki and she's beside herself having her dad back in the house. She actually thinks she's getting a baby brother. Did you ever tell Doc his name is on her birth certificate?"

"He's never asked."

"Do you really plan to have another one? I thought you wanted to be married first."

Kristy looked up from her computer. "I did, but I would like a son to go with my daughter and I won't wait forever to have him."

"Hunter once told me he loved being around you when you were carrying Nicki. I think that reaction we just saw was because he's going to feel left out."

"Hunter isn't going to be left out, shoot I'm around him more than

I am Nick."

Sarah understood. "It's like you're still living alone isn't it? He comes, he goes, he gives you a call to let you know he'll be late. You never really know where he's at. Has he told you he loves you?"

"Sarah, only you and I know how we feel about these men of ours. I've chosen to be with Nick and that's the way it's going to be. I'll make a home for him and our daughter but I also have to know I'm capable of taking care of myself and Nicki because I have too."

"Mavis, know yet?"

Kristy shrugged. "I'll tell her tonight. Grab your purse, let's go to the Lone Star for some fun."

"You're readin' my mind. I'll call Brian once we're there."

Nick shut off the engine of Big Red in the parking lot of the Lone Star and walked inside to find Mavis up to her neck is paperwork. The place was packed.

"So Doc, what can I get for ya?"

"Usual, Mavis."

"So how's our Kristy?"

"You mean you haven't talked to her recently?" He sipped the beer.

"Ain't had time. With my new place openin' tomorrow and servin' all of you in here, just ain't had time."

"Then you don't know."

Marvis' head snapped to attention and a big smile played on her lips. "Know what? Has Kristy finally corralled the old war horse himself. Lordy me, I can hear cowgirl's heart's a breakin' all over this city." She put another beer in front of him. "How'd that Hunter fella take the news?" Mavis watched Nick's expression harden.

"Mavis, we ain't getting married. We're only thinking about having a baby boy."

Mavis scowled, she didn't like the sound of that at all. "And does that mean Nicki and a baby boy will always have the last name of Williams?"

"Mavis, the kids are Chandlers, just using the Williams name temporarily."

"My daughter ought to have her head examined to love an old fool

213

like you! She deserves better. My grandbabies deserve better."

Nick grinned, picked up his beer and headed into the nosiest part of the bar to share his news with the others. He hadn't taken two steps into the noisy clamour when he felt Jez's arms slip around his waist from behind. Her fingers dipped beneath the belt buckle.

"Here's my man," Jez crooned and moved against him in time to the music.

It wasn't long until Nick found himself surrounded by other women all trying to lead him to their tables or booths. In the past he would have played the game...but as he looked around his whole game plan had changed. If he could unwrap Jez he'd tell her about his moving in with Kristy.

"Jez, you might want to get your hands out of Nick's jeans and go find your own man," Kristy said with a straight face.

Jez's expression was one that was priceless to Kristy. Sarah just grinned as she stood next to Kristy.

"Whata ya mean? How can he be your man?"

In unison Nick and Kristy laughed. Sarah started laughing. Mavis stood there grinning with three bottles of beer in her hand.

"When did this happen?" Jez almost choked on the words. "Why'd you hook up with someone with a kid? Thought she was out of your life for good. That ain't like you, Doc."

Nick thought now was as good as time as ever to tell Jez about Nicki. "You ever take a good look at Kristy's kid, Jez?" Nick asked.

"No, why?"

"Cause you're looking at her daddy." He took Kristy by the elbow and walked her and Sarah to a booth where Mavis set the three bottles of beer on the table.

Mavis shook her head. "You sure told her, Doc. Kristy, you'd better warn that Hunter fella Jez will be lookin' elsewhere."

"She'd better."

Nick couldn't miss the warning look in Kristy's eyes.

CHAPTER TWENTY

"It'll be all right, Kristy," Hunter said. "Breathe."

Kristy found herself hyperventilating at this point. It was opening night at Dallas Rhodes. She'd done everything to make sure things went right but she kept running the schedule, the timing of the publicity, the booking of talent, the menu, had they picked up their clients at their hotels, everything over and over in her mind. Did every table have a yellow rose in the vase? Had they ordered enough liquor, food…

Sarah smiled and warned, "Kristy, get hold of yourself. You don't want anyone seeing you falling apart like this." She patted Kristy on the back.

Kristy took a deep breath, held it, then exhaled. "Okay. I'm over it. I know in my mind I've done everything I should." She stood up too quickly and became light headed almost falling over. She reached out and grabbed the back of a chair to steady herself.

"Whoa," Sarah said and grabbed her.

Hunter was quick to be at her side put his arm around her waist and helped her to the couch in Mavis' new office. Sarah followed close behind.

"I've never seen you like this," Hunter said as Matt walked in.

"Like what?" Matt frowned.

"I'm fine. I got a little light-headed thinking of tonight. We all have so much money invested in this place...what if I forgot to do something? What if..."

"Oh shit, cut it out Kristy," Matt said. "You're the most organized woman I've ever met. The only thing that could go wrong is you not being out front meeting your clients."

Kristy inhaled again. "I feel sick."

"Then have a drink," Sarah poured a glass of water and handed it to her.

Hunter grinned, then taunted, "I thought I saw some of those Maverick basketball players out there and I know there are at least four Dallas Cowboys in the room."

Kristy started to hyperventilate again. Oh God, what if she loses all their money?

"Stop it, Hunter!" Sarah warned.

Nick came into the room just in time to see Matt, Hunter and Sarah hovering over Kristy. "What the hell happened?" he growled and hunkered before Kristy taking her hands in his.

Sarah shot Hunter a warning look that could kill. "Hunter scared her. She's as nervous as a cat in a room full of rockin' chairs. Tell her it's going to be all right, Nick."

"I brought that dress you forgot, go put it on and get yourself out there, there's a room full of people anxious to get their night goin'."

Sarah shooed the men out of the room while Kristy pulled on the thigh length shimmering white dress she'd worn to the California functions. She'd already put on her makeup and had her hair pinned up. Sarah sucked in her breath as Kristy slipped into heels that matched.

"Kristy, I think you're the most beautiful woman I've ever seen."

Mavis walked into the room pale as a ghost.

"Oh no, not you too?" Sarah groaned. "Like mother like daughter. Mavis where's that new gown Kristy bought for you?"

Mavis could only point to a door.

By the time Kristy recovered and had composed herself it was her turn to be surprised. Mavis emerged from the bathroom dressed in a long shimmering tight fitting black dress. With makeup and heels she looked stunning. Her hair had been colored the honey blonde it use to be and it was pulled back into a chignon. Kristy's mouth dropped open in total surprise. That was her mother!

"You're...beautiful."

Sarah's mouth dropped open too. "My God, you two...anyone can see there's a resemblance here. You look like a model again, Mavis."

"Can you still sing?" Kristy asked.

Mavis ran her hands nervously down the sides of her gown. "I haven't felt like this in thirty years. Yeah, I haven't lost the pipes yet. I need a drink." Had she done the right thing by making the restaurant reflect the true cowboy cooking...instead of Tex/Mex? The place would go over well with Kristy's clients but would the live mesquite fire grilling go over with out of towners? She had to trust Kristy's ideas, and advertise the best Dry Herb Rub Prime Rib in Dallas. My God, she groaned, with more than 70,000 restaurants and bars in Texas...would her two be any different? Would the Jordan Agency clients spread the word and send new people her way? She was too flustered to think about that at the moment! So much rode on tonight's opening. Why had she let herself be talked into something on such a grand scale? What if she lost her daughter's money? What if...

The three women fixed themselves a stiff gin and tonic before taking a deep breath and walking out into the restaurant to circulate among the patrons. Sarah stood back and watched the two most beautiful women in Dallas greet customers and shake hands with celebrities. Kristy was in her element...and so was Mavis.

Hunter came to stand beside Sarah and slipped his arm around her waist. "She's beautiful isn't she?"

"Our Kristy?"

"Our Kristy. She doesn't even know she's pregnant yet."

Sarah gasped. "What?"

"I know that glow about her. It was there the first time I laid eyes on her, and it's there now. This should be interesting to watch in the next few months."

"Oh my God, how's Nick going to take this news? Here she is out there being herself and now..."

"He'll probably be pretty pleased with himself. What he doesn't know is that when Kristy's pregnant every man she meets wants to take care of her. And since she's single...she's going to have to break more than one heart. She never got very big with Nicole but she sure was all woman. Soft and vulnerable."

"She never ceases to amaze me," Sarah said. "God, I wish I could get Brian to fall in love with me like you are with her."

"Sarah, if you want this kind of love you won't find it in a pigheaded Texas cowboy."

Sarah's shoulders slumped a bit. "Then, like Kristy, I'll have to settle."

"She doesn't have to settle, she can have everything I can give her. I asked her to marry me."

Sarah sucked in her breath. "You...you asked her to marry you? She loves Nick."

"Yeah, but he doesn't really love her, if he did he would have committed by now. She wants Nicki to have a brother and wants Nick to be the father. We'll see what happens when he finds out she's pregnant."

"She's settled, now let it alone, Hunter." Sarah pointed toward the front in the waiting area. "There's Gracie and Nicki, why don't you take them out to dinner."

Hunter smiled. "I think I'll do just that. You okay here?"

Sarah nodded. "I'm waiting for Brian, he's bound to show up sooner or later." She watched as Hunter made his way through the crowded restaurant to Gracie where he pulled her into his arms. Nicki jumped up and down until Hunter gave her a hug too. She envied Gracie. God, how she envied Kristy. Hunter actually asked her to marry him? If only Hunter could love her.

Sarah decided to wait in the new bar with Nick. "Mavis has gone all out with the Texas theme don't you think, Doc?" She glanced up at the big longhorn skull with ten-foot horns hanging behind the bar, a Texas flag on another wall, old branding irons and samples of barbed wire finished off the new look.

"She'll bring in a whole new clientele with this bar. I'm glad she kept the Lone Star, most of us feel more comfortable there."

Sarah let her gaze go to the front of the bar. "Oh I don't know, look what just came in, Jez." As usual, Jez was overly made up and wore the tightest clothes she could pour herself into. Shoot, Sarah thought, you could smell the woman's perfume a block before you saw her. She chuckled, must be to cover the scent of horse.

"Thought I'd find you here, Doc. How come you're not out there with Kristy?"

"Because I've already had supper." He nursed his beer.

"This is some place Mavis has here. Nice stage. Who's the good lookin' kid settin' things up?" Her hand automatically went up Nick's back to his shoulder.

Sarah didn't want to watch Jez put her moves on Doc so she walked over and presented her hand, "J.C. remember me, Kristy's secretary, Sarah?" Young and tempting, she mused.

J.C. took her hand in his. "Sure, how's it goin', Sarah? I saw Kristy out there in the restaurant lookin' mighty pretty."

"Do you need any help setting up?"

"Naugh, the boys will be in shortly, we did a sound check earlier. You gonna stay and hear us play?"

Sarah smiled brightly, "Oh I think so. You know Kristy's arranged to have a record producer here tonight don't you?"

J.C. gave her a lopsided grin and raised an eyebrow. "She said she had contacts...wow I had no idea. She gonna introduce us tonight?"

Sarah gave him her best Texas smile. "Yeah, she is."

"Know what she might be doin' after the show?" He continued to fidget with cords and cables as he talked.

"Well, J.C., she's kinda involved with someone right now, but I'm sure she appreciates the offer."

J.C. grinned and tuned his guitar. "Afraid you'd say that. Too bad. I have a hankerin' to get to know her better."

Nick just sat there listening and feeling pride in Kristy's accomplishments. He didn't like the fact some young musician had eyes for her though.

"Well," Jez said in her best sexy voice, "guess I'll find myself a table and watch this J.C. move his groove. Wanta join me, Doc?" Her hand slowly made it's way down Nick's back.

"No thanks."

Jez brushed against him. "Suit yourself."

"Welcome to opening night at Dallas Rhodes, I'm Kristy Williams and I'd like to introduce a new group to you featuring song writer and singer, J.C. Norton. So let's welcome this Nashville band to Dallas." She applauded as did the room full of people.

The house lights went down and the stage lights came up. The band started to play.

Kristy came off stage and into Nick's arms. She was exhausted. She'd been running on adrenalin all night. She could hardly wait for the reviews in tomorrow's papers so she could see where they'd need to improve. She was certain J.C. didn't need improving, he held the audience in the palm of his hand. He was good. And...no doubt would get that record deal by tomorrow.

"You tired?" Nick asked and slipped his arms around her.

"Exhausted." She leaned against him.

"When can I take you home?"

"I'd like nothing better then to say right now but I have to talk to the record producer first. After that we can leave."

A middle aged Italian with a very thick accent approached Kristy. "Guido Piazza, this is Nick Chandler," Kristy said, "I hope you've enjoyed your stay in Dallas. If the Jordan Agency can be of any help to you while you're here be sure to let us know."

"It is nice to meet you, Mr. Chandler. Kristy has been most gracious to me and my countrymen. The Jordan Agency has agreed to represent us here in America. I wish to thank you for a most pleasant evening and an enlightening stay in Dallas." He turned to leave, hesitated then turned back to Kristy. "Ah, may I ask one other thing...the tall blonde woman in the black dress I saw you with, may I ask her name?"

Kristy smiled. "Her name is Mavis Rhodes. She owns the restaurant and bar. Would you like for me to introduce you to her?"

Guido's black eyebrows drew together to form one brow. "You would do that?"

"Sure." She leaned over and kissed Nick. "Excuse me while I introduce this gentleman to Mavis."

Nick watched with amusement as Kristy, with Guido in hand, made her way to where Mavis sat chatting with the owner of a large prominent stable. One of Nick's clients. Mavis shook the Italian's hand and offered him a spot at her table. Kristy made her way back to Nick. "Nice move," he said. "Mavis is really something to look at now that she's all dolled up like that."

Kristy leaned against Nick and he put his arm around her. "I wonder if she has any of her modeling pictures around here. I'd like to frame them and put them around the restaurant. I can see what dad saw in her and back then she must have really been a beauty. No wonder…"

"Hell look at that old fart put the moves on her." Nick laughed.

"Which old fart, Guido or your client?"

"Both. I think Mavis is gonna come into her own now that she's gussied herself up. I think I'm gonna like coming in here just to watch the human show."

"I hope my parents never come to this place. I'd hate to think she'd have to fight dad off. And I'm sure that's just what would happen."

"Ellen can take care of Joe."

"Yes, she can. But for her to see what Mavis has become…"

"It's all thanks to you. You did this for her."

"I did it for me too. Don't you think I owed her something for giving me life? She's Nicole's grandmother. I've invested in my future and my daughter's future here. I want to take Nicki and go back to the Chandler ranch someday…if that's what I want, but I don't want to have to worry about money to do it. I need to help my parents out as much as I can."

Kristy couldn't take her eyes off Mavis. Even as the Lone Star barkeep she'd displayed a kind of elegance about her, but now…she looked amazing sitting there carrying on a conversation with an olive oil king and Texas horse royalty.

"Kristy," the record produced approached her, "I'll give you a call tomorrow afternoon."

"Did you get a demo?"

"Sure did. I'm overnighting it to LA."

"Your car is waiting outside. Thank you for agreeing to come tonight."

"We've signed the Nashville Brit you sent us. He's given the Jordan Agency full credit and wants you on his team."

Kristy shook her head. "No. I'm turning him over to Hunter at this point."

"Too bad. He's going to be disappointed."

Kristy took Nick's hand in hers. "I'm concentrating on my daughter at the moment and don't want to be traveling back and forth from Dallas to LA. He'll just have to understand."

The producer grinned. "Oh I think he does. I'll look forward to who you send me next."

"Thanks."

"Nice to meet you, Mr. Chandler," the producer said and left the club.

Nick kissed Kristy's forehead. "Now can I take you home?"

Exhausted she gazed into his eyes and whispered, "Oh please do."

Once home she fell into bed and into Nick's waiting arms.

"Wasn't that Hunter's sports car I saw in front of Gracie's?" Nick asked and let his hand play over Kristy's stomach.

"I hope so." She turned to face him and took his hardness in her hands to give him some much needed attention.

"Oh yeah...why's that?" He hissed and held his breath.

"Because she needs a husband and he needs someone in his life."

"Then...keep doin' that...you'd need a new sitter...oh..."

She wrapped her legs around him and pulled him into her, she needed to wear off the tension of the evening and this was the best cure she knew.

By the time Kristy woke the next morning Nick was long gone. She missed waking up to him and wondered why he'd let her over sleep. She also felt awful. She picked up the phone and dialed the office.

"Hi Sarah, this is Kristy. I'm going to be late. I overslept and don't feel all that great this morning."

Sarah laughed. "Well I'm not surprised."

Kristy lay back against the pillow and put her arm over her eyes. "Why would you say that?"

"Hunter says you're pregnant."

Kristy bolted upright. "What?"

"You heard me, Hunter says you're pregnant. Said he could tell because you looked just like this when he first met you. Could it be true?"

"I...I...I think I'd better call a doctor. I'll be in later."

Later that afternoon Kristy stepped off the elevator and headed for her office only to be intercepted by Hunter. She glared at him.

"What?" He asked acting surprised, "What did I do?"

"How'd you know I'm pregnant?"

Hunter gave her a deep-throated laugh. "Sarah had to tell you you're pregnant? I would have thought you'd have guessed."

She opened the door of her office and took her jacket off throwing it onto the couch. "I've been too busy to think about such things. Isn't that the purpose of birth control pills?"

Hunter gave her a funny face. "Well hell, you haven't been to busy to make one."

"That's different."

"So?"

"So what?"

"Did you see a doctor yet?"

Kristy sat down at her desk and turned on the computer. "Yes. In about seven months. Hunter...regardless of Nicki's demands to have a brother, this wasn't really planned."

Hunter grinned and sat down on the couch. "So is the cowboy happy?"

"He doesn't know yet. And how the hell did you know when I didn't?"

Hunter leaned forward resting his arms on his thighs. "I know everything about you and I always have. I knew the moment I saw your face yesterday. I hope to hell you know what you're doing."

She leaned back in the chair and looked at him. "I hope to hell I do too."

Sarah came in with a cup of coffee for Kristy. "Well? What's the news?"

Kristy gazed up at Sarah and wished that damned Brian would make up his mind one way or the other. "Would you and Brian like to join us for dinner tonight?"

"Sure, I guess," Sarah said, "I'll have to ask Brian...if I can find him. What's the news?"

"Ask Hunter, he knows more about me than I do."

Hunter just sat there grinning his answer. "You can't love a woman for as long as I've loved Kristy and not know when there's been a change in her life."

"Oh hell don't tell that to Nick," Sarah grumbled. "You going to be around when it's born?"

Kristy sucked in her breath.

Hunter stood to leave. "You bet, if the cowboy isn't around she can at least count on me. I'll keep asking her to marry me until she says yes."

Once Hunter closed the door Sarah sat down on the couch and smiled. "Have you told Nicki yet?"

"I haven't told anyone yet. I wouldn't have known except you told me. And when I had time to think about it I called the doctor. I feel…"

"It's what you want, isn't it?"

Kristy sat there still stunned by the news. "I thought it was…" Her gaze rose to Sarah. "I don't know anymore."

"The Brit, Robert, just called and wanted to talk with you. Said he heard you weren't going to be working with him on PR."

"I guess the producer phoned him. I told him I was turning him over to Hunter. I know that's not a good idea, but I can't be traveling back and forth until I have this baby."

"What about J.C.?"

"What about him? If he gets a contract he'll go back to Nashville or LA. We can do the PR from here if we have to. Unlike Robert who demands hands on attention, J.C. is much more agreeable."

"Kristy, you're life is coming together just the way you've always wanted it to."

"I guess."

"Except…you don't even know if Nick really cares about you, do you?"

Kristy shook her head and sadness swept over her. "No. But I'll have my beautiful children that are part Nick and I will always love him."

"I'll see if I can reach Brian. I don't suppose you know what their schedules are, do you?"

Kristy just stared at her. "Nick doesn't tell me anything."

Sarah headed out the door. "Neither does Brian."

CHAPTER TWENTY ONE

Nick and Brian were both missing at dinner due to an emergency. Instead, Kristy, Gracie, Sarah and Nicki sat at the table staring at each other while eating spaghetti with meatballs. Kristy shoved her food around the plate. She had absolutely no appetite. She was upset and confused.

"Well," Sarah said, "tell Nicki the good news."

Gracie and Nicki both gave Kristy their undivided attention.

"Nicki, we're going to have a baby in about seven months," Kristy said feeling a bit hesitant.

Nicki grinned and put her fork down, scooted out of her chair and came around the table to hug her mother. "Thank you, Mama. Gracie, we're having a baby."

Gracie was near tears. "I'm so happy for you and...Nick."

"Thanks," Kristy tried to smile and feel happy. Where the hell was Nick?

"Mama, can I spend the night at Gracie's?"

"Why?"

"Because daddy isn't here and I think you should tell him by yourself."

"That's not necessary Nicki. He's your daddy too."

Nicki smiled that smile of Nick's, showing the dimples beneath her cheekbones. "I know that. But you should tell daddy by yourself."

Gracie laughed and put her napkin on the plate. "She's welcome to stay with me. Besides, I'm teaching her to knit."

"You are? What are you knitting?"

"Baby things. I started about a month ago."

Kristy's mouth dropped open. Did everyone know but her? "All right, go get your pj's and I'll see you tomorrow."

Nicki came out with her backpack and put her arms around Kristy's neck. "Thank you, Mama. I think I'm going to like having a brother."

"It could be a sister, you know."

Nicki shook her head in a determined fashion. "No, it's a brother. I love you, Mama."

"I love you too, Nicki." Kristy smiled as she watched her daughter bounce out the door with Gracie.

"Well now," Sarah said and poured them a cup of coffee, "everyone knows but Nick."

"He and Brian are busy." Her heart was breaking.

"Oh like hell. They can stop for dinner now and then."

"Sarah, they think a fast food drive thru was developed just for them. You and I are just going to have to make do." She thought for a moment then said, "Hell, let's go to Mavis' place. I've had enough of a shock today, I need to be around people tonight."

Sarah slapped her napkin onto the table and stood up. "Me too. Let's go."

Kristy and Sarah couldn't help but notice Big Red in the parking lot of the Lone Star. Hunter was parked at Dallas Rhodes. Kristy pulled up next to Hunter.

As they stood in the parking lot the two women looked at each other. Sarah finally said, "Class or Trash?"

Kristy grinned. "Class, trash we can see any day of the week." They headed into Dallas Rhodes.

"Hi Kristy, Sarah," the bartender said and waved at them.

"Hi Tony, how's it going?" Kristy asked.

"We've got a full house tonight. Stay for dancin'?"

"I might."

She pulled Sarah into the office and found Hunter sitting there working on the computer. When he looked up he was surprised to see them.

"Thought you two were having dinner to make the big announcement."

Kristy sat down on the couch and put her arm across the back of it. "Oh we had dinner and made the announcement to Nicki and Gracie. Both, by the way, are thrilled."

"And?" He grinned knowing full well she was pissed at Nick. "Wasn't Nick there?"

"And nothing, we're here to have a good time. Want to do some dancing?"

Hunter pushed the papers back onto the desk and turned off the computer. "Two lovely...lonely ladies to entertain, why not."

He took both women by their arm and escorted them to Mavis' table for an evening of dancing. When he had Kristy in his arms he whispered against her ear, "I saw his truck next door. I also saw Jez's."

"Hold me tight, Hunter. Make me feel as if everything's going to be all right."

He took up the challenge and did just that. "I'll always be here for you." His lips brushed up and down her neck.

She squeezed her eyes tight. "I know you will."

"Baby, what's the matter?" Mavis said when she saw Kristy dancing with Hunter.

"Nothing." She stopped and looked at Mavis. "No, I'd be lying to you if I said that. Mavis, I'm having another baby. I told Nicki tonight."

Hunter kept his arms around her. He could feel her shaking from anger.

Mavis' smile broadened. "I'm happy for you. He didn't show up for the news did he?" Well, it looked to her like Nick had gotten his way with her daughter and she wasn't one bit happy about the way he was treating her.

Kristy shook her head and leaned into Hunter for comfort. "No, Mavis, he didn't. Sarah and I had everything planned, but as usual...nothing's worked out. Have you been next door tonight?"

"Yes, baby, I have. Yeah, he's there, she's there."

"Thanks. Hunter, keep dancing with me."

"I can keep my arms around you for as long as you want."

Sarah sat at the table with her heart breaking for Kristy. She knew Kristy well enough to know she wasn't going to tell Nick now. She doubted if she'd tell him until he noticed her rounding stomach or until Nicki said something. Stubborn as hell. She couldn't blame Kristy one bit. Oh God, why couldn't that green eyed Hunter fall in love with her? Instead of Kristy.

"May I cut in," a familiar male British accent said.

Kristy sucked in her breath and looked into dark eyes. "I didn't know you were in Dallas, Robert."

Hunter said, "You should have called."

"I tried, Kristy wouldn't take my calls. Why aren't you working with me anymore?"

Hunter led them all back to the booth and ordered a round of drinks. Water for Kristy.

"Robert, I can't keep flying back and forth from here to LA. Hunter can. I'm having a baby and I can't leave Dallas for a while."

Robert ran his fingers through his long thick black hair and leaned back in the booth to allow his gaze to roam up and down Kristy's body. "I didn't believe it when the producer told me Hunter would be my wing man. Your kid, Hunter?"

Hunter leaned forward and looked into Robert's dark eyes. "No, it's not mine. But she's having a baby, leave her alone."

Robert inhaled and exhaled, put his arms around Kristy and kissed her just below the ear and held her close to him for a short time. "Ah hell, it didn't hurt to try, besides, she's not married she's fair game." When he glanced up at Hunter he could read anger in his eyes. "All right. But I still want you doing my public relations. Hunter, I know you're good, but I can always count on Kristy."

She wasn't sure what to tell Robert. "Hunter and I will work on it together if it makes you feel better."

"Sure, if you'll make it a promise. I know you'll keep your word. Mind if I ask Sarah here to dance?"

Sarah's mouth dropped opened. He remembered her name. Robert stood and extended his hand, Sarah took it and found herself gliding around the dance floor with a very famous musician holding her close to him.

Hunter and Kristy sat there watching Sarah enjoying herself. "That was easy enough," he said. "Only about two hundred more clients to go."

She stared at Hunter in disbelief. "Hunter, Robert unhooked my bra. How does he do that so easily?" She was surprised he hadn't taken it completely off and put it in his pocket like he did the last time he put his arms around her. He must have been a pickpocket in England because she never felt a thing. The last time he pulled the bra out of his pocket and twirled the lacy item around his index finger teasing her with it when she hadn't even realized she wasn't wearing it anymore.

Hunter laughed and watched as she discreetly leaned close to the table and removed the bra through her sleeve and put it in her purse. He wanted to feel those bare breasts next to him when he held her. "What's going to happen now?"

"Nothing's going to change," she reminded him. "I'll be at work every day. I'll be here on weekends. I'll...go on with my life."

Hunter took her hands in his. "Your heart's breaking. It's always going to be breaking being around Nick. I don't think he's ever going to change."

"Okay, if that's the way it's going to be, so be it. I'll continue as I am...I suppose."

"Want to go next door?"

She looked up into his gaze. "Why do I have to keep fighting for him? What is it those women have over him that I don't?"

Hunter kissed the top of her head. "Not one damn thing. He's just been single far too long and has played the game too well."

"Why does it have to be a game, Hunter?"

"It doesn't. I think because of the age difference maybe you scare him."

Kristy drew back and stared at him. "Why would you think that?"

His mouth curled into a smile. "Sometimes when you think you might lose something it scares you."

Now she frowned. "I sometimes think he's pushing me away and I'm just fool enough to keep clinging where I'm not wanted."

"Makes you mad doesn't it?"

She sighed heavily. "Are you going next door with me?"

"I wouldn't miss it. Let's get Sarah untangled from the Brit. She's got as much at stake as you have. Let's see what underwear she's missing."

Sarah, her underwear in tact, took it all in stride as they walked into the parking lot to go next door. "Trash!" She laughed as they walked into the dimly lit place.

The jukebox blared, couples moved around the room, and every booth and table was full. Even newly remodeled it was still a haven for the locals that didn't want to be bothered by outsiders...or seen.

"Want me to get her off his lap?" Hunter volunteered when he saw Jez on top of Nick with both her arms possessively around his neck.

"No. Leave her to me. Why should you have to take care of my problem?"

Sarah gasped when she looked at Kristy's face. "Oh no, what are you going to do, Kristy?" She said, her eyes widening.

"Just watch."

Taking a deep breath, head held high and determination in her stride Kristy walked to where Nick held Jez on his lap and, as Jez looked up Kristy reared back and with a right hook let her have it in the jaw.

"Jesus Christ!" Jez yelled and went flying off Nick's lap onto the bar room floor where she landed with a thud. She grabbed her jaw. "Why the hell would you do that?"

"I warned you once, Jez. Nick's not your man." Holding her reddened knuckles in her other hand Kristy turned on her heels and marched back into Hunter's waiting arms and with Sarah following they all walked out of the Lone Star, got into their cars and left. To hell with Nick, to hell with Brian.

"What the hell was that all about?" Nick yelled as he walked into the house.

Kristy just looked at him and wondered why she even bothered loving him. "You missed dinner. Brian missed dinner."

"We had an emergency."

"Oh like hell."

"What are you talking about?"

She spun around to glare at him. "Jez is always going to be your excuse for an emergency. As far as I'm concerned, go for it Nick. Just get out of our lives, let us live in peace!" She marched angrily off to the bedroom and threw her shirt and jeans onto the chair. She grabbed her nightshirt and slipped it over her head.

Nick followed. "What the hell are you talking about?"

"We're living separate lives…or haven't you noticed? We rarely see each other, Nicki never sees you and now…"

"All Brian and I did was stop in for a beer. Sure Jez was there, so what? She's always there."

Kristy glared at him before turning on her heels and walked into the kitchen to grab a bottle of water. "And so are you. Every time I walk into that place she has her hands all over you, in your pants, running up and down your pants, you name it and I've seen it. Why the hell don't the two of you just rent a room for the night and get it over with!"

"What are you talking about?"

"You and Jez," she yelled. "Every time I see you two together she's all over you."

"And Hunter's all over you." He reminded her.

"For your information Hunter keeps…others away. Hunter knows the boundaries where I'm concerned. He isn't trying to touch me in inappropriate places."

"You trying to tell me he's protecting you? Don't give me that shit, he's admitted he's in love with you."

She threw her hands up in the air. "I'm tired Nick. I'm tired of arguing, I'm tired of seeing Jez all over you, I'm tired of being alone. I'm just plain tired these days." She walked back to the bedroom and slammed the door shut, climbed into bed pulling the covers up around her neck.

The door flew open. His clothes came flying off and he climbed into bed beside her. She turned her back to him with her heart thudding in her ears. He lay there staring up at a dark ceiling.

After a long silence he said, "Look, I'm sorry about tonight. Brian and I did have an emergency. We only stopped for a beer."

Kristy turned to face him. In the dark all she could see was his profile. "Why are we together Nick?"

"What?"

"Why are we together?"

"Because of Nicki."

She sucked in her breath. "That's what I thought you'd say." She turned her back to him again. Damn fool! He was a damn fool! The words screamed over and over in her mind. They were both fools. Why couldn't he see she'd given him Nicki to carry on the Chandler name and protect his damn ranch? Yet, hadn't she forced herself and Nicki on him when she hadn't intended to? What now? With another baby on the way that meant she'd have to raise two children alone. She knew something had to give, their living arrangement was not working for her.

He turned to face her back and placed his hand on her waist. "Kristy, I'm sorry, I know that's not the answer you wanted to hear. It's not just because of Nicki. I want to be here with the two of you."

"You don't act like it."

"We're both independent people. We're not used to thinking about someone else."

"From my understanding of things," Kristy reminded him, "commitment is all about caring about the other person."

He moved closer to her until his body pressed against hers. "I do care about you." His hand moved over her stomach and down to his favorite distraction.

She responded to him as she always did. She loved him. She would always love him and be in love with him. Nothing would ever change that. And she knew that if she couldn't have his love then she would have his body and took him to places where there were no arguments.

When she opened her eyes the next morning Nick was staring at her.

"I thought you'd be gone by now," she whispered.

"I like watching you sleep. Only you tossed and turned all night. What's the matter?"

She rolled over onto her back and stared up at the ceiling. "I feel as if my life is spiraling out of control. With the club and restaurant, the agency…Nicki. I can't seem to portion myself out the way I would like. I think the stress is beginning to get to me." She was being honest with him.

"Why don't you take some time off?"

"I can't. It's even more important now that I…Maybe in a few months I can take a break. Right now I have to make sure the clients are happy."

"What about Nicki?"

"I'm here for her after school. She's happier than she's been in a long time. She has roots, she has her horse."

Nick pulled her into his arms. She fit him perfectly in every way. He didn't want to lose her. Maybe if he could spend more time with them, be a family, give more of himself. But how? He'd also have to watch being around Jez. Shit, he'd never seen Kristy as mad as she was last night. He wondered what Jez's face looked like this morning. He picked Kristy's right hand up and looked at it. She tried to pull it back under the covers. It was red and the knuckles were bruised. He placed them to his lips.

"Where'd you learn to hit like that?"

"You don't want to know." She didn't want to tell him Hunter had made her take a few boxing lessons. She liked boxing more for the exercise than self defense, but now knew it could come in handy with the likes of Jez Bevaca.

There was a soft rap on the door and Kristy said, "Come in, Nicki."

Nicki had a small tray in her hands with a glass of milk and a mug of coffee. "Good morning, Mama, Daddy. Here Mama this is for you and the baby." She put the glass of milk beside Kristy then walked to Nick's side of the bed and put the mug of coffee on the nightstand. "This is for you, Daddy."

"Thank you, Nicki," Nick said.

Nicki threw her arms around Nick's neck and kissed his cheek. "Thank you, Daddy, for our new baby." She walked to the door and turned to look at her parents. "Gracie is packing my lunch so I'll see you after school."

"Have a good day," Kristy smiled at her daughter.

Nicki closed the bedroom door behind her. Kristy started to get out of bed to shower and dress for work but Nick grabbed her arm and pulled her back down.

Shocked by Nicki's revelation Nick said, "What baby? When did that happen?"

Kristy crawled back under the covers and laid her head on Nick's shoulder. "That's what dinner with Sarah and Brian was all about last night. Only you missed the big announcement. At least Nicole is happy about it."

"A baby? When?"

"In seven months." Kristy gazed into his eyes but couldn't read them. Was he angry? Happy? Indifferent? She couldn't tell.

Nick turned to face her and pulled her into his arms. He was grinning broadly as he thought of the hayloft. "Yep, there's nothing like a roll in the hayloft to get you pregnant." He hugged her tight against him.

"How do you feel about it? I sprang Nicki on you and now to have another one...Nick, I don't expect anything from you, I can take care of my children."

"Like Cotton said, we need lots of Chandler's to carry on at the ranch. Nicki is more than I could ever have hoped for. This one will probably be much like her. Have you told your parents yet?"

Disappointed in his answer it was what she'd expected. "Only Mavis." She wasn't going to remind him the children were not Chandler's, but Williams'.

"Mind if I give Joe and Ellen the news?"

"Not at all. It doesn't matter who tells them. I'm surprised Nicki hasn't called them. Last night she stayed with Gracie because you didn't come home for dinner and she wanted me to tell you by myself. Well...we know how well that went."

"Hunter know?"

Kristy took a deep breath. "He's the one that told Sarah, and she told me and when I had time to think about it I called the doctor."

"How the hell would he know?"

"Because he knows me. He remembers the last time."

"I only ask one thing with this one...I want to be there when it's born, not Hunter."

Kristy laughed and kissed him. "You should have been there for the first one."

CHAPTER TWENTY TWO

Nick and Brian settled, for the moment, in Nick's office. Joanie brought them both their tenth, eleventh, cup of coffee for the day, even she'd lost count. The sign on the front door said closed. But to Nick and Brian that didn't really mean anything they were on call twenty-four, seven.

"Thanks, Joanie, goin' home?" Nick asked.

Joanie was exhausted. "Unless I'm needed for anything else."

"Nope," Brian said, "go on home." He settled back into the chair and looked at Nick. "So why aren't we at the Lone Star?"

Nick grinned. "Ah hell, Jez is probably there and Kristy might find out. Did you see Jez's jaw the last time they ran into each other."

Brian let out a belly laugh. "Shit, that was five months ago, surely Kristy's gotten over Jez by now."

"I think it's the other way around. Jez runs when she sees Kristy coming her way. And with Mavis backing her, Jez is running scared."

"That's some woman you've got there. Seven months pregnant and looks as good as ever. My problem is that now Sarah's getting ideas."

Nick gave Brian a hard gaze. "How come you and Sarah don't get married?"

Brian took a sip of coffee and set the mug on the table before him. He glanced up at Nick. "Because I think she's half way in love with that Hunter fella."

"Why would you say that? You're still together."

"I can't put my finger on it, but ever since she came back from California last year she's been different. When Hunter's in the room she can't keep her eyes off him. What the hell does he have that these women seem to want?"

Nick wasn't going to tell him what he knew. "Then why don't you just ask her to marry you?"

Brian took a drink of coffee and leaned forward. "For the same reason you aren't married to Kristy, because, this practice runs us, we don't run it. I can't give Sarah my full time attention any more then you can commit to Kristy. Christ, Kristy knows your limits and lives with them. Sarah doesn't want to do that."

"Kristy knew what she was getting into when we moved in together," Nick reminded him.

"Sarah told me Kristy may have to go to California for a couple of weeks with Hunter. How you gonna handle that?"

Nick shrugged. "There's nothing to handle. She's the mother of my children. I have her heart and her love. All of which Hunter doesn't have."

"Nick...she has his love. Sarah told me Hunter's been in love with her for years. He's just waiting for you to slip up, like a vulture, he'll be there to pick her up and make her feel better about herself. Shit, you stubborn fool, you've never once told her you loved her. It's been a one sided relationship from day one. Kristy never seemed to mind though, she's been more loyal to you then you have to her. She went after what she wanted until she got it. Whether it's going to be enough for her, Sarah says she can't tell. She's with Hunter more than she's with you. He's been there to catch her every time you've slipped up. He's the one who watches over her with those high-powered clients of hers. Sarah said he runs interference for her when things get out of hand. Yet she can't stop working, she feels she still has to take care of herself and the kids. Sarah said Kristy wouldn't depend on you for anything the kids needed."

"I think Sarah talks too much."

Brian grinned. "Sarah cares about Kristy. Shit, I think she halfway lives her life through Kristy. Sarah loves working with her and Hunter."

"And why are you telling me all this?"

"Because there are changes coming. I can see it in Kristy's eyes and in Sarah's. Even Mavis has changed. I'd like to tell you to chuck it all, grab Kristy and the kids and head back to the ranch to live...but I can't, and won't. I think Kristy and Nicki would die of boredom if they weren't in Dallas. Kristy's no longer ranch material, shit, she's no longer just the ranch foreman's daughter. She's become a woman that people look up to and depend on. Look what she's done for Mavis. No one considers Mavis just a barkeep anymore."

"And Kristy knows I fully intend to return to that ranch one day to live."

"Then it had better be before the kids are grown and you're too old to do anything with that roving eye of yours."

"I may have a roving eye, but that's as far as it's gone since I moved in with Kristy."

Brian stood and stretched, flexing the sore muscle of his arm. "You have it all Nick and you don't see it. What I'm sayin' is...oh hell, don't blow it."

After Brian went home for the night Nick stared at the closed door. He couldn't change even if he tried. He'd been set in his ways too many years. He loved Kristy in his own way. She hadn't complained. Kristy knew his goal was to make the ranch self-supporting, that's why he worked so hard in his practice. She knew he wanted to go there to live someday. Sure ranch life was hard as nails and sharper than a pitchfork but it was his and his kid's heritage. Like his Uncle Jack use to say 'the land is too tough to tame, yet we're rooted here forever'.

His mind went back to the place he and Kristy had called home and had loved growing up. He thought of the main house that looked as if it were embedded in stone. To the view from the encircling screened porch that was breathtaking. His mind wandered to the canyon to the south where cattle weren't seen for days at a time, and jackrabbits died from dehydration. How those red clay canyon walls at dusk reflected colors off the entrance sign to the ranch like a rainbow. Kristy loved the ranch as much as he did, she'd grown up

237

there. He recalled that little girl that would sometimes tag along behind him asking questions and always seem to be under foot. He'd watched her grow into a beautiful woman, one that had won his heart so long ago. By all rights she should still be there, and it was his fault that she'd left in the first place. Yet, she was here with him loving him, giving him the children he needed to keep the ranch in the family. Brian had to be wrong, Kristy would return to the ranch with him.

He needed to clear his head. Big Red headed home.

The house was quiet when he walked in. Where was everyone? He went to the barn but no one was there either. What now? Go inside to do paperwork or…he piled into Big Red and headed for the Lone Star, he didn't want to be alone.

"You mean I can come to California with you?" Sarah's smile brightened at the thought. "Will we be staying at Hunter's?"

Kristy gathered the files she needed to take home so she could load them onto her laptop. "Sarah, I'm seven months pregnant and I need you as my right hand when we get there. Yes, we'll be staying at Hunters. And yes, Hunter will be staying at Hunter's. So you'd better decide how you're going to handle things."

"Gracie's not going is she?" Sarah sounded a little bitter.

Kristy shook her head. "No, she's staying here for Nicki."

"What'd Nick say when you told him you'd be gone a couple of weeks?"

She slammed the briefcase shut. "The same thing he usually says…nothing."

"Then I guess things haven't changed for you."

"Sarah, do you have the tickets?"

"No, I do," Hunter grinned as he stood in the doorway.

Sarah said sheepishly, "Can we go out in the boat for a dinner cruise?"

Hunter gazed at Kristy. "I have a surprise for both of you, we have a new one hundred fifty foot yacht now. She's got five staterooms, five full baths, two thousand gallons fresh water in the tank, Jacuzzi's, and a massive dining room. She's ready for us when we want her. I'll see you ladies at the airport at six tomorrow morning."

"Good night, Hunter," Kristy said and watched him leave.

"A hundred and fifty foot yacht? Good grief, why?" Sarah was grinning broadly. "We could go to Hawaii in something that big. Wow…having Hunter all to ourselves on a long ocean voyage…" And into her bed.

Kristy raised an eyebrow, she knew what Sarah had in mind but doubted Hunter would ever go along with her dream of seduction. "I would imagine it's a yacht for charter."

At the car, Sarah said, "Should we stop by Dallas Rhodes and tell Mavis we're leaving?"

"I think I'd like that. I have a couple of things to check out with her before we take off tomorrow."

As they pulled into the parking lot, Sarah gasped. "Oh no," she grimaced at seeing Nick's truck in the parking lot next door. "Is he still doing that?"

Kristy didn't like seeing Big Red parked at the Lone Star but knew she couldn't stop Nick from doing whatever he wanted to do. They were like two strangers living in the same house but only passing each other on occasion. An overwhelming sadness swept over her as if she'd lost something she never really had.

Inside Dallas Rhodes Mavis gave Kristy a hug. "Hunter tells me that y'all are gonna be in California for a couple of weeks. I'm gonna miss ya."

"I have to train someone to take over while I'm unavailable. Once this baby is born I can spend the time I need out there."

"How's Doc feel about that?"

Kristy hugged her and laid her head against her shoulder. "Mavis, Nick lives his own life these days. We're just the family."

Mavis lowered her gaze and put her arm around her daughter. "Seems to me that's important."

Kristy sat down. "Only if it matters."

"Think you'll have some time to see your family before the little one comes?"

Kristy smiled at the thought of going home. "Nicki asked me the same thing. I think I'm going to take a couple of weeks off when I get back and she and I will go to the ranch. It's been much too long since she's seen her grandparents." She touched Mavis' hand. "She knows you're her grandmother."

"Oh baby, I know that, she's the light of my life, but she needs to see Ellen and Joe too."

"This will be our last chance to go back until I have this baby." She leaned back into the cushions of the couch and rubbed her stomach. "I must be having a boy because I'm exhausted most of the time and he kicks like Nicki never did."

Sarah put her hand on Kristy's stomach. "How I envy you."

Mavis gave Sarah a sidelong glance. "Ah hell, honey, that ole Brian needs to know how you feel."

"He knows, Mavis, and he's not budging."

Mavis grunted, "Men! Can't live with them, can't live without them."

Sarah laughed, "Yeah, they're really only good for one thing, and even then…"

She looked up to see Brian standing there. "What are you doing here?"

"Thought I'd take you to dinner." His smile warmed Kristy's heart and she thought Sarah looked stunned that he'd even asked.

Sarah was in his arms in an instant. Mavis led them into the restaurant and to her best table. Kristy smiled. Sarah really did love Brian, and Brian was trying to make an effort with her, but…she just hoped Sarah kept that in mind while they were in California. Hunter still hadn't committed to Gracie and being so far from Dallas…

Kristy finished her business and headed out the door to her car. She hesitated. Did she really want to know? She went on automatic and walked into the Lone Star. He was there in the shadows, but he wasn't alone. Kristy turned and walked back outside and to her car. She had to pack for her trip. She didn't need to be upset, not at this stage of her pregnancy. But she did feel sad.

Once home she had dinner with Nicki and Gracie. Later, she went to the bedroom to pack. In some ways she was looking forward to getting away. She needed to feel the sand beneath her feet, hear the sound of the ocean and inhale the fresh salt air. She needed time to regroup. She couldn't change the coarse of her life, especially where Nicki was concerned, but she could stand back and take a second look at her feelings for Nick. Maybe she should accept Hunter's proposal. She never felt upset and confused when she was around Hunter. She tired so easily these days that by the time her head hit the pillow she was sound asleep.

When she woke the next morning she was alone. Nick hadn't come home. With sadness in her heart, she said goodbye to Nicki and Gracie and promised to call every night.

"I wish I were going with you, Mama," Nicki said. "I like the ocean."

"I know you do. Maybe after we have the baby we can spend some time at Hunter's house. He would let us use it for a vacation."

"With Daddy?"

Kristy's smile faded as she glanced at Gracie. "I don't know if your daddy could get away. But I'll bet Gracie would love to spend time there."

Gracie smiled, "You bet I would. You have a safe trip and don't worry about Nicki. We have everything under control here."

Kristy hugged both of them and headed for the airport.

She was about to board the plane when she heard her name being called.

"Kristy!"

She turned around to see Nick coming toward her. He looked like hell.

"You didn't come home last night," she reminded him.

"I had to operate on a horse." He removed his hat and ran his fingers through his thick hair. "I couldn't let you go without seeing you and saying goodbye. I'm going to miss you." He put his arms around her and held her close.

"When I get back Nicki wants to go to the ranch and visit my parents. I told her we should go before I have the baby. If you can make it we'd love for you to go with us. If not…we understand." Why did the conversation seem so stilted and forced? She wondered why he even bothered to come to the airport. He was like a total stranger to her.

"I'd like that. I'll see if Brian or Henry can cover for me."

"I guess I'd better get on the plane, I'm sure Sarah's already onboard." She put her arms around him and hugged him tight. "Nick…Please watch over Nicki while I'm gone." She kissed his cheek.

His hand spread over her stomach and could feel the baby kicking as if it were saying goodbye. "Take good care of yourself. Nicki will be just fine." He moved his mouth over hers and held her tight. He

241

didn't want to let her go. When he did, he watched as she walked away to board the plane. He knew things had to change, she was slipping away from him just like Brian said.

Kristy found her seat next to Hunter and Sarah. His hand went over hers. "It'll be all right, Kristy."

She found herself with tears in her eyes. "I hope so. I can't uproot Nicole again."

"Then he'll have to come around."

Kristy looked at Sarah and she too had tears in her eyes. "I think this trip is going to be our turning point, Kristy. We can't go on the way we have been."

Hunter relaxed. He would be there for her.

By the time they reached the beach house the sun was setting. Kristy opened all the doors and windows and inhaled the fresh salt air. Hunter came to stand behind her put his arms around her and spread his hands out across her stomach.

"My, he's an active little thing tonight isn't he?" He kissed the top of her head.

Kristy felt herself relaxing for the first time in weeks. "He? Why are you so sure it's a boy? I love this place. You've spoiled us rotten. Would you take us to the Crab Cooker tonight? How about it Sarah?"

"Oh that sounds good."

After dinner the three of them kicked off their shoes and walked along the beach by moonlight. Hunter held each of their hands and considered himself one lucky man. He didn't mind being a stand in for their missing cowboys. He had them all to himself and that's the way he liked it.

"Kristy, I've convinced Mr. Meyer to meet with you tomorrow on the yacht for dinner. He's bringing his wife so we can do business then. I've hired a full time chef and a permanent Captain on board the new yacht. So we can all relax and enjoy the voyage. There are other clients lined up for the next two weeks, and we've extended the same invitation to all of them. So far no one has refused."

Kristy leaned into him. "Hunter why are you the one always looking after my best interest?"

"Because Matt expects you to give one hundred percent, no matter what condition you're in, and the new yacht is a now a tax write off for the agency. Besides, I know how tiring the drive to LA and back would be on you. Between Sarah and myself we'll help anyway we can, but these clients only want to deal with you."

"What'd you name the new yacht?" Kristy asked.

Hunter took her hand and pulled her close to him. "Dallas Luck."

"How appropriate. Are you going to charter it out?"

"You know me too well, don't you? Of course it's a charter. At one hundred fifty thousand a week to rent it'll pay for itself in no time. Our dear client Robert has already chartered it four times for his weeklong indiscretions. The yacht has a compressor and we can have a full time professional diver on board at all times if the client so desires, along with the ski boat; these are just two things Robert demands. I hope the hell no husband finds out where he's romancing their wives."

"Well," Kristy said, "at least he's not chasing after me. If you don't mind, I think I'll go back to the house and go to bed. This pregnancy is really tiring. I'll remember this before I ever have another one." Her hands went to the small of her back. Why was she so exhausted these days?

Sarah laughed and patted her on her shoulder. "I'll go back with you."

"No, stay and enjoy the evening." Kristy turned and walked back to the house. She climbed into bed but couldn't sleep. She missed being held by Nick, being loved by him, yet she hadn't had either of those things in months. After midnight she turned on the lamp and picked up a book to read. There was a light rap on the door.

"Come in," she said.

"Couldn't sleep?" Hunter said and entered the room, shutting the door behind him. "Can I get you anything?"

She shook her head. How did he know? Only Hunter would know how lonely and heartbroken she was.

He walked to the bed and stretched out beside her. "Let me rub your back like I did when you carried Nicki. You always relaxed when I did that."

Kristy turned onto her side and allowed him to work his magic on her aching muscles. "I'm as big as a cow, how can you stand to touch me?"

"You never minded me touching you the last time you were pregnant. Besides, to me you're beautiful in this natural condition."

"I wish Nick felt the same way. I swear, he'd rather have his hands on a pregnant mare."

"What can I say? A mare means money to him." Hunter was sorry he'd even opened his mouth. He could see how hurt she was and that wasn't his intention at all.

When his hands spread to her stomach she didn't stop him. The baby seemed to quiet as he rubbed her belly. She didn't stop him when he turned her onto to her back and kissed her gently while letting his hands roam at will. She needed to feel wanted and loved and she kissed him back. She hadn't spent more than an hour a day with Nick since she'd gotten pregnant and her hormones had been raging out of control for months. It wasn't Nick's fault, yet she needed to feel a man's hands on her body. She didn't stop Hunter when his mouth replaced his hands.

"Kristy," he moaned with excitement, "I don't expect anything from you…just let me love you." His hands played ever so slowly over her body just the way they use to do, only this time her body responded differently. She found herself aroused and in such an emotional state that she couldn't stop herself even if she tried. He removed her nightshirt and tossed it onto the floor. His fingers played along her thighs and in-between followed by his mouth. Her back arched, her breathing came in shallow breaths and he could tell she was hungry for release. His tongue moved up to trace patterns over her breasts before taking one in his mouth. "Kristy are you sure?" Hunter asked in a husky voice.

"I need Nick," she said in a choked voice, almost breathless. "I'm sure…" She knew Hunter understood he was now the stand in and she didn't object when he slowly slipped his hardness inside and made love to her. She needed Nick, what she had was Hunter. She was willing to take what she could get. Hunter was certainly no disappointment, he lived up to every promise he'd ever made to her and she would forever be grateful to him for caring enough to love her and make love to her. He gave her what she needed and when the passion became overwhelming he encouraged her to give herself to him. Hunter was very inventive when it came to making love to a very pregnant woman. For the next three hours Hunter drew Kristy out of herself and into a world he only dreamed of until tonight.

He brushed the damp strands of hair from her face and kissed her forehead. "I love you, Kristy," he whispered. "Tonight fulfills my love for you. Don't ever feel guilty about giving yourself to me." There were tears in her eyes as he stroked her forehead and he knew her decision was killing her. It was up to him to make her feel better about herself. "You're not married, you needed me. I'm not a stranger to you, I've loved you and your body for years. Feel sleepy yet?" He comforted her in his arms.

She reached over and turned out the lamp. "Hold me Hunter. Just hold me." Hunter's arms weren't Nick's, but she not only needed to be made love to but to be held by a man. She felt so unwanted by Nick. Why was Hunter always there for her when Nick wasn't? Was she a fool to stay with Nick when Hunter was offering her everything she could possibly need and want? She may have Nick's children, but it was Hunter who'd been there for her while she was pregnant...both times.

Hunter didn't need to be encouraged he cradled her in his arms knowing she could now sleep in peace. Letting him make love to her was a decision she hadn't made lightly. He also knew he now had a chance to win her love, their relationship had come full circle and he had her to himself for the next two weeks. He intended to make the most of the two weeks whether she let him make love to her again or not.

The next morning Hunter quietly returned to his own bed before Kristy or Sarah woke. He knew they would never speak of their night together and that was all right with him. He would always have the memory of their bodies in a captured embrace and fused as one.

Their days were busy. Unfortunately they couldn't find anyone to replace Kristy. So they did the next best thing and convinced new clients they might want to visit the Dallas office. Most had heard about the fabulous entertainment the Jordan Agency provided their clients and readily agreed to visit Big D. By the end of the two weeks, the older clients had been satisfied and had enjoyed their time on the yacht, even opting to rent it from the agency for two weeks at a time. And the new clients were welcoming a trip to Dallas.

On their last night Hunter suggested they order in and relax. He and Sarah shared a bottle of wine while Kristy settled on ice tea.

Sarah felt a little sad that it was their last evening at the beach house. She also felt sad and a little hurt that Hunter hadn't tried to take her to bed this trip. "I can't believe how big Matt's agency has become. It's amazing how many people have heard about Dallas Rhodes. I'm so lucky to be a part of all this."

"We all are," Kristy reminded her.

"What happens when we get home, Kristy? I mean…things can't go on the way they have been."

Kristy looked at Hunter who was devouring her with his eyes. "Sarah, I can't answer that. I'm taking two weeks off and going to the ranch. Maybe I'll have a new perspective on my life by then. Life will go on with or without Nick." She knew Hunter would always be there for her.

"That's so sad." Sarah curled her feet beneath her on the couch. "Do you want me to come to the ranch with you and Nicki?"

"You're welcome to come. Gracie will take some time off while we're there. She'll have her hands full in another month or so."

Hunter sipped his wine while staring intently at Kristy. "You're going to have this one earlier than you think."

Kristy and Sarah both gave him a doubting look. "How would you know about such things?" Sarah asked.

He just grinned, got up and poured himself a brandy.

CHAPTER
TWENTY THREE

When the phone rang Nick answered. "Nick, it's Joe. Hell, calves are dropping like rain. We've lost seven calves in three days to Brucellosis abortions."

"Oh Christ, what else?"

"Well, Jessie's having calving problems."

"She's our best cow, what do you mean?" Nick questioned.

Joe suddenly yelled into the phone, "I mean she can't have this blasted calf. She's been trying all morning and nothing happens."

"We'll be there as soon as possible." Nick realized the phone had gone dead.

Nick walked into Brian's office and explained the phone call. Brian called Henry to let him know they were headed out to the ranch.

"Tell him I'm flying," Nick ordered. Christ, Kristy was flying home today. He quickly called Gracie to tell her what his plans were but didn't give her any specific detail.

"Brian, you can follow in Big Red. Shit, if it's as bad as Joe says, it means a quarantine mess."

"Ain't Kristy and Sarah due in this morning?" Brian suddenly remembered.

"Can't worry about them, I have to get out of here. This mess could wipe us out of the cattle business. I have no idea how many cattle have been exposed."

"Get your ass out to the airport, I'll get what we need and follow."

"Joanie," Nick yelled, "I need a ride to the airport."

Joanie made her way into Nick's office. "Going to pick up Kristy?"

"No, I have to fly to the ranch. Maybe you can intercept her and let her know where I've gone. Brian's driving Big Red."

"Sure."

Joanie had just seen Nick's plane head for the clouds when she spotted Kristy, Sarah and Hunter coming down the walkway. Kristy walked slower these days, but looked beautiful. Hunter was doing his best to help her along.

"Joanie?" Kristy said, "Where's Nick and Brian?"

"Nick had an emergency at the family ranch. Brian's taking Big Red."

Kristy was near panic. "What happened?"

"Bangs."

"Oh shit," Sarah said.

Hunter just gave them a funny look. "Bangs?"

Sarah, who had worked long hard hours with Nick and Brian explained, "Bangs is caused by a bacteria. It causes infected blood and spontaneous abortions in cattle." She looked at Joanie. "How many?"

"Joe said they've lost seven in three days."

Kristy turned pale. "I was going to the ranch, but in my condition I don't want to risk hurting the baby."

Hunter gave her a worried look. "You mean it could hurt an unborn child?"

Kristy stared at him. "I don't know, but I don't want to risk it. It's one of those diseases that can be spread by flies to man and other animals, to cattle by contact and direct transfer. With all those babies being born dead the discharges from the cows are filled with infectious organisms." She clung to Sarah's arm. "This could wipe out the entire herd if they don't get all the contaminated cattle."

Sarah looked at Joanie. "Quarantine?"

"I suppose. Look, I have to get back to the clinic. Nick just wanted me to let you know where he had gone and why."

Kristy smiled and thanked her.

"Hunter, take Kristy home, I'm going to the clinic and see if I can catch up with Brian. Kristy I'll ride out there with him if he hasn't already left."

They watched Sarah's retreating form race out of the airport. "Let's get you home," Hunter grabbed their luggage and headed toward the Dallas ranch.

Nick buzzed the ranch house to announce his arrival since the landing strip was several miles away. When no one came out of the house he found it odd. Maybe they're already at the landing field? So, with normal procedure he circled the landing area and inspected the strip from the air. In the middle of the runway was a tractor that seemed to be broken down. He circled the field as he watched a second pickup drive up and pull the tractor off the runway.

Nick landed and jumped out of the plane. "What the hell happened? Why was that tractor in the middle of the goddamn runway?" He happened to notice blood on the bumper hitch on the tractor. "Is anyone hurt?"

Joe shook his head. "No, that's cow blood. It's from Jessie."

"Just tell me about Jessie," Nick instructed and climbed into Joe's old truck.

Rowdy said, "Well…I tried to pull the calf by hand but it was too stuck. She went down on the ground when I tried to jack the calf out with the calf jack you left us."

Nick was getting worried. "And?"

"Well, to make a long story short I still couldn't get the calf out."

Nick glared at him. "And?"

"Oh hell then I used the tractor."

Nick, who had been drinking a warm Coca Cola choked and spit half of it all over the dashboard of the truck. The dust turned to mud.

"But," Joe added, "he got the front half of the calf out. Hell, the rest he left for you. Do you think we should look at the cow today?"

"Good God! Do we have any help? Is Jessie already dead?" Nick sputtered.

Joe spit tobacco out the truck window and wiped his chin. "No.

She bellowed a lot, but she's okay. Maggie's sending some boys."

"We'd better look for Jessie," Nick ordered.

"Ain't Kristy flyin' home today?" Joe asked.

"Should be home by now," Nick replied and hoped to hell she understood why he couldn't be with her. Evidently Joe had called the neighbors to round up the cattle for testing. At the same time he still didn't know how many head might have been exposed to the disease. Yet he didn't want to leave anything to chance.

"She's due in a few weeks, ain't she?" Rowdy asked.

"Who?" Nick half way listened.

"Kristy."

"Yeah, yeah, in a few weeks." The truck pulled up and stopped at the bunkhouse. Nick got out and noticed Maggie's crew were the first to show. These cowboys were as leathery and rugged as the canyon terrain. He'd known most of them all his life and as he looked at them now he realized none had changed a lick.

"So, how's it going boys?" Nick asked.

"Oh same as ever."

Nick looked at Roper and Scram sitting on the bunkhouse porch. "I need the two of you to help find Jessie."

"Yeah, yeah," they said.

Roper said, "I think she's up by the front gate."

Joe said, "Nope, I left her in the pens by the lower barn."

Scram then asked Roper, "Do we need to take our horses?"

"I told you she's penned." Joe reminded him.

Scram scratched his head and the two men climbed into the back of the truck. Nick watched as Rex arrived with his horse already saddled in the trailer. Nobody seemed to be able to tell Nick where the cow was. They decided to try the lower barn area.

Jessie was nowhere in sight. The gate had been left open. Uncle Jack came to mind, except he was resting in the family plot. Nick just shook his head. This ranch was running deeper into debt as they talked. Between Jack's management and Joe's, nothing had changed.

"What's this mess, Nick?" Rowdy asked and pointed to something on the ground.

Part of the remains of the calf were still near the pen. Nick took a quick look at it and knew it had been dead for days before Rowdy had pulled it from Jessie. He also suspected the mess was full of contaminating bacteria. "Burn and bury those remains immediately," Nick ordered.

Rex spotted Jessie not far from the front gate. He came back for Nick. "I smelled her before I saw 'er," he said.

Rowdy and Scram twitched their noses. "Yep, she's rotten all right."

The minute Jessie saw Rowdy she took off running. Nick could only guess but the memory of Rowdy pulling her calf out of her didn't set well. They blocked the road that crossed over the pond dam while Rex herded her down the path. When she hit dead end Rex roped her and tried to cross back over the dam. Scram got his loop over her neck too yet Jessie made her objections known.

Rex tied the cow to the nearest mesquite tree while Scram hung on for dear life. Nick watched as Jessie fought but then she got so mad she collapsed in anger. Her legs locked and her nostrils flared as she fell on her side and groaned.

Nick grabbed two O.B. gloves and went to inspect the damage. The discharge that rolled out of her made flies immigrate from Montana as the odor hit the air. He knew that the bacteria could be transmissible to man, it caused Undulant Fever, a serious public health problem that often plagued cattle practitioners. Yet, he didn't know if Jessie had been exposed to the infected cattle. He took extra precautions.

"Hold her good," he ordered Roper and Scram. But as he reached inside he heard:

"Oh shit, Doc!"

"Hold her!" Nick yelled and tried to maintain his position. His efforts were in vain. Jessie stood and threw him around the place like a rag doll. Her tail beat him across the face as her long horns tried to hook everything in sight. The Mexican cross-bred cow got madder and madder and Nick found himself covered with blood and afterbirth. But he hung in there.

Roper yelled out, "Hey Doc, you're bull-doggin' 'er from the wrong end!"

Scram laughed as he yelled "Just hang on, Doc. You can do it!"

Nick gripped Jessie's tail like a life line until she fell again. Quickly, he extracted the nasty decayed fetal parts. The cow fought the entire procedure as he dug the calf out, piece by piece. Jessie thrashed about. He finally got all the calf removed and flushed her out with antibiotics. He was exhausted by the time he'd finished.

"Let's load 'er up, Doc," Rex hollered.

Scram had pulled Rex's horse trailer close enough so the cow could be loaded and returned to the pens. Nick took one look at Jessie and knew she had other plans. The massive beast exploded before he could get out of her way. She pulled enough slack in the restraint ropes to whirl her body furiously with Nick in her path. He went flying into the pond while Roper, Scram and Rex fell to the ground...laughing. Nick landed waist deep and face down in the water and mud.

Roper yelled, "Ah Doc, you needed a bath anyway."

Nick failed to see the humor. "This ain't been my day," he said as he slapped the surface of the water with a handful of green moss. "I just wanted to meet Kristy at the airport and take her home."

Slinging mud and grass Nick crawled up the side of the bank. He watched as Rex loaded the old heifer into the trailer, cowboy style. Nick rolled his body into the bed of the truck and Rex stepped on the gas. When Rex slammed on the brakes at the corral gate the cow must have been glad to see the pens because she unloaded with very little fight.

"Doc fixed her," Roper said as Joe came out to watch.

Joe took one look at Nick and said, "God, you're a mess, Doc."

Nick took one look at himself and scraped off a handful of mud from his overalls and hurled it at Roper. He smelled like something dead and his overalls were stuck to his body.

"Ah shit," Joe said, "Ellen's gonna make you bathe outside."

"Anything's better than this," Nick said with disgust and suddenly wanted to be in a scented tub with Kristy pulling her legs around him and slipping inside her.

Back at the house Ellen fed the hungry men while Nick showered. After dinner they discussed plans for the roundup. Everyone knew the real work was yet to come.

Nick called Kristy.

"How's it going?" She asked.

"We'll know by tomorrow. How was the flight?"

"Exhausting. Has Brian arrived yet?"

"Yeah, he made it in time for supper."

"Do you think I should delay coming out?" she asked.

"Don't you dare set foot out here until we determine the damage. If you have to wait until the baby's born, then we'll come back later."

He talked to Nicki for a few minutes before he had to go back to work. He felt a tug at his heart and realized he wanted to be home with his family tonight but it wasn't possible.

By the next afternoon they had determined that only one third of the herd could have been exposed to the infected cattle that had been isolated in an area on the ranch. The primary Longhorn herd had not been involved. After testing seven hundred cows the State vet said they would handle the rest. Nick knew the quarantine wouldn't be lifted for months. Five days later he flew home.

The Bangs incident gave Kristy a lot to think about. Nick was the last remaining Chandler old enough to actually run the ranch. Yet, he didn't seem to want to slow down or settle down, so what now? He shouldn't be busting his butt in Dallas if his heart was at the ranch.

A month later Kristy sat in her office going over her latest client's demands when Sarah walked in.

"I'm getting married."

Kristy's mouth dropped open and her head snapped to attention. "Brian?"

Sarah's smile cheered Kristy up. "Can you believe it? He actually asked me last night."

"How old is Brian now?" Kristy teased.

"Old enough to settle down."

"I have two questions for you. When? And am I going to lose you as my secretary?"

"I'm going to keep working and as soon as I can haul his ass off to City Hall. I don't want any fancy wedding. I want it quick and legal." Sarah stood her ground.

"Then it's all arranged. Is there anything I can do for you?"

"Not one damn thing except be there for me."

Kristy pushed herself away from the desk and stood. Her back ached, she hadn't seen her feet for a month and she was exhausted most of the time. "Plan to have any kids?" She grinned and pressed her hands to the small of her aching back.

Hunter walked in. "How are you feeling today?"

"Sarah's getting married."

Hunter leaned back and grinned. "So you've finally lassoed that cowboy of yours. When's the happy day?" He walked to Kristy and put his arm around her waist to lead her to the couch.

"City Hall, any day," Sarah laughed. "If you get any bigger Kristy you won't be able to walk up the steps to City Hall."

"I told you she's farther along than she thinks," Hunter reminded them.

Kristy glanced up at him. "I think he's just going to be bigger than Nicole was."

Sarah grinned and relaxed on the couch next to Kristy. "So have you talked to Nick about the ranch yet?"

"What are you talking about?" Hunter questioned.

Kristy placed her arm across her extended stomach. "Nick's the last Chandler. Right now dad and the boys are running the place. I thought maybe I could spend at least a week each month there with the kids. It would give my children an idea of what the ranch is all about and I could help mom and dad at the same time. I think I need to help them out as much as I can. And, they would love having their grandchildren around more often."

"Oh hell what do you know about running a ranch?" Hunter growled. He didn't like her idea one bit.

"I grew up on that ranch and there's plenty I can do. For one thing I want to pave the runway. I have the money now to do that. I'd like to bring in some new breeding stock. I have the money to do that too."

Sarah touched Kristy's stomach to feel the flutter. "And what will Nick have to say about all this?"

"I don't know. Maybe if I present the fact Nicki and this new one are half Chandler's and I need a runway to land on. Oh I don't know…"

"I won't fight you on this because it obviously means a lot to you," Hunter said, "but I want you to have a home office setup because I need you working while you're there." He stood back and leaned against her desk. "Say…why don't you think about allowing some of our west coast city dudes come visit the ranch, get the feel of the real thing."

Kristy smiled at the idea. "I'm only going to be there one week of the month. You expect me to entertain and work at the same time?"

"No, make them work. Shit, let them get manure on their brand new cowboy boots, put them in the saddle to wear a shine on those new jeans they'll be wearing. Put them to work."

"Hunter, we sometimes think alike. The only problem I'll have is getting Nick to go along with it. It would mean having to build a separate bunkhouse, I'd need to…what am I saying, I can't do any of this without Nick, it's his ranch."

Sarah patted her hand. "There's time for that. I think first we should have this baby, then make plans for you going to the ranch."

Hunter sat back in the chair staring out at the skyline. "You know, Kristy, if Nick doesn't want to go along with your idea we could buy our own ranch and set it up as a kind of dude ranch. You, Matt and I already have a huge investment in Mavis, and Dallas Rhodes has more than paid back what we put into it. I'll bet we could do the same thing with a working cattle ranch."

Kristy could hardly believe anything on the scale of a cattle ranch would work, but she could be wrong. If Nick didn't want to make the ranch self-supporting with strangers riding the range…then maybe Hunter's idea was valid.

Kristy looked at Sarah. "What do you think about Hunter's idea?"

Sarah, caught off guard by the question, seemed to think a moment before she answered. "What if the ranch wasn't too far from Dallas? Just far enough out there that the city slickers would get the feel of the west, but could still come to Dallas Rhodes for entertainment…if they wanted too?"

Kristy looked at Hunter. "Maybe she's right. Nick's ranch is out is the middle of nowhere. I think she might be right. Instead of investing my money in a runway and stock, it might be wise to find something already up and running."

Hunter looked at both women. "Let me talk to Matt about this and check with some ranch brokers. We just may be getting into the cattle business after all."

Kristy and Sarah just stared at each other. Kristy wondered if they knew what the hell they were doing? Did she want her money tied up in something that wasn't going to be inherited by her children? But on the other hand it could mean an income for the entire family.

CHAPTER
TWENTY FOUR

In the month that Kristy had been back in Dallas Nick hadn't spent two hours straight with her or Nicki and felt guilty as hell. His days started early and stretched into the wee hours of the morning only to start all over again with sunrise. He was burning out but didn't know how to say no to patients or their owners. He'd started the day with two dogs, each hit by cars, then onto a downtrodden old farm where the cows were sick and dying, then back to the clinic to operate on a big fluffy white cat, then on to horse ranches. Back and forth, from outside to inside, shit he didn't know whether to put on coveralls or a smock half the time.

The clock on Big Red's dashboard read two a.m. All he wanted to do was shower, climb into bed, and hold Kristy in his arms for what was left of the night. When he pulled into the driveway the lights were on in the house.

"I'm glad you're here, Nick, we tried to reach you but nothing seemed to work." Gracie said.

"What's wrong?"

"It's Kristy, Sarah took her to the hospital, she's in labor."

Nick paled. "When?"

"About two hours ago."

Big Red's tires smoked as he raced toward the hospital. If he walked into that hospital and found Hunter hovering over her...His pager went off. Nick found himself headed into the badlands to treat a horse with colic.

Sarah gripped Kristy's hand. "Why didn't you call Hunter? Shit, Kristy he knows about this kind of thing..." Sarah was sweating as much as Kristy.

"Because..." When another contraction hit she tried to breathe. "Because...I want...Nick...here."

"But we can't find him. I'm no good at this sort of thing, you know that."

Kristy tried to smile and brushed a wet strand of hair from her face. "I'm sorry. If you want to leave you can. I know this is hard on you."

The door flew open and Sarah looked up with relief flooding her face. "Hunter's here!" She made it sound like the Calvary had just arrived in the nick of time.

"How long has she been like this?" Hunter growled and rushed to Kristy's side to take up her hand in his and place it to his lips.

"Why are you here? How'd you even know?" Sarah asked.

"When did this start?" His tone demanded an answer.

Kristy was overwhelmed by another contraction. "About...midnight."

"She called me. We tried to find Nick. Brian's out there some place lookin' for him."

"Why didn't you call me? I had to hear it from Gracie and she's upset. She said Nick came home and was headed here but obviously he got a call..." He watched her face closely and could see another contraction coming on. He held her hand tight.

Kristy wasn't going argue with him, she needed him. "Doctor Morris says he's a good size baby but not as big as he would have been. He thinks he'll be just fine."

The hours wore on and Kristy strained while Hunter coached her. Sarah was amazed at his connection to Kristy, his patience, his concern that she breathe just right. She watched as he stroked Kristy's contracting belly and talked gently to her. He fed her ice chips when her mouth became dry. He praised her when she made it through another contraction. He wiped her damp forehead. He pressed her fingers to his lips and kissed them gently as he told her over and over again how proud he was of her. He was doing everything that Nick should be doing. It angered Sarah to think Nick was missing the birth of his second child.

"Where the hell is the cowboy," Hunter looked at Sarah and growled. "Hold on. You're getting there. Inhale slowly...that's right...pant."

Kristy groaned. "He's probably arm deep in some old horse." She hoped she didn't sound bitter.

Hunter put his mouth against her damp forehead. "Don't talk. I told you this one would be early. And, by the looks of you it's time to get the good doctor in here." He picked up the buzzer and pushed it.

Hunter stood away from the bed as the doctor came in. "Either one of you going into delivery with her?"

Sarah put her hand on Hunter's arm. "But Nick's the father."

"Yeah and he was the father last time too, but where the hell is he? I'm going in. I was with her last time. Doc, point me to the scrubs?"

Doctor Morris looked up over his mask and Kristy could tell he was smiling at her frustration. "Yep, he's a big one," he said, "give me one more push, Kristy."

Hunter found himself holding his breath and hadn't realized it until he heard Kristy gasping for air and the baby squalling at the other end.

"Hear there's a ragin' storm outside," Doctor Morris said as he handed Hunter the baby. "Guess we're in for some heavy Dallas weather."

Eight pounds four ounces, twenty-two inches long. He looked just like Nicki, which meant he looked just like his father. She'd given Nick a son to go with his beautiful daughter. Hunter could kill the sonofabitch for the way he was treating her.

"Well?" Kristy whispered in an exhausted voice, "aren't you going to let me see him?"

Hunter held the baby close to Kristy so she could look at him.

"Oh Hunter, he looks exactly like Nicole when she was born." She touched the baby's cheek and grasped his tiny finger. "He's beautiful."

Hunter kissed the baby's cheek and handed him back to the nurse.

Doctor Morris patted Hunter on his back. "Yep, if Nick asks her real nice she'll give him six more just like him."

Hunter hoped to hell Nick fell off the face of the planet. He'd been more of a father figure then Nick ever had. He'd been there through both of Kristy's births. He knew her better then anyone else and she certainly deserved better then what she was getting from Nick. This could be the turning point for the two of them.

"Thank you, Hunter," Kristy whispered as they wheeled her out of the delivery room.

He bent over and placed a kiss on her forehead. "You did it. I love you."

Kristy was sad that it was Hunter saying those words of endearment to her. She was exhausted but happy and found herself falling asleep.

Sarah came to stand beside Hunter as they watched Kristy being taken to her room. "Hunter, are you all right?"

He was angry. "Hell no. I hope to hell she never sets foot on that ranch or gives that cowpoke another chance. She has her children, now she needs a husband. I don't want to see her treated this way ever again."

Sarah silently agreed with him.

The next morning Kristy propped herself up in bed and smoothed the covers across her lap. Nick stood there staring at her. God, he wished he could tell her how much she meant to him? That she had become his life, his reason for doing things. She'd given him two of the most beautiful children he'd ever seen and yet never complained when he didn't come home or had to work late. She never made the obvious demand on him to marry because she knew he wasn't ready. His gaze went out the window and could see the storm raging outside. He was glad she was safe, that the baby was safe.

Holding her son in her arms Kristy looked at Nick. "Well," she said, "what do you think of him?"

Nick pulled up a chair beside the bed and took her hand in his. "He looks so much like Nicki. You're amazing." He stood and sat on the bed beside her, holding her hand in his. His head lowered and his mouth covered hers in a long, warm, loving kiss. He lifted his head and gazed into those blue-green eyes of hers. "I'm sorry about last night...I had to operate on a horse."

Kristy was speechless but expected as much. A horse came before the birth of his own son. He was certainly telling her where she fit in his life and she had to accept it. Once again Hunter had come through for her, something she would never forget. She took a deep breath to regain her composure.

She forced a smiled. "Did you want to name him?"

Nick's smile warmed her heart. He reached out and took hold of a tiny finger. "Would you mind if I named him after my dad? John Chandler."

Kristy nodded her approval and gazed down at her son. "John Dallas Williams."

Nick raised an eyebrow. "Dallas?"

"If I hadn't come to Dallas I never would have had him. Dallas has been good to me in a lot of ways. There have been so many things happening in my life in the past few weeks that I've wanted to talk to you about...but you're never home. Do you think you could find an hour or two one of these days so we could talk?"

His sense of guilt overwhelmed him. "I'm taking some time off to be with my family." He took John from Kristy and held him close to his chest watching the tiny baby breathing. He couldn't believe he was actually holding his son. Someone to carry on his name.

"I think you should go home and tell Nicki about her baby brother. You've made her one happy little girl."

He put the baby in the bassinette beside the bed, pulled her into his arms and hugged her tight. After Nick was gone the door opened and Hunter walked in with a large bouquet of yellow roses. "How are you?" He sat the roses on a nearby table.

Kristy spread her arms and Hunter marched to her bed and sat down letting her comfort him. "I'm fine. John Dallas is fine. Thank you for caring about me and being there when I needed you a second time." After all he'd done for her, why couldn't she love him the way she loved Nick?

Hunter looked down at her and smiled. "John Dallas? Johnny D. John D. J.D. Williams. Yep, that's a Texas name all right. Although, I predict as a young sex pistol he'll be called Dallas or John Dallas by those newborn cowgirls out there."

"Nick wanted to name him after his dad, John Chandler. You know why I wanted to call him Dallas."

"Because of everything that's happen here. I understand. Has

Sarah seen him?"

"I think so. I'm afraid seeing me in labor scared her. I'm sure she'll be in later."

Hunter picked John up and cradled him in his large arms, kissing his tiny forehead. "God, he looks so much like Nicole. She's going to be elated. You've given me a hell of a lot to think about these days. I'll let the clients know you're on maternity leave." He put the baby back in his bed. "Kristy, I want you to think about your life long and hard. Is Nick what you really want? Or do you want these kids to have Taylor added to their names?"

Kristy's heart was breaking for her, for Nick, for Hunter, and most of all for her precious children. She looked away from him and out the window. "I can handle most of whatever comes up from home for the next few weeks, but I'll be back to work after that." She took a deep breath then said, "Gracie wanted this baby as much as I did, it'll give her the experience she needs." This was the only answer she could give him at the moment.

Hunter chuckled. "You're avoiding what you need to face. I'll see you later." He kissed her on the forehead and walked out of the room. His heart was breaking for her. She'd gone after something she thought she wanted and it had backfired on her.

Nick met Brian at the Lone Star that night.

Brian shook Nick's hand and congratulated him on his son.

"Shit," Brian said, "having Sarah in the labor room with Kristy is makin' her think twice before wantin' any kids."

"I'm sure you'll change her mind when the time is right," Nick assured him.

Brian shook his head, "Ain't so sure about that."

"Mavis!" Nick yelled, "You have a grandson."

By the time Mavis walked to Nick's table there were tears in her eyes. "No kiddin'. How's Kristy? So what'd you name him? Joe and Ellen know yet?"

"We named him John, after dad. Kristy gave him the middle name of Dallas. He's the spitting image of Nicki."

Mavis smiled broadly and slapped Nick on the back. "In other words, Kristy's reproduced you yet again. She's sure somethin' ain't she."

Nick's smile lit up the old Lone Star. "She sure is."

"Well hold onto your shorts, here comes Jez," Mavis said in an angry tone.

"So what'd she have this time?" Jez asked.

"I have a son."

Jez took one look at Mavis in her defensive mood and nodded before walking into the darkest part of the bar.

Mavis asked, "Did Kristy talk to you about the ranch?"

Nick scowled creating lines between his brows. "What about the ranch?"

"She wants to take the kids there for one week of each month. Wants them to get to know their roots. Hunter told her to let some of those citified dudes and dudette clients of hers come for a visit and put them to work. Those Japanese business fella's would pay big bucks to play cowpoke on a real ranch. I believe he said, 'let 'em get manure on those new boots and lose the color of their new jeans'. Kristy's been wantin' to talk to you. This would bring in money for the ranch. Kristy wants to pave the runway and build a bunkhouse for those city slickers to stay in."

"Jesus Christ!" Nick grumbled, "Where the hell have I been?"

Brian grinned and took a sip of beer. "Working your ass off so you could pay for the ranch."

Nick thumbed his Stetson back on his head. "She really wants to take the kids out there?"

Mavis threw a bar towel over her shoulder. "She said you're the last Chandler old enough to run the ranch. Joe and the others are doing it now. Even though the kids are Williams' she wants them to take pride in the place their grandparents live and work. Says she's got enough money to bring in new stock if you'll let her."

Nick sat back on the bar stool and stared at Brian. "Did you know about any of this?"

"Ah hell, Sarah can't keep her mouth shut for a minute once she gets home. She says Kristy's been afraid of steppin' on your goddamn boot toes, afraid you wouldn't let her help. Says that pride of yours is bigger then the state of Texas. But, Kristy understands. And if you don't want her help then she and the agency are going to buy their own cattle ranch and let the city slickers do their thing close to Dallas."

"She once told me that what's hers is mine and that included the kids."

"So?" Brian said, "What do you think about all this?"

"Where do you fit in?"

"Ah hell, Sarah wants to stay Kristy's secretary, says that both of us could use some time off to be with family. I don't mind runnin' the clinic while you're at the ranch, we've got Hank helpin'. It's only one week of the month...for now."

"I've got a lot to think about. Think I'll head on home to be with Nicki. I bring Kristy and John home tomorrow. Man, has my home life changed."

"Yeah," Mavis grinned, "but for the better. I'll be out tomorrow to see my new grandbaby." She watched as Nick left. If he only knew that he was about to lose Kristy he might do the right thing. "So what do you think he'll do Brian?"

"Hell if I know."

Kristy couldn't sit still, she had to be at her computer working. She loved her children but since coming home she was restless. She loved the way Nick couldn't keep his hands off Johnny, as he called him, and with Nicki in hand the three of them would wander out to the corral or barn where Nick would talk to the baby in his arms. Nicki could be heard telling Johnny all about horses. Two months old and John was already getting an education on ranch life. She was sure Nick would have him in a saddle by the time he could sit up. Gracie couldn't keep her hands off John either. Kristy knew he was one loved baby. She tried hard not to think of Hunter's offer to her and her children.

At dinner Nick said, "Shouldn't we be flying to the ranch to show Johnny off to his grandparents?"

"Please, Mama, please," Nicki pleaded.

Kristy smiled her answer. "I'd love that."

By the time the plane landed and everyone was loaded into pickup trucks Kristy could see a change occurring in Nick. He seemed more relaxed, at home and in charge. Before the sun set he'd ridden the range, checked fence line and played vet to a dozen head of cattle.

Ellen had Johnny in her arms with Joe cooing over him most of the evening. Nicki was looking at old photo albums that Ellen had brought out with pictures of both Nick and her mother in it.

Kristy took a cup of coffee to the screened porch and sat in the old swing still hanging from the porch roof and watched Nick dismount from Rascal. God, how she loved that man. He was everything to her. He'd given her two beautiful children. He was the best vet he could possibly be...yet, he was failing miserably in the fatherhood department. He was rarely home but when he was Nicki was overjoyed to have his attention. Nicki had missed not having her father around for so many years, and now it was as if she couldn't get enough of his attention. Nicki thrived on Nick's attention. Whatever the reasoning, Nicki loved her dad. Kristy realized there wasn't enough time in the day or enough of Nick to go around for her and the kids. This was something she either had to change or accept. She needed to take some time and fully analyze their relationship once and for all. Her daughter was happy, but was she?

"You look mighty content," Nick said as he slapped his gloves against his chaps. He came to sit beside her in the swing and took a sip of her coffee.

Content? She needed a distraction. "Nick, look at the floor. Aren't those our handprints in the cement?"

Nick laughed and took his hand in hers. "I do believe they are. My God you were young when we put them there for posterity."

"And now here we are, with two children. I never thought I'd be sitting here like this, with you, having your children playing in the other room. It was a fantasy of a young girl. I envisioned you here with Mallory and she having your children. After I found out I was pregnant with Nicki and left the ranch my dreams died. I was alone. I never thought I'd see you again. This is taking my breath away."

His arms went around her to hold her close. "You've always taken my breath away. I could never see Mallory out here it wasn't her style. She didn't want kids. When I saw you going into that barn that day my heart stopped. In my mind you were always meant to be at the ranch. I had no idea you'd given me a daughter. It was as if you'd jumpstarted my life when I finally met Nicki."

"I'd like to talk to you about some improvement ideas I have for the ranch."

Nick put his arm around the back of the swing and let his hand rest against her shoulder. "I already know about them. Mavis and Brian."

She laid her head against his shoulder. "I should have been the one to tell you what I had in mind, and to ask you what your vision is for the ranch."

"Seems I saw more of them then I did you. Hear you want to pave the runway."

She gazed up at him. "Are you angry?"

He pulled her closer to him. "No. I think we should pave it. Shit, if we're flying down once a month we need to know we can land in any kind of weather. Maybe we'll evidentially build a hangar too."

"I think these old cowboys of yours will like having someone around to tell them what to do. Dad said they've been getting lazy without direction."

"Nicki will have them shaped up again in no time. She told me last night she intends to have a sister she can call Sierra. Where the hell did she get that name?"

Kristy's mouth dropped open as she stared at Nick. "She said what?"

"You planning to give me more kids?"

"I hadn't thought about it. Good God, my worse nightmare. Oh no...I have to set her straight about this." She suddenly realized Nicki was trying to form a family in hopes they would actually become one. No, she couldn't let Nicki control their lives like that.

Nick laughed and pulled her back into his arms. "Sierra, huh?"

"Sierra Nevada Mountains, no doubt. We use to ride trail. Some friends use to ride the Levi's ride and tie one hundred miles before it ended. I'm afraid Nicki has to know she can't run, or plan our lives to suit her. My God, she's so much like you. I see your attitude in her every day. There won't be a man around who will ever tie her down once she's grown."

Nick leaned forward and rested his arms on his thighs. "How about two daughters and two sons?"

"Nick...your daughters would end up being the vets while your sons would be chasing every cowgirl between here and Dallas. I don't think so. My children are my responsibility and I can't and won't handle more than two of them by myself. And even now, there are times when I can't seem to give them what they need."

"Look at that sunset."

"Nick, are you happy?"

He leaned over and kissed her on the cheek. "Right now, home again, here with you and the kids, is exactly as I pictured my life so many years ago. It's not a reality yet, but maybe someday."

"Did Mavis tell you about the other half of my ranch plan?" She asked, dreading his answer.

"You mean building a bunkhouse for the citified foreigners? Hell, if they'll pay to wear chaps and sit in a saddle all day to round up cattle, why not? Give our old cowpokes a reason to get up in the mornings."

Kristy started to laugh. "Oh my God, I have visions of Guido riding range with Old Jake. Or my Japanese clients with their big hats trying to hang on for dear life when Rowdy takes them out. I think even Mom would be revived having to cook for so many new faces. And dad?" She became pensive. "Dad has his grandchildren beside him and that's all he seems to need at this stage of his life. Did you see the way he took over when Nicki put Johnny in his arms? Give him two more grandkids and he'll think he's raised a dynasty."

"Then you'll be all right with us spending some time each month out here?"

"I wouldn't have brought it up if I weren't. But...I plan to spend the rest of the time working and making sure Dallas Rhodes keeps bringing in the money."

He nibbled on her ear. "Think I could use one of those special California massages of yours tonight, what do you say?"

"Right after you put your kids to bed. I'll run the bath. I've had a long, hard day and could use a hard night," she teased. Tonight for the first time in a very long time she would have him all to herself and she intended to make the most of it. She would show him how much she loved and needed him.

266

CHAPTER
TWENTY FIVE

Kristy looked at Mavis and scowled. "What do you mean you don't sing country western?"

Mavis took Kristy's hands in hers. "Look, I married a country western barkeep, but in New York I sang Jazz and Blues. You can't expect me to fill in here when one of your acts doesn't make it."

Kristy's mouth dropped open. "Blues?" Crap, her opening act had strep throat, the backup band missed their flight. What was she supposed to do now? She picked up the phone and dialed Hunter. "Do we have a piano player who can play jazz or blues?"

Hunter had to think a minute. "Yeah, that Kenny Thornton fellow. Want me to give him a call? How about a guitar player?"

"Call anyone that can fill the bill. The acts didn't show, Mavis just informed me she can only sing jazz or blues. She's going on whether she likes it or now."

"Oh holy hell, this I have to see. I'll be right over."

"Mavis, you're going on tonight. Get out any sheet music you want to sing and have it ready for the piano player. I think we'll have a guitar player too."

Mavis stood her ground. "Like hell! I haven't sung in years."

"Get your ass in that dressing room and get yourself dolled up. You are going on."

"If you weren't my daughter I'd have you quartered and hung out to dry right now." She smiled and as she did the features of her face softened. "But...since you are my kin I don't want to let you down. Who's playing piano?"

"Someone named Kenny Thornton. Hunter's handling that part."

Kristy called Nick to let him know the situation and as she hung up could hear his uproarious laughter coming from the other end of the phone. She was glad he found her situation funny, because she didn't.

Twenty minutes later Hunter, grinning from ear to ear, walked in. "Is he here yet?"

Kristy was sitting at the bar with her face in her hands and a shot of Jose Cuevo Gold before her. She nodded. "He just got here. He's in there with Mavis." She turned to face Hunter. "I've got thirty minutes before the show starts. I have four California hot shots sitting at the front table. Two record producers who are disappointed that the acts they came to hear aren't going to show up. The club is packed tonight and what I'm left with...I don't even know if she can carry a tune."

Hunter put his arm around her to comfort her. "Can you sing?"

She leered at him. "Only if there's no one around for miles and the cows don't mind."

"But can you sing?"

She continued to glare at him. "Some. But, there is no way..."

"Let's go check on Mavis and see what's happening."

Kristy stood there stunned as she listened to Mavis rehearsing with the piano player and Joey Metcalf, blues guitarist. Hunter was just as stunned. They looked at one another and smiled.

"Ladies and gentlemen, thank you for coming to Dallas Rhodes tonight. I'm Kristy Williams and as you may have heard our opening act is under the weather." She held up her hands. "But...I don't think you'll be disappointed with the singer I'm about to introduce to you. Mavis Rhodes is the owner of Dallas Rhodes. Mavis is a Blues singer so let's have a round of applause for Dallas Rhodes herself, Mavis Rhodes."

Mavis didn't disappoint anyone in the room. Kristy sat there absolutely stunned at Mavis' ability to belt out the Blues as if she'd lived every suffering note that came out of her mouth. Hunter sat beside Kristy grinning. He ran a finger down her arm.

"I know that look Kristy. What's running around that pretty head of yours?"

Her heart pounded wildly as the creative juices began to flow. "Do you think we

could add on to the club? How does the name Blue Rhodes grab you? My God, listen to her. Look at the crowd they're eating it up. Look at their faces. And if I'm not mistaken, it looks like the drinks are coming faster than before."

Hunter took her hand in his and pressed them to his lips. "Doesn't anything slow you down?"

"Only pregnancy."

He leaned back and his eyes widened. "No, you're not."

"No, I'm not." She thought she heard him let out a very heavy sigh.

"Why don't we open up one night a week as blues night and see what the demographics will be?"

"You're right, of course. I think blues and country can go together, don't you?"

"Yeah, I do. You've heard of the Texas Blues. But let's see first."

Two hours and thirty minutes later Mavis introduced the piano player and the guitarist and thanked the audience for their understanding. The room exploded and she was given a standing ovation.

Hunter gave Mavis one of his famous smiles. "Man, those pipes of yours are really something. Why have you been hiding them all this time?"

Mavis grabbed a beer and opened it. "Blues in a country western bar? Need you ask?"

Kristy just shook her head in amazement. "You're really something. Did your husband have any idea how special you were?"

Mavis took a long sip of beer. "Hell he was so drunk he never knew which end was up most of the time."

"So why'd you marry him?" Hunter asked.

Mavis seemed to stare off into space. "Because I couldn't have Joe."

Kristy put her arms around Mavis and hugged her. "I'm sorry." Her eyes automatically focused on Hunter. She had to make a decision.

"Oh hell, all that's in the past. Look what I have now, my beautiful daughter, two grandbabies, two bars, a restaurant, men trying to get my attention every night. Life's pretty good right now." Her smile lit up the place.

Hunter picked up his bottle of beer and tapped it against Mavis'. "Kristy thinks we should have one night a week as blues night, with you as the headliner. What do you think?"

Mavis sat there looking dumbfounded. She gazed at Hunter first, then to Kristy. "Didn't my resume look full as it is?"

Kristy gave her a hug. "No."

"Mind if I sleep on the idea?"

"Sure," Kristy said, "but you'll do it. I saw how you came alive out there tonight. Anyone that can sing like you needs to be appreciated for their talent."

Mavis grinned at Kristy. "You're a slave driver. Now get on home to that family of yours."

Kristy kissed Mavis on the cheek and hugged Hunter before she left.

Mavis looked at Hunter. "You might as well ask Gracie to marry you because you know Kristy's not giving up on Nick and her family."

"That's one of the reasons I love her so much. The sad thing about it is that any woman I ask to marry me will know she's only getting half of my heart, that the other half will always belong to Kristy. Kristy still hasn't given me an answer, until then, I'll wait." He hugged Mavis and left.

Mavis thought somehow even a small amount of Hunter would be enough for Gracie. She had to admit Hunter and Kristy were good together. He'd been there every time she needed a man to protect her. How could she get the blinders off Nick in time?

Nick was still awake when Kristy opened the bedroom door. She smiled at the sight of him sitting there on the bed doing paperwork while Johnny lay next to him.

"He was restless but settled down when I brought him in here."

She picked Johnny up and kissed his sleeping face then carried him back to his own bed and tucked him in for the night. She undressed and slipped into a nightshirt.

"You're spoiling your kids," she teased.

He put the papers aside and turned the covers back for her to slide beneath and crawl into his arms. "So how did it go tonight?" He asked. "Could Mavis carry a tune after all?"

She lay facing him touching his cheek. "She stunned us. Nick, the woman can sing like you wouldn't believe. We're going to have blues one night a week. You've got to come hear her sing, she's amazing." She snuggled closer to him and pressed her lips to his. She loved the feel of his arms around her.

One late afternoon a month later at the office Kristy sat drinking tea with Sarah and chatting.

Sarah reached for her second cookie and asked, "Has Nick given you an answer about the ranch yet?"

Kristy put the cup of tea down and shook her head. "No. I take it he hates the idea."

"So what does that mean?"

Kristy's gaze went out the window and she pondered the question before answering. "Maybe the agency should go ahead with plan B."

Sarah's mouth had dropped open and she was staring at Kristy in disbelief. "Does that mean you and Hunter will be going in together on the ranch?"

Kristy was unsure about anything in her life. "I don't know." She got up from the couch and walked to the window where she pressed her forehead against the glass to look out over the Dallas skyline. She'd been back in this town for two years and nothing in her life had changed, except she now had a son. What did she want? Nick was the love of her life yet even after two years she couldn't give the kids his last name. Without the Chandler name they'd never be able to own any part of the ranch even if they wanted to. Hunter, on the other hand, would give them the Taylor name in a moments notice. They would inherit such wealth they would never want for anything. Should she listen to her heart or to her head? What was best for her children? Should she accept a California lifestyle or hold off for the Texas roots she'd grown up with? There was a heaviness around her heart because she didn't know which way to go. When she looked up

Sarah was gone. Hunter stood there.

Hunter spread his arms and Kristy walked into them feeling comfort as they closed around her. "It's killing you, I know," he said as he hugged her to him.

"Hunter, why do you love me?" she whispered. She needed to know.

He closed his eyes and pressed his cheek to the top of her head. "Why? Because you give me such delight in every day life. Your smile lights up a room. Your devotion to your kids is amazing. Nicki has been such a kick to watch these past two years. When she's on that horse of hers I'm amazed at her attention to it. I watch your face light up when your children accomplish something new. I want children with you so I can see that same elation with their accomplishments, something we could share. I want to know I have you to come home to at night, to be there to love when we need each other. We spend enough time together now that it seems as if we're already married and I love every minute I'm with you. You never cease to amaze me when you're with the clients, the way you charm them and cater to their needs. Kristy, I could give you and the kids everything you want and need, you know that. The only thing I can't give you is Nick's heart and his love. That's something he has to do for himself. It's been two years, how long are you going to wait?"

She'd been asking herself that same question for two years. It was time to stop.

When the phone rang Kristy picked it up but her eyes remained focused on Hunter.

"Kristy, this is Gracie, there's been an accident."

"What kind of accident?" Her brows drew together in concern.

Hunter came to stand behind her for support.

"Crystal Locket...the trainer was trying to load her into the trailer...she balked, Nicki went in to calm her and...somehow the horse fell in the trailer and...Nicki...Kristy, Nicki's at the hospital. Nick had to take Crystal Locket to the clinic, she has...I think he said a chipped knee or something like that."

Kristy could tell Gracie was crying. "I'm on my way to the hospital." She spun around to face Hunter. "Nicki's in the hospital it seems something happened in the horse trailer and she was hurt. Nick took the horse to his clinic."

Kristy found her daughter in the emergency room. Her left arm had been broken and she had a slight concussion. Kristy was devastated to see her daughter lying there sedated. Why had this happened? Crystal Locket had been in training for nearly two years and she was a gentle horse. Gracie held Johnny in her lap.

"I'm sorry Kristy," Gracie sniffled. "Nick feels just awful about the accident."

Kristy took John and held him tight in her arms. "I just don't understand how this could have happened? Nick's careful, he wouldn't let Nicki go in that trailer while they were loading the horse."

Gracie shook her head. "He didn't, she thought she was going in there to help, I don't think he even saw her until the horse reared up…"

Kristy sucked in her breath. She went to stand beside Nicki and ran her hand across her daughter's forehead. She loved her daughter more than life itself. She had trusted Nick to take care of her, yet she didn't blame him.

Kristy made sure Nicole was safely in a private room and comfortable before she turned John back over the Gracie. "I have to go to the clinic," she stated. "I have to know Nick is all right."

"We'll wait here," Hunter said and put his arm around Gracie and John.

Kristy looked at her beautiful daughter again. "The doctor said she wouldn't wake for a while. I have to see Nick."

Nick and Brian repaired the horse's fractured bone by securing the fragment with orthopedic screws. They did the best they could. The healing time would be long and slow, and the potential for arthritic changes could limit Crystal Locket's ability to perform.

It was late when Kristy pulled into the clinic parking lot. The lights were on and Big Red was still parked there. She walked inside just as Nick, Joanie and Brian came out of the horse surgery wing. They all looked exhausted. Joanie helped Nick and Brian from their scrubs and left, Brian followed her.

Nick looked up to see Kristy standing there. "How's Nicki?" he asked as the crease between his brows deepened.

She opened her arms and he walked into them. "She has a broken arm and a concussion. She's asleep. How are you?"

He clung to her. It was comforting to hold her in his arms. He couldn't shake the vision of Nicki being crushed against the inside of the trailer. How could he not have seen her? Kristy trusted him to take care of Nicki and he'd let her down. He cupped her face in his hands to look into those beautiful blue-green eyes of hers. He needed to know she didn't blame him, and as he gazed into them he could see with relief that she didn't. He brought his mouth down to hers and held her as close to him as he possibly could.

"I'm so sorry," he whispered. "I didn't know she was in there."

Kristy ran her hands through his hair and down the sides of his face. "Nicole probably thought she could help otherwise she wouldn't have gone in. She trusted the horse; she didn't understand there could be danger. It's not your fault."

His heart raced at the thought he could have lost Nicki, that he'd been careless with her safety. Now his daughter lay unconscious in a hospital bed and the horse would have a long painful recovery. He was sure the accident would haunt him for years to come.

"How is Crystal Locket?" Kristy asked.

"She suffered a slab fracture of the radial carpal bone in her left knee." Nick didn't want to tell her the injury could be fatally crippling. His future and the fate of the Chandler ranch might hang in the balance if Crystal Locket had to be destroyed.

"If anyone can fix her it's you," Kristy said.

Nick and Brian alternated their duties. Almost every waking moment was spent with Crystal Locket. Her rehabilitation would be slow and laborious. After the bandages and sutures were removed, Nick transferred her to hydro-rehab center where Crystal could exercise in a swimming pool designed for horses. This allowed mobility and stimulation. Crystal took to the therapy well. Paddling her legs in the water seemed to invigorate her. The motion increased circulation into the injured tissues, maintained her muscle tone, and helped in her healing.

CHAPTER
TWENTY SIX

The day Nicki was to be released from the hospital Kristy stood by her bedside. "What do you mean you don't want to come home?" Kristy asked.

Nicki shook her head. "I want to go to Hunter's in California. I don't want to go home."

Kristy stood there numb and confused by her daughter's refusal to return home. "I don't understand, Nicki. Why don't you want to come home?"

Nicki ran her hand over the cast on her left arm. "Mama...daddy's never there and it's lonesome."

Kristy knew that was just an excuse not to face what was really bothering her. The accident must have traumatized more than she thought. "Nicki, look at me." She watched Nicki's blue eyes darken as she asked, "Does this have something to do with the accident? Honey, it wasn't your fault. It wasn't daddy's fault. Crystal Locket..."

"No!" Nicki screamed, "I don't want to go home."

What was she to do now? Kristy wondered if she should call Nick. "Do you want to see your daddy?" She also knew Nick hadn't been in to see Nicki but one time during her stay in the hospital. That was no way to rebuild the confidence of an eight-year old girl.

"No!" Nicki said adamantly. "I want to go to Hunter's."

Frustrated Kristy wasn't sure what to do. "But that's not possible."

"It is too," Nicki reminded her mother. "Hunter takes care of us."

Kristy closed her eyes and took a deep breath. "Maybe you'd rather go to the ranch to be with grandma and grandpa?"

Nicki hesitated, then said, "First I want to go to Hunter's."

"We still have to go home, and I'm not sure Hunter will let us use his beach house."

Nicki looked angry. "Then call him. I don't want to go home."

Kristy did not like being manipulated by an eight-year old. Her daughter was going to need some serious counseling as the result of the accident. "Let me call your dad first."

"No. I want to go to Hunter's."

"But, we can't just go straight to the airport we don't have tickets and I have to make arrangements to take some time off."

"Then take me to his apartment."

Kristy's mouth dropped open. "Nicole, what's wrong with you? Why don't you want to see your dad? Why don't you want to come home?"

Nicki looked away from her mother. "I just don't want to."

Kristy was angry, both with Nick for not spending a little time with Nicki while she was in the hospital, and with Nicole who was dead set in getting her way. She walked out into the hall and pulled out her cell phone. She called Nick at the clinic but he was out and Cheryl had no idea when he'd be back. She called Hunter at the office and explained the situation to him.

"Hell, she can stay at my place, no problem."

"Hunter, there is a problem, she's running to you when she should be running to Nick. Something's happened to make her shy away from him."

"Just bring her to my apartment and we'll figure it out when you get there."

Damn, she thought, she didn't need more complications in her life. She walked back into Nicki's room.

"It's all right with Hunter if you want to stay at the apartment. That means Gracie will have to bring Johnny there during the day. Why are you upsetting the entire family, Nicole?"

Nicki stood her ground. "Gracie should be at Hunter's. She likes him."

"But Nicki, you need to be home."

"No."

Kristy decided to try one more thing. "Nicki, do you intend to get back on a horse?"

"No."

Kristy knew she had her work cut out for her. Nicki had to face her fears and she had to get reacquainted with Crystal Locket...if the horse ever recovered. If Nicki's attitude didn't change there really would be a bigger problem to solve, one having to do with Nick.

Kristy called Gracie, who agreed to meet them at Hunter's apartment. Hunter took Nicki into one of the spare bedrooms and made sure she was comfortable.

Kristy sat on the couch shaking her head. "Thank you, Hunter. You can see how upset she is."

Gracie put John on the carpet so he could crawl around. "How is this going to work?" she asked.

Kristy shook her head, she wasn't sure about anything at the moment. "I don't know. I can't leave her here alone and I can't expect to turn Hunter's home into a nursery either."

Hunter sat beside her. "Hey, Gracie can stay in the third bedroom, that's not a problem. If you want to take some time off until we figure this thing out you can at least stay home with John. Or, you could bring John here during the day, I don't mind. We can childproof the place if we have to."

Kristy looked around the plush penthouse apartment and just couldn't envision infant paraphernalia being brought into the place. "I'll take some time off. I have to figure out how to get through to Nicki. We can't leave it like this."

Hunter put his arm around her. "Nick and that horse are the key here. Nicki has to face whatever it is that's bothering her."

"I agree. It's going to be up to me to make that happen. But...I don't have a clue as to how I'm going to do it."

Kristy scooped John up off the floor and went in to say goodbye to Nicki. Then she headed home. How the hell could she continue working, take care of a six-month old and see to her daughter's mental needs all at the same time? She suddenly felt a sense of overwhelming uncertainty grip her.

*   *   *

That evening Kristy was finishing feeding John when Nick came home. "How's Nicki?" He asked. He took one look at Kristy feeding their son and knew something was wrong. "Where's Gracie?"

Kristy wiped John's mouth and lifted him out of the highchair. "Nicki and Gracie are staying at Hunter's apartment."

Nick stood there with a stoic look on his face. "What the hell do you mean by that?"

"Nicki refused to come home. She refuses to face her fears, and she doesn't want to see you."

Stunned, he didn't understand any of it. "But why?"

Kristy put John in his playpen. "She wouldn't tell me why. I asked her point blank. She refuses to come home. She wanted to go to Hunter's beach house and I told her that was impossible. I asked her if she wanted to visit the ranch and she didn't say no, but said she wanted to go to Hunter's first."

"He can't keep her, she belongs here at home with us we're her family."

Kristy's hands went to her hips. "I agree, but I also have a child on my hands that has obviously been traumatized by the accident. She told me she never wanted to see Crystal Locket again. She doesn't want to see you, the one person she's crazy about. I shouldn't have to impose on Hunter but he's been gracious enough to allow my daughter to stay at his place. I asked Gracie if she would mind staying there to watch Nicki, but I can't expect her to keep Johnny so I'm taking some time off. I have to straighten this mess out so we can all get on with our lives."

Shaking his head in disbelief Nick ran his hands through his hair. "I'm her father, why wouldn't she want to see me?" He didn't understand her attitude.

When John started to cry Kristy picked him up. "Nick, Nicole hasn't seen much of you for months, I think between that and the accident she feels abandoned in some way. It's going to take time to rebuild any relationship you had with her."

Nick reached out and took his son in his arms holding him tight. "I had no idea she felt that way about me."

"Neither did I."

"Should I make an effort to go see her or call her?" He asked. His heart ached to know his own daughter didn't want to see him. He'd missed out on so much of her life and now...he was devastated.

Kristy put her arms around Nick and John and hugged them. "We need to give her some space...and time. She has to face what's bothering her sooner or later."

"And how long will she stay at Hunter's?"

"I don't know, but Nick, I need to get her back here as soon as possible."

Nicki absolutely refused to return home. Six weeks later Kristy had no choice but to return to work. She would take John to the apartment for Gracie to watch, but had no idea how to help Nicki get her life back together.

Sarah walked into Kristy's office and sat down. "I think you should know that Nicki and Hunter have gotten really close since she's been living there. Even Gracie is happy."

Kristy scowled. "Well, I'm not. Nick and Nicole are so much alike I'd like to wring both their necks. How do I get my daughter back?"

"Hunter needs to talk to you. Since you've been out of the loop he and Matt decided to go ahead and buy the ranch they were looking at. Hunter put in your share of the money, he said you needed to keep your money to invest in your children's future and he didn't want you to risk any loss."

Kristy slumped in the chair. "Then I guess I won't have any say about what they do."

"Nonsense," Hunter said from the doorway. "I invested for you and you'll have a lot of say in what we do out there. I also want you to take Nicki there to live for a while. It's only a short way from Dallas, you can drive it in no time."

Kristy was confused. "What the hell are you talking about? I can't possibly take off to some ranch and stay."

"Sure you can. Look, it's a great place for Nicki to recover physically and emotionally. I've already talked to her about living on the ranch...it's just for a little while. You know about ranching, Matt and I don't. I need you out there to figure out what we'll need to satisfy our clients and make a profit at the same time."

Kristy stood and walked to the window to peer out. "Why?"

Hunter came to stand behind her. "Because you need a healthy daughter. The ranch is a neutral place for her. She can be around horses again, be around you and John. Gracie will be there too."

"And what about my clients?"

"That's the beauty of the ranch, there's a huge office and plenty of ready bedrooms, your clients will get to visit while they're here. Right now, this is the way it should be. Matt and I need your input, give us your opinion of what we need to do."

She turned around to face him. "And Sarah? Can she come out there too?"

Sarah's mouth dropped open. "But...I'm engaged."

Kristy gave Sarah a long hard look. She could read something into her words and she wasn't sure how to respond. "You're not married yet."

Sarah started to cry. "It doesn't matter what I do it doesn't change a thing with him." She looked up at Kristy knowing she would understand. "It's colic season, the scrub oaks are witherin' and the pasture grasses are turnin' brown. Those clinic doors will swing open day and night when the bellyachin' horses react to the changes in climate. Brian will never even know I'm gone. I'll be there. You need a secretary and I need...some space to think about what I've done." Large tears continued to slide down her cheeks.

Kristy understood and felt sorry for Sarah. She shook her head because she couldn't believe that yet again, she had to move even if it was for a short time. "All right, help me pack up my son and my daughter and let's get out to this new ranch of yours. I have to stop by the clinic and give Nick the news. He's not going to be happy about this."

Kristy walked into a quiet clinic. Joanie was gone, Nick was gone, Brian and Henry were no where to be found. Cheryl sat quietly at the reception desk polishing her manicured nails.

"Where is everyone?" Kristy asked.

Cheryl pursed her lips. "Big accident at one of the stables south of town." She blew on her wet nails.

"May I use Nick's office to leave him a message?"

With a wave of her fingers Cheryl said, "Sure, he won't be back for hours."

"Thanks."

Kristy walked into his office and sat behind Nick's desk. She loved his office, he'd decorated it himself and it fit him. Every piece of furniture was dark and solid. His desk, as usual was scattered with papers but the right side of his desk was clear. That's where two pictures sat, one of her and Nicki and one of her and John. She picked up the one of her and Nicki and looked at it. Nicki looked so happy in the picture. It was taken about the time they moved in with Nick over a year ago and before John was born. She set the frame back down on the desk. Once again things had turned around so quickly that it left her reeling. She had a suspicion that Hunter knew the real reason Nicki didn't want to see Nick so she intended to get to the bottom of it.

She wrote a long note to Nick explaining how, for Nicki's sake and for the agency, she had to move out of their house and out to the new ranch. She hoped it wouldn't be for long. She left the new phone number. She put the note next to his computer so he would be sure and find it. Not that it would matter to Nick, she thought, Sarah was right, he and Brian would be busier then ever this time of year and with her and the kids out of the way he wouldn't have to worry about them. The move was probably for the best.

With Hunter's help Kristy, the kids, Gracie and Sarah moved into the spacious ranch house south of Dallas. The minute Kristy saw the spread she felt at home. The huge two-story brick house looked like some hotel simply because of it's imposing size. There was a separate wing that she thought would suit her family, Gracie and Sarah. The office was enormous, as was the dining room, which looked more like a dining hall, and she fell in love with the thoroughly modern kitchen.

There were well-manicured lawns surrounding the house and lots of trees that didn't seem to be native, Kristy thought. The place was impeccably kept up. There were two big barns and several rows of stables. And there were pastures, lots of fenced pastures.

"Well, what do you think?" Hunter asked as they walked around the corrals, barns and stables before they took the Jeep out to the pastureland. When he parked his newly purchased Jeep he looked over at Kristy to see her smiling and realized he hadn't seen that beautiful smile in months. He'd done the right thing to insist on buying the place. He was doing it for her and the kids. He'd invested a huge sum of money but he convinced Matt it was the right thing to do, that with Kristy's ranch experience and creativity she would have the place making a profit in no time. Matt had his reservations, but he also needed to invest for tax purposes, so he agreed.

Kristy removed her sunglasses, propped her feet up on the dashboard and looked at Hunter. "What kind of budget are you giving me here?" She wanted to buy more horses, she needed a trainer, she needed hands to work the spread, she needed...Nick. Her heart was breaking.

"No budget, get what you need I'm footing the bill."

"I could lose it all for you."

He reached over and traced the outline of her face. "No, that's the one thing I know you won't do. I have more faith in you then you do yourself. So does Matt."

"You're putting a huge responsibility on my shoulders."

"And we know you won't let us down."

Kristy looked out over the beautiful open space and felt a sense of peace that she hadn't felt in a very long time. She looked over at Hunter. "Hunter, why won't Nicki see her dad?"

"You want the truth or want it sugar coated?"

She scowled. "You know me better then that."

He put both hands on the steering wheel and looked out over the range. "She's angry that he never spends any time with her. She so desperately wants a dad that loves her and gives her some attention. Kristy, she's asked me to marry you."

"And what'd you tell her?"

"That I wasn't her father and she had to work things out with you and Nick. I didn't tell her I'd asked you to marry me a long time ago. I didn't want her upset with you."

Kristy felt as if she'd been kicked in the stomach by a mule. "I had no idea she felt that way. She and Nick are so much alike it's like they're butting heads with neither one of them willing to give in. She doesn't understand Nick is getting older and he's not used to a private life or that everyone at the ranch depends on him financially. Having a family doesn't come natural to him, and since I more or less forced my children on him…"

"Then why not marry me?"

She looked into Hunter's eyes. She wasn't ready to agree to marry him for the sake of her children. She needed more time to work things out with Nicki. "I need to buy horses and some more cows. Let's get some Polled Herefords. Maybe get some Black Angus to feed to the clients and paying customers. I could put on a cutting horse demo in that arena if we build a grandstand for the outsiders that'll be coming out here. We need to fill that fancy stable with docile horses for the greenhorns to ride. I need to hire hands to help me run the place. I need household staff and a chef. Would you mind if I asked my dad to come stay with us to give me some ideas?"

A deep-throated laugh erupted from within Hunter's chest. "You're avoiding what you need to face, and you've been doing it for years."

She took a deep breath. "Hunter, let's get this place up and turning a profit before I make any other decisions. This will be good for me…for my children."

Hunter turned on the jeep. "Give your dad a call. Do you want a runway put in out here?"

Kristy smiled and put her feet back on the floor. "Make it a helicopter pad, we're not that far from Dallas. Can you afford to buy a helicopter?"

Hunter grinned. "Baby for you, you got it. Wanta learn to fly the thing?"

Kristy's mouth dropped open. "I think I'd like that."

Teasing, Hunter gave her another deep throaty laugh. "You're one expensive woman to keep."

She raised an eyebrow and put her sunglasses on. "But I turn a profit. Too bad we couldn't operate a whore house out here, we'd really make the big bucks."

"Maybe we ought to consider moving the operation to Nevada. I wouldn't mind sampling the goods." Hunter stepped on the gas and they laughed all the way back to the house.

Kristy could only hope he was kidding. Hell, what kind of life would being a madam be?

CHAPTER
TWENTY SEVEN

When Nick found the note Kristy left he was too busy to feel as furious as he did. Brian wasn't happy either. Their days and nights were filled with sick animals and neither looked back. Neither liked going home to dark empty homes, so they spent a lot of what free time they had at the Lone Star Saloon where the local cowgirls were more then eager to console them. Nick had been so angry he didn't even bother to call the number Kristy had left him. Too hell with her, he'd get over her and he had the women who could help him do it.

After sixty days Crystal Locket walked out of her stall bearing full-weight on her left leg. Nick was optimistic, but cautious. One false move and Crystal could be crippled for life. He hand walked her repeatedly everyday for weeks on end, while monitoring her progress with periodic x-rays. The fracture appeared to be healing well with a few arthritic changes. It took another month before Nick allowed her to trot. She was seldom out of Nick's sight or mind.

Five months passed before Nick very carefully started her back into training. Crystal Locket never missed a beat. Nick thought she had the heart of a lion and never looked back. In no time she was ready to get back to work and back in the show ring. He was beginning to have problem with her pent up energy, and turned her over to a professional trainer that he knew and respected. To Nick, Crystal Locket's recovery was a miracle.

Six months later the ranch was shaping up and that gave Kristy time to start going back into Dallas. Joe had come to visit her several times over the past six months and now it was time for Kristy to take her dad into town for some fun as her way of saying thank you to him. She knew just where to take him.

"Come on, Dad," Kristy urged, "I have to see Mavis." She took Joe by the hand and pulled him into Dallas Rhodes. She noticed Big Red parked outside the Lone Star. "Well?" she asked, "what do you think of the place?"

Joe immediately removed his hat, something Kristy knew wasn't natural for him. "You did all this?" He couldn't believe the size or scope of the place or how many people were there. And the smells coming from the kitchen made him hungry.

Kristy walked into the office to find Mavis sitting at the desk. "I did it for the agency and Mavis," she said.

Mavis looked up to see Kristy and Joe standing there. A dry lump formed in her throat. "Well if it ain't my long lost daughter. How are ya, Joe? What do I owe this visit?"

Kristy kissed Mavis on the cheek. "Dad's been staying at the ranch with me. He's helping me out until I get some things under control out there."

Mavis leaned back in her chair and smiled up at her daughter. "Hunter tells me he bought you a helicopter and a pilot to go with it. He says you've got a dozen clients comin' in from Japan next week, four from Germany and six from Italy the following week. How the hell you handlin' all that and the kids too?"

Kristy smiled. "That's why I have Sarah and Gracie. I have more free time to be with the kids now that I'm home all day. Things are coming together out there so I can come back into town to be with you."

Mavis looked up at Joe. God, how she still loved that man and probably always would. "So Joe, how's Ellen?"

Joe was still stunned by his surroundings. "She's fine." He could hardly take his eyes off Mavis. She looked as good to him now as she did when they were teenagers. To see her and Kristy together, side by side, took his breath away. Creating Kristy seemed to be the one thing he'd done right in his life. If only he could have had other children.

Mavis gazed into Kristy's eyes. "He hasn't called you has he?"

Kristy sadly shook her head. "No, I guess after six months we can call it officially over between us."

Mavis sucked in her breath. "No…don't say that. Nick'll come around."

Joe put his arm around Kristy's shoulder and he could feel her shaking.

"Did Hunter tell you why Nicki's mad at Nick?"

Mavis nodded. "Yes. Sad. She's just a kid, she'll get over it."

"She's just a kid that is so much like her father that if she does get over it it'll harden her for life."

"And Hunter?" Mavis asked. "Are you going to finally say yes?"

Kristy leaned against Joe. She needed her dad to comfort her. "I can't. I don't love him. My children will be just fine, I'll see to that."

Joe didn't like to think of his daughter taking full responsibility for her children when they had a father to help out, but he also knew she was as pigheaded as Mavis and would continue to work. "You could come back home to the ranch," he said, "your mother and I would be happy to help raise our grandkids."

Kristy all but laughed at the thought. "And there I'd be right back where I started only this time with two kids to add to your burden. No, thanks Dad, I have to support my children and to do that I have to be where the money is."

"But…but…you need to be where you have roots, and that's the ranch," he reminded her in no uncertain terms. "Think about it. Don't automatically toss out the idea. It's where you were the happiest."

Kristy shook her head. "And I was happy because I hadn't been away from the ranch yet. No…I've been through enough to know I have to throw myself into my work to keep from thinking about…"

"Damn that Nick," Mavis swore under her breath. She looked up at Kristy. "Why don't you take Joe next door, let him relive some bygone memories. Hunter's due in here anytime. I'll send him over."

Joe gave Mavis a hint of a smile. The old gal remembered the fun times they'd had.

286

Kristy scowled. "I saw Nick's truck parked out there."

"So? If you're not with him anymore what difference does it make?" Mavis wanted Kristy to see Nick, she knew how much she loved him and it would serve as a reminder. It wouldn't hurt for Nick to see her again either, remind him of what he's missing.

"Come on daughter, let's go." Joe took his daughter by the hand and led her into the Lone Star Saloon where memories of his wild younger days came into play. He ordered beer and walked into the dimly lit room to slide into a booth.

"Well Dad, is it like old times for you?"

"Ah hell, not until Mavis gets here."

Kristy kept her chuckle to herself. She also couldn't help but notice Nick, Brian, Jez and four other cowgirls neatly tucked into the darkened recesses of the room. His back was to her so he didn't notice. He had both arms around his woman.

Joe leaned forward toward Kristy. "You okay with this? Can you handle it?"

Kristy took a deep breath and exhaled. "I have to handle it. I know what he does in here. I've seen it before. He's like a stranger to me now."

"Ah the hell he is, you've got two kids with him."

"They're just his biological children, it takes more than that to make a parent and you damn well know it."

Joe held up his hands. "Okay, I'm not going to argue with you. Hunter's lookin' for you anyway."

She looked up to see Mavis and Hunter heading toward their booth.

Mavis held out her hand to Joe. "Dance with me?"

It didn't take Joe but a second to agree and it warmed Kristy's heart to finally see her mother and father in each other's arms. She couldn't understand her feelings at the sight of them moving around the floor together. Except...they were her parents and she was the result of their love.

"So, how do you feel about seeing them together?" Hunter asked.

She continued to watch the two of them hold each other and move around the floor. "They must have been something in their younger days."

Kristy couldn't keep her eyes off Nick. She missed him so much that her body ached at the sight of him. She knew she wouldn't be able to sit there for long, she would have to leave it hurt too much to watch him with Jez.

When Nick looked up long enough to see Joe and Mavis clinging to each other and moving around the floor like they'd done many times before, he knew Kristy must be in the room too. He sat up and removed his arms from around Jez. Did he even want to see her? Hell, did he care what she thought?

"Hello, Nick, "Joe said. "How you been?"

Nick nodded. "Joe. Things okay at the ranch?"

Joe nodded in a stilted manner. "Expect to see you later this fall." He pulled Mavis back in his arms and moved about the floor. He didn't want to argue with his boss and the man who signed his paycheck. He had Mavis in his arms and he liked it that way. Nick and Kristy would have to work their own problems out without his interference.

"I need to check something next door, you be all right here alone?" Hunter asked.

Kristy smiled. "Of course, my dad's here."

With Hunter gone and her dad on the dance floor Kristy put her face in her hands to rub her forehead. Why had she agreed to come here? Her heart was breaking into pieces at the thought of Nick and Jez being together. When she looked up it was to see Nick walking past her as if she were a stranger. She looked away.

Nick had every intention of walking out of the place just to get away from her, but as he passed the table he stopped short of the door. Hell, he had to hold her in his arms one more time just to prove there were no feelings left for her. He turned around and headed back to her table.

Kristy looked up to see Nick standing there. He held his hand out to her. Automatically, she took it and found herself wrapped so securely in his long arms that she was nearly breathless. Their bodies moved to the slow music. Words didn't seem necessary. When she gazed up into his eyes his mouth came down to hers and she was tasting beer and inhaling Jez's perfume. It didn't do much for her emotions but she had him in her arms, right then, right there and she was going to make the most of it. Her lips parted slightly allowing him to probe and savor her mouth. His hands moved slowly up and down her back until they came to rest on her hips. When the kiss ended his lips brushed against her cheek. She could feel his heart beating loudly against his chest and was sure hers was beating just as fast. She wanted, and needed him. When the music stopped he took her by the arm and without a word led her out of the bar and to Big Red. She would be going home with him tonight and she didn't object.

It pained her to walk into the house he'd shared with Mallory and not see her things scattered about. The house was big and empty. And quiet. He led her to the bedroom and kissed her with a passion she'd never felt from him before. Without a word, clothes went flying in every possible direction until they were naked and fell across the bed wrapped in each other's arms and fused as one. There was no foreplay or sweet words, just plain good old-fashioned hot and heavy sex. Their bodies spoke for them. Kristy's head and body were reeling from the sensations his hands and body created and together they found the place that always made them happiest. Six months had been far too long for both of them.

When their breathing slowed, Nick rose up on one elbow and gazed down into her eyes. "You're tearing me apart."

Kristy closed her eyes and pulled his head down to rest against her shoulder. "I don't mean to do that." It felt so right to have him in her arms and their bodies entwined as one. Even with the hint of Jez's perfume still clinging to him she considered herself lucky to be holding him in her arms, making love with him. She didn't want it to end.

She was still wrapped in his arms when the phone rang. "Call Brian," he said and went back to loving Kristy. That, to Kristy, was not at all like Nick. Was there a crack forming in his self imposed armor?

The next morning they slept late. Nick stretched and yawned and realized he hadn't slept like that since she left. He turned to look at her sleeping beside him. He missed having her there with him. He missed having the kids underfoot. He pulled the sheet away and leaned over to put his mouth on her breast.

The sensation surging through her woke Kristy. "You sure know how to start my day," she whispered. He didn't stop there.

Later when she lay quietly in his arms he said, "Shouldn't we talk?"

"Wouldn't it spoil our time together?"

"How are the kids?"

She put her hand on his taut stomach and looked up at him. "Johnny is starting to walk. Nicki is at least looking at horses again."

"Why's your dad here?"

She tensed at his tone. "Look, I'll pay his wages for the time he's away from the ranch. I needed his advice on a few things."

He flinched. Did she think he was asking her to pay to have her father visit her? "I wasn't thinking about wages. I was just wondering why he was here. The way he held Mavis last night…"

She closed her eyes and covered them with her arm. "Oh my God, I forgot about them once I was in your arms. I wonder where dad stayed last night?"

Nick chuckled and ran his hand along the contours of her body. "I couldn't believe you were there last night. I wanted to walk out and forget you. I couldn't."

"Nick…" Her fingers reached out to touch the cleft in his chin. "I will never get over being in love with you. Dad told me I should quit my job and bring my children back home to the ranch so he and mom could help raise them. I told him I'd be right back where I started only this time with two kids and I couldn't expect them to help me out. My children are my responsibility."

"Crystal Locket is ready for the national futurity. I'd like Nicki to be the one to show her. What do you think?"

Stunned, she wasn't sure what to think. "She won't come here. To her Dallas is where her worst nightmare happened. But…what if you bring Crystal out to the ranch?" She hesitated then said. "Nick, that could be the answer. If Crystal Locket's in the stable out there Nicki would have to face her fear. I could work with the horse. Nicki's been watching me on my horse when I entertain our clients and I can see it in her face, she wants to get back on a horse. I think she just needs a little coaxing."

"And what about me? I take it she still doesn't want to see me?"

"Nick, she's a little girl. I think if we take it slow, she'll forgive."

He pulled her tight against him. "I miss the kids. It's hard to believe Johnny's walking already. Mavis tells me you've turned the ranch into something Matt and Hunter are very proud of. She also told me Hunter wouldn't let you invest in it for fear you'd loose your money. Is that true?"

"He thought I should invest in something my children will inherit. I haven't lost the agency any money, nor will I. That's one reason dad is staying with me, he's helping me to find some studs for breeding the next generation of horseflesh. He suggested we get into Quarter Horses, do some racing. I'm not sure about that idea yet. I figure selling well-bred Quarter Horses to my west coast clients would bring in enough money to cover buying the stallions. For some reason they think a Texas bred horse is better than one that's California bred. I don't tell them California has some six hundred forty five thousand horses in the state, that's more than other states. The ranch has also become the hottest place around for event planners. We find ourselves hosting some big events that have nothing to do with horses and still make a lot of money doing it. We've even had some pretty strange weddings take place out there."

"It seems to me you'll do well no matter where you live."

"I suppose." She looked at the clock. "I'd better get dressed and go find dad. I hope he didn't..."

Nick hugged her one last time. "So what if he did?"

"I guess there's no stopping the old fool if that's what he wants to do. Maybe it's his way of finding closure with Mavis."

"Closure?"

"Yeah, you know, what could have been and all that." She looked around the room for her clothes. "Where'd my jeans go? My underwear? Shoes?"

He watched her leave the room. The words 'what could have been' tattooed in his mind.

The day Nick brought Crystal Locket to the ranch Kristy made sure Gracie had taken Nicki into town for the day. She didn't know how Nicki would react to either Nick or the horse. Once the horse was safely in her stall she took Nick by the hand.

"Let me show you around the place."

Nick was impressed with what a little money could do. He was even more impressed by the fact Kristy had created most of what the place had become out of her fertile imagination and ranch upbringing. They'd built a covered grandstand where people paid money to come and watch weekend rodeos and horseshows. There were plenty of sponsor's signs and banners placed around the arena. There was a huge indoor arena where big functions were catered when it wasn't being used for upscale horse shows and auctions. The house had so many bedrooms it resembled a small hotel and every room had an occupant. She even had spillover entertainment from Dallas Rhodes where they would perform their shows for high end clients at their pricey weekend barbeques.

Nick looked up to see a half dozen Japanese gentlemen moseying toward them. He had to suppress his urge to stare…or laugh. They wore white rhinestone shirts, white pants with rhinestone designs down each leg, white ten gallon hats and boots so pointed even a horse would be terrified. And…they each had two Nikon cameras dangling around their necks, one of the two he knew to be a three thousand dollar digital camera. He was impressed.

In broken English and trying to imitate the Texas accent one of the gentlemen said to Kristy, "Kristy san, good mornin'."

Kristy replied in Japanese. "Signore san, Ohayoo gozaimasu. How are you today?"

Signore replied, "Okaga sama de. Very well thank you."

Kristy smiled at the charming and so polite gentlemen.

As Nick turned to look at Kristy he could have sworn that as her clients walked away they were trying to imitate John Wayne's gait. Lord…what a sight. He wondered what Kristy was charging them to live out their cowboy fantasy.

Kristy took his hand and led him to the separate wing of the house. "I have a surprise for you," she said and opened the door.

Nick took one look at Johnny standing there with Sarah and watched as his son walked with unsteady footing to where he stood. Nick picked him up and hugged him. "He's gotten so big."

Johnny pulled at Nick's hat and babbled dada. Sarah walked over to where Kristy stood and put her arm around her.

"Looks so natural to see Johnny in Nick's arms. He looks so much like him. I just wish Nicki would forgive."

Kristy smiled. "She will, Sarah, I'm working on her attitude."

Nick came to stand before Kristy. "What happens when you finish your job here? Where do and the kids go then?"

"I don't know, I haven't given it much thought. First, I have to get my daughter back on a horse." She didn't want to think about an uncertain future.

"How's Brian?" Sarah asked.

Nick didn't know how to answer Sarah. "He misses you."

Sarah managed a smile before she left the room.

"Where's Nicki?" he asked.

"I had Mike fly her and Gracie to Dallas."

"Was that so she wouldn't have to run into me?" How in the hell could he repair his relationship with his daughter if he couldn't see her?

"I haven't had time to tell her about Crystal Locket yet. If you have some time on weekends to come back I promise things will change. I could have Mike fly you out here to save time driving."

He set Johnny on his feet to watch him toddle off across the room to grab a toy from a chair. He'd missed watching Nicki go through the toddler stage, and he was missing Johnny's development. His future and the future of the Chandler ranch stood there chewing on a toy horse and babbling something only a baby understood. It suddenly struck him that life was a journey, not a destination. He'd been so focused on being the prodigal son his father wanted that he was missing the big picture of life. It had always been about the ranch and keeping it going. His dream had been to someday return to the ranch to raise cattle and horses and his idea was to get there no matter what it took. Becoming a vet gave him that financial security the ranch needed, yet it wasn't his driving force, being the best vet he could be was what drove him. He realized as he looked at Johnny that he was missing the journey of watching his children grow and interacting with them. Shouldn't he have some input into their developing years to help shape them into what they would become? Nicki showed all the signs of becoming a vet, yet how could she fully explore her options if he wasn't there to show her and guide her. And Johnny? He'd always wanted a son he could mold and shape into a fine young man. Instead, Kristy was both mother and father.

"Well?" Kristy asked.

Nick shook the cobwebs from his mind. "I'll think about it."

Kristy watched him looking at John but couldn't read the expression on his face. She went to stand before him and slipped her arms around his waist. "Thank you for the other night," she said and wondered if it would be another six months before they made love again. God, she hoped not! Hunter began to look too good to her after that length of time and she didn't want to encourage him.

Nick's arms went around her to hug her tight against him. There was no doubt about it, she was embedded in his heart...something he swore he'd never let happen again after the Mallory incident. He never wanted anyone to have the kind of power over him again where they took everything from him but his dignity. Yet, as he looked at that little boy in his image poking his tiny hands into every nook and cranny in the room...his heart softened.

"It was my pleasure." He inhaled deeply then said, "I have to make tracks back to Dallas."

Kristy picked John up and held him in her arms. They walked Nick back to Big Red. Her heart was breaking as she watched dust billowing behind retreating taillights of the horse trailer.

CHAPTER
TWENTY EIGHT

The next afternoon Kristy took Gracie aside and asked her to bring Nicki and John to the arena in an hour. She then went to Crystal Locket's stall saddled and bridled her and took her out into the arena to work her. The horse didn't need much training. She just needed more conditioning after the accident. But more important Nicki needed to face her fears.

She pretended not to notice as Nicki came to stand just outside the fence. Gracie came to the fence and stood behind Nicki for moral support. Kristy continued to put the horse through her paces. When she finished she nudged the horse to the fence.

"Gracie, let me have John." She reached out and lifted him in the saddle before her and made her way back into the arena. She turned the horse toward the fence and sat there facing Nicki letting John pull at the mane while slapping his small hands against the horse's neck. She was forcing Nicki to come to terms with whatever it was that scared her. If Nicki saw that John wasn't afraid of Crystal Locket, maybe she wouldn't be afraid either.

Nicki finally made her move. She opened the gate and walked into the arena. She hesitated at first. Kristy and the horse didn't move.

Nicki took a few more steps toward Crystal Locket. "Mama...she didn't mean to hurt me, did she?"

The horse stood quietly. "No baby, Crystal didn't mean to hurt you."

Nicki came closer. "I scared her...when she was going into the trailer." There were tears in Nicki's eyes. "Mama, I didn't mean to scare her."

Kristy kept the horse perfectly still. "I know you would never do that. It was an accident. She's okay now, your daddy took care of her."

Nicki came to stand about two feet away from the horse. Slowly, she reached out and put her hand on Crystal Locket's forelock, before reaching up to pat her neck. The horse didn't flinch. Nicki came closer until she could reach up and touch her mother.

"Mama, may I ride her?"

Kristy handed John down to Nicki and dismounted. With John straddling her left hip, Kristy helped Nicki reach the stirrup and walked to where Gracie stood.

"Aren't you going to put her saddle on?" Gracie asked.

"Not now. I want her to get the feel of Crystal Locket again. She doesn't need her own saddle to do that. Besides, she's almost outgrown it. I think it's time to get her a new saddle."

Slowly, Nicki walked Crystal Locket around the arena, then loped. Within minutes Kristy could see the change in her daughter. She was almost the same self-reliant, confident outgoing Nicki that she was before the accident, now...if she could only get her to open up to Nick. Somehow she thought that might be a harder feat to accomplish.

"Mama, has she been worked enough today?"

"I think so. Do you want to put her in her stall?" This was going to be another test she hoped Nicki would pass.

Without hesitation Nicki took Crystal Locket into the stable. Kristy watched as Emanuel helped Nicki remove the saddle and together they groomed her. Nicki was born to be around horses. At that moment Kristy had no doubt that Nicki had faced her fear and settled it in her mind. Now, she had to concentrate on getting Nick and Nicki back together.

"So she did it," Hunter said.

Startled by the sound of his voice Kristy turned around to see the biggest smile she'd ever seen on Hunter. "When did you get here?" She smiled back at him.

"Earlier. I drove. Thought I'd spend the week out here. Nick must have been here if that's Crystal Locket."

"He brought her out yesterday."

When Nicki saw Hunter she ran out of the stall and jumped into his arms, wrapped her legs around his waist and hugged his neck. "I did it, Hunter! I did it!"

Hunter hugged her tight. "I knew you would kiddo. I'm so proud of you."

It hurt Kristy to see what was unfolding before her. It should be Nick giving her daughter praise and affection, not Hunter.

Hunter took one look at Kristy's face and knew what she was thinking. "Nicki, don't you think it's time to forgive your dad too?" He could feel Nicki stiffen at Nick's name.

With her arms wrapped securely around his neck, Nicki laid her head against Hunter's shoulder. "I never see my daddy. He doesn't like me."

Hunter's eyes closed as he hugged her again. "Nicki, your daddy does too like you. He's always loved you. Your daddy doesn't have the kind of job that gives him the time to be with you and John. It's going to be up to you to make sure he knows you love him."

Kristy was so touched by Hunter's words to her daughter that she walked over and put her arms around both of them and hugged them tight. Why couldn't she give her love and devotion to Hunter instead of Nick? She was wasting her time on someone that didn't give a damn about her or his children.

Hunter put his arm around Kristy and with Nicole in his arms they walked out of the stable.

"Nicki," Kristy said, "would you be interested in showing Crystal Locket in the national futurity?"

Nicki wiggled out of Hunter's arms. Her hands went into her back pockets and she turned her face up to face her mother. "Can I?"

Kristy felt as if she was looking down into a miniature version of Nick as Nicole stood there with her hands in her pockets and those dimples showing. She smiled. "Yes you can. We'll get you ready."

Nicki strolled off to be by herself, her hands still stuck in her back pockets. She wasn't alone for long; one of the ranch dogs joined her along with three of the Japanese make believe cowboys with their Nikon's hanging around their necks.

"Nicki san, Konichi Wa...hello, good afternoon."

Nicki became animated as she headed toward the corral with them.

Hunter kept his arm around Kristy's waist. "If Nick ever shows up again I think she'll see him."

"Hunter, what would I do without you? Dad's going back to the ranch next week and I'm going to miss him so much."

"Marry me and you'll never be without me."

"And what great adventures would await me?" she asked. When his lips curled into a devilish smile, Kristy took one look at the front of his jeans. "I didn't mean eight inches of unleashed fury!" she laughed.

"Then how about a trip to Milan, or Hong Kong, anywhere on earth you want to go and I'll take you there."

She leaned into him. "I don't need to leave the country to be happy. I'm happy where ever my home and children are." Sadness swept over her because she realized she had no real home.

"We could live in Newport Beach, or I could buy you a horse ranch in California. Hell, I could buy you another ranch here in Texas if that's what you want. It's time to put real roots down Kristy, those kids need a full time father and you need a full time husband. I don't want to watch you growing hard as you age. That's what happens with women who choose this kind of life. You've spent your share of time getting things done and entertaining, now it's time for you to be the one who's pampered and entertained. You need to be loved on a regular basis. I've got the money...and the assets to do all those things."

She certainly understood his meaning. He was right, if she stayed on managing a ranch she would grow hard, she'd seen it before. She didn't want to be a tough as nails cowgirl doing a man's job all her life. She missed dressing up for evenings at Dallas Rhodes and having power business lunches at the best restaurants in Dallas where the conversation was stimulating and so was the company. She missed closing deals.

"I know I've kept you waiting far too long, but would you mind if I wait until the national futurity? I promise...I'll give you an answer then."

"Since you know what deadlines are I'll go along with your decision." He took her hand and brushed it across the front of his jeans. "Let's go to the loft and let the stallion out of the corral."

For half a second she was tempted to go for what she knew would be an incredible ride. "No loft. I tend to get pregnant in places like that."

Hunter's deep-throated laugh filled the air. "Now I know where we'll honeymoon."

She led him toward the corral. "Let's go have lunch with our clients and try to sell them next spring's foals." He slipped his arm around her waist. "This ranch is going to need a full time vet," she added.

"You asking Nick?"

"No. I contacted several vet schools and put out the word we'd be needing a vet. I've received forty-five applications. I've narrowed it down to half a dozen."

"You think a vet who's just graduated is good enough?" he asked.

"They're cheaper. They need first hand experience and I'm sure they're more than qualified. The ones I've chosen have ranch experience both here and California. Sarah's setting up interview schedules." She gazed up into those sexy green eyes of his. "Hunter, I think we should also think about hiring someone to replace me. You're right when you say my children need roots and security. This ranch of yours and Matt's has been wonderful for my family, but I need to get back into an office setting. Sarah's getting restless. And thanks to you and our investments I have a passive income that will more then see to my family's financial needs for years to come and put my children through college."

He chuckled. "Does your dad know he's set for life? All right, I want you back in town anyway. Does this mean you'd be moving back into your old home?"

She shook her head with uncertainty. "I think after the national futurity I might go back to the ranch for a couple of weeks to get my head together. I'll decide what to do then. I suppose I could rent an apartment again. Mavis told me I could bring the kids and move in with her."

"No," he said, "you promised to give me your answer, if anything you'll be moving in with me and we'll decide what we want to do together."

She smiled up at him and let him hug her. In truth, her heart was breaking. She cared a great deal about Hunter. But if she married him it would be because she was grateful to him for all he'd done for her and her children, not because she was head over heels in love with him. To Kristy, love, family and home meant everything to her and these were the things she wanted to instill in her children.

Nick sat in Mavis' office listening to the latest gossip while sipping a beer.

"Yep, Kristy's hired a full time vet for the ranch. Says he's out of Texas A&M. I think she hired him because of the love story between Dan and his wife. Seems they grew up on the 6B ranch in Denison and fell in love as kids. But when it came time to go off to college both sets of parents wanted the kids to part company so emotions would cool down. Dan went to Texas A&M and became a vet while Angela was shipped off to Cal Poly at San Luis Obispo in California. Well, true love always finds a way. Angela got her degree in Animal Husbandry and went to work for the branch 6B Ranch in Grass Valley, California and waited for Dan to finish up his education. Somehow these two kids got back together and got married behind their parent's backs.

Kristy said she liked Dan the minute he skidded to a stop in a battered old blue pickup truck that he musta had since high school because it looked as if it'd worked the range as much as he had. That old blue truck was so loaded with vet paraphernalia in the front seat that Angela showed up following in her white jeep that had crossed Apache arrows painted on the hood. Yep, Apache Indian and Texas cowboy, what a volatile couple they make Kristy said. She's hired Angela to take her place and manage the ranch while Dan will be the ranch vet. Kristy said having a real life Indian run the place is a great sales pitch to her foreign clients. "

Nick had the image of her Japanese clients flash to mind. Kristy really knew how to market Texas!

Mavis continued. "Nicki had to put her two cents in on his hirin', said Dan had to come with a clock that ran backwards and she wanted to see him with the animals first." Mavis watched Nick's expression soften.

"How are the kids?" he asked.

"Well maybe if you went out there once in a while you'd know. Nicki made friends with Crystal Locket and is gonna show her in the national futurity. John's in the saddle with Kristy every time she gets on a horse. Hunter's given her a deadline to accept his proposal. Kristy and the kids are movin' back to Dallas." That should be enough to grab his attention, Mavis grinned.

Nick's head snapped up. "Hunter asked Kristy to marry him?" Had the two of them become that close?

Mavis leaned back in her chair. "Ah hell, he asked her long before John was born. He's been pretty patience waitin' for her answer wouldn't you say? Guess he wants to get on with life so he gave her one last chance to say yes. He wants his own children."

"And?"

Mavis picked up a framed photo of Kristy and the kids from her desk and looked at it. "This is the most beautiful thing I've even seen, my daughter and grandbabies. Kristy doesn't love Hunter, if she marries him it's to give the kids what they need, a hands on father."

Nick scowled heavily creating creases across his brow. "They have a father."

Mavis leaned forward and rested her arms on her desk. "When was the last time you saw them?"

He felt guilty. "They have a father."

"Did you know that Nicki finally said why she wouldn't see you?"

Nick stared at Mavis. He was sure she was going to tell him whether he asked or not.

"Nicki told Hunter you didn't like her because you never spent any time with her. Her way of dealing with rejection was to reject you."

Nick scowled again. It felt as if his heart was being pulled out of his chest. "And what'd Hunter have to say about that."

Mavis leaned back in the chair and folded her hands in her lap. "Hunter told Nicki that you loved her, but you had a job that didn't give you much time to spend with her. He told her it was up to her to let you know that she loves you."

Nick stretched his long legs out in front of him and leaned against the back of the couch lacing his hands behind his head. "Tell me something Mavis, what do you think your life would have been like if you'd married Joe?" He was amazed at the change in her facial expression. A what might have been look, as Kristy would have called it.

"Ah hell, if life had been perfect I would have given Joe the dozen kids he wanted. We would have worked a ranch and been happy. But it didn't happen and now Kristy and her kids are all Joe and I have left in common." She gave Nick a long hard look. "It's a sad thing when you have nothing left in life except to look back at what could have been. Life's too short for that. We all have a path to follow."

"Did Kristy say where they'd be livin' when they move back here?"

"Hunter wants her to move in with him. I asked her to move in with me."

"She has a home she can come to."

Mavis picked up her reading glasses and put them on. "Nick, it's too late, Kristy has to do right by her children." She turned her attention to the computer.

Nick thanked Mavis for the beer, got in Big Red and headed to the solitude of his home to wait for the next emergency call. With his hands jammed into his hip pockets he walked from empty room to empty room. Why had he continued to live in Mallory's house where echoes of arguments and accusations resonated from every room? Mallory had said to him, after they were married, that she had no intention of having children with him or being tied down to some unproductive ranch. Why had he fought so hard to keep the house when he'd bought it for Mallory? Hell, she got everything else. Was it just a hollow victory that he got to keep the house? Or was it something else?

He had to let himself think back to the year he'd asked her to marry him. Why did he ask her? He'd spent so many years in college to become a vet that by the time he actually started practice and slowed down enough to realize he needed to start a family she was there. He was in his early thirties by then and had met her at some social function. There was nothing special about her except she gave him the attention he wanted. She seemed to want the same things in life he did, or at least that's what she said. He recalled something he was told by a mutual friend two weeks before he married her, that she thought her daddy's money would get him what he wanted faster. It would free them up to travel the world. He'd felt betrayed and lied to yet knew he was committed. When he went home to the ranch he found himself in the blackest mood of his life and spent most of his time at his favorite thinking spot.

That day he went into the barn and saw Kristy moving about with such grace and beauty he wanted to lash out at Mallory. He wanted to hurt her just the way she'd hurt him. He was angry. Kristy meant nothing to him she was just some kid that grew up on the ranch. She was always there every time he'd come home from school. He rarely noticed her before that day. But anger blurred with desire and he needed to vent.

He followed her up into the loft after he watched her trim hips and long legs lead the way. She had no idea he'd go up there. He intended to use her and leave it at that but what he hadn't expected were the emotions that swept over him that day. He had no idea she was a virgin, it surprised the hell out of him. How could someone that beautiful be untouched and innocent growing up on a ranch full of cowboys? What started out as revenge and lust ended up as something completely different. Kristy got into his heart that day. He'd used her for his own desires, yet at the same time he knew she wasn't to be trifled with. She cared about him. She wasn't superficial and greedy. She was innocent and yet gave herself to him so thoroughly that day it haunted him for years after that.

He walked to the front windows to look out over the expanse of manicured lawn. The next time he saw her was at the ranch when she was going into the barn. The sight of her took him by surprise. An overwhelming desire to know her again had come over him and when he learned about Nicki…the idea of him having a daughter was staggering. And to learn that she'd loved him all those years she was growing up blew his mind. He had no idea how she felt. Was he blind? So self absorbed in himself and his goals that he couldn't see what her feelings for him were? Shit, he ate at the same supper table she did every summer that he returned home to work the ranch. What he was looking for in a life partner was right there under his nose and he never even saw it. They had the same lifestyle, the same goals. She gave him Nicki and Johnny because she wanted his children. And now? Was he ready to hand her and his kids over to Hunter? Hunter no doubt was a good man, but not one that should be raising his children. Nicki and John needed to be on the ranch where their grandparents live, and are buried, not in some smog ridden California city where he would never get to see them.

He envisioned John the last time he saw him chewing on that toy horse and babbling some kind of nonsense. His tiny son toddled into his arms as if he missed him. That would change as he grew up, just the way it changed with Nicki. His own daughter thought he didn't like her because he didn't spend any time with her. And even when he did spend some time with her it couldn't be considered quality time, it was time spent in-between barn calls. Kristy was devoting her life to those kids and making sure they were happy and cared for. She never once asked for his help to support them, she was doing it all herself. She'd discovered a talent she didn't know she had, and combined with her common ranch sense, it had no doubt given her the money she needed to care for herself and the kids.

He missed her presence in Mallory's house and the ranch house they had shared, then sold. He missed the kids. He missed having her in his bed at night and waking up to see her beautiful face. He missed everything about her. And now...she would be Hunters. He couldn't handle it. He got in Big Red and peeled rubber pulling out of the driveway.

CHAPTER
TWENTY NINE

The Williams family gathered at the coliseum in downtown Ft. Worth the day Nicki was to ride Crystal Locket in the Futurity. Even Ellen had agreed to attend the event and Kristy thought that was very special since her mother hated leaving the ranch for any reason whatsoever. Mavis was there, sitting with Joe and Ellen. Gracie, Sarah, Brian and Hunter sat with them.

Kristy held John as she walked around with Nicki and could feel the exciting electric atmosphere in the place. Nicki had never ridden in such a grand scale event before. Kristy couldn't sense any nervousness from Nicki, but maybe she was covering up how she felt.

"Mama, those red white and blue banners up there in the ceiling are kind of pretty don't you think?"

Kristy smiled and put her arm around Nicki. They took time to walk behind the scenes to the corrals where the entrants gathered. "Kind of remind you of the Cow Palace?"

"Oh yes Mama, I remember those shows. You were great to watch when you worked Chartier in the arena. Annie use to yell so loud I always thought you could hear her. It use to hurt my ears when she whistled."

"What do you remember the most about showing?"

"That you had to be one with the horse. Oh Mama, I forgot that's what you used to say to me when you showed Chartier."

They located a quiet area where they found bales of straw. John plopped himself onto the bare floor and began picking up pieces of the dried yellow straw. Kristy and Nicki sat on the bale. "Nicki, I only want you to do this if it's what you really want. Do you think you're ready to ride out there in front of all those people and put Crystal Locket through her paces?"

"Do I have to win?"

Kristy shook her head. "No, just do what you can do. Winning isn't everything, not to me or John."

Nicki looked up at her mother. "How about Hunter?"

A knot formed in the pit of Kristy's stomach. She had given Hunter her answer that morning, a resounding no. "It doesn't matter to Hunter either. We want you to enjoy what you've learned. I want you to go out there and show this crowd that you know what you're doing and how to do it."

Nicki took the straw out of John's hands and picked him up. "John, what do you think?" She started to laugh. "Do you think Johnny will ride in this place someday?"

Kristy took John and sat him on her lap. "What do you think? I'm so proud of you. And someday you and John might ride here together. I look forward to watching my two children competing for top prize. I love both of you so much." She put her arm around Nicki and hugged her.

"I'll try my best, Mama."

Together they started to walk back toward where the family waited.

"Nicki, your dad is riding Rascal in the Maturity event for the Texas Cutting Horse Championship. Are you ready to see him?"

John grabbed Nicki's hat and tried to pull it off. Kristy removed his hands and switched him to her other hip. "Yes, Mama, I think I need to see him. I know Hunter isn't my dad but he's always been there for me...for us. Do you think my dad will want to see me?"

Kristy and Nicki failed to notice Nick had spotted them and had headed in their direction.

"Yes, I do want to see you," Nick said from behind them.

Kristy spun around and her heart sped up at the sight of him. She smiled. "Nicki and I were just discussing what she needed to remember going into the arena."

Nick looked into his daughter's eyes and locked on. "Nicki," he said, "do you think I could get a hug from you?"

Nicki let go of her mother's hand and lunged into Nick's arms hugging him as if she were drowning and he was her life preserver. Nick's gaze went up to Kristy.

"I'm sorry, Daddy. I didn't mean to be mad at you. I love you."

Nick hugged Nicki tight in his arms. This was *his* daughter, the light of his life he was holding. He never wanted to be away from being able to hug her again. He loved her. He loved Johnny. When she let go of him she stood back. "You look mighty pretty in your show clothes," he said.

Nicki smiled up at him. "Mama and I used to show at the Cow Palace. She was reminding me what I should remember to do. Mama, may I go sit by grandmas and grandpa to watch daddy?"

Kristy couldn't take her eyes off Nick. "Sure."

Nick reached out and took John from Kristy. "I hear Hunter's asked you to marry him."

Kristy's smile faded and she looked away from him. In a whispered tone she answered, "Yes, he has." She reached out to take John but Nick backed away.

"So what are you going to do?"

All right, she thought, if this was some kind of game he wanted to play she'd go along with it. "I've turned him down. I'd rather live as a single mother then to be married to someone I couldn't fully love. Hunter understands."

"Do you think he's accepted your answer?"

She glared at him. He had no right to question what she did or didn't do. "Yes, he has. Hunter loves me and wants what I want."

"And what do you want?" he asked.

She shook her head and reached out for John. "It doesn't matter what I want Nick, it matters what I do." She took John and walked away.

Nick caught up with her and grabbed her by the arm. "I hear you're moving back to Dallas, where do you plan to live?"

She jerked her arm away from his grip. "Why do you care where

I live? I'll probably move in with Mavis until I can find an apartment."

"No. No apartment. We've gone through this before, the kids need open space."

She was becoming frustrated. "Nick, just let me be!"

By the time she got back up into the stands and sat down she was out of breath. Mavis put her arm around her while Joe took Johnny. "Honey," Mavis said, "you've made the right decision, he'll have to live with it."

Kristy's first instinct was to seek out Hunter for comfort but she thought better of that move. She was on her own now whether she liked it or not.

"Mama, there's daddy on Rascal."

Kristy couldn't help but admire Nick's ability with Rascal. He looked every inch the cowboy he really was. He belonged on his ranch, using Rascal like he should be used, cutting cattle for real. Nick, now at forty-two, could still be a vet but needed the freedom to do what he always planned to do, raise cattle and horses. The choice wasn't up to her and she knew it. It was over between them, and it was over between her and Hunter. The choices she made now were for her future and the future of her children. She loved watching him and was ecstatic when he won the grand prize. She was sad when she didn't see him after he'd won.

Nicki's event was later that afternoon. Kristy put Nicki on Crystal Locket. Nicki leaned over and kissed her mother. "Mama, you can go back with the family to watch if you want. I like it when I know you're in the front row where I can see you."

"Okay, if that's what you want. I'll come back here after you show."

"Thank you, Mama."

Kristy went back to the stands and sat nervously on the edge of the seat. The family held hands as Nicki made her way into the arena. Kristy watched her beautiful daughter work Crystal Locket like an adult and she felt such a sense of pride and joy. Nicki and John were her greatest accomplishments in life and she so welcomed the thought of watching them grow into what they would become.

Nicki won the National Futurity.

After the award ceremony there was dead silence in the building until she spotted Nick on Rascal at the far end of the arena, Nicki was on Crystal Locket beside him.

Over the loud speaker, in front of thousands of people, Kristy heard Nick say:

"Kristy, I love you, will you marry me!"

Kristy sat there stunned, she couldn't move. She looked first to Joe then to Mavis, both were smiling. Sarah leaned over and kissed her on the cheek. "They're riding in this direction," Sarah said and pointed at Nick and Nicki.

Kristy's mouth dropped open, a lump had formed in her throat. She couldn't move.

Nick slid Rascal to a stop and leaned from his saddle to the fence where he tipped his hat at Mavis and Ellen before shaking Joe's hand. Nicki stopped beside him wearing the biggest smile Kristy had ever seen.

As Nick dismounted and planted his boot heels on the ground Kristy slid over the rail where he caught her in his arms. As they looked into each other's eyes Kristy said, "Yes." Nick's mouth lowered to hers and the crowd went wild with applause. Kristy was left breathless.

Joe handed Johnny to Nick. "Let's go to the ranch, there's been enough time wasted."

A loud whistle echoed from behind the corrals where Jez and Rowdy stood. Nick tipped his hat to the audience before offering his right arm to Kristy. He grabbed Rascal's reins, motioned to Nicki and the four of them made their way out covering the length of the arena.

"Mama, Daddy says we're going home," Nicki said. "Where's home?"

From the stands where the family stood applauding, they heard, "We'll see y'all at the ranch!"

Kristy couldn't stop shaking. "Does that answer your question, Nicki?"

"Yeehaw!" she yelled.

Johnny got excited at hearing and seeing Nicki and threw his arms about and something akin to yeehaw came out of his mouth too.

That evening after they put the kids to bed and were in their bedroom Nick noticed a framed 8x10 photo on his dresser. He picked it up. "When did you have this taken of Johnny?" he asked.

Kristy came to stand behind him and put her arms around his waist. She smiled. "That's not Johnny. That's you. Mom must have found it in the album and had it framed."

Nick did a double take. He was stunned that he couldn't tell himself from his son. "I guess the Chandler genes are pretty strong."

"They have to be to live in this part of Texas. Strong genes produce strong sons."

He smiled. "And daughters."

"Are you thinking of Nicki?"

Nick put his arms around her. "You and Nicki both. It takes a strong woman to produce strong children. The Chandler's are finally home again to their Texas roots."

"Nick, are you sure getting married is what you want? What happens to the clinic? Or my job?"

Nick slowly undid one button of her shirt at a time. "That is exactly what I want. I sold the clinic to Brian and with the money I won at the show I can do what I want out here. As for your job...maybe you want to spend one week a month in Dallas, but the rest of the time I want you here with us." His lips brushed against her neck as his fingers continued their journey. "We still have two more Chandler's to produce."

Her breath came in short gasps as his hands brushed lightly over her body. "You've been talking to Nicki again!"

"Yep, she told me after we have Sierra she wants another brother that she can call Jack. But what she wants most is to see her parents get married up there on cemetery hill so she can call herself and her brother Nicole and John Chandler."

Kristy closed her eyes and savored Nick's mouth on hers. Then teasing, she said, "You mean I won't get my Nicholas Junior?"

Nick drew back. "I'm too old to play daddy to that many kids."

"I think the two we have are enough. This house isn't big enough for more kids."

Nick laughed and pulled her onto the bed. "What happens, happens."

It took another week before it hit Kristy that Nick had actually proposed to her. Then the idea of a wedding at the ranch became overwhelming to her. Sure, she'd help plan the weddings they'd had at the agency's ranch, but she was detached from those people, and they were just weddings, money in the bank gladly paid by total strangers.

She woke early one morning before the sun had come up, made coffee and sat on the front porch. Her mind was reeling. What kind of wedding did she want? Wouldn't she have to invite her clients...from all over the world? Oh my God, she thought, there would be a guest list long enough to choke a horse. And of course Nick's clients and colleagues would be invited, then there was friends and family. Even with the roughest guesstimate there would be well over a thousand people they needed to invite. Maybe she needed to call Greg in San Francisco and ask his opinion? Good Lord, she'd have to invite Greg and Jed. What if Jed came in drag? A quick trip to Las Vegas was beginning to sound extremely good.

When she heard the screen door open she looked up to see Nick standing there in his bare feet and shirtless. "Couldn't sleep?"

She handed him her cup of coffee. "Nick, I...maybe we should just live together for the rest of our lives."

He sat down beside her. "Getting cold feet? I thought I was suppose to do that."

"The logistics of a ranch wedding is mind boggling."

Nick took a sip of coffee. "How's that?"

"With everyone we'd have to invite I'd find myself becoming me right back in a professional capacity. The scheduling of flights and rooms for my clients...the..."

Nick leaned over and kissed her to shut her up. "The trouble with you is you think too much. Turn the job over to Mavis or Sarah. We are getting married up there on cemetery hill whether we have two people or two thousand. Set a date."

Kristy leaned close to Nick and laid her head on his shoulder. "Can I give you a wedding gift of a decent runway?"

He gave her a sidelong glance. "Am I going to be shocked when I learn what you're worth?"

She smiled. "What's mine is yours."

Kristy decided to spend a week in Dallas to pull things together. When she entered her office she found Sarah sitting at her desk looking forlorn. "What's the matter, Sarah?"

When she saw Kristy she came to life. "Oh my God, it's so good to see you here. This place is dead without you." She quickly stood up and came out from behind her desk where she hugged Kristy. "What brings you to Dallas?"

"A wedding. I need help."

Sarah grinned. "Yours?"

Kristy nodded and sat down on the couch. "I don't even know where to begin."

"Then let us handle the arrangements," Hunter said from the doorway.

Kristy looked up. He looked tired and drawn. Her first instinct was to hold him in her arms but had second thoughts about that. Instead, she simply said, "I plan to spend a week each month here in Dallas. The rest of my time will be with my family at the ranch."

Hunter made his way across the office and sat down beside Kristy. "Are you happy?"

"Yes, I am."

Sarah watched the disappointment glaze over Hunter's face. She'd seen him pull away from everyone he'd become close to since Kristy turned him down. And that included Gracie.

He reached out and traced Kristy's jaw line with his thumb. "Then all you have to do is show up ready to marry Nick. We'll take care of the rest. Give us four weeks to pull it together. Sarah knows what to do."

He stood to leave but before he could reach the door Kristy said, "Wait!" He turned around and she walked into his arms. Hunter's eyes closed as he held her against him. "Thank you for being you, Hunter, and for loving me. I'm sorry I've hurt you. You've been the one person who's been with me through every possible disaster and supported me the most."

Hunter gazed down into those beautiful blue-green eyes of hers that he loved so much, cupped her face in his hands and lowered his mouth to hers. She was the one thing he'd wanted the most and the one thing his money couldn't buy. "I'll always be here for you when you need me," he said and left the office.

Kristy didn't want to dwell on what might have been between them so she quickly turned to look at Sarah. "Will you be my bridesmaid?"

"Of course. Do you want the traditional cowboy wedding? You want it catered?"

Kristy plopped back down on the couch. "Think I can find a lace gown that allows me to ride on a horse without revealing too much leg?"

Both women laughed at the image of a bride looking more like a hooker.

Sarah suddenly had a thought as her face lit up. "I saw the perfect dress for you, a lace corset style bodice with a train and flounce and the front of the skirt comes to just above those fancy wedding boots you'll have to buy. And of course you'll wear a felt cowboy hat with a pearl band and lace with a long veil in the back." Her mind was reeling. "Maybe you should arrive in that buggy they've got stored in that second old barn. How about Ellen bringing out the chuck wagon and we'll hire chefs to do the cookin'...oh my but I'm gettin' excited." She started to pace around the room with a million ideas running through her head. "Thanks, Kristy, I need this wedding to take my mind off..."

"Off Brian?"

"Yeah, off Brian."

Kristy stood and took a deep breath. "Well...I guess we have four weeks to get our act together."

"You just leave it to me...and Hunter, we'll give you and Nick the wedding of your dreams."

Kristy had the feeling she'd really be getting the wedding of Sarah's dreams. "Want to join me at the Lone Star?"

Sarah beamed. "You bet."

Mavis was overjoyed to see Kristy come into the bar. "What brings you into Dallas? Doc with you? The kids?"

Kristy kissed Mavis on the cheek. "I'm alone. I came to town to get help planning my wedding. Hunter and Sarah have volunteered to help me out."

Mavis smiled. "That Hunter is one sad man, but he'll no doubt get over you. Thank God Doc finally came to his senses and decided to be your husband instead of your man. So...is he a happy man these days?"

Kristy shrugged. "I certainly hope so. The kids are overjoyed to have him with them everyday."

"And how are you doing livin' back at the ranch with the family?" She could see that Kristy was happy, but something seemed to be missing.

Kristy managed a smile and looked at Sarah. "We're doing fine at the ranch. Dad is happy to finally have his grandchildren living on the ranch with him. Mavis, you should see him with them, I really wish I'd grown up with brothers and sisters. He seems to thrive on teaching those kids something new everyday. But I plan to spend one week a month in Dallas. I can't give up the best job I've ever had I would miss it too much."

Mavis nodded, she was sad not to be able to see Joe with the children, but understood. "Sarah, what about you? Brian's in the other room."

Sarah hung her head slightly. "We had a fight and I told him about me and Hunter. I guess he'll never forgive me for cheating on him. I have to move on."

"Ah hell, what's good for the goose is good for the gander," Mavis said. "Brian's no puritan ya know. Why is it...there seems to be a double standard when it comes to their egos?"

Sarah laughed. "Mavis, I couldn't tell you a single thing about men. I love him, I lost him, and now I'll have to let him go."

"Well...just the same why don't you go on in and see him."

Kristy watched as Sarah made her way slowly into the dimness of the other room. "He's not with Jez, is he?"

Mavis shook her head. "Lord I hope not. Naw, he's been moping like a love sick puppy since he found out about Hunter and Sarah. You warned him though and he didn't take it seriously, he should have expected her to find the lovin' she needed somewhere else."

"Just the same...it must have hurt Brian. He'll never find anyone who loves him as much as Sarah does."

"Well hell, if Doc can come around, so can Brian."

Kristy looked at the other room. "Nick has children, Brian doesn't."

Mavis raised an eyebrow. "Then maybe Sarah should do something about that."

"Mavis! That's not Sarah's style...and I never set out to get pregnant either, but it happened."

Mavis just shrugged and grabbed her bar towel. "You and Doc were always meant to be together."

"If that's true why has it taken ten years to get here?"

"Because the first seven years he didn't know about his daughter, and Mallory did a real number on Doc. She hurt him before he married her and she hurt him even worse after they were married. It's taken him a long time to get over losin' everything he had."

Kristy looked at Mavis. "Then I'm sorry he thought I'd hurt him like she did. I love him and want what he wants. Nick and our children are my world. My children and I are financially independent so he won't have worry about his money."

Mavis came out from behind the bar and put her arms around Kristy. "I know they're your life. You're going to have a wonderful life with Nick and my grandbabies. And I fully expect you to bring those precious children to me when you come to Dallas so I can have some time with them."

"You have my promise. I will never keep those children from seeing you."

"You gonna wait for Sarah to come out?"

"No…I think I'm going in." Kristy sat in the darkness of the inner bar and watched Sarah and Brian at the far booth. Sarah was doing most of the talking. In her heart she wanted those two to make up, but Brian was no doubt as stubborn and proud as Nick and it would take more then words to heal his wounds.

"Mine if I join you?"

Kristy looked up to see Hunter standing there. "No, not at all."

"What are those two fighting about now?" he asked.

"You."

"Ah shit, she didn't tell him about the time in California did she?"

"She did."

"Then I think I'd better make myself scare. Want to join me at Dallas Rhodes?"

Kristy took a final look at Sarah and Brian. "That might be a good idea."

Once in Dallas Rhodes Hunter asked Kristy to dance with him. "So," he said as he held her tight against him. "Did you ever tell Nick about us?"

She looked up into those green eyes of his. "No. I did tell him early on that we lived together and I'm sure he thinks we had something going on between us. I never bothered to tell him any different."

Hunter kissed the top of her head and relived in his mind the one time she let him make full passionate love to her. "I love you, and would like nothing better then to spend the rest of my life telling you that, but I know you love Nick. I'm letting go. Just know that I'll always be here for you." He pulled her tighter against him.

"Thank you, Hunter, for letting me follow my dream. And for putting up with me."

"You deserve to be happy."

"So does Sarah. I just hope Brian will eventually forgive her. They belong together."

"And if he doesn't?"

Kristy smiled up at him. "I wonder if she can wait ten years to get her man?"

Hunter's laughter filled the room.

CHAPTER THIRTY

Kristy was banned from planning her wedding, and she didn't mind. She was a nervous wreck no matter what she did or didn't do. Hunter and Matt absolutely wouldn't hear of her paying for it or getting too involved other then to give her approval on everything done. Sarah was given full rein to hire the best consultants in Dallas, the best caterer, order the best food, and she even had two secretaries sending out invitations and making follow up phone calls. They made reservations for flights in and out of Dallas, booked rooms, accepted gifts at the office that would be taken to the ranch, and by the time the day arrived some two thousand guests were scheduled to attend.

The press had been notified and even Advertising Age was sending a reporter who wanted to do a piece on the Jordan Agency's miracle Ad Executive, Kristy Williams, and how she turned ordinary cattle ranching, a saloon and a restaurant into a profitable adventure for the firm and their world wide clients. And since two famous musicians, Kristy's clients would provide the entertainment, two tabloid magazines made an offer that couldn't be refused. Kristy did maintain the right to choose which photos and articles would be used.

For a week the ranch swarmed with busy strangers transforming the place into a suitable venue for the biggest cowboy wedding anyone in those parts could remember. Kristy was amazed but not allowed to help. Ellen took charge of any duty Kristy might have had.

A huge wooden dance floor was erected outside and another inside the barn. Picnic tables appeared and western decorations were everywhere. The day before the wedding bales of straw that would be used as seats were decorated with rope and wild flowers. Tables set beneath canopies had bouquets of wild weed, wild flowers, sunflowers and colorful Zinnias in old buckets, boots, old cowboy hats, baskets, mason jars and even old tins were used as containers and coils of rope at the base tended to add to the theme and hide the containers.

The barn had swags and bows made of calico and gingham materials everywhere. Bales of straw lined the dance floor. Nothing was left undecorated. Anything that even hinted of the old west the decorators found a place to display. A huge longhorn skull with horns now adorned the chuck wagon, and there were so many rolling barbeque pits set up no one would possibly go hungry. Piles of dried ten-year old mesquite wood was delivered by the truckload and placed near the cooking area. Beef, pork and chicken were going to be the foods of the day. Barbequed, dry herb rubbed, and plain cooked meat was on the menu. There were going to be so many side dishes even Kristy was amazed at the selection. A famous pastry chef from California offered his services because he wanted to attend an authentic cowboy wedding to get the feel of it. Along with the traditional bride and groom cake, every guest would have their own individual miniature wedding cake to take home.

Tumbleweeds and denim seemed to be the overall theme. Kristy thought she'd stepped into a western movie set and expected John Wayne to come riding through at any moment. She had never seen so many galvanized tubs in so many sizes and various states of condition ready to be filled with ice for beer, soda and champagne. She couldn't help but wonder what they'd do to cemetery hill!

During the week of commotion Kristy hadn't seen much of Nick and wondered if he was now having second thoughts. She certainly wouldn't blame him if he did. The day before the big event Nick was nowhere around and Kristy knew just where to find him. She rode up to his favorite thinking spot. Hadn't he done the same thing right before he was to marry Mallory? Maybe she should give him the option to back out. The last thing she wanted was for him to feel forced into marrying her. She intended to marry for life but if he felt different she should know ahead of time.

She found him lying there on the grass with his long legs stretched out, his hat pulled over his eyes and his arms beneath his head. Rascal grazed lazily nearby. She watched him for a moment deciding whether to intrude on his quiet time. Just the sight of him made her heart beat faster. She loved him beyond words. She turned to leave.

"Where you going?" he asked.

"You looked so peaceful I didn't want to bother you."

"Come lay by me."

She did and rested her head on his arm. "It's so quiet up here. I'm sorry our wedding has turned into such an extravaganza. I know it's good publicity for the agency, but..."

"It's all right," he assured her.

"No, Nick it's not at all what I dreamed of as a little girl growing up here. I had no idea working for Matt would turn into something so big. He let me go with my imagination and his and Hunter's money and I made all of us more money. I've always wanted to be a wife and mother here on the ranch, not some big shot ad executive. Even articles of our wedding will bring in more clients. I've already let Matt and Hunter know I'll only be in Dallas one week a month and they've agreed." She turned onto her side and put her arm across his stomach. "Are you getting cold feet yet? If this isn't what you want..."

He tipped his hat back and looked at her. "No I'm not getting cold feet. You'll still be a wife and mother on the ranch, with a part time job in Dallas...for now."

"Nick, I love you."

He hugged her, then reached over and unbuttoned her blouse. "I've always wanted to make love you to up here, I think now is the perfect time, don't you?"

He didn't have to ask twice.

The day of the wedding Kristy looked out the front windows to a sea of limo's, sports cars, pickup trucks, vintage and new Harley motorcycles, sedans and horses. There were even seven helicopters sitting in a nearby pasture, one of them belonged to the agency. Sarah told Kristy the guests would be taken to cemetery hill by horse drawn hay wagons, buckboards and carriages and anything else they could throw bales of straw on and attach a horse to. Neighboring ranches pitched in with wagons and even sent their own cowboys over to help drive the guests. They were all dressed for the occasion. Kristy was sure there were a lot of deserted ranches that day, at least within a two hundred mile radius. They were guests at her wedding.

Kristy was a nervous wreck! She shook so much she didn't even have coffee that morning, let alone eat breakfast. Ellen, Sarah, Gracie and Mavis separated her from Nick and the children. The only male allowed near Kristy's room was Hunter.

"Mind if I come in?" he asked. He smiled as he watched Sarah helping with Kristy's hair.

Kristy flew into his arms and clung like a vine. "I'm so nervous," she moaned.

Hunter grinned and kissed the top of her head. "This is what you wanted, isn't it?" He could feel her body shaking.

She nodded. "Yes...but..."

"Take a deep breath," he ordered. "I came in here to tell you Matt and I have made you a partner in the agency, if you want it."

Kristy pulled back and her mouth dropped open. "You've got to be kidding!"

Hunter smiled. "Nope, this wedding of yours has already more then paid for itself in new clients. No matter what you do you brings in clients, which in turn brings in money."

"Hold still!" Sarah yelled at Kristy as she pulled the laces tighter on the back of the corset style bodice. "Where's that pearl necklace Mavis gave you?" She found it on the dresser and put it around Kristy's neck.

"But...I don't want to work more than a week a month."

Hunter picked up her wedding hat and placed it on her head. "As a partner you won't have to work that much. You'll have input into where we want the agency to go. We can do video teleconferencing on a daily basis. Kristy, we can't lose you."

"Sit down," Sarah ordered. "Put these fancy lace boots on." Her mind raced, something old...the pearl necklace, something new? Something borrowed...the bible, and something blue? "What do you have that's blue and something new? It won't do to break with tradition!"

Kristy was torn by Matt's offer, but not for long. She laced up the white Victorian style wedding boots and stood to face Hunter. "I'll do it. Give me some time off to be with Nick. If I can arrange my schedule so it fits with his…thanks Hunter." She reached up and kissed him.

Hunter raised an eyebrow as his gaze slowly moved up and down her body. "I never thought I would say this about any bride, but God, you're gorgeous." He quickly turned to Sarah and said, "And you, Sarah, you're just as gorgeous in that dress you're wearing. If Brian doesn't get the picture after today you'd better give up on him."

Sarah gave him a devilish grin. "You available?"

Hunter winked. "You just never know." He didn't mean to tease her but it was his nature. There could never be anything between him and Sarah other than that couple of times he'd had her in California. She didn't suit him like Kristy did.

He kissed Kristy on the cheek and handed her a small velvet box he pulled out of his jacket pocket. "Here's something new, a gift from me."

Kristy reluctantly accepted the gift and opened it only to gasp at the sight of a pair of large diamond ear studs. She gazed up at Hunter as she put them in her ears. "Thank you, they're beautiful."

Sarah's heart began to pound against her chest. "Kristy put on the garter." They still needed something blue. Her mind raced as her eyes darted around the room looking for something blue. What was she forgetting? Now she knew how Kristy felt the night Dallas Rhodes opened.

Hunter hesitated before leaving, watching Kristy pull her white dress up and slip the garter on that gorgeous long leg of hers, the sight took his breath away. Every memory of his hand running up and down that same leg came flooding back to him. He also removed his sapphire pinkie ring and put it on Kristy's ring finger of her right hand. "Here's something blue."

Kristy stumbled with her words. "I…I'll give this back after the ceremony." My God, she thought, she must be wearing a cool ten to twelve thousand dollars worth of jewels!

Ellen came into the room and handed Kristy a Chandler family bible that had a grouping of wildflowers tied by soft rope encircling it. "This is your bouquet. We have a real one you can throw later on."

She smiled at her beautiful daughter. "Your dad is ready."

Suddenly Kristy wasn't nervous and wondered why? Hunter had given her the news when he did on purpose because he knew that would give her a future to look forward to. Nick and the kids were her life, but he also knew she needed to have that creative outlet. It would work out, it would!

Old Jake drove Kristy and Joe in an open flower decorated carriage up to cemetery hill. Rowdy drove the bridesmaids. The altar was located between the posts at the entrance of the cemetery and beneath the overhead hand carved sign that read Chandler. Wheat, wild flowers and Zinnias were intertwined along the newly whitewashed fencing around the cemetery with tumbleweeds placed here and there. Nick's mother's headstone had fresh flowers adorning it as if she were part of the whole affair. That was how Nick wanted it, to be married before the entire Chandler family resting there as if he was letting them know there were and would be new Chandlers to keep the ranch going for future generations.

Old Jake pulled the carriage to a halt where the red carpet started. Joe helped Kristy out. When Old Jake reached beneath the seat of the carriage and pulled out a shotgun that he put in Joe's hand, Kristy gasped in horror.

"You wouldn't!" she whispered.

Joe grinned as he looked at Kristy. "Ah, daughter, it's just for effect, a real cowboy wedding." What he was really thinking was, Nick was damn well going to make things right this time, and just maybe the shotgun would serve as a reminder.

Kristy was amazed at the number of western dressed guests seated on bales of straw. Denim and diamonds mixed all together into the most informal wedding she'd ever seen. And she liked it that way. J.C. Norton stood near the altar with an acoustic guitar strumming traditional country western wedding songs. Kristy held her breath as she looked at her beautiful little girl dressed in a long white lace dress and acting as her flower girl sprinkling yellow rose pedals on the carpet. Gracie and Sarah were beautiful as her bridesmaids.

Kristy couldn't take her eyes off Nick as they walked toward him. Dressed in his western cut black tuxedo he resembled something out of the old west. Wearing a black Stetson he looked all cowboy, handsome and virile radiating strength and charm at the same time.

Brian stood beside him looking almost as handsome. And in-between the two men stood John, dressed exactly like Nick in the cutest little tuxedo, black hat and cowboy boots Kristy had ever seen. She was overwhelmed by love for both of them.

Nick couldn't believe the vision of his Texas beauty walking toward him. But what in the hell was Joe doing carrying a shotgun? When Johnny reached up and took hold of his hand...Nick knew the symbolism and smiled at his soon to be new father-in-law.

Somehow they made it through the ceremony. Kristy and Nick exchanged gold cigar band wedding rings that had the ranch brand etched into the outer circle. Kristy knew, wearing the Bar C brand meant she was now part of the Chandler family forever. When the preacher pronounced them man and wife and Nick kissed his bride, John yelled "Yeehaw" in his tiny voice and the guests, who had each been given miniature cowbells, rang them scaring every horse standing patiently attached to the wagons. Seasoned ranch hands from many different spreads scrambled to grab reins and soothe horses to prevent a stampede.

The preacher announced, "I give you Doctor and Mrs. Nick Chandler, their children Nicole and John Chandler."

Nick and Kristy turned toward their guests grabbed the hands of their children and arm in arm walked back down the red carpet to the carriage. Cameras flashed everywhere. Old Jake whisked them back to the ranch house for what looked to be one hell of a cowboy reception.

Ellen took charge of the children and quickly saw to it they were changed into more appropriate clothes to celebrate in. Mavis was in tears as she hugged Nick and Kristy, and then went to find her grandchildren. Joe put his shotgun away. They lined up to greet their incoming guests from cemetery hill.

By the time the last guest was thanked for attending wonderful smells of the mesquite fired grills permeated the air. Children ran around frolicking with other children and dogs chased after them. Kristy circulated among her foreign clients and adored the Japanese who returned with their ten-gallon hats and rhinestone outfits. The Germans and Italians were also there dressed to the hilt as cowboys. Guido must have seen too many spaghetti westerns. He wore a bandelero of fake bullets, which was Mexican, not American western.

He seemed to be having a good time. Greg from San Francisco came dressed to look like Doc Holliday while his life partner Jed, came as Big Nose Kate, Doc's girlfriend. Jed was so convincing no one even knew he wasn't female. Greg and Jed made over Kristy like a long lost sister and couldn't get over her precious son John or how Nicki had grown. Annie too was just as amazed and cried the first time she saw how grown up Nicki had become.

Hunter tended to watch over Kristy from afar. He couldn't win her as his wife, but she would still be in his life and that was important to him. He watched her now with the same amazement as the first time he'd seen her with clients. Every client they had loved working with her. She'd made the Jordan Agency the hottest new business in Dallas while making them all wealthy, and that included Mavis. It would be interesting to see if she gave Nick any more children. Somehow he doubted she wanted any more knowing Nick wasn't around to help her with the birth of the last two. He was glad she'd put her foot down about paving the runway. They really needed one out here since she'd be flying to Dallas and back on a regular basis. Maybe he should give her the helicopter since she had her license. It would probably cost them close to a thousand dollars an hour if she used the Aerostar. Which usually meant she would bring in an income twice what he spent on her. And she wouldn't have to depend on Nick or her dad to fly her to Dallas in Nick's plane. Maybe he should convince her to learn to fly Nick's plane. He smiled to himself. Wait until she saw the next surprise he had for her.

"How do you feel, Hunter?" Sarah said and handed him a glass of champagne.

He couldn't take his eyes off Kristy. "Like I've gained a best friend." He loved Kristy beyond words and would always be available to her needs no matter what they were.

"Come on, let's get some of that barbeque I'm starving," Sarah said.

By the time the cake was cut, toasts made, food devoured, bouquet and garter thrown it was time for Nick and Kristy to get on their horses and ride into the sunset. Which was actually riding to the airplane and had nothing to do with a sunset. Nick refused to tell her where they were going.

They landed in Dallas only to get on another plane, destination unknown by Kristy until they were airborne and the Captain said welcome aboard the flight to Orange County California.

Kristy put her hand on Nick's arm. "Why are we going to California?" She was totally surprised. She hadn't expected a honeymoon at all.

He leaned over and kissed her cheek. "Seems the agency wanted to pay for our honeymoon as well as our wedding…only catch is Hunter bought a horse ranch outside of Santa Barbara that he wants you to look over and me to inspect the horses. He said you had a key to the beach house and to his yacht. He's ordered someone to take us by boat up to Santa Barbara and then has someone else picking us up there to take us to the ranch. Says we can use the boat any way we want."

Kristy chuckled. "Wow, just what I've always dreamed of…a working honeymoon." She wondered how many millions she'd make for them on her honeymoon.

Nick laced her hand in his. "Or you'll be working all right…when we're alone. I'm kind of looking forward to seeing this beach house where you spent so much time with Hunter."

It was late by the time they got to the beach house. Kristy walked from room to room opening all the windows and sliding door that led out onto the deck. She opened the refrigerator and took out a beer and handed it to Nick, then took his hand and led him down the hall to the bedroom she'd always used while living there.

"I never in my wildest dreams would have thought I'd see you in Newport Beach," she grinned and unbuckled his belt. "Thank God it's off season, you might actually enjoy it."

"Didn't have time before." His fingers undid each button on her blouse.

Kristy unsnapped each of his buttons and opened his shirt to place kisses along his chest and neck, followed by her hands. "Wait until you see the tub in the master bathroom," she teased and led him to the sunken tub with resting benches and water jets. She filled it half way with water leaving the center bench an island and threw in some lightly scented bath salts she'd left behind when she returned to Dallas. She also found some candles and lit them.

Nick took one look at the enormous round tub and said, "Looks like a Texas swimming pool."

Kristy gave him a sly look. "Hunter likes the best."

Nick drew his brows together. "I'll just bet he does." He cocked his head and asked, "Did you and Hunter spend much time in here?" Did he really want to know? What was in the past should stay in the past.

Kristy was glad he cared enough to ask. "No, I was never in this tub at the same time as Hunter." She stepped out of her clothes, piled her hair on top of her head and climbed into the tub. She crooked a finger at him and said, "I think it's time to give you the full California treatment."

Nick couldn't get out of his clothes fast enough and into the tub where he lay stretched out on the island bench to enjoy the view of his new bride naked and turned on as scented water swirled around her from the jets.

Kristy put one leg on each side of him and sat on his stomach while her hands went into his hair and she kissed him with a passion of a woman that loved her man. Her breasts brushed against his naked skin sending a rush of excitement through both of them. Slowly, she drew her mouth down across his chest to his stomach where she teased him with her tongue and lips. Nick knew just what to do and took them both to heightened pleasure. Before they sank lower into the tub Nick's lips brushed against her ear and he murmured, "I love you."

After the relaxing bath, Kristy led Nick back to Hunter's custom made oversized bed and gave him a back massage that soon led to other things and every time they made love Kristy showed him a new twist to 'California lovin'. With the sound of the ocean crashing against the shore Kristy gave Nick her body and soul.

They slept late the next morning and only woke when the phone rang. Kristy answered it. "Give us an hour," she said. When she hung up she turned to Nick and ran her fingers lightly over the stubble of his unshaven face. "I love you Nick Chandler, and I'd like nothing better then to stay in this bed and show you, but…our yacht awaits."

Nick grinned. "Ah, and just when I was getting the hang of California lovin'."

Kristy snuggled next to him. "You'll never get the hang of it, I'll always throw in something new. We need to get dressed and out of here."

Nick tossed the covers aside and said, "But I'm hungry."

Kristy took one look at him and raised an eyebrow. "We'll have breakfast on the boat…it'll take a while to get to Santa Barbara. I promise by the time we reach our destination you'll have a breakfast fit for a king…and me."

Nick pulled her into his arms. "How do feel about being Mrs. Nick Chandler?"

She looked at the brand on her wedding band. "Like I was born to the position. And…our two children thank you for officially making them Chandlers. Did you hear Nicki introducing herself to everyone as Nicole Chandler, she didn't even use Nicki."

Nick chuckled as he thought of his daughter. "She seems to be the best of you and me."

Kristy grinned. "A future vet with an attitude and ability to give orders. I'm going to love watching you with the kids now that we're all on the ranch. John should really be something to watch as he grows up and learns from you."

Nick put his arms around her and hugged her tight. She was the love of his life and he could hardly wait to get her back on the ranch so they could start the rest of their lives together.

When the yacht reached Santa Barbara a limo waited for them.

Kristy asked the driver, "Is the ranch far?"

"No Mrs. Chandler, about twenty minutes."

The ranch was beautiful with green irrigated pastures, rolling hills, large oaks and white vinyl fences edging the road and long drive up to the ranch house. Some of the finest looking horses Kristy had ever seen grazed lazily in several pastures. They walked around the place until they came to the stables, which were modern, clean and filled with pregnant mares.

"My God," Kristy said, "why did Hunter buy a place like this?"

Nick remarked, "You tell me."

She shook her head. "I can't imagine what he was thinking of, this place looks like it can run itself. How's he going to make any money here?"

A strapping muscular middle-aged gentleman walked out of the stable office to greet them. "Good afternoon, I'm Clay Sterling, you must be Doctor and Mrs. Chandler."

Nick shook the man's hand and said, "Yes, we are."

"Good, you've seen part of the ranch. As you can see we have a good many mares that we'd like you to take a look at. We do have a vet but Mr. Taylor wanted your opinion."

"Then, if you'll excuse me," Nick said, "I'll go back to the stables."

Clay looked at Kristy and said, "I think you might be interested in the ranch house itself. There is also a letter waiting for you from Mr. Taylor."

Kristy was totally confused by the turn of events. Why had Hunter bought this place? Why did he want Nick to check out the mares? No, there was more to this than just a horse ranch.

"Clay," Kristy said as she looked around the enormous silent house. "Doesn't anyone live here?"

Clay shook his head. "Not formally. The place's been empty of people for some time now. But as you can see there are still plenty of furnishings."

"Don't you live here?"

"I live in another house on the property. I manage the place."

"Who owns all those horses?"

"Mr. Taylor."

"You mean, other people really own them and board them here but Mr. Taylor owns the place?"

Clay shook his head. "No, he owns everything, including the horses." He walked over to a baby grand piano sitting in the music room and picked up an envelope and brought it back to Kristy.

"He told me to give this to you after you saw the ranch."

Kristy was more confused then ever. She opened the envelope and pulled out what looked like a deed to the place. "What's this?" Clay handed her a second envelope. It read:

My darling Kristy,

I bought this ranch for you while we were living in California. If you'll look at the deed you will see Kristy, Nicole and John Chandler are the owners. But as partner of the agency we thought you might want to lease it back to agency after you decide what you want to do to it to make it profitable. It was signed Hunter.

Kristy stormed outside and pulled out her cell phone to dial Hunter's number. When he answered she yelled, "You sonofabitch! Why'd you do this?"

Nick came to an abrupt halt at hearing how angry Kristy sounded.

Hunter said, "The ranch was going to be a gift to you and the children as Williams', but since you married him I put Chandler on the deed. I bought it for you when we were in California before John was born. Why are you so upset?"

Kristy scowled as she blew off steam. "And who the hell is going to pay the taxes on this place?"

Hunter started to laugh. "If you can't figure a way to turn a profit, I'll pay the taxes. If you'll calm down enough to walk around the ranch you'll come up with some idea of what you want to do. Hell, if you can't I'll take the place back. Don't rush to judgment until you've looked the place over."

"Now you sound like a kiss ass lawyer. I told you I only wanted to work one week a month, at the most. Even if I am now a partner, how the hell can I do that?" Her gaze suddenly settled on the front pastures and she had a vision of what to do with the place. "Ah...Hunter," she felt much calmer now.

"Oh my God, you already have an idea?"

Nick followed Kristy's gaze. What the hell was she looking at?

"Yeah, I do. Play golf? Remember Sonoma Mission Inn?

"What?"

"I've got this enormous ranch house and pastures coming out of my ears. Why would we need anymore horses when we can turn the friggin' place into a golf course, restaurant and spa? We're twenty minutes from Santa Barbara, probably ninety minutes from LA. I'm sure there's even enough room for a runway for the LA crowd. We'll call the restaurant The Headquarters House. We could do upscale cooking, with a little Texas mesquite on the side. We'll get some Black Angus for the back pastures. We wouldn't have to depend on foreign clients to support the place when we have enough big shot clients in LA who all have big shot friends. And...it's secluded enough for privacy for people like our Robert when he's not chartering the yacht."

Stunned by her actions, Nick leaned back on his boot heels. How did she do it so easily?

Hunter was laughing at the other end. "Told you you would find something to do with the place. I'll let Matt know about your ideas. Want to cut us in or keep it to yourself? And how's the honeymoon going?"

Kristy suddenly noticed Nick staring at her. "Thank you for the use of the yacht and beach house. As you can imagine I'm making good use of it." There, she hoped Hunter got the picture loud and clear!

"I thought you would. Hey, I'll see you in a day or two."

Kristy turned off her cell and took Nick by the hand. "Let's take another look around the place since your son and daughter own it."

Nick stopped dead in his tracks. "What the hell?"

Kristy laced her arm through his. "Nick, you have to understand, there was a time when I thought the kids and I would be leaving Texas to start a life out here. John hadn't been born yet and even though we were living together we never saw each other. You were never around to give me any kind of encouragement about our future. I didn't think we even had one."

Nick scowled. "So what does that have to do with this place?"

"Hunter bought it for me when we were in California, when he asked me to marry him. I honestly didn't know he'd bought this place until Clay handed me the deed. Hunter just told me. I had no idea he put the children's name and mine on the deed. He said he'd be glad to take it back if we decide we don't want it. If anything, by getting the agency involved I'll be making even more money for the kid's future. Unless…we keep it for the kids, especially Nicki. If she has her heart set on going to UC Davis this could be her place to spend some time."

Nick wasn't sure what to think. "Shame to waste the horse flesh here, could think about bringing them to our Texas ranch."

Kristy put her arms around his waist and hugged him. "Then why don't we pick the cream of the crop and anything else we might want to send back to the ranch…before I think about giving half of the ranch back to Hunter. I'll be given free rein to turn this place into something. We can keep a small part for horses, maybe a stable for the spa goers. If Nicki does decide to go to Davis she can still spend part of her time here…on weekends, because her summers should be spent at the Chandler ranch learning to be a vet from her dad."

"Are we ready to go home yet?" Nick asked. "We could give Clay a call about the horses I think we'll want."

Kristy nodded. "I need to be home, where we could escape to your favorite thinking spot. We need to get our lives started as the

Chandler family."

The next morning they boarded a plane headed toward the sunrise and a new beginning. Kristy was happier then she'd been in years.

CHAPTER
THIRTY ONE

The morning after they returned to the ranch from California Kristy woke early, she knew she'd have to help with breakfast and wanted some quiet time before she got her day started. She checked in on the kids and they too were awake. She'd have to forego any quiet time she was hoping for.

"Good morning, Mama," Nicki said and pulled a tee shirt over John's head. "Johnny couldn't sleep so I brushed his teeth and got him dressed."

Kristy walked into their room and hugged both of them. "Want to come down to the kitchen to help me cook breakfast?" She picked Johnny up and they walked downstairs into the quiet kitchen. She flipped on the light and set Johnny down on the floor to play among scattered toys that Ellen left there. Nicki took the egg basket and went out to the hen house.

The sun was just beginning to lighten the sky as Kristy looked out the kitchen window to a view she'd always loved as a kid growing up there. How many mornings had she helped mama make breakfast for the ranch hands? Or looked out this same window at the view. She always felt as if she belonged in the kitchen cooking for the ranch and a family. That was probably because of her upbringing, but now it was reality. Her little boy played happily on the floor next to her and her daughter gathered eggs just like she'd done. Her heart swelled with pride as she watched the dusk fade to dawn.

Nicki returned with the eggs and sat the basket on the counter then went to sit at the table to read a book. Kristy smiled and thanked her. Nicole Chandler. There was a time when they lived in San Francisco that she never expected Nicki to have the Chandler name, let alone be back on the ranch with two Chandler children. Now, Nicki would wear that name proudly for the rest of her growing up years. And someday she too would stand at this same window looking out and waiting for the sun to rise with her own children playing at her feet. Well…probably not, Nicki was too much like Nick. She doubted children would enter into the picture for years and years, if at all, especially if Nicki did become a vet. That girl, even at nine, was as career driven as her dad. Her early years without her dad had some negative effect on her Kristy could see it. Having children would probably be John's role in life, unless he too became another Nick. She thought back to Hunter's prediction about John. She certainly didn't want to think about John's teen years when the hormones kicked in and developing cowgirls became more attractive to him then horses. Maybe she and Nick should have other children just to ensure the Chandler legacy lived on, there should be at least one Chandler that would grow up wanting to stay on the ranch. Money would never be the issue again for any of them.

"Mama," Nicki said, "do you think we could have scrambled eggs with cream cheese, bacon and pancakes for breakfast?"

"I don't see why not." Kristy ground coffee beans and started the three automatic coffee pots then set about getting the ingredients together. She couldn't remember a time when she felt more content. This was now *her* kitchen. Not the ranch kitchen as she always thought of it, but hers. It still hadn't soaked in, but it would…eventually.

Nick woke to an empty bed and wondered where Kristy went. He pulled on his jeans and shirt then walked downstairs where he noticed the lighted kitchen and heard voices. He waited quietly in the dark part of the outer room enjoying the sight before him. Kristy stood there looking out the window and mixing something in a bowl while the aroma of fresh brewed coffee filled the house. She was a natural in her role of wife and mother. He smiled as Johnny tugged at her jeans wanting her attention. She bent over, picked him up, sat him on the counter next to her and kissed his pudgy cheek. Nicki seemed to be reading a book. That was his family. It was still hard for him to believe he and Kristy had created this beautiful family together over the years. Why did it take him so long to see that Kristy loved him and their children? He couldn't remember a time when he felt more content and at peace with himself. He was actually in love and home again. This was their first day as a family on the ranch and he could hardly wait to see what life dealt them.

He walked into the kitchen and both children's faces lit up. Nick walked to Nicki first and kissed the top of her head. "You're up early."

Nicki looked up at him and smiled, her dimples matching his. "Good morning, Daddy. Johnny couldn't sleep."

Nick walked to the counter and put his arms around Kristy's waist, pulled her back against him and kissed her neck just below her left ear. "Good morning, Mrs. Chandler."

Kristy turned her face up to his and closed her eyes. She loved him more then life itself. "Good morning. The coffee's ready. Better grab a cup before the *boys* get wind of it and invade the place."

Johnny reached out to Nick and started talking in an alien language that Nick knew he'd have to learn sooner or later and today seemed like a good time to get started. After pouring a mug of coffee he took Johnny in his arm and went to the table to sit beside Nicki.

Joe and Ellen came out of their bedroom, which was just off the kitchen and Ellen automatically reached for the apron, which hung on a peg next to the bedroom door.

Joe wore a big grin as he gave Kristy a hug and kiss. He grabbed a mug of coffee and went to sit with Nick and the kids. He was one happy, but confused man. Now that his daughter had married the boss…what was his role on the ranch? Did he still accept a paycheck? "Mornin' family," he said and kissed Nicki's cheek, then John's.

Nick nodded and watched as Nicki kissed her grandpa on his cheek. It felt odd to be sitting with his ranch foreman, who was now his father-in-law. How did this work anyway?

Kristy had been watching both men and knew they would never speak their minds. She would have to do it for them. "I'm glad we're all here around the kitchen table, I have something to say." She turned toward Ellen. "Mom, come sit down."

Once the family was seated and giving her their undivided attention she leaned over and kissed Nick.

"Dad, you're probably wondering if you're still the ranch foreman. As far as I'm concerned you are…but you will no longer need a paycheck, I've made you richer than you can imagine. I've set up a savings account for you and all you have to do is take mom into Dallas and both of you sign your names. You'll never have to worry about money again. Do what you want with it. Nick…our children and any future children have trust funds set up in their names and their futures are taken care of. I've made sure Mavis too will never have to worry about money. I'm sorry if I disappoint any of you, but this is how it is. And Nick, your name is going on my accounts whether you like it or not. There are going to be things we need out here…especially if we have more children. We'll either have to build another house or add on to this one. You're free to do what you want with the money, it's just going to keep coming in anyway so we might as well use it to improve the place."

Everyone seemed to be in a state of shock and remained so silent you could hear a pin drop. Then Joe said, "Well hell, we could use a new mattress Ellen, that sagging old thing has given me a back ache for years."

Ellen just grinned. "Only because you insist on bouncing up and down on it every night."

Kristy turned red and went back to mixing her pancakes. Nick came to stand beside her. "What are you going to do with the Santa Barbara ranch?"

Kristy couldn't keep her hands off him and ran them up his chest. "I'm sending Gracie home to California. I'll let her run the restaurant and spa. She and Hunter were never meant to be, she'll love the idea. But you and I need to make one more trip out there to choose the horses we want brought back here. I'm thinking of asking Sarah to come to the ranch and be my secretary for a while. There is so much phone work to be done with renovations to a place like Santa Barbara that I can't devote my time to making the calls and the kids at the same time."

"Who's going to watch the kids when you're in Dallas if you don't have Gracie?"

Kristy turned them both around toward the table. "Their grandparents. Look at dad, he loves those kids so much. If I take them to Dallas then Mavis will watch them."

Nick smiled. Yep, life on the ranch was certainly going to change from what he remembered of his younger days. Now he had his own children on the ranch to teach them the values he was given. Kristy would insist on making their lives easier whether he agreed or not. He might as well get use to it. She knew what she wanted and went after it. Life was pretty good he had to admit, then poured another cup of coffee and headed upstairs to shave.

A month and a half later Kristy drove to Dallas and went to the office.

"Sarah," Kristy said, "wanta move to the ranch?"

Sarah's mouth dropped open. "Why?"

"Why not? I still need a secretary, especially now that we're going to renovate the Santa Barbara ranch. You know how much phone work there is, I need someone I can trust to get the job done. Unless you and Brian are back together."

"Brian and I seem to be over. I have to admit it's pretty dull around the office unless you're here. Do you have a home office yet?"

"I'll use Jack's old office for now. Jack's bedroom is available. It won't be forever, just until we get the spa up and running."

Sarah smiled broadly. "I think that sounds good to me. I've saved all the articles about your wedding for you. I think the one that's priceless has a photo of Joe escorting you up the carpet with that damn shotgun tucked in his arm, and the caption reads Old Fashion Cowboy Shotgun Wedding."

"Well, you have to admit, with our two kids as part of the ceremony, it was kind of appropriate," Kristy reminded her and laughed at the thought of her crazy family life.

Hunter walked in and when he saw Kristy he reached out and pulled her into his arms. "Do you know how many cowboy weddings are now being requested after the articles came out about yours? We've had calls from six wedding planners that wanted to know the secret. Not only that...but the Japanese now want to use our ranch for their cowboy weddings and are flying entire families in from Japan to participate. And, instead of a shotgun they're using Samurai swords tucked in their arms. God, woman, it doesn't matter what you do, you create some kind of stir."

Kristy sighed. "I'm taking Sarah back to the ranch with me for a while, until we get the Santa Barbara place up and going. Nick and I are bringing most of the horses back to the ranch. I've asked Gracie to go out to California and run the place...and she's agreed. She needs to be back home anyway. And Hunter...I want to thank you for giving me a life I could only dream about ten years ago. I will always love you for that."

Hunter's gaze traveled over her body before he gave her that devilish grin of his. "Ah, you might want to stop by the doctor's on your way back to the ranch, you're pregnant." From the look on her face she was once again surprised. He would make sure he was available if she needed him again when the time came. He also knew he never wanted children if it couldn't be with Kristy. She was the love of his life, but...he had to let her go and there were plenty of women in Dallas who could ease his pain.

Kristy's mouth dropped open, surely those damn pills hadn't failed her again? "Oh no...no, I don't think so. That's not possible."

Sarah was smiling. "Well...just in case, Kristy, let me give the doctor a call."

Hunter reached out and put his arm around her. "I knew that California tub would be useful for something sooner or later."

Kristy kept the doctor's appointment before they gathered up Sarah's belongings and drove toward the ranch.

Sarah pulled on her sun glasses. "So how do you feel about another baby?"

Kristy was still stunned. "I don't know. But I can tell you one thing...I'm switching to the patch after this one. I can't believe it happened again."

"Think Nick'll be happy about it?"

"I certainly hope so. Nicki will be thrilled. So will my parents and Mavis. In some ways it's like a miracle and in others...like a nightmare. I'm glad I have my job to keep me from getting bored."

"Kristy, you were born to be a mother. Those kids of yours are lucky. It's going to really be something to watch them growing up on the ranch with Nick teaching them ranch things. Do you think Nick will be around when this new one is born?"

Kristy shrugged. "I don't know." She turned toward Sarah and smiled. "It seems a shame to have to break in a new birthing coach. Since Nick is use to birthing animals and not humans...maybe I should consider keeping Hunter on call."

Now Sarah laughed. "And I'm sure Hunter won't mind one little bit. You're the one great love of his life...the rest of us have just been his distractions. You're right about Nick, animals mean money to him. You're just producing the next generation of Chandler's for him."

Kristy glanced over at Sarah. "I do love him with all my heart. And I love our children." Thinking back to before John was born she recalled how lonely and unwanted she'd felt. Would Nick reject her again? Hunter had been there for her back then...but she couldn't let him be there this time. She'd made her choice, now she would live with that choice.

That evening at the dinner table with every ranch hand and family gathered Kristy decided she might as well let everyone know. She looked at Sarah who was sitting there grinning from ear to ear and Kristy wasn't sure if it was the announcement or that she was just glad to be back in the thick of things. She'd become like family to her.

Taking a deep breath Kristy stood beside Nick and said, "Before we bring out dessert I have something to say to everyone here at the table." She still wasn't sure how she felt about her news.

Nick couldn't imagine what she was going to do now. He was kind of getting use to her way of looking at things.

"I guess there's no special way to say this...Nick, we're having another baby."

Nick leaned back in his chair and looked dumbfounded. Hell, they hadn't been near the hayloft. Then he thought back to the beach house and grinned. That tub beat the hayloft any day.

Old Jake grinned and said, "Yep, we'll need a lot of new Chandler's to keep this place goin'. Ain't nothin' like kids learnin' to work the ranch. Good for you, Doc." He remembered Nick as a youngster learning to do things at his father's knee. That little Nicki was a dead ringer for Nick at that age with her self-confident attitude and manners. John too would be like Nick he could see it already.

Now it was Nick's turn to give his children the same upbringing he'd been given. It was about damn time too. He couldn't recall a time when Nick looked happier. He seemed ten years younger.

Kristy looked at her dad and he had tears in his eyes. He was one happy grandpa. Nicki clapped her hands and yelled, "Sierra!" Johnny imitated his sister only instead of Sierra, the name Sarah came out.

Nick pushed his chair back and stood at the head of the table. He took Kristy's hand in his and put it to his lips. "If you'll excuse us Kristy and I need to go out to cemetery hill and tell my parents."

When Kristy looked back over her shoulder Rowdy had pushed his chair next to Sarah and was in deep conversation with her. Ellen had her head on Joe's shoulder and they were hugging each other. Nicki was wiping John's face and hands. Old Jake just sat there looking at his extended family and smiling. Tex, Scram, Roper and Cotton shook Joe's hand and congratulated him.

Nick hadn't missed the action in the dining room either and put his arm around Kristy's waist. "You would have made my parents very happy."

Kristy smiled up at him. "You said we needed to produce two more children. But just once…I would like it not to be a surprise."

Nick just grinned and helped her into Big Red.

Printed in the United States
41676LVS00004B/175-252

9 781413 763119